AF488755

Eroded Ember

Bree Ireland

Copyright © 2026 by Bree Ireland

All rights reserved.

No portion of this book may be reproduced in any form without written permission from the publisher or author, except as permitted by U.S. copyright law.

ISBNs
Paperback: 979-8-9951031-1-0
Hardcover: 979-8-9951031-2-7
Ebook: 979-8-9951031-0-3

Published by Bree Ireland

To the person who stayed up into unhealthy hours of the night listening to my ramblings, who gave me my love for romance, who never closed the doors on my dreams, and can't handle sour things.
This one's for you, Mom. I love you.

Pronunciation Guide

Characters:

- Ariella: (Ar-ree-eh-luh)

  ○ Ari: (Ar-ree)

- Anders: (An-derz)

- Evelyn: (Eh-vuh-lin)

  ○ Evie (EE-vee)

- Zadar: (Zay-dar)

- Searlas: (Sear-less)

- Kaida: (Kay-duh)

- Killian: (Kill-ee-ihn)

- Kell: (Kehl)

- Kiernan: (Keer-nen)

- Keagan: (Kee-gin)

- Kaid: (Kayd)

- Adrielle (Aye-dree-el)

- Tuuli: (Too-lee)

- Brisa (Bree-suh)

- Melten (Mehl-ten)

- Rhodion (Road-ee-uhn)

- Eryx (Ayhr-ix)

Greek:

- Agapití: (Ah-gah-pee-TEA)

- Dákry: (DA-kree)

- Týpos: (TEE-pohs)

- Peirasmós: (Pee-rahz-MOSS)

- Kallías: (Kah-lee-ahs)

- Patér: (Pah-tEYr)

- Mitér: (Mee-tEYr)

- Basileús: (Bah-see-LEvs)

Location:

- Agrond: (Ah-grond)

- Esrin: (Es-rihn)

Part 1

S he was beautiful as she hurried along, gripping the forest green jacket around her petite figure to produce the warmth she evidently lacked. She shivered as she walked, a completely *normal* movement for any *normal* person. I watched unmoving, unfazed by the bitter weather from high up in the trees, as she surveyed the deserted woods, entirely unaware of my presence.

Human. Human girl. Not a danger. Not a threat. Just a girl.

But she was more than that.

The air through which she moved swirled welcomingly around her, batting those crimson curls about, the wind playing with its new companion, and I tilted my head in observation, wondering as to what manner of loveliness was able to encompass one being. The forest didn't befriend others often.

Curious little thing. You walk alone today.

She glowed, and yet she moved as though wanting to be hidden, rushing to the visitor's center while completing her job. Her skin seemed to be touched not by the sun, but the sun's tears, a pale shade that held the illumination of stars, and I'd always wondered what it'd be like to feel the galaxy against my palms.

One slow blink had me shutting away the temptation, closing out the impulse to reach for her, see if the trembles that racked her body would still if I touched the sky in her skin because I could never be that close. Her need to stay oblivious was just as vital to my need to find her not a threat, yet I couldn't.

Using a rock I picked up earlier, I threw the object against a tree to my right, the stone slamming into the wood and crashing into ferns at the stump. She spun around, and I drank in the sudden movement, taking in her reactions in the most minute detail. Her face, now in my view, allowed me to study the tightening of her eyebrows, jaw clenching from the cold, and breath coming out smoky from her nose.

And there it was, the reason I found her, the reason I watched her, the reason she was now in danger.

Those eyes. The depth-filled violet hues of her irises. The hauntingly precious way her anxious gaze fell from one thing to the next, captivating like glittering amethysts.

Only one creature had eyes like those.

Yet, it was human legs that had her retracing her steps, following the rustling sound the stone created, violet sights skipping over the land bare of people, still not looking up.

"Hello?"

Something inside me shifted at the sound of her voice, soothing and gentle in a way that made the air easier to consume, and I stopped myself from calling out in response. The forest hushed at her sound, stilling in hope for her voice to claim the now aching silence, but it didn't, and a desperate need for more had me thinking irrationally, readying to rip down trees if it meant I could hear her scream. The idea had me pausing, only solidifying why she could never know I was here. However, these thoughts were not stopping me from moving closer, recklessly settling on a branch nearer to the girl, not ready to lose sight of her.

This innocent thing knew nothing of the danger near her, because that's what she was—innocent, and I would do everything in my unbridled power to convince my brothers. I'd seen too many effects of the death of the innocents.

And somehow, after she gave me the evidence I searched for, I knew I would come crawling back to these trees, to watch her in secret until the day she was no longer a curiosity.

But then the branch snapped.

Chapter One

His piercing screams, normal as they were, never ceased to wrench me from my sleep, and the consistent urgency to find him every night never lapsed. It had become like a silent dance at this point, a memorized sway from one room to the next, steps formulated in precise movements that only came from years of repetition. I could do it in my sleep, and sometimes, I did.

The metal door handle to his room was cold just like every other freezing object and secluded corner in this house and gripping it felt like grabbing hold of all his darkest fears and twisting them away before releasing. But that was the difference between Anders and me. I could let go of the door handle.

Anders had mostly calmed by the time I reached him. I couldn't ignore the improvements he'd made, how what was once panic attacks and continuous screaming now faded into an initial yelp of anguish. Though it'd been over ten years since these night terrors began, Anders was getting better, or he was hiding his fear more efficiently. It was hard to tell.

Tonight, his back was straight, and body unmoving as he sat in his bed, dark blue blankets tangled around his limbs, while his unseeing, ocean-colored eyes stared blankly at the bare wall in front of him. Carefully, I reached for him, pale skin touching dark, and the unexpected contact caused Anders to jump.

"Sorry," I whispered, nervous that loud noises would jar him further. His anxious gaze found its way to mine, and I watched as realization and ease sank in the vibrant waters of his vision. I situated myself next to him while Anders identified his surroundings, relaxing in the understanding that he was *here*, safe with me, and not in the terrible places sleep carried him.

"How bad was it?" I spoke again less timidly but keeping my soft tone. Like a delicate flower, Anders wilted, muscles too tired and brain too dizzy to keep him upright, and acceptingly, I pulled him closer, running gentle fingers through his dark, curly hair. "That bad, huh?" The silence that followed was confirmation. "Do you want to talk about it?" I questioned, concluding that it might be one of those nights we don't talk. I could do that, sit with him in peaceful silence with my presence as an assurance of his safety.

I'm here, little brother. You have nothing to fear.

He was so still; I thought he had fallen back asleep until he spoke. "It was about you," he answered in a voice on the edge of puberty but possessing that tiny, little tone I loved so dearly.

Again?

Questions built on my tongue tasting like a vile pill that couldn't quite be swallowed as it dissolves into a sickening substance, but I was determined to keep it down, allowing Anders control of the conversation. And to my solace, he kept going.

"There was something stalking you..." A shaky breath fell from his mouth, one developed to prevent tears that were slowly forming. "It had bad intentions, and... um... things didn't end well." The emotions he fought to hide away finally bubbled to the surface. I felt his tears dampen my shirt; I heard his breathing hitch; I saw his helpless state; And with every sign of consuming grief, my heart broke more.

"Breathe, Anders. I'm okay. You're okay. None of it was real," I soothed, loving touches falling from his hair to form careful circles on his back, and for a moment, Anders softened from the contact.

"But it felt *so real,*" he breathed, exhaustion dripping from every word as though he had been running for miles and without any progress.

"I know," I answered, remembering the hundreds of nights he'd say the same thing, "I know."

I hated seeing him like this, and I hated how frequently it happened even more.

Anders was the only ray of sunshine I had in this dark world, the only sense of warmth in a sea of ice, and when clouds engulfed him, dangerous shadows were cast. I tried to be the sister he needed, the companion he deserved, bringing light to the narrow hallways of his life, but when a storm appears, what could a candle do for the sun?

Though we were half-siblings, that did not affect my love for him. His past, however, was a mystery I never solved. I was five when Mother got pregnant with Anders, and though memories of then were hazy and confusing, I could not recall seeing her with any men after Father's death, and when she chose to stay silent about the situation, I understood it was for a reason and never brought it up. I tended to the baby as best as a child could, calming him as he cried and waking up with him throughout the night. Even then, he had nightmares, and after Anders' dependence on mother waned, she did what she'd always done and detached herself.

With no father and the lack of a mother, I raised Anders. It was difficult at first, not because Anders was defiant or problematic, but because I was a kid, and despite being a fast learner, carrying on the responsibility of raising a child wasn't a task easily comprehended. Maturity had taken root in my heart, aging my mind faster than the rest of me, and few thoughts crossed my mind that did not concern my family. Still, it wasn't enough. *I* wasn't enough.

"Will you sing to me?" Anders implored, voice barely over a whisper. His head drooped over my shoulder, and I rested my cheek on the fluff of dark curls.

"Of course," I answered, a wave of guilt crashing down on me instantly. It was a promise I had broken again, and again.

"Your voice is our little secret, okay? Don't share it with anyone else." Father's voice rang in my ear. His face was blurry, but the memory of the ocean crashing against rocks on the shore sang clearly. All my few remembrances of him were on the beach, the same beach right outside our house, the same waters he drowned in. It was unclear why Father insisted I keep quiet; he might've given an explanation in the small time I knew him alive, but that was years ago, and I was too young to retain. There was a part of me that detested disobeying him, but my desire to relieve Anders negated all rules.

So, I sang.

> *Wind on the ocean;*
> *Song on the sea.*
> *Wished for the sky;*
> *Drowned in grief.*
>
> *Lost in a gale;*
> *Torn from the land.*
> *Promises failed,*
> *Just as you planned.*

Melodic chorus, sweet somber songs,
Turned to a wail.
Come, teardrop of hope, invert the blight,
And ravage the bonds of the deep.

Follow my song, rest for long,
I offer all that you need.
Heed my voice, take my choice,
Let your heart lead you to me.

It was a lullaby Father taught me before he passed, allowing me to sing with him when we were alone. It was unlike anything else I'd learned, with warping tones and minor cords that were strangely beautiful, but it inevitably subdued Anders' hysteria which was more than I could ever ask.

After the chorus, Anders fell asleep, and the clouds vanished.

The next morning unfolded like any other, a continuous cycle of the same basic activities ending in preparation for the next day's identical procedure.

Get up. Make breakfast. Take Anders to school.

The monotony wasn't so bad, helping me maintain a stable mindset with things to do, but it was after Anders was gone, and life became still, that preoccupying my brain was a challenge.

Our house with the tiny orange door gave the illusion of welcoming. Larger than most of the neighboring homes that lined the sloping cliff leading to the shore of Pebble Beach, the structure contained two stories when the majority of the town had one level, yet it wasn't big enough to forget the additional people living inside, even if they hid themselves in rooms with doors that were *always* closed. Mother could pretend she was alone, secluding herself in her enclosures because her mind was quiet, along with the rest of her world, resting in the peaceful bliss of silence for eternity. I, however, could hear everything, and the clinking of her paintbrush against the glass bowl filled with murky water echoed through the house, haunting the unlit corners of my mind like the hollowed ghost she was.

She's here, but never for you. You disappoint her. She can't stand to look at you.

Shuts the door to avoid seeing you. Pretends you aren't there. She can pretend. I wish I could too...

Pushing past the prickling noise of my thoughts, I flipped on the television to bring some semblance of life to the deadened stillness of the open kitchen as I began cleaning up from breakfast. The news started when I grabbed the pan used to make pancakes, and I half-heartedly listened to the sturdy, serious voice that sounded, comforted by the illusion of company. While running the warm water for the dishes, I watched the town start their long day from the small kitchen window, seeing every car that passed carrying someone with different motives and ambitions than the rest, many of them wearing an uneasy expression and a rigid posture.

Crescent City's beauty was immeasurable with roaring beaches on one end and towering redwood forest covering the other, but aside from the immense trees, endless sea, and occasional tourism, it was a humble little town. The people were thoughtful, willing to help those in need or brighten their day with a kind word, and in a town filled with good, you wouldn't think bad things could happen, but the world was not that simple.

"Twenty-five-year-old Justin Harris and thirty-nine-year-old Brittney Moore were reported missing last night in Crescent City, California," the television blared, causing me to ponder if discouraging news was better than silence. "Police investigating the situation say the kidnappings were likely committed by the same person who—" I turned it off, and the room instantly reclaimed the painful quiet I endeavored to avoid. After recollecting recent memories and constructing quick mental math, the shock of the number caused the dish to slip from my hand.

Five. Justin and Brittney were the fourth and fifth individuals to be abducted *this month*. My heart mourned for these people and their families, knowing very well they would never be found.

As tragic as it was, frequent kidnappings were common in our small town, and living here increased the chance of disappearing without a trace like many before had.

It started in 1964, after the tsunami destroyed much of the infrastructure, leaving chaos to ensue, debris to corrode, and crime to go unnoticed. He was cautious back then, only taking a few and distancing the time between each victim, but it'd been nearly twenty years now, and he'd grown increasingly boldened by the year. The police were still as clueless now as they were in the '60s; he seemed to sneak in and out of places without a trace, taking those he willed along the way. There was no pattern to the madness, no consistent tell to predict who was next on his list, and nothing for authorities to build on but the two things the crimes had in common: one being the danger, though bleeding into the surrounding cities, was most prominent in Crescent City, and the other that people who went missing were never seen again.

Locals gossiped, calling him the "Silent Killer," worrying their lives were on the line. And though there was no proof of murder, it was highly presumed.

I finished drying the dishes by the time I noticed the cold, plated pancakes stacked in the corner of the countertop. I silently scolded myself, remembering I'd set them aside for Mother over an hour ago. The hand towel fell from my grasp as I quickly grabbed the plate and a fork and rushed to her room before abruptly halting at her door.

She didn't like it when I entered her domain. Mother usually left her room at random times of the day to grab food herself, but I went out of my way to make her something, and sure, they might've lost their warmth, but I was trying. She had to see that.

Maybe then she would let me in. Maybe she would keep the door open. Maybe she would look at me. Maybe she would *smile*.

Releasing a sharp exhale, I opened the door and was met with the blinding sunlight streaming from the wall-length windows along with the overpowering smell of saltwater candles. Mother had lived thirteen years without her hearing, and her other senses were heightened because of it. The room was perfectly clean, the bed against the wall flawlessly made, clothes organized in the closet, and even the watercolors were lined in pristine order as she painted. Despite not hearing the door open, or my footsteps enter, she knew I was there. I watched as she tensed, posture straightening, her back facing me.

"I brought you some pancakes," I spoke, understanding it was of no use, but I believed it to help lighten the tension. "They are cold, but I thought you still might want them. It's okay if not. I just assumed you might be hungry since I haven't seen you get food this morning."

I waited for her to move, to give any acknowledgment of my presence, but there was no response as she sat still in the sectioned-off painting corner of her room, her hand holding a brush hovering just above a nearly finished canvas of the ocean.

Please look at me. I'm here. I love you. Don't pretend. I'm sorry I disappoint you. I'm trying to be good. Please just look at me.

Her chair screeched against the wooden floor as she stood, causing me to flinch at the abrupt sound. My heart practically stopped when she turned to face me, empty, brown eyes meeting mine, and I froze, hope burning in every inch of my body because she was *seeing me.*

I didn't dare move; afraid she would remember why she hated me if I did. This moment was delicate, fragile like thin ice over a glistening lake, and while it projected an eerie beauty, sudden movements were dangerous. Mother, however, was not frightened as she stepped in my direction, pausing beside the wall separating her painting room from her bedroom before sliding the door shut, parting us without one word.

Everything bright and pleasant bubbling inside of me died, and the emotions piled in my throat, making easy breaths impossible.

Closed doors; can't stand to look at you.

I blinked a few times, forcing the tears back as I set the food on her nightstand, leaving quicker than I had entered. I passed a mirror in the hall, causing me to pause, scrutinizing the girl looking back at me, violet eyes that glinted sorrowfully searching for answers I would never have. Apart from the long, scarlet red curls and similar complexion, Mother and I were remarkably dissimilar. She was beautiful with a long, proportionate face, possessing gentle features and soft tones. Nothing like mine, all sharp curves, and pointed details, skin too pale, eyes bright violet and unnatural. Everything about me looked wrong, inhumane, harsh. I understood why she refused to look at me; I didn't want to look at myself either.

Finishing school will make her proud, I'd told myself, then graduated from homeschool at sixteen and was met with days empty of work rather than praise.

Cooking and keeping the house clean will make her happy, I'd told myself, then stole the dust from vacant rooms and made food for a table fit for four, only sitting two.

Raising Anders will help her, I'd told myself, am *telling* myself, hoping that one day she would return to the Mother I used to know, and then she would finally tell me I'd done well. It'd been thirteen years, but I hadn't given up on that dream despite being nothing more than a disappointment.

Gradually, I slid down the wall I'd leaned against, pulling my knees to my chest, and sobbed as the weight of not being enough crushed my heart.

The item in my pocket poked my leg as I squeezed tighter into the ball I'd formed with my own body, compelling me to release the pressure and pick the item from its hiding place. Examining the seashell with blurry vision replenished my mind with memories of Father. He always looked at me, watched me with such adoration even as a toddler. He'd tell me I was special, that I would do remarkable things when I was older. Rubbing the gold lining of the gift felt like rubbing his cold hands while we sang with only the ocean to listen to us.

Tipping my head against the wall, I closed my eyes and pictured the splendor of *back then*, before Mother lost her hearing and Father died, when singing was allowed and dancing was a way to express joy, back when life was good, and fear and pain were nonexistent.

I couldn't help but wonder how different my world would be if none of it had changed.

Chapter Two

Thanksgiving felt like any other day, Anders and I alone at the dinner table, sharing stories of recent happenings, or rather, Anders talked, while I listened. He'd tell me of school, and all it encompassed. From memorable friends to lengthy, procrastinated assignments, along with the occasional stranger exchange, there was plenty to listen to. I found contentment in the soft pitching of his voice, how he spoke so positively of each interaction, viewing life with a type of excitement I lost long ago.

Proud of you, Sunshine.

I was grateful for the school he had, for the escape from cold floorboards and whispering walls of a house that could only be called home when he was present, but after Thanksgiving break ended, I was forced back into my bitter routine of loneliness.

I attempted to preoccupy myself, cleaning already spotless rooms, sleeping to the point of restlessness, trying new hobbies that were never worth the effort, and the shortage of distraction formed a paranoid sense of anxiety. Half the time I convinced myself someone was in the room with me, the undeniable feeling of eyes tingling at the back of my neck, but I was alone, and that feeling only occurred every few months.

I was reading the newspaper one cloudy morning, prioritizing each syllable with intense focus, when I felt the lightest tap on my shoulder. Tossing a glance in the direction of the touch, my eyes widened when catching vibrant, ruby hair.

"Mother!" I shouted, scrambling to my feet to face her like a soldier at attention. My heart pounded in my chest as I racked my brain for explanations, but the rumbling chaos dissolved the moment she looked at me and smiled.

It was small, the faintest upward pull of the lips, but it was a smile; a smile directed at me.

"I found you a job," she signed, fingers forming in swift, easy movements. My eyebrows drew together, confusion lining every harsh angle of my face. Pulling something from her pocket, Mother handed me an application for a ranger position at Redwood State Park, only adding to my befuddlement.

"Where did you even get this?" I signed, setting the paper on the table to concentrate solely on Mother, who I struggled to believe was truly standing in front of me, communicating as though this were a common occurrence.

"I think you will like it there," she answered, completely deflecting my earlier question.

She doesn't want to talk to you. Be quiet. Be respectful. Be grateful. Smile. Nod. She's watching you. Don't mess it up.

I bit down on my tongue, refusing to let words slip out. I forced a smile to my face, adding a predetermined nod, and folding my arms behind my back as they pressed harshly against each other, pushing past the fierce desire to hug her. It wasn't acceptable now, but maybe one day, if I proved myself good enough, it would be.

Mother left after I acknowledged her recommendation, which felt more like a request. The interaction was peculiar and random, things not clicking into place where they should, but I couldn't complain. Mother was thinking of me, went out of her way to find a position to keep my mind busy when I was sure I'd slowly been falling into madness. I hadn't considered working at a job, not when I had asked last year after finishing school and been instantly turned down, but I liked the concept of getting out of the house, breathing in lungfuls of oxygen surrounded by trees, and the idea of me working made Mother so happy.

Without another thought, I sat down at the table and filled out the application.

The interview was shorter than I expected, with a straightforward list of questions that oddly didn't relate to the forest: name, age, medical conditions, legal guardian, home life. It confused me why queries of a present father were necessary in a job of tending a forest, but I didn't ponder it long. I was here to learn, not to already know, and the man explaining the rules to me was remarkably kind yet stern, owning the authoritative demeanor of a district ranger.

"Best keep clear o' walkin' near the base o' secluded trees if ye can. Their roots only reach about ten feet down, and they're shallow because o' that. Steppin' on them does harm, and in time, the tree'll fall," the ranger explained as we walked through one of the trails, stopping occasionally to thoroughly observe specific tourist locations and review important facts.

"So, the redwoods are top-heavy?" I questioned, taking in the landscape in small increments to avoid overstimulation.

"One could see it that way," he answered evenly, "Some grow near three hundred sixty feet tall. Without a bit o' proper structure, say in a storm, they can seem awfully top-heavy, aye."

I replayed his words in my head, committing another guideline to memory.

"How come it's only secluded trees we need to be careful around?" I recalled, the ground squashing against my feet as I followed his long strides. He slowed his pace after noticing my struggles to keep up, my boots catching on outgrown roots and slipping on mud, and the discreet gesture tugged a smile onto my lips. It could be easily overlooked, but by the way he attentively glanced in my direction, left enough time between each topic to let me speak, listened to me as I talked, it was clear he thought I was worth the patience. I didn't understand why he believed I was deserving of this thoughtfulness, but I couldn't deny the gratitude that gathered inside of me.

"They've got support, ye ken. The roots twist in wi' the trees round about, keepin' them steady, and together they draw what they need tae thrive." He turned to me, with a meaningful smile on his face. "Growin' strong takes a bit o' help, an though we cannae see it, the roots reach far." The blues of his irises were almost luminous in the shadowed landscape of the forest, a fierce contrast from the deep ebony of his skin. The stare he held could be seen as intimidating to some, but I saw kindness. "They're no as alone as ye think," he finished, looking off into the endless terrain of the redwoods.

It fell quiet, the forest hushing to match our somber silence. I wished he had kept talking, continuing to explain guidelines even if my brain was crammed with beginner information. It was nice to hear someone else speak apart from Anders and the voices in my head, and in a way, it felt normal, as though human interaction released pressure I hadn't known was building.

Droplets fell from the wet branches, appearing like sparkling crystals in the sunlight stretching between the trees. The leaves held onto the water from the previous night's storm, providing a leisurely rain that dripped cold against my body. The ranger proceeded with his tour without acknowledgment of the soft showers upon us. It was strange how the rain seemed to soak into his skin, like a part of him was missing without it. I didn't voice my curiosities, afraid he'd lose the toleration he so graciously gave me, and after spending most of the day with him in training, I was determined to earn his fondness. Maybe then he wouldn't have to fight to maintain patience around me.

We came to the end of the looping trail, stopping to review the significant regimes before heading to the next location.

Help the visitors. Preserve the plantation. Watch for animals. Never leave the trail.

It wasn't a lengthy list, but I replayed the guidelines multiple times, ensuring its commitment to my memory. The ranger strictly emphasized the last rule, telling me of all the dangers and tragic incidents that came from vacating the designated path. Yet that rule was the easiest to follow.

"Any questions?" He asked after I recited the routine. I bit my lip, wondering if the intrigue lingering in the back of my mind was appropriate to talk about. His head inclined in my direction, yet again showing patience as he waited for me to speak, and the directed attention calmed my uncertainty.

"What part of Scotland are you from?"

I was very familiar with the accent he had, understanding everything he said like it was second nature. Mother was originally from Scotland, and her accent was just as strong as his back when she spoke. Hearing the different inflections filled me with a sense of familiarity, and I felt a connection to him despite just meeting him today.

A laugh was not the response I expected from the ranger, but it sounded so joyful, reminding me of how Anders giggled when I'd playfully chased him around the house.

"I meant aboot the park," he restated, an amused expression lighting up his face.

"I know," I answered sheepishly, lowering my head in shame as though I disappointed him.

"Ariella Rowe," he called softly, quiet chuckles abruptly changing to tenderness. I was impressed he memorized my name, followed by guilt of forgetting his. Another failure of mine.

I glanced up at him, directing my focus to his eyes that held many years of wisdom past his age of what I assumed was his early thirties.

"I'm no upset wi' ye," he stated, "Just caught me aff guard, is all." The ranger scanned my face. "There's somethin' else ye're wantin' tae ask, isnae there?" He read me so easily, as if I wasn't trying to conceal my worries, as if I wanted him to know each concerning thought that crossed my mind.

"I cannot remember your name, I'm sorry," I caved, knowing silence would not help me solve anything.

"Will ye please look at me?" He asked. I complied dutifully; unaware my vision had found its way back to the damped soil. "My name's Zadar," he said clearly while staring into my eyes as though he could commit the name to my memory himself. "And you've nae reason tae be anxious."

His ability to read me like a book made me wonder if I had always been bad at hiding my emotions, that Anders could see all that I felt through my expression or posture. I hoped it wasn't true.

"If ye'd still like tae know," Zadar started again, tone easy and light. "I used tae live in Drumnadrochit, near Loch Ness. "

"Why did you move here?" I prompted before thinking. That genuine smile returned, and I began to believe he might truly enjoy carrying on a conversation with me.

"That's a long story," he said making his way to the vehicle used to bring us to our location, "an' the day's near done. Maybe another time, aye?"

I nodded, more than satisfied with the conclusion as I followed him back to the vehicle.

My two-week training consisted of speaking to strangers, which I quickly found did not come easily to me, along with mapping out the trails, and managing the front desk. Interpretive ranger wasn't a complicated job, not requiring me to carry a gun and fight like the officer rangers protecting the park, or recall the differences and specialties in each plant to support a thriving forest like the backcountry rangers, but reinforcing the rules to visitors was tough at times. Zadar told me that it would get easier and after a month or so, confidence would settle in and take over the jumbled mess of words in my head, but I struggled to believe any confidence would come once he was gone.

Zadar briefly mentioned his plans to relocate after Christmas, saying how all district rangers move to different areas of the woods from time to time, though he worded it differently. His promise to return to the Jedediah Smith area of the Redwoods after a few weeks was my only security in seeing him again. I disliked how dependent I had become on his counsel, more afraid of disappointing him than losing my job. Talking to him, even if it were entirely boresome work scenarios, was easy and enjoyable, and listening to his accented responses filled me with a comfort I couldn't explain.

My heart hollowed a bit after learning of his upcoming withdrawal, but I recognized the opportunity it presented. Perhaps I'd form relationships with my other coworkers, or I'd make a fool of myself and have no one to turn to, and I inwardly sighed, realizing the latter was more likely.

The forest had been immensely quiet today, allowing me to think clearly without the buzzing noise of disarray. The winter wind bit my skin, tinting my pale features with a vibrant pink. I shivered as I huddled farther into the half-warm embrace of my coat, my body unable to give off enough heat to withstand the chills running down my spine.

The year was almost over, and though most people were away visiting family, I complied to make my usual rounds when Zadar requested it. I blinked away the tears that formed from the frigid air, struggling to detect humans in my watery sights. Trees, ferns, and dirt blurred together in colors of red, green, and brown, differentiating them merely by height and texture. The majestic beauty of the redwoods was temporarily overlooked by my sheer determination to embrace the warmth of the visitor's center as soon as possible. Anyone choosing to hike in this cold lacked sanity.

The sharp wind had calmed to a chilly breeze as I began looping back around to the entrance of the trail, bones rattling with each step, easing the air enough for me to hear something collide with wood behind me. My muscles tensed, worrying I'd missed a visitor in my hurry to get inside, but when I turned, no one was there, yet that unnerving sensation of being watched remained. I followed the direction from where the sound came, leading me to a tree with a minor scuff on its wet bark. Staring at the dent with perplexion, my eyes fell to the large rock at my boot, nearly the size of my foot in length, only adding to my bewilderment. It matched the size of the tree's wound, and judging by the height, it seemed to have fallen from the sky. I scanned the surrounding area, and unable to find a reasonable cause for such an oddity, I spoke in hopes of a response.

"Hello?"

The world hushed.

Then a *snap* of wood rang throughout the grove, followed by the *thud* of gravity forcing it to the ground, and any remnant of heat left in my body turned cold.

My head whipped around, finding a massive branch that had fallen in the ferns.

Only, it hadn't fallen.

The wood appeared perfectly healthy as I inched forward to examine it. The end was broken off, jutting out sharp pieces of redwood from the disconnection, meaning it hadn't fractured naturally. A significant amount of pressure must have caused it to snap, and after viewing the size of the branch a second time, it was clear that no human had that strength.

Animal.

Another chill shot through me, but not from the freezing, lingering stillness. I evaluated the mental the list of creatures Zadar warned me about, but as my brain scrambled for answers, a dark figure caught the corner of my eye. My vision was still watery from the air as I watched the large, shadowy being slip behind the trees in a swift, singular movement. Though it was brief, and my sight was impaired, I knew of only one creature native to these woods that matched my observations.

Bear.

I quickly brushed my palms against my eyes, wiping away the remaining tears to clear my vision. Slowly, just as Zadar had instructed, I backed away from the tree where the black bear was hidden, holding my breath unknowingly while I moved. My sights never left the darkened red bark of the tree, legs yearning to sprint with each careful backward step I took.

The bear remained hidden behind the tree, as if my presence were frightening to him, but that didn't stop me from quickening my movements the more distance I gained. My foot caught on a rock, causing me to stumble to the ground, and a grunt slipped out of me. I froze, hands wet from the dirt, waiting for the bear to respond. Surely, he heard me; surely, he'd use this moment of weakness to attack, but the only acknowledgment given was the brisk slash of his tail against the ferns peering from behind the wood. The action was concise, and my frantic brain might've been playing tricks on me, but it seemed the dark ligament was painted with rigid scales.

Not a bear.

I bolted, hyperaware of every twig cracking and leaf rustling under my boots, panic mixing them with the sounds behind me. I was able to glance back, repercussions hitting me head-on when the wind yanked my hair over my eyes, causing me to nearly trip again, but I was able to keep myself upright, refusing to slow until I reached the transportation vehicle.

Nothing followed me.

The cozy enclosure of the visitor's center was just as inviting as I hoped, leaving the chills that permeated my body outside the door. As expected, no guests were wandering about the building, and the atmosphere felt hollow as a result. The shelves were fully stocked with souvenirs from the recent replenishment of items. I'd spent an hour last week properly tagging it all when the day had been particularly uneventful, and now they remained untouched, shirts limply hanging as they awaited a customer's ownership.

I scanned the spacious room once more, quiet and empty, posing as a roof for the weather rather than a shelter from danger. Most of my coworkers were on break this Christmas Eve, but I'd volunteered to work, knowing the holidays were never a priority to Mother.

"Oh, good," Zadar voiced, appearing from the backroom, that kind smile warming his face, "Ye're just the one I was wanting' tae see."

Relief gradually evened my heart rate, knowing I wasn't alone anymore, and though I would have taken any company at that moment, Zadar made me feel safe in ways no one else could.

"I ken ye've yer ain work tae get on wi'," he continued, oblivious to how I glanced behind, preparing for something to break down the door as he grabbed the papers from the front desk, "but I was hopin' ye could give me a haun sortin' out some files."

Subconsciously, I moved to him, eyes fixated on the entryway.

"Ariella?" Zadar inquired, looking up from the papers and noticing my odd conduct.

"Yes... yes, I can help, sorry," I fumbled, tearing my attention from the door to Zadar, whose focus now shifted from me to the entrance, but he didn't question it as we walked to his office.

I couldn't knock the urge to run, even after I sorted through papers for ten minutes, fidgeting with the shell in my pocket when my hands were free, a bad habit I had gotten myself into years ago. The shell's surface was smooth, soothing to rub my thumb against in stressful situations, and rejecting that mindless desire did more harm than good.

"Are ye feelin' awricht?" Zadar spoke, and with the documents taken care of, there was nothing else to distract him from my behavior.

I debated telling him what I saw, thinking if there was a threat, Zadar would know how to handle it, but the longer I tried to formulate the occurrence into words, the more ridiculous it sounded in my mind. The last thing I wanted was for him to question my mental stability.

"I'm fine," I resolved to answer, but Zadar was convinced otherwise, skeptically glancing me over, his eyes fixing on the hand fidgeting in my jeans.

"Whit's that in yer pocket?"

My fingers tightened around the shell, pulling it from its hiding place, the light reflecting off the gold lining.

"It was a gift from my father before he passed," I responded, my fear temporarily bypassed for sullen grief that I still hadn't completely accepted.

"It's bonnie," he said, though his tone dipped, examining the thing with strong fixation that was difficult to read, like he wanted to display it and crush it under his boot all at once, "Far too bonnie tae be hid awa' in that pocket o' yours." He moved as though to hold my shell, thinking better of it when he crossed his arms, meeting my eyes. "Ye should wear it. If ye tied a wee chain roon the top, it could make a fine necklace."

I nodded in response, pondering what Father would have thought of the idea. I wondered if he liked jewelry, if he would be disappointed that I hadn't thought of it first, or if he wanted it kept secret, hidden from all eyes but our own, just like my voice. In either scenario, I had failed him, and asking forgiveness from someone who was gone was an impossible task. I felt my jaw clench in agitation.

I'm sorry for misusing your present. Don't be upset, Father. I can obey. I don't sing. I keep quiet, just like you wanted. I'll make you proud of me.

"Why dinna ye head hame?" Zadar offered. I had forgotten he was there, distracted by thoughts of the past and the desire for a different present.

"I still have three hours of my shift left," I reminded.

"Aye, I ken. I'm lettin' ye off early. It's Christmas Eve, efter aw, an' ye look like ye could do wi' a bit o' rest."

I didn't argue, not when I wished to get away from whatever was hiding behind the trees. Ending my shift took only a few minutes, and I was prepared to leave when my tenacious curiosity finally got the better of me.

"Hey, Zadar?" I started, already regretting speaking up.

"Aye?"

"What kind of bears live in the redwoods?"

He looked at me curiously.

"Black bears. Mind? We went ower this in yer trainin'." His tone was not accusing, but the statement seemed to end almost with a question.

"Right, of course," I replied, quiet and shaky laughter pitching from my voice. I began to leave, stopping only after I gained enough confidence to continue speaking. When I turned to Zadar again, his eyes were fixed on me in that stern set that reminded me of the reasoning behind my hesitance. "Black bears don't have... tails, do they?" The question was formed slowly, but I was able to complete it without interruption. Zadar kept his intense gaze, sea-blue vision, searching for hidden information.

"They dae..." he answered, skepticism dripping from each word, "but they're no that long."

"I knew that" I stated, uneasy guilt clutching my throat as though I had been rightfully accused of a terrible crime. My feet resumed their delayed parting immediately after, hoping to escape the awkward stillness I had created.

Why do you speak? Obey the rules without question. Be seen and not heard. You want him to like you? Keep quiet.

"Ariella," Zadar called, forcing me to halt at the door. I faced him once more, every muscle of my body itching to leave as I respectfully listened to what he had to say. "Did ye see somethin' in the forest?"

There was silence for a moment, but eye contact remained.

"No."

It wasn't a lie; I truly hadn't seen anything, only glimpses of animals and an overactive imagination led me to this point. There was no evidence of potential danger, and I regretted having brought the topic up in the first place.

"I hope you have a Merry Christmas, Zadar," I conversed, unable to handle the feeling of disobedience any longer. I left the room without shutting the door, allowing Zadar the option to call for me again, and he never did.

There were few days Mother didn't paint, choosing Anders and I over her seclusion, and while those special moments were arbitrary and scarce, Christmas was the one consistency. There was something magical about the holiday, how it seemed the world agreed to live peaceably with loved ones, leaving sorrow and regrets to be picked up after the New Year when life started fresh again.

Before I started my job, our lone source of income came from the artwork Mother sold, and surprisingly, we lived a comfortable life with the money, though it wasn't enough to afford presents, so our small tree remained bare both on the branches and underneath. And this year, when I found a small box beneath the tree, I was shocked, followed shortly by confusion, as I saw my name on the present. I knew it hadn't come from Mother, and Anders was too young to think of this on his own, but it had to have come from one of them. I tried to ask my family about the mysterious box, and when there was no clear answer, I decided to open it, revealing a shiny, silver chain atop a plum, velvet cushion. I stared in awe for quite some time, noticing how the metal glittered like starlight, and though the person behind this generosity was a mystery, I couldn't deny my wish to keep it, placing it in my room so no one could steal it away as I continued the holiday with my family.

There was once a time when Mother danced around the tree with me, out of breath and giddy with laughter, back when her eyes were still bright and she sang with joyous love, but now she sat on the sofa, quiet and somber as always, and the memory of her voice had long been forgotten. I still danced with Anders, or rather, skipped around the house with him to the beat of the jingles pouring in from the radio. Mother watched her son laugh as he nearly slipped on the slick floor on multiple occasions, and I could see her faint grin appear while she imagined what his giggles must sound like. I waited for her to look at me, noticing how heavy my breathing had become, or the large smile that pulled at my cheeks, but she never did.

I should've been used to it by now—the constant neglect and insensitivity, should've learned how to nullify that unyielding craving for acceptance, but not even years of apathy could deter the love I felt for my mother. So I sat motionless when we ate dinner together, glimpsing my only living parent as often as I could, committing each feature of her pale face to my memory, witnessing the loss of life in her chocolate eyes and the few grey strands of hair contrasting the deep red. Mother was much too young to display such rapid aging, and I feared she was losing years of her life, whether through stress or anxiety or some other cause, I could not discern, but one thing was abundantly clear: her health was declining.

Mother and Anders sat together, while the chair beside me remained unoccupied. I failed countless times when trying to picture Father beside me, unable to think of him anywhere but by the water.

Four wooden chairs made for a family of three, only used by two, and yet this one, never used, stood out more than the rest.

But now as I stared at the vacant seat, I felt as though something very prominent was missing.

Chapter Three

Zadar had been gone for a week, and though work felt longer without him, I was beginning to get the hang of things. As it turns out, giving directions and instructing visitors was considerably easier when familiar with the forest.

Each day, I fell in love with the redwoods a little more: the towering trees, the vibrant colors, the tranquil silence—how feeling small and insignificant blended with the sensation of security and comfort. I tried not to be miffed at my new manager when he instructed me to work the front desk for a week, concealing me from the beautiful nature and allowing my coworkers to make the normal rounds on the trails.

We were still in the holiday season, meaning everyone was with their families, and since it was New Year's Eve, I hadn't expected to see a car full of people pull into the parking lot. Just before they entered, I tucked my hair away from my face and rolled my shoulders back to assume a more proper position from where I'd rested on the worktop.

"Welcome to the Jedediah Smith State Park," I greeted enthusiastically, hoping it didn't sound fake, even if I had been exceedingly bored mere seconds ago, "Is there anything I can help you with?"

The act must have been convincing enough because when I scanned the group for faces contorting with disapproval, I found bright eyes and mischievous grins. There were a boy and two girls, all appearing close to my age and clearly invested in the story the dark-haired boy performed, the girl with twin braids periodically chiming in. I didn't mean to stare, but as they laughed together at a joke I missed, I had the sudden desire to join the conversation, just so I could feel my face heat from a shortage of proper oxygen like the girl, or have a hand memorably patted on my back like the boy did to calm his friend.

The girl with the blonde perm was the first to compose herself and acknowledge my greeting.

"Yes, we were hoping could you tell us the best place to spot Bigfoot," she requested with such sincerity that the absurdity of the question caught me off guard. I almost choked endeavoring to keep my amusement down, and bit my lip to avoid smiling. Of all the strange requests I'd dealt with, this was the most absurd, and I looked forward to sharing it with Anders over dinner.

"I'm not sure I can help you with that. I am sorry," I offered as honestly as I could.

"But you work here. You must know where he lives!" complained the girl whose braids fell past her shoulder blades. I cleared my throat to extricate the giggle bubbling there. They expectantly waited for my directions, glancing at one another as if they, too, were trying to keep back laughter.

"You are aware Bigfoot is not real, right?" I suggested, supposing it was some peculiar joke from their poorly hidden amusement.

"Not with that attitude he's not," the boy said, lazy smile forming on his lips. *Teasing. They are not upset. Just kidding.*

My shoulders loosened at the realization, only to tense again at the sight of the girl unhappily looking at the boy, her face hardening in a scowl when glancing me over.

No, you definitely did something wrong.

I glimpsed at my outfit, wondering if I had mistakenly worn something to offend her.

"You are really pretty," the female blonde spoke up, negating the continuation of the thread of our conversation, and I was grateful for the change in topic. "Where did you get your contacts?" she continued before I could thank her for her curt yet generous compliment. My eyebrows drew together at her curiosities.

"My what?"

"Contacts," she repeated, tapping beneath one of her grey-blue eyes, "You know, the glasses you stick in your eyeballs that change colors." The two friends on either side of her stayed perfectly quiet, either content with the entertainment of our exchange, or disinterested in conversation after the subject shift.

"I'm... not wearing contacts," I answered.

"How is that possible?" she questioned, leaning over the counter to get a better look, and reflexively, I took a step back, "They are purple! No one has purple eyes."

With her this close, I noticed the small, thin braid she kept barely visible in the mass of her poofy hair.

"Maddie, you cannot just get into people's faces like that," the other girl scolded, pulling Maddie off the counter. Maddie did not fight her friend as she was moved, like a child obeying a parent after years of repetition, compelling me to think this wasn't the first time Maddie had invaded personal boundaries.

"She doesn't mind, Heather," Maddie argued, turning back to me. "Do you?" I wasn't sure how to answer, afraid honesty would be rude, and Maddie took my silence as confirmation, determinedly trying to figure me out. I stood there awkwardly as Maddie scrutinized every part of me. The dark-eyed boy whose haircut was rather unfortunate also focused on me, but the glow in his gaze caused me to believe his reasoning for staring was different than Maddie's.

"You live in that house by Pebble Beach with the orange door," Maddie concluded, clapping her hands in triumph like she had solved some grand mystery. An unsuppressed anxiety clamped down on my lungs, while I grappled for a manageable explanation.

"I—how did you—?"

"I'm a mind reader," she stated plainly, giggling at my stunned expression. Heather placed her head in her hand, pinching the bridge of her nose as though she could push the embarrassment away. "I'm just kidding," Maddie went on, unaware of her friend's disrepute. "I know everyone in this town apart from that house, and since I hadn't seen you before, I put two and two together. It's common sense, really."

"Common sense?" I questioned before I could stop myself, compelling the boy to chuckle at my bafflement.

"Well, maybe not common sense," Maddie considered, "but process of elimination, yes. I have a talent for figuring strangers out."

"Really?" I asked, not sarcastically, but rather with genuine curiosity. Maddie nodded with her head held high.

"I could tell you your favorite color right now."

"Okay," I agreed, fully conscious of the fact that I did not have a favorite color, but her enthusiasm was too amusing not to encourage.

"Yellow."

Mother often used that color for painting sunlight and sandy beaches, and I hated how the hobby she chose over her children affected the color, but every time I viewed it, all I could see is the harshness of its vibrancy.

"No." I expected Maddie to be saddened by my denial, but she already had her next guess out before I could finish responding.

"Red."

The color of my hair, the cause of unwanted attention. The color of blood, a sign of pain.

"No."

"Blue."

Beautiful memories with Father were rich with every hue of the ocean, and while that should've caused me to favor the color, blue played as the reminder of loss, and the sea to mock me from my window.

"No."

"Green."

There are many shades of green, some more pleasant than others, but my first thought was of the subtle, cool green of the redwoods, how magical it felt to walk alone in the never-ending forest, and while pondering, I realized I did have a favorite color after all.

"Yes."

"I knew it. See? What did I tell you?" I accidentally let a giggle slip and watched as Maddie's jaw set in a determined line. "Oh, you don't believe me, huh? Alright then, I'll prove it to you," she challenged, resting her arm on the counter and pointing her finger at me as though she could pick out every aspect of my life. "You like..." Maddie's eyes narrowed, concentrating intensely on my face, and I feared the eccentric conclusions she was formulating, "to dance."

It was a random guess, I could see it in her unsure yet hopeful stare as she waited for my answer, but I felt personally attacked, my smile dropping from my face. Mother started my love for dancing at a very young age, and I had tried to recreate those joyful movements with Anders, constantly trying to give him the childhood he never had, but it wasn't the same. And after last Christmas, I had to accept that it never would be.

"I do," I mumbled, losing focus of her game as my eyes fell.

"Well lucky for you," Maddie started again, "I am having a New Year's Eve party tonight, and there will be plenty of dancing. You should come."

"Please do," the boy added, smirking much too smugly for my comfort.

"Jason, be quiet," Heather grumbled, and while Jason playfully fussed and Heather harshly criticized, I gave my attention back to Maddie.

"I don't think I could," I responded, not enjoying how my heart seemed to sink at the refusal, and Maddie looked equally disappointed.

"But why?" she complained, "Do you have other plans?"

"No." It was quite the opposite. Anders and I would eat supper together and possibly play a game or two, but that was no different than any other night. I wasn't even confident he would make it to midnight awake as he had failed many times in the past, but Anders wasn't where my concerns lie. Mother would be furious if she found out I went to a party without her consent, and I knew she would never agree to it.

"Then I don't see the problem," Maddie cheered, ushering her friends to the door, "We are going to go find Bigfoot now, and I will be at your house at seven to pick you up."

"But—"

"See you tonight!" she called, allowing the closed door to end the conversation, and I sighed, realizing no matter what I did, someone was going to be disappointed tonight.

Closed doors; doesn't want to listen to you.

"What all did you do today?" I asked Anders, setting the pasta and chicken on the table. I used my best efforts to make dinner as fancy as possible, even buying us a bottle of sparkling juice to share, a fun tradition that made us feel older than we were. Anders happily served himself with enough food to appease the appetite of an almost teenage boy.

"I read a book, talked with Mom a little, and—oh, Ari! I finally solved my Rubik's Cube!" he conveyed, preparing a sizable bite of pasta on his fork.

"Oh, yeah?" Anders nodded excitedly, and I wished I shared his energy to give him the supportive reaction he deserved, but I couldn't move past the rest of his list. "What did you and Mother talk about?" I asked, keeping my eyes on the plate as I poked at the food, appetite suddenly lost.

"Just random things," Anders answered at a considerably slower pace, picking up my emotional detachment from the conversation.

I took a sip of my drink, the carbonation feeling like stabbing needles slicing down my throat, and I made an effort to focus on the discomfort more than the ache pricking my heart.

One day she will talk to you too. Be patient and make her proud. But how can she be proud when she never notices how hard I try? Wants to hate you. No other explanation.

"How was work today?" Anders questioned, a beam of sunlight piercing the darkness, and with the rays came an escape that I took without a second thought.

I met Anders' ocean-eyed stare, concern drowning in its waters, and I remembered all of the wonderful things the world offered while seeing his dark face.

Thank you, Anders.

"It was good," I responded, adding a smile that wasn't as forced as I expected. "I met some interesting people, but they were very kind. I even got invited to their party tonight." Anders' eyebrows lifted in an expression I could not recognize with the glass covering half of his face as he drank. "Don't worry. I'm not going," I explained before he could fret.

"Why not?" He asked, placing the glass back on the table, and I watched the action while debating how to answer such an obvious question.

"Because I am not just going to leave you alone on New Year's Eve," I reasoned and my brother playfully rolled his eyes.

"I am almost thirteen. I can take care of myself. Besides, I go to bed at nine anyway. The only person who'd be 'alone' here is you."

Early bird. Perfect child. Mother's favorite.

"Don't be a lemon curd," he taunted, his nose crinkling as he smiled at our inside joke, reminding me of how his face contorted after he had eaten that lemon tart years ago.

Anders was only five when I offered him a piece of what I called "lemon cake". Not accustomed to the sour tang of lemons, he exclaimed that the dessert was not made from lemons, but rather lemon *curd*, and I laughed myself hoarse at his puckered lips and eyes squeezed shut. I teased him for months afterward, and as time went on, it became an ongoing joke to use lemon curd as a sort of slang.

To this day, he refuses to eat anything with the word lemon in it, no matter how hard I try.

"I am not!" I defensively responded.

"Then go to the party! You deserve to have fun too, Ari. I will be fine here." I exhaled heavily, struggling to fight my own wishes, let alone his stubbornness.

"I can't, Anders. Mother will—"

"She won't even notice you are gone."

He sounded so optimistic saying it, as though that solved all my problems, and wasn't the root cause of them. Unlike Anders, I couldn't see such positivity, and his words hit me harder than stones ever could.

He was right. She wouldn't notice.

And maybe it was the principle that prompted me, or the desire to experience life with people my age, but the decision had been made the moment I saw Anders' promising smile.

"Alright," I caved, forcing down the remaining ache and choosing to focus on my bubbling excitement, "I will go."

Chapter Four

T rue to her word, Maddie picked me up at seven o'clock, and since her house was only a few minutes from mine, I didn't have much time to prepare myself for the pounding music heard even from her enclosed car.

"Couple things you should know," she advised, putting the vehicle into park. "Your goal is to find a partner for the midnight kiss, so dance with every boy that offers. It's the best way to see the chemistry you have."

"Midnight kiss?" I echoed, already fidgeting with the shell that once hid in my pocket, now resting just beneath my collarbone, hanging from its silver chain.

I had imagined what my first kiss would be like, just like any girl had, standing on the beach with the sunset behind us, or in a secret garden in the middle of spring when the flowers were blooming. But my fantasies never took me to an unfamiliar house late at night with someone I barely knew. It sounded more scandalous than romantic, and I could almost see the heart attack Mother would have.

"Obviously. It's *New Year's Eve.*" She answered as though I had asked her if chocolate was sweet. Maddie clearly misread the unsure lilt of my brows, easing her tone when she spoke, "But don't worry, with a face like yours, you'll have plenty of options to choose from."

My stomach twisted into several knots, and I weighed the benefits of going back home, which were looking better by the minute.

"You can take your hair down now," Maddie directed, and I paused my debating to reach for the mess of a bun atop my head.

"Why?" I questioned, obediently removing the pins.

"You mean you were going to leave it like that? You are definitely new."

My hair fell past my shoulders, down my back, and I wished I could conceal my apologetic expression in the crimson curls, but Maddie was too focused on her own hair, fluffing up the already poofy coils in her perm.

"Hair is everything," she verbalized, pausing between each word to create emphasis, "It's how you silently communicate. Flip it to a side part. Toss it over your shoulder. Twirl it around your finger. Do all this while maintaining eye contact, and you have mastered the art of hair flirtation. We'll talk about *how* to use your eyes next time. Can't have you stealing all the boys tonight," she played, giving a little scrunch to her nose as she exited the vehicle. The music was louder without the barrier of Maddie's car door, and I made no move to join her until she was at my door, opening it for me.

"And one more thing," she said, tugging me from the car, dismissing my timid requests to remain in the vehicle. "Don't eat the cookies. Those aren't chocolate chips in them."

Inside was more unruly than what I had prepared for.

Beaming neon colors of blue, red, and green flashed formations of luminous shapes on the walls cluttered with picture frames and decorations, providing an uncomfortably dark environment. Projected on the farthest wall was the countdown to the New Year, which, for the people here, was a countdown to find a partner. With the squeezing sensation stirring in my gut, I couldn't picture myself making it to midnight.

The room was exceptionally large, well-made furniture pushed to the side to form an extensive dance floor where most of the guests mingled. The refreshments table alone displayed the house owner's wealth, adorned with artful cakes and delectable snacks that appeared to have taken a considerable time to make.

But the blazing lights and appetizing smells did not overwhelm me like the pounding songs that seemed to flood in from every corner of the house. My ears ached with the sounds of boisterous laughter and off-key singing, incoherent shouts and names being called, making me completely deaf to the subtle noises, such as paranoid whispers and quiet shuffles following me. That scared me more than anything, making me wonder if the same fear drove Mother's isolation.

"Come on," Maddie giggled, moving me from where I stood frozen in the doorway. The crowd we approached didn't take note of us, swaying mindlessly to the music as they carried on with their conversation until familiar dark brown eyes caught notice of mine. Jason promptly dismissed himself from the group, joining us, to Maddie's great pleasure.

"Oh, Jason, good. I was just about to—"

Maddie's name was yelled from an unknown location, her face lighting up in response to the recognition. She almost moved to the voice, halting before the first step could be made to look at me with uncertainty.

"I've got her, Maddie. You can go," Jason offered, and Maddie turned to me.

"Alright then. See you around... uh, what is your name again?"

It was a ridiculous idea to fuss over, but the fact that we had spent this much time together, even bringing me to a party in her own car without asking once for my name, left me momentarily stunned.

"Ariella," I answered when I sensed she might leave without a response if I hesitated much longer.

"Pretty. I'll see you around, Isabella," she cheered, practically bouncing off to where she was called. I couldn't decipher whether she wasn't paying attention when I spoke, or if she couldn't hear me properly over the babbling noise, but she was gone before I had the chance to correct her.

Jason took another step closer to me, and despite being in a room filled with people, it strangely felt like it was just the two of us.

"Fun, right?" he began, gesturing around us, and I tensed as his hand nearly brushed my arm.

Don't let him touch you. Mother would be upset. Shouldn't be here. Disobedient. Rebellious. Disappointment.

"It's not what I expected," I responded, letting my eyes fall to where Maddie had rushed off, wondering if calling for her would bring her back. Jason's head dipped into my line of vision.

"You don't need to be so shy, you know."

I stared at him for a moment, then looked away, masking my insecurity with silence.

"Do you want to dance?" he offered, still smiling, but my mind registered his words differently.

Do you want to kiss tonight?

Though it may have been rude, the speed at which I backed away from him, I could not find it in me to apologize.

"I don't plan on dancing with anyone tonight," I said honestly, surprising myself at the clarity in my voice.

"I thought that's why you came. To dance."

He wasn't wrong, but after viewing the dances performed, I quickly decided against it. Until this party, I hadn't realized there were so many techniques for dancing apart from the peppy skipping and twirls that Mother taught, and the spontaneous movements made on the dance floor unconnected with the music looked overwhelming.

"I did, but I don't feel well at the moment."

That wasn't a lie either. The throbbing beat of the music began to affect my head, causing the refreshment table to appear like the most delightful thing here. "I'm going to get some water," I explained, dismissing myself.

"Would you like me to come with you?" he suggested, following in step behind me.

"I'll be fine on my own. Thank you," I answered, entering the crowd of dancers before I could convince myself otherwise.

For as appetizing as the refreshments seemed, placing the table on the other side of the room had become a damper for me. So far, there were no slow dances, allowing me to slip past people dancing individually, but that didn't stop the irritated glances I was given.

Disappointment.

The voice was in my head, repeating the same words I thought daily before I even fully registered the strangers' bothered faces.

Annoyance. Failure. Worthless.

I apologized, but the music drowned out my words, seeming to get louder with each word I spoke, digging into my ears as though clawing into my brain. My heart beat a little faster, trying to make up for the dismay I caused, but more groups kept appearing, the room never-ending, the songs stuck in a painful loop. I had held my breath in hopes of sneaking by undetected, but didn't remember to loosen it, forgetting entirely how to breathe.

Just make it to the wall. So close.

It was a lie, and the moment I realized I was lost, I stopped persisting. Everything I had been familiar with was far out of reach, and I regretted not letting Jason join me. Releasing the air from my lungs came out sharp and wrong, and inhaling felt even worse, caving my chest in. I gripped my necklace, grasping for any sense of comfort, but it only caused the chain to pull tighter around my neck.

Can't find a way out. Never making it out. Can't hear you. Too loud. Want to scream. Get out. Get out! Terrible sister. You shouldn't have come. Alone. Trapped. Scream. Need to scream. No one will help. Can't breathe. Need help—

A fierce heat engulfed my wrist, shooting sharp sparks through my entire body. I had lost count of how many people I mistakenly made physical contact within the crowded chaos, but this touch was deliberate as it loosely held my arm. I jolted from the extreme temperature change leeching near my hand, and my head whipped around in search of the cause.

There, staring back at me, were the most beautiful eyes I had ever seen.

They couldn't be described as green, not when the color was so much deeper than that, not when glittering emeralds and rich jade paled in comparison, and the flecks in the iris stole all surrounding light, reminding me of how the sun rays enhanced each hue of trees and ferns and every other thriving thing in the forest.

No, his eyes were not green. They were the color of life.

"Are you alright?" he asked, tone soft despite the blaring music practically making him yell. I was frozen, unable to break my gaze even as he glanced over me, checking as though I had been harmed. "You look a little lost."

His hand still lightly held my wrist, leaving plenty of space for me to pull away, but my hand fell limp from the inviting warmth he put off. The contact had my breath returning, my muscles relaxing, my heart easing. I hadn't known a single touch could bring relief.

"I'm Kiernan, by the way," he started again, glancing away occasionally from the stare I maintained while he pursued conversation.

For the first time in years, my mind was quiet, and with no thought, words felt useless.

It was dark, the only sense of light came from the flashing neon beams against the walls, and though his mouth was scarcely visible in my peripheral vision, I heard the smile he formed as he continued.

"You know, when someone gives you their name, they typically get a name in response."

"Ari," I managed to get out, incapable of reciting my entire name, but I always had a preference for the nickname Anders used.

"So, you can speak?" he teased, but my mouth wasn't functioning as I hoped it would, as though I had forgotten how words were formed, yet there was no irritation in his gaze, or really any emotion at all. Just a blank stare and a pleasant smile.

"Well, Ari, care to dance with me?"

I wasn't entirely sure how my head was able to nod when it felt too light to move, or how my legs fell into effortless steps as I was led farther onto the dance floor, movements not made of my own accord, and I did not fight the way he gently brought me closer to him. His hand slipped from my wrist to carry my hand, and I involuntarily shivered when powerful heat was pressed against my back.

The position we kept was comparable to a waltz, with two people facing each other, hands joining together or resting on shoulders or sides, but the steps were faster and more elaborate than the slow, rhythmic motion of a waltz. I struggled to keep up at first, but after misstepping several times, I caught on to the pace and timing, and confidence followed closely behind.

We eased past the groups dancing in place, drastically standing out from the rest of the crowd, and I was very aware of every head turning in our direction, but I was enjoying myself too much to be insecure about the attention or the fact that our movements contradicted the beat of the music. The emotional release of moving in such a carefree manner replenished me with such blind happiness and hazy thinking that I had become numb to the fingers tracing my spine and the outline of my hands, oblivious to the eyes examining with great intensity. He spun me in tight twirls, causing loud and genuine giggles to tumble from my mouth, and when he dipped me, giving me a new angle to the world, I could at last understand why people enjoyed these parties. I dangled just above the floor for longer than necessary, but that was part of the fun, not following the rules and moving however the music charmed you, and no one else could judge when they were doing the same thing.

My companion moved to lift me, dragging my reality upward to normalcy, but my foot slipped, and his posture swiftly changed from supporting me to catching me. Hands that'd been nothing but gentle suddenly fastened around my middle with demanding force, and I curled my head into him to keep it from hitting the floor. His scent permeated my nose, smelling like clean earth and smoky wood, like fresh rain and robust campfires. I laughed freely after

I caught my footing, forcing myself into stability, but he must not have been convinced since he still held on to me even after I stood.

"Sorry," I managed through a giggle, looking back at him.

He did not return my smile or the liveliness of my spirit; in fact, his face was altogether drained of emotion, leaving an unnervingly insipid countenance that made me question if he was the same affable boy who asked me to dance no more than ten minutes ago.

And now our dance had fully halted, standing motionlessly in the center of the dance floor as everyone apathetically moved around us. Without the easy breeze that came with swaying and pivoting, I was suddenly conscious of the emphatic warmth embedded in my chest, feeling the sweat trickle down my back.

His stare alternately searched between each of my eyes, as if I had answers to questions that were forbidden to be uttered. Confusion and determination pulled his eyebrows downward in a solemn focus, and I found myself unable to look away as the green burned into my vision, not until his sights shifted to something behind me, and the concentrated lines on his forehead slackened.

In an instant, all physical contact we shared concluded as he abruptly backed away from me, and despite perspiration dotting my forehead, I inwardly felt frigid. Without another word or glance my way, he moved into the crowd, disappearing entirely from my vision.

Disappointment.

The voice returned, sending chills across my skin where his touch had been, and I wrapped my arms around myself in hopes of imitating the relief he brought.

I lost track of how long I stood unmoving on the dance floor, staring perplexedly at nothing in particular, as I replayed the events in my mind, trying to pick out what went wrong. My memories gradually fused together while recalling each remembrance one by one until the whole occurrence evolved into an uncanny fever dream, but I remembered clearly how quickly the moment ended once he glimpsed behind me.

Glancing over my shoulder, I found sharp, green eyes glaring with such vehemence it couldn't be mistaken for anything but a threat. He was not the boy I danced with, knowing well I could not agree to be close with someone that intimidating, but it was evident the two were related. Every handsome line of his face was hardened in a dark scowl, the glare promising violence if

I so much as breathed the wrong way. It shouldn't have been that difficult to identify my mistakes, especially when I had accustomed myself to it for years, but I couldn't imagine my offense was comparable to the petty things I'd beat myself over with the look he gave me, staring as though I had murdered a loved one.

We watched each other for no more than a few seconds, feeling like hours of scrutiny before he at last turned to walk along the wall he'd been leaning against, giving no explanation for his actions.

Annoyance.

Dancing had left me back where I started, near the entrance, far from the refreshments, and no amount of cake was worth another nervous breakdown. I could sense another stirring in my chest, and I wrapped my arms tighter around myself, searching the crowd for aid, finding Jason's eyes instead. He stood across the room, his brows drawn down as he stared at me with a look I couldn't decide whether to be irritation or hatred. Suddenly ashamed, I dropped my gaze.

Failure.

My headache increased, pain extending from my brain to behind my eyes and inside my throat. I was without companions, security, answers, and steady legs, becoming more desensitized to the impoverished lighting and creeping deafness by the second. The only thought that diffused my anxieties was of fresh air free from congested turmoil, and the exit met my line of vision.

There wasn't a breeze as I had hoped, but the air was bitingly chilly nonetheless, cooling the skin that felt on fire. Before I could sip the frozen oxygen and refresh desperate lungs, my attention was drawn to the dispute held just around the corner, hidden, hushed, and not meant for outside ears.

"—and nothing happened. You saw for yourself," someone reasoned, statements mundane apart from the fight in it. I identified the voice without difficulty, his words, *'You look a little lost,'* ringing in my ears like a warning siren.

I knew I should have left immediately, but morbid curiosity kept me in place, only having enough sense to back into the door, pressing myself into the planned escape route.

"It doesn't matter," argued a harsher tone, "Something *could* have happened. Your recklessness could have—"

"I know," he cut the other short, unapologetic and uninterested. A sigh sounded, and I couldn't decipher who it belonged to.

"Killian would have expected more from you."

"Don't bring Killian into this," the recognizable voice snarled back.

There was a deep, rumbling noise that reacted, something close to a growl but with more imperious demand.

"I'm only going to say this once." The conversation had significantly quieted, and had I not given all my focus to the heated discussion, I would have missed it. "*Stay away from it*," he spat the words with disgust, as though verbalizing them appalled him. If there was a response, it was too low for me to hear, but the gruff voice went on with barely a pause. "You wait here. I'm going to get Keagan, then we are leaving."

There were footsteps next, heavy and precise as they neared, and I found my hand had never left the door handle, resulting in an undetectable re-entry of the home.

I took no comfort in my hurried movement being masked by the unforgiving volumes, knowing their sight was unaffected, and their eyes felt sharper than most.

Not safe. Get out. Get home. Never should have come.

I frantically shoved past teenagers, my erratic heartbeat shrouding their voiced complaints, hunting for an escape. My mind flashed back to a few days ago, when I ran for my life in the woods from a threat that did not pursue, and the heat returning to my veins burned like scorching lava.

If I could just find Maddie, I could go home and later laugh at my paranoid self, but at the moment, I did not feel ridiculous in my distraught search, and spotting a popular girl in a room packed with people seemed more impossible by the second. I was alone and lost again, but I preferred that over being found and in possible danger.

Heather's low, flirtatious giggle should have been too quiet for me to hear, but in my attempts to pick out each softened sound, finding her location was the simplest thing I'd done that night. I didn't run to avoid unwanted attention, but my unsteady legs formed brisk steps in her direction, halting solely after spotting another one of *them.*

He smiled brilliantly, teeth radiant and perfect, undoubtedly aware of the effect it had on the girls crowding him, as though he had the antidote to every broken and lonely heart, and it would've been a lie to claim there was no draw to listen to the story he enthusiastically told.

His dark hair was longer, not like the mullet Jason had, but on the top, the perfect length for running his hands through when speaking, which he did on more than one occasion. He must've known of Maddie's hair flirtation methods.

I watched as each girl near him seemed to melt, intoxicated by the vibrant eyes and upmost confidence, the charming manner in which he spoke to each individual as if he were sharing an intimate secret. Heather was no exception.

I took a timid step closer to her, preparing to whisper my request in her ear, but my attempts at subtlety fell through when his eyes slid to mine, piercing me with green for the third time that night. He abruptly paused the story, captivating the audience that would have done anything to gain the intense attention he granted me. His pleasurable front slowly drained from his flawless face, unease teasing every confident muscle of his body, but unlike the other two, his stare was concerned, unsure of what was the most appropriate move.

"Excuse me, ladies," he spoke, his voice soft and charming, matching the rest of his disposition. He offered each girl a brief look, eyes lingering a moment longer when reuniting with mine before passing in the direction opposite, and while several girls followed him, unwilling to give up on a possible midnight kiss, most of them faced me with a stern scowl. I swallowed, sensing the pure jealousy and irritation press in on me, and I wanted to explain my innocent intentions, but the girls had already started dispersing into different crowds, not that I thought they would believe me anyway. In truth, I wanted to leave just as much as they wished me gone.

"You'd better have a good reason for interrupting," Heather grumbled once the group had left, clearly not wanting to be associated with me when there were witnesses.

"I need to find Maddie," I hurriedly answered, disregarding the sore edge in her tone.

Heather released a labored sigh before unexpectedly yelling Maddie's name, and my heart practically leaped out of my chest at the impending attention.

"Oh my gosh, Isabella!" Maddie's enthusiastic profile emerged seemingly out of nowhere, and I wondered how much trouble I could have saved by simply calling for her. She rushed to us, giggling as she came, sweat dampening the tight, yellow curls framing her face, and I was glad to see I wasn't the only one swelteringly hot, though our reasons were likely dissimilar.

"I saw you dancing with a Turner!" she exclaimed like a proud mother to an accomplished child. Maddie faced Heather to ask, "Did you see which one it was?"

"No," Heather clipped, glancing about the room to see which group looked the most intriguing to join, or maybe she was searching for the boy, a *Turner*, I mentally corrected; either way, Heather showed no interest in our conversation. Maddie shrugged her off, turning back to me with a much too excited expression.

"What did he look like? Was he handsome? Well, I mean, they are all ridiculously beautiful, but exactly *how* attractive was he?" she pressed, growing louder with each question.

I couldn't remember, headache clogging the proper flow of my thoughts, clouding everything apart from...

Brilliant green lighting up the dark. Life in his eyes. Warmth in his hands. 'Dance with me?' Airy twirling and giddy laughter. What was his name?

I shook away the thoughts, hoping to move past them and forget the occurrence altogether.

"I don't know, Maddie, but—"

She paused to catch her breath, and I tried to convey the irrelevance of this topic, but she was spewing out more statements before I could get more words in. "It's okay, Isabella, we will find you your midnight kiss. Don't stress."

"That's not my na—"

"Was he really flirty with you?"

There she was again, using her mind-reading process of elimination on me to discover things I didn't want others to know.

"No," I reluctantly complied, understanding Maddie would not give up on it.

"So not Keagan. Was he kind of scary?" I shuddered remembering that hard glare he held.

"Definitely not."

"Not Kell, then. Which leaves Kiernan."

Kiernan. That was his name.

I nodded, regretting it the instant Maddie exploded into a new level of excitement.

"Oh my *gosh*! You have to tell me everything! What did he say? How long did you dance for? Did you use your hair like I told you to—"

"Maddie!" I finally cut in, realizing just enough built-up anxiety to compose myself. "I want to go home."

Maddie's expression remained huge, simply swapping from excited to surprised. "Go home? But it's still hours from midnight. We haven't even done karaoke yet."

"I can't sing," I replied abruptly, extracting a smile from Maddie's countenance, no doubt believing I was just being shy.

"Sure, you can. It doesn't have to sound pretty; it's just for fun. This is a judgment-free zone." After my recent experiences, I had a difficulty believing that.

"I *won't* sing," I corrected, watching as her brows furrowed.

"Why not?" she asked, lips puckered.

"I'd rather not get into it."

That was the wrong thing to say to a hostess determined for you to have fun.

"I will take you home after you do karaoke with me," she challenged, an impish grin making her cloud-colored eyes sparkle.

Betraying both parents in one night raised a lump of guilt in my throat, and though neither of them would ever know my wrongdoing, that didn't make it okay. It was a mistake to go partying; I knew that, and went anyway, digging myself deeper into the mess while trying to get out of it.

"One song?" she pleaded.

I peered at my surroundings, not a trace of trouble in sight, and I assumed the Turners must've left after overhearing their conversation.

"One song," I caved, and Maddie squealed.

She ushered me through the dance floor, hand clasped around my own, dragging me past groups that didn't seem as bothered by being bumped into when noticing the owner of the party leading me.

There was a platform just a step above the floor holding equipment for music, and when Maddie switched off the party songs, starting the microphones in the silence that rang louder than the previous music, it announced the end of dancing and the beginning of singing.

A well-known tune was presented through the speakers, compelling several teens to cheer in acknowledgment. Thankfully, I recognized the popular song as well, used to humming along to the radio at home when cleaning or cooking, and the slightest bit of confidence allowed me to rest my hand by my side without it bunching in my skirt. Maddy was jumping to the beat of the intro, microphone already to her mouth in preparation, and I found it in me to giggle. Though she was aloof and abrasive at times, I admired Maddie's enthusiasm.

She began to sing, lyrics fitting in perfect timing, many voices joining with her in a mish-mashed sing-along. Subconsciously, my smile grew, my head gently bobbing to the music, forgetting about the many people watching us. Some returned to the habit of dancing, while others took the opportunity to get refreshments. Maddie sang with her whole heart, unfazed by anyone else's decisions, and I wished I knew her secret for that. As her part of the song neared an end, she pointed to me, the last friendly boost I needed.

I'm sorry, Father.

Pressing the microphone to my lips, I followed up with Maddie's verse, lungs releasing pent-up emotion in full, lively notes, finally remembering how to breathe. At first, it came out in strong gasps, flowing into decisive words and satisfied stanzas.

I closed my eyes for a moment, reveling in the lightness of my chest, setting free crushing weights gained from years of silence, and there was a second that passed where I believed gravity did not apply to me. I wished to stay in this warped sensation of certitude, but when I was forced to regain reality, Kiernan's stunned face being the first thing I saw, it didn't seem like an incomprehensible idea.

Maddie was right to call him ridiculously beautiful, with his sharp jawline and dark, wave-textured hair falling just above perfect eyebrows; I couldn't think of a better description. Heat bloomed across my cheeks, recalling how close we had been not long ago.

He stood across the room, his eyes were wide and alive, as though he was seeing the world for the first time. His lips parted as he opened his mouth the slightest amount, longing to speak things that never made it past his throat.

Apart from a quick stutter, my voice persisted in a lovely melody until the two remaining Turners surged into the room, hands shoved aggressively against their ears, yanking Kiernan to the exit. Kiernan appeared not to notice as he was dragged, gaping at me with what looked like hope, but again, they disappeared with unreadable glances as their sole communication, and I was left with an eerie dread to rest in the pit of my stomach.

I stopped singing then, utterly disturbed and unable to continue, but there weren't complaints about me ending mid-song as I had expected or any reaction at all.

Drawing my focus from the bizarre event, I found all attention on me, each person having expressions similar to Kiernan's, and I regretted not listening to my father's instructions. Silence filled the room when the wordless music muted, and people began to move like they had control of themselves once more. Applause and astonished smiles burst from the guests, Maddie undoubtedly affected by something, causing her to cover her gawking mouth.

"Do you know how *beautiful* you sound?" she shouted, and I didn't like how she looked at me, like she'd be willing to jump off a bridge if I asked her to.

"Home. Please," I reminded, longing to block out each plea for me to stay and sing more, Maddie especially trying her best to keep me. It took more fight than I had, but eventually, I convinced her to take me home.

The car ride was silent, Maddie hoping to prove her reluctance through the stillness, but it was a nice break from the persistent sound. I wished her a Happy New Year as my goodbye for the evening, incapable of relaxing until I was inside my house behind a locked door. My family was asleep as expected, and while I planned to do the same, lying in bed wide awake as the hours went on, my mind couldn't rest, too immersed in thoughts of the party.

And I rang in the New Year thinking of the color green in more ways than one.

Chapter Five

The Silent Killer found new victims.

It had been over two months since the last kidnapping, and just when it was considered that the crimes had faded into the background again, three were announced missing on the same night. The year had only begun, and death was the topic of every conversation.

I was terrified of what the future held.

In my rush to make it to work on time, I missed the details the radio provided of the tragedies. Restlessness kept me awake most of the night, causing me to miss my alarm, and if it hadn't been for Anders checking on me, I would've been hours late to my shift, which I feared to start more than usual.

My job was safer than most, with armed officer rangers patrolling the forest, ensuring protection for all on the park grounds, but even if every citizen of Crescent City worked to keep the redwoods a secure place, it wouldn't be enough to cover the forest's entirety, especially not with the rapid population decrease from disappearances and people moving away out of fear. Leaving was never an option for my family however, a comfortless realization I came upon several years ago when I saw how attached Mother was to this little town in her paintings, but Mother didn't seem bothered by this Silent Killer, or that multiple deaths were assumed each year. I started to wonder if there was anything she cared about enough to leave her room for. I strived not to focus on her, the news, or how alone I felt walking the trails, instead understanding that if I stayed on the path, visible through the gapped trees, where screams could be heard, I'd be fine.

Keeping to the familiar soil was simple, unlike the precarious thoughts demanding in, similar to bees swarming a hive, and when the buzzing became intolerable, I resolved to hush them with my voice.

No matter how hard I tried, I couldn't forget the karaoke incident, or the unconventional event that preceded it, shocked faces and clamorous cheering burned into my memory, but now that I was on my own, singing didn't feel unlawful. It still didn't feel right, either, but forcing out words in song made me breathe, which tended to be otherwise difficult when I had myself worked up.

The redwoods were complacent as I continued forward, eliminating any sound that could play as a distraction while my voice encircled clearly around each tree, supplying my chest with fond levity. Even though it was wrong, I loved the way it felt to sing freely and openly, a desire unknown to me, until Maddie introduced it by coercing me to the microphone.

My anxieties had nearly diminished when detecting movement in my peripheral vision made my heart skip a beat, cutting my song short.

My first thought was of an animal, remembering the last woodland creature encounter, calming after placing the figure as human, walking off path, and vanishing behind a distant tree.

"Excuse me!" I called out, hoping to grab their attention from where I could see the ground, fearing to lose myself in the sea of ferns, but when there was no response, I was forced to follow after them. Not every visitor was conscious of the dangers this place held, diverted by the majestic atmosphere, and their safety was my top priority.

I shouted again, trudging deeper into the woods, trying not to trip on hidden roots and rocks, gradually misplacing the path back in my mind, and just when I convinced myself that my imagination had gotten the better of me again, I spotted him.

"Kiernan?"

He paused his strolling and twisted to see me, his face lacking the surprise I carried. Now viewing him in the daylight, surrounded by greenery, his eyes didn't illuminate as a silent argument appeared to be held behind them, but seemed to blend with the environment, like he belonged here and was meant to disappear into the brush. There were many inquiries my mind summoned, lingering on my tongue, but thankfully, the only question that slipped out was a sensible, "What are you doing out here?"

Kiernan shifted to face me fully, and with the blinding muddle of last night, I somehow missed the deep tan of his skin and the notable toning of his arms from where he wavered, short-sleeved in the early January weather. I felt cold just looking at him, more queries catching in my throat.

Comparable to flipping a switch, Kiernan's countenance changed, arms folding and posture loosening.

"Hiking?" he posed, as though it were obvious, glancing about the forest.

"You can't hike off the trails. It's against the rules, not to mention dangerous. There are *bears* out here—" I was interrupted by Kiernan's soft, breathy chuckle, like I was not worth the energy of a full laugh but too comical to ignore, and feeling like a naive child, I scowled asking, "What is so funny?"

"Nothing," he answered, grin telling me otherwise, but when he refused to elaborate, I tried again.

"Will you please come back to the trail with me?" I explained, pondering if he knew where the trails were.

"Where? Those commercialized, little pathways you walk? Don't tell me that's all you've seen of this place," he seemed to reprimand though he wasn't truly upset, exposing perfect teeth in an off-kilter smile that did odd things to my stomach.

"It's all any of us are supposed to see," I insisted, standing firm even when my legs strangely felt like buckling, and his eyes turned mischievous as though he knew my feigned strength.

"Well, that would make living out here rather difficult."

My eyebrows pulled together.

"You... live here?"

"Not exactly in *this area*, but in the redwoods, yes."

I blinked in surprise, but I believed him because, interestingly enough, it made more sense than anything else.

"Is that legal?" I asked, my face pinched with uncertainty, while Kiernan gave an unbothered shrug.

"I have been here for nineteen years and haven't gotten in trouble yet," he said, offering another smile that was startlingly beautiful, but it didn't quite fit right, similar to a piece forced into the wrong puzzle. "I could show you some beautiful places if you'd like," he proposed, hand gesturing further into the grove.

My denial should've been quick and without thought, yet there was something about the way the wind nudged me forward and opened the gates to endless passages, something about *him* pulling me in with the false sense of security he emitted, reminiscent of when we danced together. I could hear my thoughts ringing like warnings, especially when they sounded like Zadar.

Help the visitors. Preserve the vegetation. Watch for animals. Never *leave the trail.*

Easy, basic, simple rules he had given me, and I believed my brisk consideration of breaking any of them to be a betrayal of Zadar's trust.

"I can't," I answered, attempting not to show emotion just as he had demonstrated.

"Okay. Another time then, Ari."

I had heard Anders say my name countless times, but it sounded different playing on Kiernan's lips, like he practiced it several times to see which way felt most appealing.

Another time. He wants to see you another time.

Kiernan then walked off, and I returned to the trail.

"You sang?" Anders shouted, the shock of his knowing I never shared my voice publicly making him louder than usual.

He'd been more than curious to hear *every* detail about the party, and while I had no problem telling him of flashing lights, loud music, and large friend groups with plenty of dancing, I was careful to leave out the parts involving the Turners.

"Yes, actually, and a lot of people seemed to enjoy it."

"That doesn't surprise me," he responded, meaning the compliment he gave entirely. "What was your favorite part?"

Dancing with him.

The thought arose so quickly that I physically flinched, and I didn't appreciate how the movement yanked Anders' attention, action not matching my words as I drawled, "I don't know..."

Hands catching you from falling. Eyes searching for answers in your own. Fresh rain and robust campfires.

"Probably the cake," I concluded, remembering how I failed to reach the refreshment table. Anders didn't need to know that, or the other memories rushing through my head that I tried to push away.

"Were there any *boys* interested in you?" he taunted, voice overly playful and excited, ready to give me a hard time if the opportunity presented itself. My eyes shot to him, a quick rush of panic firing through me at the thought of him reading my mind, but I easily calmed myself once noticing how ridiculous this was.

"No," I answered, trying to hold back the smile forming. Anders cocked his head, mischievous grin taking over his expression, making my smile break free. I could have told him about Jason, but I tried not to think about that either.

"Alright, Ari. Who do I need to fight?"

His exaggerated protection ripped a laugh from my lungs, earning little giggles from my younger brother, echoing happiness through the house. Even though it was all just a joke, the love he showed was real, and if it ever came down to it, I knew Anders would fight to the death for my safety.

The teasing was interrupted by a demanding knock at the door, our heads whipping in that direction. No one visited our home, and the expectant pounding against the entrance stole the room's cheerfulness.

"Did you invite anyone over?" I questioned Anders in a lowered voice, and after he shook his head, I was compelled to answer the call.

Cautiously, I opened the door, only to shove it aside when recognizing the girl with the perm doing her best to hold back tears.

"Maddie?"

Maddie looked nothing like her usual peppy self, posture slouched, makeup smeared, and hair disheveled more than I thought possible of a perm. She stared at me speechless for a moment, and I watched, stunned, as ample tears slid down her air-chilled pink cheeks.

"What's wrong?" I inquired, and that was all the invitation Maddie needed. Stepping into the house, she wrapped her arms around me in an aggressive hug, squeezing until my breath had been nearly taken from me.

"I'm so sorry for your loss," she sobbed onto my shoulder, "I know you were close to her too."

Carefully, I rested one arm on her back, the other I used to close the door, keeping away the winter wind that requested in as well. Anders neared as I brought Maddie to the couch, setting her down to better understand the situation.

"Tissues," I communicated to Anders through sign language, and while he ran to his room, I took the seat beside Maddie and placed a comforting hand on her shoulder, thumb gently rubbing against her shirt as she continued to cry. "What happened?" I questioned tenderly, experienced in calming with these situations, and Maddie relaxed slightly from my touch.

"Heather," she choked out, "she's dead."

My hand stilled.

"What?" I uttered understatedly; despite the shock I felt.

"She was one of them who didn't make it home last night."

One of the taken.

A surreal uneasiness came over me, realizing I was one of the last people who would ever see her again, wondering what might have happened to me if I'd stayed longer. Heather did not particularly care for me, but I would never have wished this on her or anyone. The unknown was such a terrifying thing, and I couldn't imagine what Maddie must have been feeling. I pulled her back into a warm embrace, offering consolation in any way I could, but Maddie had stopped crying, grief coming and leaving in waves. I didn't want to guess how many tears she'd already shed throughout the day.

Anders' footsteps hurried down the stairs, rushing around the corner to hand me the box of tissues, which Maddie gladly took for herself.

"Who is this?" she asked. She sniffed once and pulled a tissue from its container.

"This is my brother Anders," I introduced, before facing him and explaining, "and this is my friend Maddie."

The smile he gave her was warm and bright, lighting up the room like the sun, and Maddie thrived off of it. Anders exhibited his ability to brighten the world around him, making it impossible to be sad in his presence, and I was greatly appreciative of the distraction he brought.

"Which one of you is adopted?" she questioned, tone already near normal, which made it easier to respond honestly.

"Neither," I answered more in a question than a statement, puzzled by how she came to that conclusion. Her eyes flicked between us, not wanting to state the obvious, but unable to believe we were related.

"You look nothing alike," she claimed, fully moved from the last conversation to this one, and if it had been anyone other than Maddie, the drastic change would've concerned me.

She wasn't wrong, though. In the looks department, Anders and I were very dissimilar, skin light and dark, hair curly and coiled, eyes purple and blue, but our hearts, habits, interests, and sense of humor made us unmistakably alike.

"We have different fathers," I put simply, which Maddie interpreted as an entirely different thing.

"*Oh*." The tone she used gave away her judgmental notions, and because my guard had been down to express vulnerability, my protectiveness took over.

"Before you think poorly of my mother, she was not a cheat," I snipped, a bit more defensively than needed. "She lost my father a year before she had Anders."

"So, your mom remarried?"

I shifted, uncomfortable with the topic and how Anders was listening intently to every word.

"No," I muttered, wishing she would drop the issue.

"Mhm," she hummed matter-of-factly, as though she perfectly understood the subject I wasn't bringing up, determined to take some source of scandalous gossip from the conversation.

"No, Maddie, I—" my eyes shot to Anders, my wonderful beam of sunshine, and though the idea of that light dimming broke my heart, he was old enough and deserved to know. "I don't think she had a choice in the matter."

I had never said those words out loud, even if I had believed them for years. Like many things, Mother refused to talk about Anders' father, a secret that never sat well with me, and of all the conclusions I developed, this made the most sense. It explained why I never met him, why Mother wouldn't leave the house anymore, and why she tried harder to show her son love and acceptance. She was afraid, worried he wouldn't feel as though he belonged, but my mind refused to see Anders as a casualty of violence, not when he was the only thing holding this family together.

Thankfully, Maddie didn't push the subject further, for once reading the room and quieting, but it wasn't her reaction I was concerned about.

Glancing at Anders, I found his brows pulled together, face full of pity and sorrow, not for himself, but directed at me. I wished to understand what he was thinking and see his reasoning for looking at *me* with sympathy when I clearly didn't deserve it. At least I knew who my father was, and that he would never hurt Mother, but Anders was always selfless, and the idea of him prioritizing my feelings didn't surprise me.

Unfortunately, expecting Maddie to stay silent for long was unrealistic, and when it looked like she might explode if she didn't say something, she started a new, unneeded topic.

"Has Kiernan tried to contact you yet?"

My heart stuttered a beat, pinning her with a look she evidently did not catch on to.

"Kiernan?" Anders echoed, speaking up for the first time since Maddie arrived.

"No, he hasn't," I answered pointedly.

All three conversations were difficult to deal with in their own way, and I was starting to worry what might come out of Maddie's mouth next if she stayed much longer.

"You are lying," Anders observed, staring at me curiously like he could see all the secrets written on my face. It may not have been the best cover up, but how fast and confidently he called me out had us both startled.

"I knew it!" Maddie exclaimed, momentarily ripping my concentration from Anders, and I could practically see the questions piling in her lungs. I panicked, shooting to my feet and grabbing her wrist to tug her with me.

"It was wonderful to have you over, Maddie, but I have *tons* of chores to get done, and I wouldn't want to bore you with that," I insisted, ushering her to the door before she could bring Kiernan's name up again.

"Is she lying about that, too?" she questioned my brother as she scurried beside me, exiting without a response. "Thanks for showing me your house, Isabella. We can finish our conversation later," Maddie said with a wink, shutting my door for me, the stress leaving with her.

"Were you planning on telling me about Kiernan?" Anders asked softly, almost sounding hurt about my keeping situations from him, and I sighed, repressing the guilt I felt.

"Listen, Anders, a lot happened last night, and there are some things that I just would rather not talk about," I explained in complete sincerity, watching as his expression melted into understanding.

"Okay, but Ari, if something important happens, do you promise to tell me?"

I held his gaze and reached for his hand, hoping to help prove my pledge through two points of contact.

"I promise."

I squeezed his hand, and while Anders smiled, his expression wilted, as though all he saw in my eyes were lies.

Chapter Six

Anders' guttural scream pierced my heart.

I shot up, almost tripping on air as I stood, blood rushing to my head in dizzying pulsations. It wasn't uncommon for him to shout after a nightmare, but in all the years of listening to his anguish, never had I heard him scream like *that*.

The world wouldn't stop spinning, even as I reached my doorframe, reluctantly pushing forward, neglecting how the floor seemed to twist, and that I may not have been fully conscious. Anders' cries drove past his door and through the hall, the sound reverberating through my bones.

It felt like hours had gone by before I had, at last, made it to his room, finding him crumbled on the ground a few feet away from his bed, head lowered and knees pressing against the wooden floorboards. His arms were fastened tightly around his abdomen, constricting the sobs that puffed out in uneven gasps.

"Anders?" I spoke, unsure whether it came out in a yell or whisper, but he heard me either way, ocean eyes brighter than they'd ever been when finding me.

His tense muscles shifted rapidly, finding his footing long enough to grab ahold of me and nearly pull me back down with him. Balancing our weight, I was able to haul him into a complete hug, helping him remain upright as he cried.

"You died. You died. *You died!*" Panic rose in his voice, his entire body in tremors that worsened with each word. "He killed you—I saw it!" His hands fisted the back of my shirt, gripping like I'd disappear if he let go.

"It wasn't real," I soothed, managing to keep us stable even with my brother's trembling.

"But it was real," he choked, barely catching his breath before going on, "I could see too clearly for it not to be: the colors, the room, the man, the darkness, how the sick murderer had you draped over his arm, the wound in your stomach, and the *blood*. So much blood..."

"Don't think about it," I whispered, the command directed to us both, trying to erase the vivid picture he'd painted in my mind.

"I can't get the image out of my head!" he echoed back, agony soaking his voice, incessant tears returning.

"I'm alive, Anders. It wasn't real," I repeated, but it did not change the way he continued to wail into my shirt, dampening the lapel.

Sharing the same hopelessness Anders experienced, I defaulted to humming the lullaby while my fingers gently traced shapes on his back, knowing he would calm eventually, and I was willing to comfort him for as long as he needed.

Overhearing Maddie cry about Heather's death from upstairs was the only explanation I could formulate that would trigger such a nightmare about the silent killer. Death had a way of haunting, even those young and healthy, a taunting reminder of inevitable fate, and if dwelled upon, could consume the living. I envisioned Anders fighting that battle as his cries quieted, and my trapped voice hushed.

"I'm scared," he mumbled, words groggy but calm, and I was relieved to hear his breathing had regulated.

"About what?" I questioned, moving back to see his face, and besides the puffy eyes, he looked completely normal.

"That I am going to lose you."

A piece of my heart chipped off hearing the pain and honest fear in his tone, like he knew the future, couldn't prevent it, and dreaded the outcome all at once.

"You couldn't get rid of me even if you wanted to," I teased, poking at his side until a smile broke on his face, eyes still carrying sadness, "You should go back to bed. Tomorrow is your first day back to school from Christmas break. You need the rest."

Reluctantly, Anders nodded, crawling into bed and tangling himself in the sheets. I examined his movements, and when he appeared at ease, I was able to leave his room.

I couldn't sleep much after that, and it was safe to say Anders didn't either.

I wouldn't say my walk along the trails was mindless, focused on one thing rather than being filled with nothing, but I was oblivious to anyone who might have crossed my path, which made my job of searching for people in need pointless. Heather and I were not friends by any means, but I was acquainted with her, and knowing the face opposed to simply learning a name on the radio seemed much more *real*. I felt personally tied to the tragedy, like a witness in a murder, but parallel to the other cases, there was no evidence to present. While I always felt sorrowful for the victims, terror nipped at my heart thinking of what happened to Heather, what could *still be* happening to her.

If Anders were ever to be taken, I could only picture the hysteria that would destroy me. It was clear he was thinking the same thing from that torturous nightmare, his mind traveling to the darkest places beyond reality and exercising fears that shouldn't have been strengthened.

The forest was louder today, not in the sense of wind rustling leaves or birds chirping, but in gentle humming, like the trees hoped to lull me past their barriers, forever losing my way back. As I stared at the off-trail path I had taken yesterday, I pondered how bad of a thing it would truly be, to exist forgotten in a place as beautiful as the redwoods, in return forgetting the painful life outside of peaceful silence and vibrant colors.

"Don't do it."

I jumped, startled by the taunting voice behind me interrupting serene stillness. Kiernan stood just enough off the path to be a bother, but not an actual issue, ferns coming up to his shins as his slanted posture leaned against one of the oversized trees. "It's dangerous, remember? Bears and all," he mocked, but his face didn't match his tone; a hollowed expression and deep, emerald eyes overcome with nothingness. "Plus, you are still new here. If you plan on going off trail exploring, which I do recommend, at least go with someone who knows the forest well."

He stood a bit taller, a clear gesture to himself.

Contemplating how he managed to sneak behind me without a sound, I missed his offer, my face contorting as I looked at him.

"How do you know I am new?"

The question of how he even learned I worked here was undoubtedly answered with the dark green uniform I wore, which he didn't give much notice to.

"The trees have ears," he responded, placing a large palm on the damp bark, the kind touch you would give a close companion, "and they whisper about you."

It was an absurd statement, one that shouldn't have been encouraged, but I couldn't refrain from the curiosities compelling me to ask, "What do they say?"

His gaze slid to mine from where he beheld the top branches of the tree, the intensity making my heart stutter.

"I can't share that. It's personal."

My brows pulled together in doubt, suddenly concerned about the opinions of plants.

"How come you get to know?" I contested, wishing my tone hadn't sounded as aggravated.

"They are my friends," he put simply, taking another look at rich leaves dangling near hazy clouds.

"The trees?" The vexation I held began to slip, intrigue filling its place to which Kiernan mistook as humor.

"Are you going to start laughing?"

It would have been a more appropriate response to delusions I was oddly growing more fascinated in, but instead, I stuttered, "No, I—I want to be friends with them too."

His hand fell from dark wood, moving to the trail in my direction, and I tried to discern why I stepped back.

"How do you expect to be close with the forest when you only see the parts everyone else does? Anyone can make small talk and tread the comfortable areas in their lives, but it's the deep conversations and sharing things nobody else knows that creates true friendships," he illustrated, stopping just in front of me, the heat radiating from him, instantly pulling my mind back to our dance, the sole circumstance I couldn't bring myself to regret from that night. "So do you want to stay on the trail just like every other acquaintance, or would you like to come with me and listen to the trees whisper their secrets?"

This close, I had to tilt my head upward to meet his gaze, and Kiernan had no issue looking down at me as his eyes darted across my face.

"I don't even know you."

He hummed in acknowledgment, his sight never wavered as its curious search persisted.

"Well... I speak a little Greek, midnight is my favorite time of the day, and I hate the rain. There, now we are friends too."

He motioned an amicable greeting, his scent claiming the air around us, smoky yet sweet, reminiscent of burnt marshmallows.

"My manager would be upset," I resolved, ultimately shutting the idea down, and to my surprise, I expressed more disappointment than he did.

"I won't force you to do anything that makes you uncomfortable," he answered easily, stepping past me and on to prohibited territory, pausing long enough to call out, "But if you were interested in knowing, the forest is very fond of you."

Then he was gone again.

I hadn't struggled parting ways yesterday, but now my feet stuck to the dirt, legs denying any movement that didn't follow him or the wind's pushing.

Stay on the trail. Stay where it is safe, where everyone has been, where you want to be. Small talk and comfortable treading. Secure and simple. Only, that's not what you want. A crave for deep conversations with whispered secrets, hidden and carefree. A friend of the forest.

"Kiernan, wait," I called out.

The clean air tickled my skin in a friendly welcome as I ran after Kiernan, jumping over fallen branches and ducking under low-hanging limbs. He wasn't too far ahead of me, as he hadn't been given enough time to be unreachable, and the farther I went, the more puzzled I became to find him not around the corner.

I shouted his name again, a bit breathless, smile teasing my lips, but he did not respond.

I ran farther, my heart racing in exhilaration, dissatisfied when forced to pause in front of a fallen tree blocking my path. Moss lined the bark and ground, like a large, green blanket draped over the sleeping nature. Still, there was no sight of Kiernan.

I quickly concluded all the casualties coming from attempting to climb over the enormous trunk, accepting that if Kiernan had done so, he was already long gone.

Irritated for not accepting his offer sooner, I turned back, contemplating the beauties I was missing out on.

I tried again to call for Kiernan, glancing around me for any indication of him, search cut short after detecting that wasn't the tree I originally believed it to be, or how all my surroundings looked unfamiliar.

Oh, lemon curd.

I was lost.

"Kiernan!" I yelled, alarm lining my voice, vision overanalyzing every bark grove and smashed clover, anything to spark my memory. I spun hastily, hunting for a way back until dizziness caused the world to tilt and my hand to grip a tree for support.

Just when I had gathered enough air to yell for help, black fur moved into my field of vision, terror clogging my lungs from exhaling.

The bear's eyes met with mine, sharing the same expression and stillness I carried, and I couldn't decipher if he wanted to retreat or attack; both of us locked in a frozen stare.

Zadar had told me not to run, instead to stand tall and make loud noises, but Zadar felt so far away now, and I couldn't find my lungs to breathe, let alone scream.

The bear footed closer, leaving massive prints in the dirt, and with each step he progressed, I could feel myself shrinking. Slowly, the fear in his coal, black eyes waned, realizing I was not stronger than him, how easy of a target I would be, and compared to his claws and teeth, I truly was helpless.

"Go away!" Kiernan demanded, grabbing the beast's attention when he appeared seemingly put of nowhere.

My knees buckled, relief lasting a mere second as I tumbled down. Though I wasn't alone, that didn't make me safe, only sharing the danger with someone else, but Kiernan showed no signs of fear as he boldly stood between the bear and my crumpled figure.

"Leave," he ordered, dark and threatening, but the bear fed from my vulnerability, continuing to advance to remove the interference. I swallowed hard, forcing down the desire to vomit, gripping my shell with enough pressure to break it.

A deep rumbling reverberated through the solid earth beneath me, rattling my bones and settling in the pit of my stomach, the growl playing as what

I assumed was a last show of strength before the bear ran off, yet somehow overlooking the fear that had returned to its eyes.

Kiernan's face was a mask of emotionlessness when he turned, glancing over me with enough dullness to make me wonder if we had witnessed the same thing.

"Are you alright?" he spoke, feeling wiped clean from his tone like an entire town missing from a map. I didn't blink as I shakily nodded, afraid I'd miss something if I lost sight of him for even a split second.

He offered a hand to me, something twisting under his skin, snaking down his arm, and I flinched away on instinct, regretting it when he recoiled faster than he lended. Kiernan's gaze darted to the side, somehow looking like an ashamed child despite his vacant expression.

Warily, I stood, legs wobbling to find a solid stance, but Kiernan kept his eyes on the dirt, his posture tight and unreadable. I opened my mouth to speak, not entirely sure what to say, but he pointed to my left before I could make a sound.

"The trail is that way," he spoke, his mouth in a thin line matching the tensity of his tone, "You should go back."

My legs complied before my brain could register, stumbling in half-steps closer to safety, watching him carefully as I moved, muscles remembering how to ease away from past animal encounters.

Kiernan didn't speak again, my brain too scrambled to request an explanation, and when he was out of my line of sight, I sprinted to the trail.

Chapter Seven

I t had been a week since I last walked the trails.

Graciously, my manager agreed to let me work at the front desk when I asked, never questioning me or my change in behavior, not caring enough to give the proper attention, and my aching miss of Zadar grew by the day. It worked out, however, to be overlooked and ignored, allowing my incident to escape unnoticed. Maybe it was a mistake to keep a bear encounter a secret, but I feared my job was at risk if I confessed to breaking the rules, and if I was being honest with myself, the bear wasn't the reason I avoided my normal rounds.

Each exchange I shared with Kiernan felt off, like an anomalous dream, the kind in which you wake up sweating and dazed, and more times than not, his exchanges ended with me in a panicked state. While the problems may not have been his fault, I couldn't deny the bad luck charm he seemed to carry, and yet when I was around him, I dared to do things I never would have considered before.

I had plenty of time to think it all over from behind the counter, aiding the post-holiday groups trickling in as we slowly inched our way to February. Days were longer when cooped up in a visitor's center, invasive thoughts stuffing my head when forcing confidence to talk to strangers wasn't distracting me, and by the beginning of the next work week, outside adventures sounded like an escape more than a danger.

Strange or not, Kiernan had saved my life, and at the least, he deserved a thank you.

I resolved returning to the woods when the rain had calmed and the sun could aid my journey, only calling for Kiernan once before spotting him standing in the center of the trail.

He looked different than before, friendly smile gone, arms folded over his broad chest, stance implying he had been expecting me to show up for some time. The rain darkened his hair in half-hearted waves falling over his face, still attractive despite its solemn edge.

Hates the rain.

I swallowed, risking my comfort to be near him, life-like color tracking my motions.

"I wanted to thank you for..." I still didn't want to admit it, even if he had witnessed the occasion himself, "last week."

That was the lightest way to put it.

"It was nothing," Kiernan spoke, bored in every aspect, and though he may not have looked sore, anger was the only rationale for his replies.

"It wasn't nothing. You saved my life! Let me repay the favor," I presented, hoping to make up for not just my rescue, but also his patience that I frankly didn't deserve.

"There is no need."

Another short, uninterested response, this time involving him turning away, announcing the irritation my avoidance caused, and my guilt provoked me to block his departure.

"Please don't be upset with me," I implored, stepping in front of him, grateful that he didn't press forward, "I should've come to see you sooner. I know. I'm sorry. You did nothing wrong, and I was—I just—" I was fidgeting again, and Kiernan's focus prioritized the quivering hand tightening around my necklace like he didn't understand the action but wished to. I dropped my hand, self-conscious and regretful, sucking in a breath to add, "There has to be something I can give you."

Even as I said it, I had no idea what to offer, but with my promise, I hoped his smile would return, unable to handle him looking at me as Mother always did.

"Are you trying to make a deal with me?" he questioned, and if that was how he wished to think of it, I had no issue agreeing.

"Yes, I want to make a deal with you."

Just please stop looking at me like that.

His countenance did shift from dull to curious, his eyes glazed with a light of suspicion, and I worried I'd done another thing wrong. I watched as his gaze lingered just beneath my neck, staring at my shell with enough stillness to appear zoned out, but his sight refocused on mine before I could question his presence. That silent debate he held behind his eyes from our first conversation in the forest returned, both watching each other, waiting for a response that I feared the longer the speechlessness went on.

"Will you sing?"

He wasn't asking if I *could* sing, but if I would choose to sing, a request, rather than an expectation. I was surprised by his proposition, mind running through solutions, wondering how he came to that idea. My tongue felt heavy as I tried to refuse, recognizing how simple the appeal truly was, and though I tried another time, the denial never came.

I let my eyes fall to the ground as I began to sing, shame melding my words into unassertive mumbles, but the lullaby's tune was clear even if the lyrics were not. Kiernan didn't speak, and I didn't ponder if it was out of annoyance or interest, concentrating on not allowing the guilt to constrict my throat. I had already lost track of how many times I had broken my commitment to Father this year, not just with Anders, but for strangers as well.

But I had disappointed Kiernan too, and if this was the only way to fix my faults, then I decided it was worth it.

I couldn't have him hating me like Mother did.

I sang, my voice seeming to go nowhere and everywhere at the same time, reaching out past places in my field of vision, nothing echoing in response like it had in Anders' room. I was just as quiet now as I had been with my younger brother, making it easier to pick out the bubbling chatter growing closer.

My head whirled behind me, voice cutting off instantly as I tried to catch sight of the visitors, feeling a warm hand grasp mine a second later.

"Come with me?" Kiernan whispered, urgent yet hopeful, like he didn't want to be found, but didn't want to leave me either. His eyes were wide and bright when I spun back to him, emeralds glittering and nature awakening. "It won't be like last time, I promise."

I glanced back to the trail, the guests nearing, knowing if I decided to leave, it would have to be immediate before I was noticed. Kiernan's grip was the same as at the party, welcoming but loose, free will promised through mindful touch, and parallel to that night, and I was sparked with unrecognizable ambition.

Kiernan hurried us off the trail, hold tightening as we trudged through overgrown plants, and I could practically feel his projected excitement in our linked hands, much like how Maddie dragged me to do karaoke, but I didn't dread going wherever Kiernan had planned. With him, in his home, I knew I was safe.

We plunged deeper and deeper into the brush, disregarding pinning landmarks to find my way back, not giving thought of fleeing time to circle my mind. He helped me over fallen trees that were still a bit slick from the rain, and though wet soil caked to my boots, the scenery appeared lusher and richer with the plump droplets resting on leaves reflecting their colors. I wished to take in the fantastical beauty for hours, but Kiernan didn't slow his pace, playfully tugging me along which quickly became a game to see how long I could keep up before he had to pull me back to him, and I giggled every time I fell behind. I finally got the hang of how he stepped without tripping through plant-infested territory, stride swift and effortless from experience when he halted, ending our little competition.

In front of us stood a nearly open meadow, not large but big enough to cast all attention on the single tree standing in the center of the clear ground. Its branches were peculiar, jutting out in different directions and angles; its base was smaller than the surrounding trees, making it accessible to climb if desired.

My hand slipped from Kiernan as I moved closer, recalling Zadar's warnings about secluded trees and how walking near its base was damaging, but he was talking about redwoods, and it was evident this tiny tree did not share those genes.

"This is my favorite place," Kiernan said, coming up from behind me.

"It's beautiful," I agreed, lifting an arm to reach for its moss-covered bark.

"Not yet," he instructed, nudging my elbow forward to touch the dampened wood, "Climb."

I was careful when stabling my foot on the slanted stump, fearing the abnormal thing would snap under my weight, or that I would slip and snap something of my own, but neither occurred as I successfully hooked my other foot in the crevasse of a lower branch. Kiernan hoisted himself up in pursuit when I approached the top, finding it much higher than I expected from the ground. Removing my gaze from the dirt, I saw why this place was Kiernan's favorite. The stunning landscape could be seen for miles, its grandeur forever surpassing my understanding. Watery, clean air consumed my lungs, the breeze humming enthusiastic salutations, and I could practically hear the whispers fluttering through rustled leaves.

Friend of the forest.

"I wanted to apologize as well, and I hope this view will help me earn your forgiveness," he uttered, bringing my concentration away from nature.

"What could you possibly be sorry for?" I questioned, straining to think of a time he was anything but wonderful.

"You weren't treated fairly at the party. Some of that was my fault, but also, my family can be... insensitive at times."

He looked deeply regretful, and I nearly reached for him, showing reassurance through touch as I had with Anders, but I quickly stopped myself, offering a warm smile instead as I said, "I understand. My family is kind of a mess too. My younger brother is the only one who will really spend time with me."

"I can relate to that," he agreed, situating himself more comfortably in the tangle of tree limbs, "Tell me about yourself. I gave you three things about me the other day, and you said nothing."

"Well, I can only speak English, but I know sign language, my favorite time of day is sunrise, and I greatly love the rain," I answered teasingly, and Kiernan smirked.

"Those answers sound strangely influenced. Can't imagine why."

It took all my willpower not to laugh, making it impossible to hide a smile, yet I had no issue continuing the joke.

"If you aren't happy with honesty, then I don't know what to tell you," I responded with a shrug, and Kiernan gripped the branch I rested on to pull himself closer, stealing my relaxed demeanor.

"Tell me something no one else knows about you."

My smile fell. His voice was soothing, his eyes scouring, his body near enough to touch, and it frightened me how easily I could confess the darkest part of me to him.

"I tell my brother everything."

Liar.

Kiernan stared at me a moment longer before lowering himself to where he originally sat, while I battled the flush creeping up my neck.

"All right, then, tell me about your parents. What are they like?"

I shifted, content to move past whatever those last seconds had been, yet struggling to find a proper response.

"Mother is... well..."

Traumatized. Callous. Repressed.

"Absent, I guess you could say," I reasoned, finding the perfect branch to perch myself on while facing him, "She doesn't care for me very much, and we never talk, mainly because she likes to paint alone in her room." I trailed my hand along the bark, moss tickling the tips of my fingers. "And my father is gone."

"So is mine," he added, tone surprisingly light for such a dark topic, "I knew we could find something in common."

A laugh broke from me, and I instantly covered my mouth, his teasing entirely catching me off guard, and Kiernan's smile allowed me to forget how sad I was supposed to be. After all, the only parent who cared for me was dead, but for the first time, it didn't hurt to talk about Father in the past tense.

"Tell me more," he insisted, resting his chin atop his arm that lay on a branch beneath where I sat, looking up at me like I held the world.

"Like what?" I asked, a warm and cozy sensation snuggling inside of me.

"Everything. Leave nothing out."

I couldn't contain my smile, or the way I rambled on about each little thing that popped into my head, and Kiernan listened intently to it all, never showing signs of boredom or disinterest, even as my stories dragged on for hours. I wasn't sure if I had ever talked so much in my life, legs numbing from where they dangled far above the ground, and just when I felt guilty for chatting endlessly, he'd join in long enough to start me on a new subject.

And through it all, my mind remained quiet.

By the time the sun began its descent, I truly believed he enjoyed the sound of my voice, absolutely fascinated with something about me I wasn't able to figure out.

"I need to go," he stated, almost startled, glancing up at the sky that was now a pale shade of pink, "You should too."

I matched his abrupt urgency, scrambling down the tree while Kiernan instructed me how to get back to the trail, a little disappointed he couldn't walk with me, but it was clear from the quickened way he scampered into the woods that whatever demanded his attendance was important.

"When will I see you again?" I shouted, already lost sight of him after reaching solid ground.

"Whenever you choose to come back here!" I heard him yell from a distance.

So, I returned to the tree the next day, and many days after that.

Chapter Eight

"**Y**ou died again," Anders spoke, poking at the oatmeal he still had yet to taste. I watched him intensely, analyzing each intake of air and subtle tremble produced, but he didn't meet my gaze as he studied his uneaten breakfast.

"In your dream?"

He hadn't been able to speak last night, only screaming indecipherable messages and sobbing uncontrollably until my singing calmed him to the point of exhaustion. It was the same dream for the past seven nights, somehow worsening each time, and I was grateful Mother couldn't hear her son's agony as I struggled experiencing it myself.

Anders didn't respond, stirring his spoon in the same circling pattern, the sound of metal steadily scraping against the glass bowl, ringing in my ears.

"Anders, are you okay?"

"Your hair was wet," he went on, ignoring my concerns like he never heard them, "and your dress was blue," Anders paused to clear his throat for the fifth time that morning, hoping to bottle up emotions stronger than he was, "It had golden flakes on the skirt," his hand clenched around the utensil, "and the moonlight hit them just right where they cast sparkles on the walls."

"Anders, look at me."

He did, but I almost wished he hadn't, his eyes red-rimmed and filling with tears, pain leaking from the blue, and a sickening anxiety curled in my stomach.

"What is going on?" I pleaded, worrying that the only person who could answer that question was a doctor.

Hiding something. Doesn't want to talk to you. Isn't comfortable. Stop pushing him!

Anders' lips were sealed in a thin line, eyes shifting from my face to lock on something behind me, and instantly his breathing went still. His face was an image of pure fear as he released his spoon and placed a palm on the edge of the table like he might shove out of his seat and run for the door. I couldn't decipher why my brother's countenance changed, but I did detect the cool draft that breezed in from closed-off walls, and my back straightened.

"Ari," Anders whispered in a terror-pitched tone, his breathing hitching as though he strived to speak more but was restrained.

"What is it?" I questioned, feeling panic rise along with him, "What are you looking at?"

The deep hue of his irises illumined as his sight chased upward, over my head, and above the ceiling. He was stuck in a paralyzed state, unresponsive to the distractions I tried to cause, and my muscles were locking up.

One word escaped his mouth.

"Monster."

I jumped from my seat, spinning so quickly I had to grip the table to avoid falling, my abrupt movements jolting Anders back to life, and I pulled him behind me, acting as a human shield.

There was nothing present but an empty hallway ending with a closed door.

Thin air; that's what had terrified him.

Fighting night terrors had been one thing, but I never considered dealing with such strong imaginings in broad daylight. Anders was no longer dreaming; he was confusing delusions and reality, and I feared it was only a matter of time before he couldn't differentiate the two.

"You are very quiet today," Kiernan observed, playfully bumping into me, the heat shooting life through my body and grounding me in the present. It strangely seemed as though he had always been there for me, knowing exactly when to pull me from my thoughts, even though we had only been seeing each other regularly for two weeks now. "Talk to me. What's on your mind?"

I only allowed myself an hour or two with him before continuing my rounds, still needing to do my job despite wishing to be around him my entire shift. It seemed he wanted the same thing most days, choosing to walk the trails with me after the time I allotted for him was up, but the minute a visitor appeared, he was gone.

Though I wasn't sure the exact amount of time, I knew we had been wandering together with no destination in mind for a while, and that I hadn't said a word. It should have been guilt that prodded at me, not contentment, but I enjoyed not needing constant conversation, just being near him was a comfort, and my voice came out surprisingly even as I said, "I think Anders might be schizophrenic."

Kiernan stopped walking, and I had enough sense to do the same, realizing how serious and random the statement sounded.

I waited for him to affirm I was overreacting as I had convinced myself, but Kiernan examined my face with that unreadable expression I had grown especially accustomed to.

"You assume this because he has vivid dreams?" He questioned, pure curiosity tainting his words, and I shook my head.

"He's now seeing things that aren't even there."

"What kind of things?"

"I don't know," I exhaled sharply, "He's always been good about describing his dreams, but with this, all he could say was 'monster'."

I could have sworn I saw a muscle shift in Kiernan's jaw, but it was easy to dismiss as he prepared to speak.

"Maybe he can't find words to describe it." My lips bent to form a dissatisfied frown, and Kiernan resumed our casual strolling. "You said your mom likes to paint. Maybe Anders would find it easier to draw the image instead of verbalizing it."

"Do you think that would help him?" I asked after giving it a moment of thought.

"I think it's worth a try."

I longed to thank him for more than just his advice, but when I saw him, facing those life-filled eyes, I ended up swallowing the words down.

It became quiet again, but Kiernan didn't attempt conversation, just as content in the blissful silence as I had been.

"Here," I said to Anders, setting a blank piece of paper from his notebook overtop the pre-algebra homework, "The thing from this morning, I want you to draw it."

My younger brother blinked up at me.

"Why don't you? We saw the same thing."

I pursed my lips, allowing him to believe he wasn't alone in his experience, and I wasn't confident I could keep that notion up much longer.

"But you are the better artist. Mother definitely gave you the talent in that department," I proposed, and while he looked unsure, Anders began to sketch.

The illustration he created was rough in the nicest terms, which I found strange, as he truly was a good artist, but the picture broke into different details, as though the pencil wasn't certain how to piece it together. I brought the page closer to my view, enabling me to catch four clawed legs, two large wings, and a pointed snout; not a clear visual, but enough to understand Anders' dread.

"You didn't see it, did you?" he guessed from how my gaze darted across each sharp angle and smooth divot of the sketch.

"No—I did," I answered, struggling to tear my focus from the paper, until he lowered the page himself and gave me a long look.

"You are lying again."

"I'm not," I tried a second time, and Anders grimaced at my words.

"Please stop." He looked exhausted and hopeless, like he couldn't remember how to smile, and I was hit with another wave of nausea. "Did you see anything at all, Ari?"

His eyes pleaded for honesty, and I feared deception would hurt him more than the truth.

"No," I spoke softly, monitoring how Anders' throat bobbed as he nodded, evidence of spiraling thoughts exemplified through his tense body language, and I regretted giving in to openness.

"I'm going to bed," he announced while gathering his schoolbooks from the kitchen table.

"I haven't made supper yet," I contended, hoping to keep him longer, troubled more when he rejected my gaze.

"Not hungry," he mumbled, moving to the stairs with his arms full.

Scared. Hurting. Hate seeing him like this. Fix it.

"I love you," I blurted, grasping for anything to lift his spirits, certain he had already convinced himself he was going insane.

He didn't smile, but he did pause in the doorway, tilting his face my direction long enough to mumble, "I love you, too."

My shoulders drooped in defeat, an unseen weight pulling me down as I plopped into Anders' seat. With him gone, I could freely analyze the picture, and I chose to skip dinner to do so.

For hours I sat studying, unable to knock the sense that I knew what this creature was.

Chapter Nine

I took the drawing with me to work the next day, mindful to keep it hidden until Kiernan and I were alone.

"What do you think it is?" he questioned, his expression colorless as it usually was, a concept about him I had stopped worrying about and grown accustomed to.

"I don't know," I mumbled, twisting the paper to different angles, viewing every possibility through the tangled lines, "but I never wish to see it like he has. It seems terrifyingly dangerous."

"Maybe not," Kiernan countered, pointing to one of the crooked arches outlining the creature, "That sort of looks like a hump. It could be an oddly shaped camel."

I laughed, because, to me, it seemed to be the most appropriate response. Kiernan made a joke to lighten the tension, and I gratefully accepted, yet he stared at me as though I'd been the picture that didn't make sense, focusing on the lines of my falling smile rather than the lines between my brows.

"You're serious?"

"Did you not want me to be?"

"No, I did, but I didn't think you'd really mean that. Looking at this is…" I glanced at the paper once more, hoping they'd somehow reshape into the form I'd been searching for, giving me the answer I held in my hands if I only knew how to read in this way. "It's clear this thing is nothing less than a monster."

His brows lowered while darting his eyes away from mine, hurt flashing across his features for the briefest moment, and I was instantly pummeled with guilt, wishing I could take back the argumentativeness in my tone.

"I'm sorry. I didn't mean to come across harsh." My apology blended with an exasperated sigh, leaning against the tree we sat at the base of. "I'm just incredibly stressed about the situation. I mean, what if this becomes normal?

What if all I can do is sit and watch as my brother is tortured by his own mind, and I can't save him because there is *no real threat.*" I buried my face in my hands, pushing against my temples in an attempt to rub the aching out. "I'm so scared, Kiernan. I can't think of what would trigger something like this."

"Ari."

His voice was softer than any blanket or pillow I had ever touched, and the desire to curl into the sound and rest washed over me.

"Hm?" was all I could offer him.

"Dance with me."

I removed my face from my palms, finding him already standing by my side with a hand lent.

"What?" I asked, aware of what he said but not how we came to that conclusion, eyes squinting in the sunlight as they fixed on his hand, then to his face.

"Stand up," he instructed more slowly, reaching for my arm and hauling me to my feet, "and dance with me."

It wasn't a question or demand, sounding close to a plea, though his body language remained indifferent.

"But there is no music," I offered, and Kiernan leaned forward until his lips were hovering right above my ear.

"Music is everywhere. You just need to listen for it," he whispered, his voice even softer than before, the hum of his words sounding like a song I would willingly listen to for hours.

I could practically taste the singed sweetness of his scent as I kept my breath even, Kiernan in no hurry to back away.

"I was a mess the last time I danced," I murmured equally quietly, "I didn't know what I was doing then, and I still don't."

"I can teach you," he settled, taking three steps backward, enabling me to focus on more than his breath against my ear. "It's simple once you get a hang of it. Steps are made in groups of six, like this," he spoke, feet outlining a square, the patterning seeming easy enough. "Try it."

Back. Left. Forward. Right.

I kept my eyes on his shoes, numbers and movements mixing as I brutally tried to match his steps. It wasn't until I tripped on nothing in particular that Kiernan started again, tone gentle and forgiving as it always was.

"I'm going to count to six, and every time I say one and four, take a step."

I nodded, brow furrowed as I held my focus on the ground, my cheek sore from nervous biting.

"One."

Back.

I was able to shift without much difficulty, the struggle beginning when my other foot dragged weirdly into place during the "Two. Three."

"Four."

Left.

Again, my leg snagged against the damp grass, producing an unexpected squeak beneath my boot, and I tried not to cringe, ignoring the unpleasant quiver it shot through me. Kiernan, however, didn't seem to notice, too focused on his leading, "Five. Six."

"One."

Forward.

Kiernan backed a step as I advanced toward him, mirroring my actions with flawless ease, mind wondering how many times he must have practiced being this pristine, thoughts interrupted by, "Two. Three."

"Four."

Right.

It hardly felt like a success as I completed the square, Kiernan's cheerful, "Five. Six." sounding as though he believed otherwise.

He started again without pause, repeating the numbers and movements till my creeping confidence allowed me to look away from our feet, noting how his body swayed with the steps. He was in perfect rhythm with his directions, loose and comfortable apart from the fists clenched at his sides, displaying an agitated tension I took personal responsibility for.

I was messing up, and he was frustrated.

My eyes found his next, cool jade reflecting nothingness, while a half smile played on his lips. We swayed on the same beat, mentally reciting the numbers to keep an equal pace, and the surrounding sounds enhanced to encourage us.

Water dripping from leaves, wind whistling sweetly, birds chirping in the distance; I had become habituated to those noises over the last several months but hearing them now was like listening to nature's orchestra, the symphony of the wild played just for us.

Our dance was near-perfect, except for the distance between us, a barrier of air keeping us out of touch and taking away the unity of dancing. I didn't like it, and judging from the way Kiernan's fist stayed bunched, it was clear he didn't either, at last lifting a hand and instructing me to place my palm on his. He began walking at an excellent tempo, steps landing on *one* and *four*, and I was surprised at how smoothly I followed, both of us marching around our adjoined touch in a perfect circle.

As my right hand rested upward against his, I noted the vast size difference, unable to view the length of my fingers reaching barely above his upper knuckles when my hand was being held.

After several steps, achieving the number Kiernan had in his mind, he turned and resumed walking the opposite way with our left hands pressed together. Though I hadn't been familiar with the movements, they were straightforward to perform, strolling in a circle while listening to the song the forest sang for us, until Kiernan's hand moved from my hand to grip my wrist and pull me behind him.

"Under," he instructed, and I followed, ducking beneath his arm in a twirl while he grabbed that same wrist and spun me into place in front of him, assuming the position learned from the party.

I hadn't realized I needed to brace myself for how close we stood until it was too late, his heat-ridden touch smothering any trace of the fading winter's cold, and I couldn't ignore the thought of what it would feel like to be hugged by him.

Warm. Wanted. Safe.

I blinked several times, pushing to concentrate on the dance instead of how easy it would be to lean into him, upset for even allowing such ideas into my mind.

"What does that look mean?"

I stumbled, craning my head upward to meet his stare, finding pure curiosity in the ivy jewels as they studied my face.

"That I am thinking," I answered before I was able to say something I would later regret, hoping he couldn't hear how loudly my heart was beating.

"About?" he pressed, and I became all too aware of the warmth bleeding through my jacket from where his palm rested on my waist. My gaze shot to the side, seeking a response to a question that had several possible answers.

"Ferns," I lied, glimpsing the forest's ground, the urge to fidget with my necklace causing my fingers to twitch, and Kiernan's gently squeezed around mine.

"Good," he spoke in a pleased tone, like his goal was to keep me distracted and had achieved it, like there were things he didn't want me to dwell on, but whatever that might be, I couldn't consider it at the moment.

"What are you thinking?" I parroted, lacking the collective nature he carried in his voice.

"How pretty your hair would look if I spun you," he replied without hesitation.

And that's what ruined me.

He lifted his arm to twirl me, and while I did spin, my hair swirling around me like a blazing fire, the flustered mess of my brain reorganized my footing wrongly, and I fell into him, dizzy and disconcerted. Kiernan didn't budge the slightest, only grasping my upper arms to hold me in place, hitting me with a solid wall of heat, and while my eyes tried to readjust to the spinning world, my mouth thought it was excusable to speak.

"You are so hot."

I wished to undo the words as soon as they left my lips, and in alarmed humiliation, I pushed away from him, needing to clutch the tree to keep from falling. "Wait—no, I—" I could feel the heat flood my face, a violent shade of pink tainting my cheeks. "*Warm*. I meant warm."

Kiernan didn't respond, neither with words nor his expression, and I didn't know if that made things worse or not. He studied my redness, as though I had shape-shifted like a chameleon, overlooking my incidental compliment.

"Does that bother you?" he asked, his gaze dropping to where I notably rang my fingers in nervous fidget, "My heat?"

"No," I answered, wondering why his focus went there when there were so many other problematic things about that statement.

"Your cheeks are pink," he observed, brows knit together in pure confusion as he scrutinized my face, "How did you do that?"

"I'm just embarrassed," I admitted, self-consciously wrapping my arms around my stomach.

"What does embarrassment feel like?" he asked, and I guessed he was joking to cheer me up until I saw the sincerity in his eyes.

My first thought went to how strange a question it was, but I scanned the interest in his beautiful face and the rest of him; it wasn't difficult to figure out. If I had the looks and confidence he did, I wouldn't have had a need for embarrassment either.

"It's associated with regret, like a bad feeling you get after a mistake, but more short-term."

That choppy explanation was the best I could present, but Kiernan nodded as though he understood.

"So, you regret dancing with me?" he asked, still baffled that I had the ability to blush.

"Not at all!" I scrambled to fix, unburying my arms from my waist in order to offer him one. "In fact, I'd like to practice with you again if you're up for it."

He took my hand a second time, willing to drop our earlier conversation, and I forgot all about the paper stuffed deep into my pocket.

Once every couple of months, Mother gathered her paintings and delivered them to the local art store, leaving me enough time to clean her room without bothering her. It was the only time she allowed me into her place of seclusion, and on normal occasions, I was in and out of her private space with plenty of time to spare, but when Mother's paintings might explain Anders' drawing and her little artwork area caught my eye, I couldn't help but make sure the room was *spotless*.

Displayed on the farthest wall, hidden from the sunlight, was a painting of my Father's eyes, amethyst in the shape of irises illuminating the darkness. I studied them every month, hoping to uncover details of unanswered secrets, that colors on a canvas could tell me why my life happened as it did, but they were nothing more than the eyes of a dead man. Those same eyes stared back at me in my reflection, and it was the only reason I chose to look in the mirror.

Other unfinished portraits piled in the corners: beaches with no sand, skies with no clouds, houses with no windows. The farther back in the piles I investigated, the more completed the canvasses became. For the most part, they looked the same, beautiful ocean scenery with different tides and displays of all times of day, but there was one piece of artwork tucked in the very back that was unlike the others.

An abnormally large horse was painted in the center of it, trotting along to the beach while the water splashed and the wind tussled its mane.

The portrait looked majestic, and nothing like Mother's style.

While studying it, I heard the front door unlock, and I raced to put everything back in its original place. Unsurprisingly, Mother came straight to her room, not bothering to check on the household or the people who lived inside, finding me on her carpet pretending to clean out a stain, even if we both knew she was too careful to stain her floor.

Mother paused in her doorway, questioningly looking at me, knowing I never took this long to refresh her room, and I obediently shot to my feet.

"I wanted to talk to you. It's about Anders," I threw out, knowing it was true but never guessing we would get here, remembering all the things I had wished to speak with Mother on in the past.

Mother blinked three times before I realized that she was waiting for me to continue, willing to listen, and I understood how lightly I needed to approach the subject.

"He's been seeing monsters recently that he truly believes are real, and I had him draw—"

"He's fine."

Short, sharp, brutal: I never thought two hand movements could have such a cynical impact. I was used to the neglect, but now that her dismissal affected Anders, a surge of anger rose in me.

"He's not fine, Mother!" I fired back just as abruptly as she had been, "He can't sleep at night and can barely differ between illusion and realities during his waking hours! His fear is driving him close to insanity, and you have the audacity to claim he is *fine*? That is not normal, nor is it okay, and if you would ever give him the time of day, you would recognize that!" I snapped, physically yelling along with signing, and I was grateful Anders had a longer day at school so he could avoid overhearing this argument.

"He's fine," she clipped again, and my rage built only to dissipate seconds later, recognizing that glint in her chocolate eyes.

"You know why he is acting this way," I pieced together, cooling my temper seeing she had the solution.

She averted her gaze, walking past me and shifting some of her art back around, a silent dismissal of conversation, but that was all the confirmation I needed. I touched her shoulder.

"Please give me something. My brother isn't well, and you won't tell me why or how to help."

There was a painful twinge in my heart, and I wondered if the ache arose just because of Anders as I spoke, "I've done everything you wanted my entire life. Just talk to me."

I was shocked to find her apologetic, as though she wished to answer my request, but her lips formed into a half-hearted smile as she mouthed the words, "Not yet."

Her hand lifted close enough to my face that she might have lovingly brushed her fingers against my cheek if she hadn't decided to grab the door handle and shut it with the faintest of clicks.

Closed doors; not worthy enough.

Chapter Ten

"**S**he is unbelievable!" I shouted, grateful only Kiernan and the trees could witness my rant, "How can she act like nothing is wrong? This is her son!"

Hours.

That's how long I had been venting, or at least that's what it felt like, caught in a whirlpool of anger that drowned me more by the minute. I couldn't find it in myself to let it go like I had so many things in the past with Mother, not after Anders had another episode last night, and she ignored the sketch hanging by magnets on the fridge when getting breakfast. With the image fresh in his mind, Anders was able to add more details to the drawing, sharp jagged lines appearing as scales over its beastly form. It reminded me of illustrations in children's books, a fantastical creature with large wings and a pointed tail, except the talons looked sharp, and the mouth contained too many teeth to be put in lighthearted fables such as those.

I turned to Kiernan, finding him staring back, long arms crossed over his chest as he contentedly waited for me to start fuming over a new reason to be upset, but I was tired of how consumed my mind had become, and the wind tousled my hair like it wished for me to clear my head as well. I blew out a breath, bracing my hand on a limb as I slid out from where I rested on the tree branch.

"Could we go on a walk?" I requested, watching as Kiernan joined me on the ground, realizing how long I'd taken to be with him, and the trails needed to be examined.

"I have a better idea. Let's play a game," he offered, his voice echoing through me more than it normally did, and I blamed it on myself for keeping him silent most of the early morning while I complained. He'd seemed perfectly satisfied to listen to me for hours more, yet I wished I'd quieted sooner if only to hear him speak in the calming tone he always used. "I'll run, and you try to catch me."

"So, tag?" I mused, but Kiernan only gave me a confused glance.

"What's a tag?"

I blinked at him twice, my mouth partially open with an answer I struggled to give. Kiernan wasn't as strange as I'd formerly believed him to be, but it was random times such as these that made me question why normal things were foreign to him.

"Never mind," I responded, careful to avoid dismissal while glimpsing the beaten path behind him, "Do you want a head start?"

Kiernan chuckled, and I detested how off it sounded, a beautiful song played in the wrong symphony.

"If I had a head start, Ari, you would never be able to catch up to me," he provoked, and from the lilt in his voice and the light in his eyes, I could tell our game had already begun.

"What are you trying to say? That I am slow?" I couldn't remember the last time I'd teased like this, even with Anders, whose job it was to pester each other as siblings, but recent events left no room for jokes, and I missed smiling this way.

"Not at all. I just have longer legs."

I lifted my eyebrows in response, observing how Kiernan mirrored my movements mockingly.

"Are you implying that I am short?"

He simply smiled, looking down on me in a way that made him seem incredibly tall. I loosed a threatening laugh, standing on my tiptoes that still didn't measure anywhere near his height, but close enough for him to see the determination in my eyes as I voiced, "Well, now you have angered me, Turner."

I noticed his hands clamp into fists while something in him bristled, but before I could wonder what I said wrong, he spun around and darted into the woods.

I hadn't believed myself to be a clumsy person until tripping over invisible rocks and roots chasing my friend through plant-infested terrain.

Friend.

The title sang over the wind in my ears as trees darted past in a blur. I had a friend, one who enjoyed my company just as much as I appreciated his, and the realization made my heart beat a bit faster.

Kiernan wasn't like Maddie, all loud ideas and undesired drama. He was thoughtful and gentle; someone I could ramble to, yet share quiet moments without awkward silence. He made work exciting, giving me something to look forward to, a light in the dark.

Anders would forever be my sunshine, but Kiernan had become my moonlight, serene and benevolent, glowing hope in such a despairing sky.

And here I was, playing tag at almost eighteen years of age, fulfilling a missing piece of my childhood that I hadn't realized was hollow.

For as much as I denied it, I truly was slow compared to Kiernan, losing my footing in ferns and clovers while he glided by without faltering. He acted as though he wasn't purposefully slowing his pace to give me a fighting chance, but it was painfully obvious, feeling closer to a taunt than an act of mercy.

He darted behind a tree, disappearing from my view, and I peered behind it, but he was gone. Confused, I walked the base of the stump a few times, giving me a moment to catch my breath until I felt a light object land on top of my head. I reached for it, feeling the woody stem of a slender stick, drawing my attention to the branch above me, Kiernan comfortably resting there.

"How did you...?" I plucked the stick from my hair, scowling up at him as I called, "Get down. You are cheating!"

"Not necessarily," he countered with an easy smile, annoyingly long legs dangling from the outstretched tree limb. I huffed, glancing at my surroundings for a solution, and the palm-sized rock at the tree's base looked like the perfect answer. I picked it up and chucked it at him before Kiernan had time to blink, but that didn't deter his impeccable reflexes from catching the stone in one swift movement.

"Choosing violence now, are we?" Kiernan shook his head in fabricated disappointment, twisting the pebbled-looking rock in his hand before his act was broken by the light tap against his boot. The attempted strike played as a distraction for me to tag him with a running jump, sprinting onward without a pause.

"Cheater!" I heard him shout in the distance.

"Not necessarily," I laughed back, already losing my breath once more.

I wasn't sure how long it would take him to get down from where he was perched, but I didn't allow myself to glance behind me, prioritizing every step I could get ahead of him. My heart pounded in my ears, making listening for his footsteps much more difficult. Anticipation tingled through me with each snap of fallen wood beneath my feet, and the distant sound of trickling water posed as my only possible escape. My eyes fixed onto the nearby stream, not large but wide enough to slow Kiernan down while I decided my next plan of action.

I plunged into the clear tides of the Smith River, the temperature drop shocking my body, releasing an elated yelp from my lungs. I turned for just a moment, finding Kiernan stopped short at the river's edge, movements abrupt enough I thought he might tumble in from loss of balance, and my laugh was nothing short of challenging as I watched him take a few steps back.

"What's the problem? You afraid of a little water?" I taunted, the freezing stream biting into my legs telling me that I shouldn't be in the water either, but the chilling rush of it pulsed through my veins like an addictive adrenaline. Kiernan peered at me, then the water, a hesitant set to his face that I hadn't seen in a while, as though he was, in fact, frightened by the water. I could feel my pants soaking up the liquid as I witnessed another internal battle wage behind his eyes.

Hates the rain. Maybe he doesn't like being wet.

Thoughtfully, I began moving back to dry ground, wondering if I'd become insensitive until a loud splash rippled to me, followed by the raining of water wetting the entire right side of my body. I slowly turned, mouth hanging wide open in utter betrayal as I found him crouched in the middle of the stream, cupping handfuls of water, preparing to drench the other half of me. Kiernan lightly chuckled at my dumbfounded expression before flinging more water my way. I blocked most of the impact with an outstretched arm, a surge of emotion compelling me to kick the icy pools back at him, which he avoided with little effort. It rained brutal showers as he successfully repeated my attempts, and though I should have been frustrated, my shrieks were of pure delight.

I found it entirely unfair how droplets dotted my face and curled the ends of my braided hair while he remained completely dry apart from the after-effects of splashing, so in my mind, shoving him off his feet was rightly justified. Judging how easily he collapsed, we must have shared the same thought, though the sudden grip on my wrist pulling me down with him wasn't according to my plan.

It was frigid and utterly enthralling, and if I hadn't been so out of breath or worried that I'd catch a cold, I could've played these games for the rest of the day. My giggles continued even after I stood and returned to dry ground, body trembling from chills and laughter alike. I was unable to suppress the joy pouring into my heart, yet the giggles died away.

"I'm so happy," I verbalized, plopping down on a patch of grass near the glistening stream, grin so wide my cheeks began to hurt. I removed one of my boots, shaking it a few times to draw out lingering water, though most of it had already soaked into the shoe's soles.

"What is it like?" Kiernan asked, claiming the ground next to me as a seat, ringing out the front of his shirt.

"What is what like?" I questioned back, half of me listening while the latter part of me fought to remove my other boot.

"Happiness."

My hand slipped on the slick heel, driving my palm into the unwelcoming dirt and earning an irritated grunt before his words registered. My focus shifted to him, noticing the droplets clinging to his long, dark lashes, anticipating my answer rather than blinking them away. The light in his eyes had dimmed a bit, but I could distinguish the earnestness clearly through them, as though he wasn't familiar with the feeling.

I scanned his face: the tan of his skin, the smooth edge of cheekbones, the slight furrow in dark brows, the soft line his lips formed, and while we had known each other for almost a month, it felt as though I was seeing him for the first time. He was handsome in ways that made me forget my train of thought if I stared too long, but viewing him now in such a fragile moment, I could perceive the pained features hidden on his face, dulling the sense of life I saw in him.

I thought for a moment, wondering how someone could exist without greeting happiness at some point, how long I'd complained about my life when he was struggling equally, guilt draining me of joy as well.

Selfish. Always talking. Never listening.

I decided to give him the answer he sought, only, finding the explanation was a challenge, and the reason proved to be more complicated. But like the saving grace he was, Anders appeared in my mind, and everything else fell into place.

"It's like... sunshine," I smiled a bit at the word, "wrapping warm around you when the damp, cold earth tries to pull you down; like the sensation of chilling air shocking your lungs as you breathe in the beauty of living. It's—"

"Freedom..." he said so quietly I almost missed it, but when I faced him, he stared at the stream below us, his expression lost in whatever loop his thoughts developed. I wished I could see what darkness trickled into his head, if only to glimpse at what kept him so still and silent all the time. "Like the lightness of the heart and innocence of the mind when the world releases its weight, and you can just...*fly*, even if your feet never leave the ground."

His eyes flicked to mine, a brilliant flash of green, and I had to swallow the strange emotion clogging in my throat before speaking.

"Yeah."

It was all the answer I could give. Finally forcing my other boot off, I waited for Kiernan to say more, and it appeared as though he might, but whatever debate he silently held died, and his familiar mask of drained features returned. I tried to read him, but his emotions always seemed to be ripped from him like pages torn from a book, and I simply wanted to know his story.

"So, you do know what happiness feels like, then?" I prodded.

Please say something. I know you are hurting. Tell me why.

Kiernan leaned back into the grass, onyx hair sliding off his face as gravity pulled him down. I relaxed beside him, gazing at the clouds passing by through the branches.

"Only with you," he said so quietly I almost mistook it for the whispering wind. A phantom heat grazed against my fingertips, relieving sensitive skin of painful cold, but that too vanished like the breeze, making me question if it truly happened at all.

Kiernan didn't speak again, and I lost track of how long we lay in blissful silence, listening to the periodic bird songs, in the stillness of late winter, as the river lazily rippled by.

In the time it took me to walk back to the trail, my clothes had dried, and once I reached the visitor's center, my manager was ready for me to clock out. I was in the process of writing on my timesheet when my attention snagged on the box atop his office desk.

"What's that for?" I questioned, curious as to what secrets the package contained, but instead of pulling something out of the box, he grabbed his personal items and placed them inside.

"Packing up. I'm being relocated to a different district."

I tried to contain my smile as I finished clocking out and tame the way my leg began to bounce in excitement as I left the building. I didn't want to appear thrilled over his departure, but if this manager was leaving, it could only mean one thing.

Zadar was back.

Chapter Eleven

For the first time in weeks, Anders didn't make a pained noise the entire night. Had it not been for my relentless anticipation for the following day, it would've been the most sleep I'd gotten in years, and at 4 a.m., I officially gave up on rest and headed downstairs.

The house felt quieter, like every creaking floorboard tensing for a natural disaster, afraid of making noise lest it draw attention, but the days went on one by one, uncaring and unchanged. The temperature, however, remained bitterly frigid, though I supposed it fit, a home with no warmth, for a family with no joy. It wasn't like the exhilarating chills that I experienced with Kiernan, it was lonely, a numbing hold of lifelessness, and I regretted not putting socks on as my bare feet sneaked down the icy staircase.

A lean figure stood in the hallway, nearly causing my heart to leap out of my chest at the sight of crimson hair. I knew Mother's sleep schedule wasn't what it should've been, but she never was up during these hours, yet glimpsing her shadowed form wasn't as startling as the way she signed in serious conversation to someone hidden behind the wall.

She looked panicked and exasperated as she formed her silent words, pausing long enough to grab the picture from the fridge and force it onto the countertop. I remained around the corner, afraid to interrupt an important discussion, yet I couldn't contain the curiosities compelling me to watch. I couldn't remember the last time I witnessed Mother embody such intensity, her cool indifference slipping for the first time since my childhood, but what had my attention the most was the other person involved in the conversation.

Who they were, I couldn't see, but Anders had been in his room when I checked on him only minutes ago, and we were the sole occupants in this household. It was someone Mother clearly trusted, as Anders' name was brought up multiple times, forming uncertainty in my mind that he truly was as fine as she claimed him to be.

I was contemplating emerging from the shadows when Mother loudly huffed and turned to her room. I scrambled halfway up the stairs, peeking through the banister to see her enter her domain and close the door, conversation evidently over as the stranger hadn't followed her. Listening for the front door to signal the person's departure proved to be a waste of time as I decided to enter the kitchen after a long period of silence. I glanced into the living room first, surveying the area where the stranger had been, and found no one. Secretly, I hoped it was a doctor that Mother was seeking help from, acknowledging her son's needs instead of brushing them off, and from the shortage of answers that she claimed to have, I'd been powerless in aiding the situation. Worries of bills and appointments dissipated when my eyes fell on the paper lying crumpled over the countertop.

I finally recognized the scribbled creature from the extra details Anders must have added last night. I'd seen pictures of dragons from some of the books my brother read, and though the sketch was a terrifying visual, I was relieved to have some understanding of the condition.

Anders wasn't schizophrenic or crazy; he was simply a boy with an over-active imagination who loved stories. There were still important facts that needed to be dealt with, but my whole body seemed to sigh in relief with the reassurance that there wasn't something bigger going on.

All I could think about then was sharing the news with Kiernan.

I didn't see Mother or Anders again that morning, which wasn't unusual for weekends; Mother painted, and Anders slept in while I went to work, but the idea that I was being avoided crossed my mind on multiple occasions as I drove to the redwoods. Willing my focus on the paper crinkled inside of my pocket instead of allowing hurt to seep in from assumptions, I clocked in quicker than normal, movements fidgety and mind aloof.

"Someone's no wantin' tae waist time," Zadar chuckled, tearing apart my anxieties with a familiar calm, his Scottish accent reminding me why I originally wanted to start my job early. I twirled in his direction, red hair swishing into my face and causing a rather uncoordinated greeting.

"Zadar!" I exclaimed, both surprise and delight pressing into my throat. I didn't know why I expected Zadar to look different, but I was a little surprised to see him the same, as though I wasn't meant to recognize his face. He was handsome as before, meaningful smile, warm eyes, dark skin and hair, along with the assured air about him that announced his leadership strength in the way he walked. I hadn't forgotten how much I respected and enjoyed his presence, not entirely that is, but I also hadn't remembered the familiarity he brought to my heart, feeling more like a caring parent than Mother ever had.

He opened his mouth to speak, and I was unexpectedly flooded with the urge to hug him, emotions of acceptance and admiration building until a release was necessary, and I feared I might do something I'd regret.

"I should go," I said before Zadar had the chance to verbalize his thought, awkwardly backing to the door. Disappointment tainted his welcoming expression while an unreadable emotion swam behind his eyes, and immediately I wanted to apologize for failing his expectations.

"Where are ye aff tae in such a hurry? Ye've only just got here," he asked, not bothering to disguise the confusion in his tone.

"The trails. It's my turn to do rounds."

Zadar's brows drew downward, but his smile didn't waver.

"Ye're awfu' keen tae go searchin' for strangers when I could hardly get ye tae speak tae me a couple o' months back."

My hand rested on the door handle, the sketch weighing heavy in my pocket, promising a distraction if I got out of this conversation.

"A lot has changed since you were here last," I clarified, ignoring how shy I came across, "I'll catch you up during lunch break!"

I didn't give him the chance to respond, darting out the door and to my work vehicle, and while there was a twinge of guilt pulling at my heart, I knew Kiernan was waiting for me. I had this drawing to show him.

My fingers rhythmically drummed against the steering wheel as I drove to the trails, trying to understand why I was acting so strangely. Zadar wasn't one to judge harshly, and we'd gotten decently close before he relocated, but I was terrified of ruining the fondness he found in me.

I didn't feel like myself today, and I chose to blame it on how little sleep I got.

The path to the tree, to where Kiernan and I ran away together, was permanently ingrained into my mind. When he had first brought me, every brown and green plant looked the same, but now that I knew what to look for, the scratched red bark and dying yellow vegetation told me exactly where to go. I used to think I knew the forest with all its majestic beauty until Kiernan showed me that there was so much more, going from fond of the forest to friend of the forest in some of the shortest days of my life. He used that first week I spent with him to make me well acquainted with the woods, showing me all the ins and outs, the hills and rivers, what habitats were owned by animals, and where it was safe for me to wander. I thanked him on multiple occasions, but it never felt like enough. Nothing I did felt like it could make up for the generosity he offered.

"You should slow down. You tend to be very clumsy when you run."

That smooth, thoughtful voice jolted me to a stop, and it was an effort not to spin on my heals until I spotted him, but as I slowed my thoughts, I recognized the sound to be above rather than around, compelling me to lift my head toward the clear sky.

There he stood, concerningly high in one of the redwoods, arms folded, and one ankle crossed over the other as he leaned against chipping bark. His hair was a mess of ruffled inky waves, looking like a shadowed lake, and the tan of his skin made his smile glow bright in contrast.

"I am not clumsy," I argued, wishing to scowl instead of mirroring his expression, but his happiness was incredibly contagious as he stared down at me, the amusement in his eyes bleeding green.

Only with you.

My heart did a little tumble remembering yesterday's events, the chasing, the teasing, the splashing, the pure joy, and I could almost feel that phantom heat graze my fingers once more.

"Ari, I have watched you trip thirty-seven times over the most random things since I have known you. That's not counting the moments you have entirely fallen over, which is nine, if you were curious," Kiernan explained, crouching on the branch to better view me, a position that appeared close to animal-like but lacked predatory edge.

I blinked at him several times, registering his words. He'd counted the number of times I had faltered, believing me to be worth the attention and time to memorize the numbers. I felt my cheeks heat, but it hadn't been out of embarrassment as the past presented, but more of an euphoric settlement in my chest. Kiernan's bright smile wavered when he saw the sudden pink on my face. I hated the idea of ruining his joyous expression, especially when he was so impassive most of the time, and a topic change seemed like the perfect solution for ending my flush.

"How do you keep getting up there?" I questioned, wanting to sigh in relief when his grin not only returned but became playful.

"Don't worry about it,' he quipped, lowering himself on the branch, and my breath caught seeing how it shook beneath him.

"Kiernan, get down! You are going to fall!" I yelled, or at least I think I did, because he didn't appear to be moved by my fear-driven command.

"I'm not going to—"

The branch snapped.

Kiernan came tumbling down, and from the height he was at, a serious injury was the best possible outcome. The impact from the ground knocked the air from his lungs, and a shout broke from mine.

"Oh, my lemon curd!" I exclaimed, rushing to him, "Are you okay?"

When I reached the body crumpled at the base of the tree, I found it shaking, not from pain or shock, but from fierce chuckles. It wasn't until that moment I realized I had never heard Kiernan truly laugh before, which was a shame. It was such a beautiful sound, lively and bright, like the song a bird sings when it is finally released from its cage. It then became my mission to make him laugh more often, if only to memorize the wonderful sound until I knew it by heart. He said I could make him happy, and it strangely felt as though it was my main purpose in life.

"What did you just say?" he wheezed.

I shook my head, feeling the blush of embarrassment begin to creep in, but Kiernan was too amused to be distracted by my redness.

"It's a saying Anders and I joke about. Sometimes it just slips out," I spewed, disturbed that we were talking about the phrase rather than how he just fell out of a tree.

"Lemon curd," he pondered, smiling unlike I had ever seen from him, "It suits you."

"*Are you okay?*" I tried again with a demand in my voice that was unavoidable. Kiernan sat up, scanning over his limbs with more exaggeration than seriousness, emphasizing how unharmed he was.

"It would look that way," he prodded, but the relief was too fresh for me to match his easy spirits. He brushed back the loose hair dangling just above his laughter-crinkled eyes, the movement long enough for me to catch something bend beneath his skin, muscles twisting wrongly along his forearm, and there was no thought in my mind while I reached for him. My skin grazed his, hot and vulnerable, certain my hand was going to burn while I brought his wrist to my lap. He had always been warm, but a new wave of heat scorched the tips of my fingers trailing his arm, similar to the unforgiving torridity sickness brings. Kiernan didn't pull away or move at all, a stone, sweltering statue that held his breath as though his lungs were truly filled with rocks.

"That doesn't look okay, Kiernan," I mumbled, my focus never leaving the veins bulging in snake-like formations, concerned he had pulled a tender joint that caused this spasming. There was a pause in his response, the sort of hesitance that could only be derived from either insecurity or secrecy, and from the way he spoke, it sounded like it could be both.

"That's not something to worry about," he muttered, his voice low, "It's just some hereditary condition. Nothing serious."

The unnatural movement centered in his palm, and I followed its trail, tracing the outline of his hand, and the straining seemed to calm the slightest at my touch. Kiernan's hands were soft, lacking the callouses I would have assumed for a person who lives in the woods, something I had missed when we'd danced, or the times he had grabbed my wrist.

"Is it painful?"

I could feel his eyes on me, could almost see the green from my peripheral, burning nearly as intensely as the heat beneath my fingers, but I kept my stare on his palm, watching the spasms begin to dissipate.

"Yes," he answered tightly, and my hand was gone in a flash, fearing I was hurting him further. Kiernan flinched from my sharp break of contact, and I wasn't sure he was thinking either when his arm stretched for mine, grabbing hold of my hand like he'd forget what touch felt like if he let go. "Don't stop." It nearly came out as a plea, and he denied eye contact as he voiced, "It helps."

The bizarre straining returned to his skin, finding its new home in the hollow of his cheek, veins pulling as though they were fighting to break out, and I remembered the last time I viewed this happen to him. It had been like a snake down his arm, and my brain hardly registered the movement as my thoughts were consumed by the bear that almost attacked us, but in this moment, we weren't in danger, and all I wished was to take away his pain.

Timidly, I reached again for him, brushing gently against the sharp curve of his cheekbone, sensing the twisting lines morph into something more edged and brutal.

"That has to feel terrible," I said, making sure to speak calmly and keep my touch feather-light, opening the option for an explanation of his condition.

"It's not so bad," he exhaled, breath on the brink of labored, "Not right now."

He leaned into the contact, allowing my hand to fully cup his cheek, his eyes loosely closed as my hand stung from the pure heat. I bit the inside of my cheek, pondering whether conversation was the best idea at the moment. He hadn't elaborated on what exactly was hurting him, and I didn't want to push him, not when his eyebrows were knit together and eyes clamped shut from unseen pain but getting him to talk about a different topic could prove beneficial.

Distraction.

It rang in my ears like a promise, recalling all the times he had done the same for me when I was hurting. Carefully, I brushed the hair from his forehead, wanting to sink my fingers into the onyx waves, but I pulled back before I stopped using my brain again.

"Why midnight?" I asked, a distraction for the both of us.

"What?" Kiernan's eyes opened to find mine, turning his head to position my palm against the front of his cheek, thumb sweeping underneath glittering emeralds.

"You said that midnight was your favorite time of day. Why is that?"

His eyes shifted between both of mine, dark lashes tickling the edges of my fingers as he blinked, and something about the action felt especially intimate, sending a shiver down my spine. When Kiernan closed his eyes again, the muscles in his face loosened, the cutting pulsing at last resting, and he appeared relieved in more ways than one.

"It's when the stars are out."

I felt the smile he created as he responded, forcing one of my own to appear.

"You like the stars?"

He nodded, shifting my hand the slightest, and I allowed my arm to fall back to my lap. If my touch's retraction bothered him, he didn't let it show, continuing the conversation with eyes blinking awake.

"They are fascinating. Tried to count them all once," he told me, lifting his head to the sky, studying the clouds blowing by, "Gave up after 482."

"You can't give up," I encouraged, and the smile he gave me was thoughtful.

"It's impossible to count every single one, Ari."

"I don't like that word."

"What word?"

"Impossible."

He chuckled, giving an easy shake of his head. "You are helplessly positive, you know that?"

"I think you are just discouraged because you don't have anyone to aid your cause," I answered, shrugging off his words, worried the compliment would cause me to blush if I thought about it too long.

"That is possible. How do you feel about stargazing with me tomorrow?"

"Tomorrow?" My brows rose, attempting to piece together how the conversation evolved in this direction. I was simply trying to create an easy exchange, only to end up invited to a night of star counting. I couldn't complain, however, it sounded like the loveliest idea, staring at the endless night sky with him next to me.

"The tree is the perfect place to view stars. We could—" he broke off, clenching his teeth and grasping his arm while a grunt escaped his throat. The movement under his skin returned, except it didn't look like veins anymore, pointed, ridged figures scraped in its place.

"Is there anything I can do?" I pleaded, hating to watch him suffer and being incapable of stopping it.

"No. I should probably go home," he resolved, struggling to get to his feet. I bit my lip, mind running through possible solutions after seeing the short effects of touch, until I allowed myself to offer the gift I promised I never would.

"Will it help if I sing?"

Kiernan's hand was braced on the tree he fell from, veins and sharp angles alike stretching in his fingers while he looked down at me, eyes focusing on mine, then my necklace, and back up to my gaze.

"Your voice always helps," he agreed, after a beat of silence, placing himself back on the ground near me.

So, I sang, sweet and guiltless, and Kiernan didn't make a move to leave for a long while.

"Ye were attacked by a bear?" Zadar exclaimed, ocean-blue eyes wide in shock, and I smiled at how prominent his accent was when he was concerned.

"*Almost* attacked," I corrected, pointing my fork at him as I chewed. After talking with Kiernan, my nerves had been more forgiving, enabling me to carry on conversations with my boss just like I had in the past.

"How did ye get oot o' that?"

I swallowed a piece of chicken, sitting a bit taller in my seat, proudly stating, "I followed your training."

Satisfaction flashed across his dark face briefly before concern lined his well-proportioned features.

"Whit did the management say aboot the bears bein' that close tae the trail durin' the day?"

And suddenly, I found my food to be *very* interesting, shoving the rice to the corners of the clear container as I failed to meet his gaze.

"Ye *did* tell management, Ariella, did ye no?" Zadar pressed.

"Well, the bear wasn't *exactly* near the trail..." I drawled, immediately regretting looking at him once I saw his expression.

It wasn't quite the disappointment I feared, but the pride he held in his eyes seconds ago faded away, and I felt like a child preparing for a proper scolding.

"Dinna tell me ye went aff the trails," he said in a tone I wasn't accustomed to and never wanted to be, not angry but not without purpose, and I found my eyes widening as though that could aid my defense.

"There was someone off the trails and I tried to call for them, but they couldn't hear me, so I had to chase after them, then we ran into the bear and..." I trail off, disguising my hesitance by catching my breath from my rambled speech, "It all happened really fast, but I am fine!"

"Did the visitor get back tae the trails all awricht?"

"Yes."

My voice didn't waver, nor did it sound like a lie, aligning perfectly with the story, yet Zadar gave me a questioning look as though my dishonesty was blatantly obvious. I didn't think he'd take the topic of Kiernan very well; after all, following a boy into the woods alone every day didn't sound like the brightest idea, but he didn't know Kiernan, and I eventually planned to tell him.

His stare settled on my necklace from my absent-minded fidgeting, and the kind gleam in his eyes returned, though his face remained solemnly set.

"I missed ye, ye ken."

"You did?" My eyebrows drew together as I forced myself to take another bite. "Why?"

"Because we're friends, Ariella."

I struggled to accept the concept of having one friend, and having two seemed impossible, but it felt right, even if my relationship with Zadar and Kiernan was drastically different. His statement posed as an opportunity to open up, and I got the impression that was what he wanted. Friends talked to friends after all; Kiernan and I had been sharing in conversation for several months, or at least he listened as I spoke, but it wasn't the same with Zadar, believing respect needed more than casual exchanges.

His eyes scanned my face, oceans washing over my emotions in search of a response, and the only topic I could think of was my companion in the forest.

Yes, I would tell Zadar about Kiernan, but not today.

Instead, I smiled and answered, "I missed you too."

Chapter Twelve

Whatever progress I assumed we were making with Anders altered seemingly overnight. He began talking openly with his imaginings when he thought I wasn't around, carrying on entire conversations with empty air until I entered the room. He'd cut off his own words, staring wide with guilt, and he no longer answered my questions, entirely avoiding me at any chance he could get.

Anders spent most of his time home from school in his bedroom, hidden away to laugh and babble about random things, treating my presence akin to an unnoticed photograph of a distant relative. I was used to Mother's rejection, but learning to deal with Anders' was much worse. His midnight screaming sessions had stopped, and it was depressing to think I was the reason they occurred in the first place, but my absence from his life was the only thing that had changed. And yet, I couldn't keep myself away from him.

"But I don't want to close my eyes," I heard him mumble from down the hall, across from my bedroom, "Are you sure it will help?"

I listened for a response, and again there was silence. I couldn't handle it any longer.

"Anders, could I see you for a second?" I called, and Anders, obedient as ever, hurried to my doorway. I patted the side of my bed, welcoming him to sit with me, an invitation he once accepted without hesitation, but he only watched and returned my gaze without moving closer. I tried to diminish the pain in my voice while speaking, "I was hoping to talk to you..." I was unsure of how to finish the sentence, nor did I know what I was hoping to convey, but Anders nodded in complete understanding.

"If this is about my visions, you don't need to worry anymore." He smiled brighter than the sun could shine, and all I wanted was to believe it as much as he did. "It's okay, Ari. It's been getting so much better. He has been helping me."

"Who has?"

"Dad."

I sensed the tears coming, and I didn't want him to see me cry, so, giving him the most encouraging smile, I responded with, "Okay. That's all I had to say."

Anders was back in his room in a matter of seconds, steps peppy and filled with life, and I rushed to close my door before he could hear the sob clutching my throat.

He convinced himself that he was fine, that the father he never knew was supporting him, and he looked *so happy.*

Your fault. You weren't a good enough parent, good enough sibling, good enough friend. He'd rather create imaginary people to talk with than spend time with you. Just like Mother.

Only a few months ago, Anders had cried in fear of losing me, and here I was, crying because I believed I had already lost him.

Work was long and unforgiving, and my heart yearned for the stars and a distraction from the internal aches I kept shoving aside. Kiernan had always been the perfect distraction.

"Why the stars?"

There wasn't a need for the question; the galaxy's beauty was answer enough for anyone to favor them, but I wanted to hear him say it. He had yet to open up to me as I had to him, and I was determined to change that tonight.

Kiernan kept his sight on the sky above us, thoughtfully pondering his response.

"Have you ever wanted to escape this universe? To leave in search of a world where you belong, or simply fly amongst them and never come back down?"

The ground wasn't particularly comfortable where we lay, but near the tree, where we'd sneak away to see each other, was the clearest spot to view the heavens, and surrounding ourselves with nature, far from man-made light, encouraged the stars to brighten. I hadn't considered existing anywhere away from Mother and Anders, but seeing the many planets and possibilities this galaxy presented, I could understand why that idea had crossed his mind.

"No," I ultimately responded, "I have not."

When it came to deep feelings similar to the ones he was expressing, honesty was always the best answer, and with that honesty came trust that allowed room for more elaboration, unless you were Kiernan, in which case you'd never expand on the subject.

I turned my head to see him, expectant and unwilling to move past the issue, and though he still faced the sky, I knew he understood my want from the clever smile he formed.

Kiernan hummed in contemplation, either unsure of his response or drawing it out to be a pest. It looked like a little of both.

"It makes me believe in happiness," he confessed after he found my unsatisfied scowl, the end of his statement lilting in a soft chuckle.

Freedom.

He had compared happiness to freedom at the little river when he spoke freely for the first time, and I had the smallest glimpse of who he truly was. It wasn't much to work with, but I was grateful for the few pieces Kiernan gifted me for his elaborate puzzle.

He felt trapped, even if he had an entire forest to himself, he still felt contained, and I could understand.

Closed doors; can't get out.

His eyes darted over my face like they had across the sky, viewing the patterns of my features as though he were memorizing constellations, while I studied the illuminated galaxy peering back at me. Abruptly, he tore his focus back to the night sky, and I watched as his hands tensed into fists.

You've upset him. Doesn't want to talk. Stop making him.

There was so much to be said, but I kept quiet, and I knew Kiernan was avoiding the topic as he began explaining the different constellations and their stories. Tales of a girl chained to a rock for her beauty, a mother and son both changed into bears, a man induced to murder his wife and children, and many other captivating stories from the mythology of Ancient Greece painted in the stars.

"What's that one?" I questioned once he had finished his telling of Orion and a scorpion's mutual demise.

"That's Draco the Dragon," Kiernan answered, observing the constellation I pointed to, and a story of my own occurred to me.

"Dragon! Oh, my lemon curd, Kiernan! I forgot to tell you. That's what Anders' sketch was," I informed, sitting up from my relaxed position to better view his countenance, "He is seeing dragons."

Kiernan sat up with me, eyebrows pinched together, asking, "That doesn't scare you?"

I could've laughed from the relief pent up inside me at some rationale of his behavior, choosing not to think about the new, unexplained habits my brother had undertaken just this morning, and accept one accomplishment as a victory.

"Not at all. I finally have the information I needed," I said, repositioning myself to aid the leg that fell asleep, "So Anders likes to read when he's by himself, and most of the books are fiction. He has an active imagination, *of course* he is going to picture the creatures of that world in this world. I do the same when I read. Not quite to that level, but still. I know how to help him."

It felt so nice to share my burdens with someone, and even better to deliver improvements. I could understand why people such as Maddie desired to have numerous friends. "Only non-fiction books from now on," I cheered, lifting my head toward the trees and catching the stars in my sights. Guilt, sharp and incisive, penetrated my chest with recognition of how I invaded his stories, ending the one time he had been content to talk freely. "I interrupted you. I'm sorry. I talk too much," I apologized, slumping back to the ground.

He matched my actions with more grace, words assuring as he verbalized, "You don't talk nearly enough."

Immediately, the guilt was gone, and I dared to say, "You never talk at all."

"I'd rather listen to you. Your voice is a sweet healing."

He said it with such casualness, close to how the weather is talked about, and I could feel the heat rising to my cheeks. I hoped it was dark enough that he couldn't pick up on it, but my stare never left the sky, just in case.

"I thought we were supposed to be counting the stars," I diverted the conversation, acting as though I hadn't also been distracted by stunning scenery and engrossing tales.

"I remember," he spoke plainly.

It was still too cold for crickets, so silence sang its sweet song louder than the forest's normal quiet. I scanned the sea of planets above me, searching for the best place to begin. I was barely past a hundred when Kiernan's voice cut through the silence.

"Count them," he said, not in a demand but as a reminder, incredibly gentle as always.

"I am."

"Out loud."

I half-heartedly exhaled, losing my place in the sudden conversation.

"But then you can't focus on your number," I replied, finding my beginning spot.

"That's all right," he told, almost in a whisper, each word he uttered quieter than the last.

I had already lost my original count, needing to start again, and decided verbalizing them might make it easier.

My voice recorded the number of each star I tracked, tracing constellations to avoid getting lost, though I doubted losing myself in the night's glittering jewels would be a dreadful thing. At first, one section of the sky was fixated on, adding planets bright and barely visible to my never-ending sum, until I was sure some stars were counted more than once, and the assignment became inefficient.

Kiernan was right about this being an impossible task, but I wasn't about to let him know that, so I continued counting.

My vision skipped across the sky, numbering random stars until my words uselessly weighed the air, losing all purpose and meaning, but it was more fun this way. By the time I made it to the thousands, I wished I'd brought some water, throat drying as crisp air cooled my tongue.

Kiernan's silence was different than usual, and I assumed he had given up on our undertaking when I turned to see him motionless, eyelids closed, breathing lightly.

"Oh," I exhaled, hushed by his sleeping figure and the fear of waking him. There was a sort of peace on his face that reminded me of Anders when he'd cry all his tears and then fall asleep to my song, every feature of his face smooth and without pain. He looked young, the kind of youth one has before age and stress take their toll, and I wondered if this state was normal for him when he slept.

I was scared to breathe, let alone move, lest I ruin the calm that washed over him, but I convinced myself he couldn't fitfully rest if I was near. The leaves and grass betrayed silence in my attempt to sit up noiselessly, crunching and swishing beneath my palm, breath held as Kiernan shifted to lie on his side facing me. Taking this as my cue to leave, I wasn't prepared for the warmth that curved around my stomach, bringing me back to the solid earth with little force and much tenderness. Kiernan's touch treated me as if I was fragile, and feeling his heat press into my back, my body chills releasing in unsuppressed shivers, I also believed I had become the most delicate thing in the world.

"Stay with me, *Agapiti*," he whispered in my ear, his voice unwound in a way that could only mean he wasn't entirely conscious, before nestling his nose between the chilled dip of my neck and collarbone. The words stuck to my skin like the sweetest honey, and something fluttered in my ribcage, reminiscent of a butterfly trying to break free from its prison. Yet as her wings tickled my heart, I didn't desire to laugh, but rather lean into him, and melt away into nothing. It was nice to be nothing, void of hurt and expectation, and I would have been content to lie there with Kiernan holding me for eternity.

In truth, I was breakable, and I feared that if he ever chose to let go of me, I would never be able to piece myself back together.

The ground didn't feel uncomfortable anymore, and the tips of my ears burned with the rest of my face, grateful he couldn't see the red plastered to my cheeks. I worried he could feel my heartbeat aching through me with his arm securely tucked around my waist as I could feel it in my stomach, but Kiernan had slipped back into unconsciousness, his soft, easy breaths warming my neck. I concentrated on matching those breaths instead of how close his lips were to brushing my skin, or how I inwardly wished them to.

I didn't know this feeling, or why it had such an effect on me, but I never wanted to let go of it, holding on to the butterfly flittering inside as I held the hand that so carefully touched me.

Warm. Wanted. Safe.

My sight turned dark, and I became nothing.

Something shifted beside me, and my muscles braced to run for Anders' room, but I couldn't recall hearing his screams, and when I glanced around, I found I wasn't home. My skin felt hot all over, but it was a comfort to wake warm rather than rise frozen as usual. My surroundings were surveyed with heavy eyelids, sluggishly collecting the oddly shaped tree through the dark cloak of night, and the smell of sweet campfires told me Kiernan was close.

I began to doze off, fighting rest taking more energy than I was willing to give, but a twig snapped in the distance, pulling both Kiernan and me from sleep. In an instant, Kiernan was up, moving swifter than I could process, and the next thing I knew, he was hovering over me, hands braced on either side of my head. I tried sinking into the ground, watching the fierce gleam in his face, something animal-like and foreign to the rest of his features, scanning over the forest with primal instinct.

"Kiernan?" I soothed, brushing a calm hand against his arm, and I jumped when his head snapped to me. He blinked multiple times, observing my startled expression under closely-knit eyebrows.

"Ari?" He asked, confusion prominent, "What are you doing here?"

"We were stargazing, remember?" He blinked again, a clear indication that he did not. "We were counting the stars, and you fell asleep—"

Kiernan's eyes widened, and he shoved off the ground before I could finish my explanation. I stood up as well, tense from the way he moved and spoke like someone was hiding in the woods, preparing to shoot us.

"I have to go," he said, his tone sharp with urgency, staring like he wanted me to run, as though *I* had to go.

"What's wrong?" I pressed, following his fixation into the forest when it broke from me.

"I was gone too long," he muttered, glancing over his shoulder and then peering over mine. I gripped my shell, fear creeping into my heart, and I opened my mouth to ask more questions, but Kiernan began speaking before I could.

"Someone is looking for you. I need to go," he repeated and didn't look back as he ran into the forest.

I stood unmoving for several minutes, hand still clutching my necklace, trying to decide the next best move with a lethargic brain. The wind whispered inaudible messages, and I imagined it was an explanation for what Kiernan didn't have time to say, the sound gradually morphing into a solid voice, one that I knew and was calling my name.

"Ariella!" Zadar shouted again, the strain in his voice revealing how long he had been yelling.

"I'm over here!" I answered, rushing to his call.

Illuminated, blue eyes pinned on me, and Zadar was by my side in a matter of seconds, pulling me into a solid embrace I was not expecting.

"I'm fair relieved I found ye. Are ye awricht? Are ye hurt?"

It wasn't like Zadar to stumble over his words, and I struggled to reply at first, too stunned to relish in the hug.

"No, I'm fine."

He drew me back to see if my statements matched with my appearance, both his hands gripping my upper arms, firmly holding me in place.

"Whit happened? Yer shift ended hours ago."

Hours?

It had only felt like minutes.

"You were told how dangerous the woods are at night," he continued when I hesitated, adding a gentle shake that nearly made me lose my footing.

"I got lost. I'm sorry," I forced myself to answer, and Zadar scowled, clearly not buying the lie.

"Ye're awfu' warm," he observed, releasing my left arm to feel my forehead with the back of his hand. "Have ye got a fever?"

I shook my head, struggling again to find my voice, and I could almost hear the questions he wished to berate me with, but his features eased, picking up on my sensitive countenance. His eyes slid over my shoulder to scan the trees behind me, face full of suspicion, before leading me by my arm and softly directing, "Come on then—let's get ye hame."

He escorted me to my car and didn't remove his focus from me until I had shut my door and driven off, and I wondered how a man who never left the trails knew his way around the forest.

Zadar watched me clock into work the next morning, eyes hardened with an emotion I couldn't read, and it wasn't long until he verbalized his thoughts.

"I want ye workin' at the front desk for a wee while."

"Why?" I questioned. Realistically, I had a good guess.

"Ye're getting' sunburnt bein' ootside so much," he answered, and while my skin hadn't reacted the best to the sun, that wasn't the only reason he didn't want me to leave. We both knew that.

"I like the forest," I countered, my face set in my decision to see Kiernan, and Zadar took it as a challenge.

"Aye, I noticed. Especially the bits that are meant tae be aff-limits."

It was the closest he had sounded to being upset with me.

"It was dark. I couldn't see and went the wrong way."

I'd practiced the lie multiple times for the possibility of this exact conversation, but it didn't do much to benefit me.

"And where exactly were ye tryin' tae go? I cannae quite believe it was yer car."

Now was a terrible time to talk about Kiernan, and I resolved to drop the subject, ignoring the pride that begged me not to. I wasn't going to win this argument; that was clear, and I was quite fond of this job, deciding to back down before my resistance got me fired.

Lowering my head, I blew out an agitated breath, trying not to sound disrespectful when I asked, "How long?"

"Let's start wi' a week."

What was one week became two, then three, and we were just a few days shy of a month when Zadar finally agreed to let me back on the trails. I'd gone to bed that night more aggravated than pleased, convinced he drew it out for so long as a form of punishment, never feeling more like a child. I willed not to focus on it as I lay down, promising myself a chance to clarify my absence to Kiernan, and each time I closed my eyes, I remembered him cradling my back, filled with ease and comfort.

And that became the last night I slept soundly for a very long time.

Chapter Thirteen

It had been an entire month since I last spoke to Kiernan, and there hadn't been a day that went by that I didn't think of him. That evening we spent together was permanently ingrained into my memory, good events and bad alike, and I often stressed about him thinking of it too. When I avoided him for a week, he'd been waiting persistently for me to return, and if I were in his position, I'd have convinced myself I'd upset him that night. It was the furthest thing from the truth; I'd never felt so wanted.

I'd hear the door open, signaling a visitor's approach, and my head snapped to the sound, foolishly imagining it was Kiernan coming to talk to me, wishing he would walk through the door, find me with those life-filled eyes and smile.

He never did, yet I still hoped every time.

I recalled all our interactions in the long days away from him, noting how nearly every moment we shared was in secret, hidden from the rest of the world's eyes, and in my darkest moments, I questioned whether he truly existed. Kiernan was too kind, too thoughtful, too patient, too wonderful to be real, and if Anders managed to imagine the father he never knew, maybe i was no different.

I didn't greet Zadar that morning, barely even looking in his direction before heading to the trails, and though it was petty, I felt justified. Soon, I would let go of it, unable to hold grudges for long periods of time even if I wanted to, but my current priority was finding Kiernan and explaining everything, because he was real, and he'd be waiting for me. I didn't allow myself to believe differently, even if what we had was too good to be true.

Who would choose to spend time with you? Family avoids you. Selfish. Annoying. Unwanted. Made him up to cope. He never held you. Never listened to your stories. Never wanted you near. Doesn't exist. Crazy. Insane. Alone.

I ran faster, desperate to find him and prove the voices wrong, but they became louder with each step. The forest felt off, wrong, like it didn't want me to enter, like its friendship had only been an imagining, and I took it as irritation for my absence, pressing forward with hopes of regaining its favor. Kiernan wasn't waiting at the trail, and when I came to the tree of secret gatherings, he was nowhere to be seen.

Delusional girl. None of it was real.

I shook my head, not allowing the thoughts to completely overtake my mind, calling for him through cupped hands. The air carried his name away, returning sounds of movement behind me in response. Catching a flash of green eyes and dark hair in my peripheral vision, relief flooded through me, my eyes falling shut for a moment as the voices quieted. When I re-adjusted my sights, I noticed he'd disappeared behind a tree, and I smiled while advancing his way.

"Kiernan, I know you are there!" I chuckled through a relieved sigh, peering around the massive bark, unsurprised to find he hadn't remained there. How he got from one place to another so quickly, I would never understand, but I glanced up at the branches for good measure, a little disappointed to not find him resting up there with a taunting smirk on his face.

Another sound of movement at my back, and I spun on my heels faster than before, making sure to keep my balance as grass ruffled in different directions. He wanted to add more stumbles to his tally, and I made a point not to trip to spite him.

I couldn't find him, but with hustled actions made when I wasn't looking, it was clear he wanted to be caught, and I was more than happy to play along. I paused the chase, closing my eyes to focus on the next sound cue, and when Kiernan purposely kicked a rock on my left, I darted in that direction.

"Over here, little songbird."

I stopped dead in my tracks.

That was not Kiernan's voice.

"Little witch, I should say," he spoke from no certain place, voice shifting through the wind and echoing back to me with unnerving ease.

Danger. Danger. Danger.

I could hear the trees whisper, and I wanted to run, but couldn't detect where the threat was coming from, or which path led to safety. Subconsciously, I took a step back, gripping my shell as I took in every subtle movement and faint noise, trying to find someone hidden in broad daylight.

"What's the matter? Only like messing with my brother? Don't play favorites now, you'll hurt my feelings."

His tone was light, but the heaviness of his words couldn't be overlooked.

"I don't know what you are talking about," I answered, coming out like a plea for my life.

"You *are* good. And here I thought Kiernan was purely gullible, but no—" A large branch that could've served as a miniature tree slammed on the ground to my right, and I screamed, skittering away like a frightened deer. "You act just like a normal human. It takes time to master their little ticks and habits to blend in so seamlessly. Makes me wonder how long you have been around them. Twenty years? Thirty even?"

"I'm seventeen!" I exclaimed, wishing he would take it as my claim to innocence in the crime I hadn't yet been informed of.

"Seventeen years free from the ocean? I'm impressed." Another snap of wood and another jolt of fear panged through me. "I'm curious though. How much longer were you waiting to attack? You had him right where you wanted that night: alone, asleep, and vulnerable."

My throat went dry, and no amount of swallowing was going to fix that. He had seen us together a month ago, possibly even before that, and I imagined a pair of inescapable eyes watching every time I thought I was alone.

"I wasn't going to hurt Kiernan."

Kiernan had known he was there, and I realized that was the reason for his waking in a panic and leaving, thinking back to all the times he had taken off without explanation.

"Who are you?" I questioned, hoping the shake in my voice wasn't perceptible, though I doubted the trembling in my legs went unnoticed from wherever he hid.

"You don't want that answer."

Confident, skilled, like he had done this before and planned to again many times in the future.

Silent killer.

Tears prickled at the back of my eyes, blurring my search for a feasible escape, and the air suddenly felt too thick for my lungs.

"Are you going to hurt me?"

A chilling breeze blew down my spine, one that didn't match with the patterns of the wind. Then there was a dark, guttural rumbling sound just like the one I had heard from the bear before he ran off, and I could practically feel the individual hovering at my back.

"You don't want that answer either."

His voice was near me, and my head whipped around, seeing him just a few feet away. I knew his face; he'd been the one to send vengeful glares my way at the party, and I gave myself the briefest second to memorize his features.

Then I was running.

Not daring a look back, muscles groaning in protest from my drastic sprint, my lungs allowed a single scream before they demanded rejuvenation. It was shrill and desperate, and I knew I was too far for anyone to hear, but I'd seen the murderer of countless victims, and I was going to do anything I could to get that information to someone else.

I just needed to escape.

It began to rain, and the mixture of sweat and water soaked through my clothes, giving new weight to my already heavy limbs. What started as a light drizzle quickly evolved into a downpour, and the sound of droplets crashing into the earth masked every surrounding noise of danger approaching. The dirt converted to mud, turning what was solid into a slick surface, and now more than ever I had to stay on my feet. Falling didn't mean giving Kiernan another tally to his count of my stumbles; it meant I would be added to the tally of deaths in our little town.

I tried screaming again, but it snagged in my throat, and it seemed one cry for help was all I needed.

"Zadar!" I shouted with all my remaining breath, but he was already running in my direction like he expected this to happen. He halted when he reached me, trying to catch sight of what I was fleeing, but I grabbed his arm and pulled him away.

"I heard ye scream—"

"*Run!*"

It was all I could say, and Zadar didn't hesitate to follow. His legs were much longer than mine, enabling him to continually glance back and keep up with my sprint. Rain poured, air misted, and my boot slipped, covering my knees in mud, but Zadar lifted me from beneath my arms before my sleeves got ruined as well.

"Keep goin'! Ma car's just up ahead!" he shouted over the thunder, shoving me back to my feet, and when I brushed away the hair sticking to my face, I could see the outline of a grey vehicle. Zadar hurried in front of me to unlock it, immediately locking the doors when we were securely inside. I watched out the window, tainted by water, waiting for a glimpse of Kiernan's brother to emerge from the forest, but Zadar was driving off before I could make out anything.

"Whit in the name o' the wee man happened back there?" he shouted over the droplets pounding against the car while I shut my eyes and rested my head on the back of the passenger's seat.

"We have to get to the police station," I heaved, head still spinning and heart still racing, "I found the silent killer."

"The whit?"

"The one responsible for all the kidnappings in Crescent City. He was going to kill me if you hadn't shown up," I explained, processing the incident multiple times in order to keep it fresh in my mind, and my brows drew closer with each recollection. "How *did* you get to me so quickly? I wasn't by the trail."

Zadar's hands tensed on the steering wheel.

"Ye've no been actin' like yersel since I got back, and because ye wouldnae to tell me the truth..."

"You *followed* me?" I exclaimed, but he didn't flinch.

"Aye, I did," he admitted, stern and unapologetic, "and it saved yer life."

"You can't just do that!"

"Aye, I can, and I'd dae it again if I had tae. I had a strong feelin' somethin' like this was coming', and I wanted tae make sure ye were safe. Now, I'd like ye tae tell me exactly whit this person looked like."

Setting aside my irritations, I racked my brain for details in that three-second window I gave myself before taking off, searching for the things that didn't look exactly like Kiernan.

"He was tall: over six feet, I want to say and looked to be in his early twenties. Straight, dark hair, tan skin, square face shape—"

"Whit colour were his een?"

Of all the things he could have asked, I hated how it was about the most prominent feature shared with Kiernan.

"Green," I resolved and watched as Zadar's jaw clenched.

"Did he give a name?"

"No." I folded my hands in my lap to keep them from fidgeting. "But I know his last name." He watched me from the corner of his eye, posture stiff, facing the road as he waited impatiently for me to carry on. My fingers pressed into my legs with enough tension to bruise, thinking of the times Kiernan chose to keep quiet about his family and how he may have been forced to silence. He'd never hurt another person, not when he put himself in harm's way to save me from a bear, and I hoped the authorities would leave him out of this as I answered, "Turner."

Zadar pulled to the side of the road without warning, and I threw my arms on the dashboard to keep from flying forward.

"What did ye say?" he questioned with more intensity than I prepared for, his body turning at an uncomfortable angle, allowing him to search my eyes for any signs of deception.

"Turner," I repeated, shrinking into my seat, my tone timid from the way he stared me down. Zadar muttered something under his breath, brows lowering and face set with a decision I hadn't caught on to when he unexpectedly pulled back onto the road with more urgency than before.

"You know them?" I assumed, hoping to distract myself from the speed that I was confident had been over the limit.

"I ken *o*' them, but last I heard, they were aw deid a decade ago."

I stared out my window, the picture of a tiny Kiernan cold to the touch with those sparkling eyes lifelessly prominent in my mind, and it made me sick. An unpleasant shiver snaked down my spine, erasing the terrible images with it, choosing instead to watch the houses that breezed by, recognizing my neighborhood one building at a time. I was still deep in thought when Zadar drove up to my house and parked the car.

"What are we doing here?"

He didn't respond, hurrying out of the vehicle and barging through the orange door without looking back, and it took me a moment of sitting in confusion for me to tentatively join him. He'd left the front door open as well as the one to Mother's room, and a surge of emotions overcame me at the sight of doors widely open that were *always* closed. The floorboards creaked with each step I took down the hall, half expecting to be disciplined when I peeked into her domain, but she gave me no notice, her attention fixed on the man before her. I examined how Mother's countenance shifted as Zadar drew near to her, her posture lifting, her face alive in a way I only remembered from the brightest parts of my childhood. I should have intervened once Zadar brought a dark hand to cup her pale, freckled cheek but was stunned by the sight of her *smiling*, truly and brilliantly, like the rainbow after a heavy storm.

That beautiful beam, however, was stripped from her the longer she stared into his eyes, as though a silent conversation was created before them that filled her heart with deep peril. Mother heaved a sigh, standing from her painting stool, gravely nodding, and headed to her closet. Zadar watched her every movement and I took that as my opportunity to confront him, Mother catching sight of me as I stepped past her doorframe.

"Start packin'. We're movin' in the mornin'," my manager instructed, head pointed in my only parent's direction while his command was directed at me, plainly aware of my mother's hearing condition. A spike of protectiveness motivated me to march straight up to him, stepping into his line of sight for Mother, my stare challenging, fists clenched in preparation to fight.

"Who do you think you are? Believing you can't just *waltz* into my house, dare to touch *my mother*, and have the audacity to demand that I move. You are not my father, nor were you invited into my home!"

I was impressed with how steady and confident I sounded, not leaving room for fear when it came to my family.

"Naw, I'm no," he agreed, his voice easier than mine, "I'm yer stepfather."

I wanted to laugh, to write it off as some ill-mannered prank, but the situation was humorless, and Zadar's eyes were more honest than they had ever been.

"I don't know what kind of cruel joke this is, but it's not funny," I insisted, feeling tears of either anger or pain prickle behind my eyes, and it frustrated me further.

"It's true," Mother answered for Zadar, reading our lips just as she had read the room, "He is my husband and Anders' biological father."

The silver ring on her left hand seemed more prominent now when she signed, the same ring I believed she kept out of love for *my* father. I almost slipped up, denying that claim in trust that she would have told me something as significant as her remarrying, but this was Mother, I recognized, and my argument was invalid.

"How could you not tell me?"

The tears came then, along with a lump in my throat that broke my words as I spoke.

I hadn't been in love before, but I imagined it looking the same way Zadar looked at Mother, features softened yet stern with the promise of protection. He exhibited that same protection when he faced me, along with the unbending front of authority, steadily defending, "I'm sorry, Ari, I didnae mean tae keep it from ye this long, by ye cannae be upset wi' yer mam. It wasnae the right time."

"And when was the right time? When Anders was an adult and had no need for a father anymore?"

"I've been there for Anders every day that I could, and right noo, I'm here for you. There's somethin' verra dangerous here, and we cannae stay."

His lack of detail only added to my aggravation, prompting me to shout while they both remained soft-spoken.

"What's so dangerous? The silent killer? I hate to inform you, but he was here before I was born. There is nothing new about that, and instead of moving away and hiding from the issue, we should be heading to the police station to tell them everything about what I saw."

Even as I spoke, I recognized the flaws in my argument, how the killer had been committing crimes for over twenty years, and yet the man I met that day looked barely over twenty himself, but regardless, I didn't allow my accusations to falter.

"The man that attacked ye isnae the silent killer," Zadar confirmed, and what was supposed to be a relief merely fed my stirring anxieties.

"You know who the killer is?"

Zadar helped Mother hastily gather all her clothes and personal items, piling them on her perfectly made bed before tossing it all into duffel bags with immaculate disorganization as he reluctantly replied, "I ken who the man is."

"Great. Then we can inform the police together."

Zadar huffed, not from irritation with my questions, but from built-up stress, adding, "This isnae somethin' for the authorities. This is aboot yer safety."

"And what about everyone else in this town? Is their safety not important?" Mother stepped in again, exhibiting an actual existence that had me second-guessing if she was the same person I had lived with for the last seventeen years.

"Why are you fighting us on this? We are trying to protect you," she sighed, obviously bothered, judging from her exasperated expression.

"For the first time in my life, I am happy here. I can't leave now," I made sure to sign in response, taking full advantage of her absorption of my words along with her willingness to talk with me.

"Ye'll be happy in Scotland an aw, I promise," Zadar tried again, but the calm in his tone began to wane, "I've a hoose where we can aw thegither as a family. You'll meet new folk and make plenty o' friends."

They wanted to take me away from everything I knew to a different country, and from the extent that Mother packed, I could tell we weren't coming back. They were content to pretend my life in California never existed, that my childhood and everything I knew was pointless, and that strangely hurt more than anything else. There was a day when I'd given anything to escape this town and find a place where I was wanted, but now I'd found that person who wanted me, and he was to be shoved aside.

Kind words and gentle smiles. Playful chasing and friendly teasing. Heavy eyelids and warm embraces. 'Stay with me.'

And I would stay.

"No," I decided, even if I was the only one left living here, even if I truly was in danger, "I'm not leaving."

Mother and Zadar paused their packing and stared at me, her gaze scrutinizing, while his held bafflement.

"Whit's so important aboot this place?" he demanded, as though I hadn't been here since I was born.

"It's a boy," Mother answered, her eyes wide with the realization dawning on her, and the room suddenly became very hot.

"It's not," I insisted, trying to keep my voice as even as it had been before, but Zadar simply took one look at me and knew the truth.

"She's lying," he signed, and I physically felt the pained gape she sent me.

"It's not what you think!" I shouted, throwing my hands up in surrender, "He's my friend! That's all!"

"Is he the reason ye've been actin' sae strangely?" Zadar questioned, and my head lowered, attempting to obscure the flushed state of my face as my fingernails bit into the palms of my hand. "It doesnae matter. Ye won't be seein' him again anyway," he firmly stated, "I'm goin' tae pick Anders up frae school, and when I get back, I'd like tae see progress wi' the packin'."

It was an order, parent to child, but he would never be my father; I didn't care what he claimed.

I heard him kiss Mother goodbye, pausing briefly at my side to mention something, but he remained silent as he headed to the door. I glanced at Mother once Zadar was gone, seeing the light in her countenance dim as she crawled back into her distant shell, unable to look me in the eyes for longer than two seconds. Carefully, I watched her, taking in the fading loveliness, the mother I had known transitioning back into the mother I knew.

"How did you meet this boy?" she asked after a mutual moment of silence.

"Work."

"What is his name?"

"I'd rather not say."

She blinked at me, dull and emotionless, unbothered with the same mentality Zadar had. I was never going to see him again.

"I had you start that job to form a relationship with Zadar, not some random coworker."

"Why didn't you just tell me you got remarried?" I asked in the deepest sincerity, and with that question, she shut down completely, closing me off with painful familiarity as she climbed the stairs to Anders' room to gather his things. I wanted to shout at her, force her to give me answers to questions that shouldn't have needed to be asked, but I had no words, only tears to scream how I felt, and she didn't even notice as I walked out of the house, away from the doors that she closed herself.

Chapter Fourteen

Tears blurred my vision as I walked along the beach, and I was unsuccessful in my attempts to pinpoint the reasoning. It may have been that I was lied to most of my life, or that I was nearly killed earlier, but I told myself it was because of my father.

I remembered the last day I saw him, unable to forget how cold his hands were as he held mine, his eyes bleeding the same emotion Mother had framed on her hidden wall. We never said goodbye because he promised he'd be back, gifting me my shell as an emblem of his words.

The day I was informed of his death was the day I realized not everyone kept their promises.

Mother told me he died in a shipwreck, that he was coming home to us when a storm disrupted his path, and the waves he spoke so fondly of became too strong. Father loved the sea, teaching me to favor it over grass and sand, and I never understood why the thing he cared for the most would cause his demise. It was a betrayal I couldn't release, and in my bitterness, I refused to enter its waters.

Often, I wondered how different my life would have been if he had lived past my childhood, but now there was an ache like none other, longing to have him near, to talk with him, to sing with him. It had been so long since I last heard his voice, and the memory of its sound felt far yet scarcely within my reach, like the illusion of an ocean's coast being near. I stared out at the crashing waves, drawn to their depths, pondering whether drowning would be nostalgic. It certainly would bring me to him again, just as death reunites the forgotten, but I didn't want to die, not now, not yet.

Instead, I sat at the shore, shutting away my vision and picturing myself back then, when I was given his permission to use my voice. The ocean's hum was much different from the whisper of the forest that I had become accustomed to, but when I began to sing in reminiscence, the water welcomed my song as the trees had, washing over my feet with a gentle caress.

Wind on the ocean;
Song on the sea.
Wished for the sky;
Drowned in the grief.

The lyrics stood out to me more than when I'd sing them to Anders, feeling a deeper meaning and understanding in how the tone dipped, and though I could sense sobs ready to clutch my throat, I continued my song.

Lost in a gale;
Torn from the land. Promises failed,
Just as you planned.

Mother appeared in my mind then, her quiet deception and broken solicitude, words hurting as opposed to healing as they had for Anders.

Melodic chorus, sweet somber songs,
Turned to a wail.
Come, teardrop of hope, invert the blight,
And ravage the bonds of the deep.

I squeezed my eyelids a bit tighter, imagining him singing with me, but all I heard in response were mocking seagulls and crunching sand.

Follow my song, rest for long;
I offer all that you need.
Heed my voice, take my choice,
Let your heart lead you to me.

I used the last stanza as a call, wishing to bring my father back along with all the wonderful memories, and with me blind to the surrounding earth, I could almost feel him at my side until he pressed a heated hand on my shoulder, and fresh tears poured down my cheeks.

"Ari?"

Kiernan's voice mixed with the music of the sea didn't match up, something in it sounding comparable to alarm bells, and the noise jolted me from my imaginings.

"Kiernan!" I exclaimed, jumping to my feet, "What are you doing here?"

My attention shot to the houses on the hill, knowing anyone walking around the neighborhood could notice us, including my family, and I didn't want to find out what Zadar might do if he saw Kiernan. Zadar knew I had a friend along with the knowledge of the Turner name, but he wasn't aware that the two topics were connected, and I wished to keep it that way.

An unbelievable warmth caressed my cheek, brushing a tear from my face, and I quickly pulled away, viewing how Kiernan's expression lilted.

"You are crying," he observed, feeling the moisture on his fingers.

The look he gave me was fragile, and something about seeing him away from the overgrown woods, standing in a normal environment, was alarmingly unnatural, like a waterfall in an open desert.

"Please don't. You'll make this so much worse," I huffed, desperately trying to keep the ever-persistent tears down.

"Make what worse?"

I pulled him from the shore, tucking us under the hill leading to the beach, hiding away from any unwanted attention. I wasn't fully comfortable with our location, but the earnestness on Kiernan's face told me I didn't have time to find somewhere else.

"I'm moving," I informed, resolving to the fact that I was just shy of eighteen, and couldn't legally stay on my own. Kiernan, however, didn't appear to be resolved to the idea.

"What? But I—" he stopped himself instantly, swallowing harshly enough for me to see the bob of his throat, "Do you think you will ever come back?"

"I wish I could say yes."

"Where are you going?"

"Scotland."

I barely had the word out before Kiernan was protesting.

"No!" he shouted, and I jumped from the unexpected denial, forgetting tears and reaching for my shell in substitute. His tone changed the next second, willing a calm over himself as he softly added, "I'm not sure that is the best idea."

"I don't even want to go," I admitted, matching his solemn tones.

"Then why are you?"

I was hesitant to answer, afraid of how he'd react to my attack, and the longer I waited, the stronger his curiosity grew.

"Ari, what happened to you?" he inquired, observing the dirt and scrapes on my uniform.

"Your brother..." I began slowly, unsure how to word my experience lightly, but Kiernan's entire countenance darkened, and I worried explaining the interaction would only make things worse.

"When?" he demanded in ominous quiet, and I didn't like the fire in his eyes, forests burning with each flick of his sight.

"This morning," I answered in a small voice, desiring to be the water for his flame, but he wasn't looking at me, focusing on the ground in deep thought.

"Kell always takes things too far," Kiernan muttered, not to me, I realized as I watched him subconsciously examine each grain of sand, but as a conclusive factor to himself. His stare was hard, brows knit taught together while those life-filled eyes held their silent debate, and it urged me to take a step backward. The movement yanked his attention back to me, and I observed how his gaze softened, reminding me of the look Zadar had earlier for Mother.

"Do you trust me?"

I weighed those words just as I weighed the severity with which he presented them, and I knew no matter how I answered, the repercussions would be significant, so I determined the truth.

"Yes."

"Follow me," he instructed, wasting no time to execute whatever he had planned, and with less thought than I should have given, I complied.

I chased after his hurried steps, nearly running through sand, up to the edge of the redwoods neighboring our town, through mud still slick from the previous storm, all the way to the sea lining the forest's end, far from outside view, while in walking distance of my home.

"What are we doing?" I questioned perhaps too late, halting just beyond the ocean's reach as he did.

"I need you in the water."

"Why?"

"I can't say at the moment, but I wouldn't ask this of you if it wasn't important."

I gazed at the line where the sky met the sea, viewing the shift in days, changing colors as it prepared for the sun's descent, and in that lighting, the water appeared deceptively calm.

"I don't know how to swim," I admitted, picturing the sensation of liquid trapped in my lungs and my last cry for help inaudible as I was dragged into the deep. Too many times, had I pictured Father in that position.

Kiernan must've been lost in his imaginings as well because there was a moment of silence that lasted an uncomfortable amount of time before a cautious hand wrapped around mine and a tentative voice responded.

"Then I will go with you."

Water crashed into my legs, sand slipping from under my feet, sinking into the ocean's hold, already having a sensation of drowning. Half of my body submerged, the tide beckoning me to follow, and something hidden deep within my chest uncoiled at its touch, long lost familiarity pressing into me.

"I have you. Don't worry," Kiernan promised with a careful tug on our interlocked hands, reading my body language, and while his affirmation was reassuring, I didn't miss the shake in his voice. I wanted to ask why he needed this in the first place, but my focus was diverted as the water lapped at my collarbone, and a sudden dizziness overcame me.

"I feel strange."

It wasn't a sense of fear or dread, more of a type of sickness, one overwhelming enough to weaken every part of me.

"We can go back now," he agreed, appearing to be highly pleased with whatever result he had been looking for. Kiernan moved in the direction of the shore, and my legs gave out, gripping his arm with all the strength I was slowly losing. The action forced his attention back, his eyes locked on something beneath me, dread and terror morphing his face into someone I didn't know, and in his state of shock, his grasp loosened, mistakenly gifting me to the current.

Immediately, he snapped out of it, plunging in after me, and I watched with perfect sight as he swam in my direction, distress written all over him. I, however, was content to rest in the deep, and if I had enough strength, would have forced Kiernan down with me to experience the same serenity. Breathing was easy, head light as though I was in the clouds, ears filled with the ocean's quiet lullaby, my body limp with the kind of peace I hadn't experienced since Father died, and I had entirely forgotten I was underwater.

There was a creature swimming beside my slack figure, beautiful scales leading to a delicately layered fin, adorned in shimmering colors of teal, turquoise, along with varying shades of blue, and when the sun hit just right, a deep violet. I had the sense to touch the thing despite only catching its lower half, and when my fingers grazed the dazzling skin, slick and smooth, I felt the faintest tingle in my leg.

Kiernan reached me then, hooking a hand under my arm while his other limbs fought against the sea as I viewed curiously the creature following, glittering in the light I was pulled to. Our heads broke the surface, breaking whatever spell had been cast over me, and I was hit with a wave of terror. I felt as though I experienced a nightmare, the chilling atmosphere awaking me from my prolonged sleep. My body was numb, and I swallowed mouthfuls of water while attempting to stay above, needing to choke and gasp for oxygen, but there was no air to grant me that.

"Swim!" He shouted, but I could hardly hear him over the water clogging my ears, hauling me from the sea's grasp.

"I can't!" I had warned him of that, and the toll of keeping us both alive was beginning to prove visible.

"Yes, you can!" he shouted as if he were begging for his life, "Please, Ari, you—"

A wave swallowed him whole, consuming me in the process, and with the same clear vision, I saw his desperate struggle to reach the surface, air escaping from him in grievous bubbles. He was exhausted, fighting too long and hard for safety, and I realized I was going to watch him die.

No. Can't let him go. Not like Father.

Flashes of blue and violet floated in my vision before flipping behind me, and with strength I didn't know I had, I caught Kiernan. I forced my legs into submission, kicking both in unison after finding them unable to separate, surprised when gliding through the water came easily on the first try. I didn't rejoice as we neared the shore, feeling Kiernan completely unresponsive, and my heart raced aggressively enough for the both of us, terrified that I was already too late.

Can't lose him too. Please don't go.

Solid ground seemed so far away, and air seemed even further, unable to reach the surface as I pushed for the shore. I searched for the creature, prepared to beg for help, but as I spotted that glistening fin, I found it was already helping.

It was attached to me.

I didn't have time to think or properly register; all I could do was force the fin into a quicker pace until the water thinned, the ground rose higher and higher, and the beach was at my fingertips. Scales drip off me, like a shimmering mist dissipating into air, leaving drenched clothes to cling to my trembling form. I grip handfuls of sand, outstretching for land in desperation, leaving me breathless, water catching in my lungs as I tried to scream. Kiernan made no movement beside me, and I was left to helplessly stare at his unmoving chest, recalling his last words to be pleas for help.

Failed him. He needed you. Weren't enough. Murderer.

Relief didn't come, not even when Kiernan rolled to his side and coughed up the water in his throat, because I nearly killed the only person who still wanted me. Tears poured from my eyes, mixing with the ocean on my skin as I watched Kiernan's body reject the sea that tried to claim him, and the moment he could breathe, he was on his feet, pacing back and forth.

"What was that?" I choked out, weak and frail, trying to gather the events in a way that made sense. Kiernan kept shaking his head, blinking a billion times while poorly managing uneven breathing. "What *was that?*" I screamed, finally able to use my lungs, and the muscles under his skin twitched pointedly, something wanting to break free. "Kiernan!"

"It's what I feared!" he snapped, looking incredibly pained but managing to bring his voice down as he spoke the words that permanently changed my world.

"You are a siren, Ari."

Everything cold and unpleasant tingled through my body, matching the sensation I felt when touching the fin, once again losing the air I strained to find.

Kiernan went back to pacing, sharp lines like scales scratching under his bare arms, and I wondered if they might bleed.

"This wasn't supposed to happen," he insisted, stressing worse than I had seen from Zadar. "You are human. You aren't like them. I don't understand!"

I didn't either, nor could I figure out why the existence of sirens was so easily believable to him.

"What does it mean?" I implored, unsure what to say or think, and he clearly knew everything.

"It means you are in danger, and Scotland is not the place you should be."

"Where should I go?"

Kiernan watched me for a moment, and I feared what he was going to say until his eyes went wide and shot to the forest behind him.

"Home. Now," he demanded, lifting me to my unstable feet from where I sat frozen on the beach, "I will explain everything, I promise."

Another sharp look over his shoulder, and when his voice came again, it was much quieter, "Just not right now. Whenever you can, come to the forest and sing again. I will hear you."

I knew that look, and with the events earlier that day, I knew what it meant.

We were not alone.

I took off, running for home without looking back, thinking only of how wrong it felt to have legs.

Chapter Fifteen

Wet, cold, and scared, I entered my house. Zadar had yet to return with Anders, but I doubted they would be much longer. Mother was too busy packing to notice her sopping daughter rushing to her room, though I imagined if I had come home covered in blood, she'd hardly bat an eye either. Shutting myself off from the rest of the house, I huddled in the corner of my room, body quivering with chills that wouldn't cease. Soaked clothes still clung to me, but I couldn't move from my balled figure, stuck with events playing in my mind on an endless loop.

Kiernan almost died.

I almost died.

My head was still spinning, and I felt like throwing up when thinking of that *thing* attached to me or Kiernan's claim of what I was. I wanted to believe it was all a dream, that I would wake up in a cold sweat and that would be the worst of it, but Anders barged into my room, forcing me into reality.

"We are going to Scotland!" he shouted, practically jumping with excitement, "Dad told me all about it! We are going to live in the Highlands and see the hairy coos! They have castles there, Ari, *castles*! And we leave tomorrow morning! Can you believe it?"

I believed it a bit too much, realizing what little time I had to sort through it all. During everything that happened with Kiernan, I failed to mention how soon I was moving, which meant one thing. If I were ever to see him again and get answers to questions I couldn't ask anyone else, it would have to be tonight when the household thought I was asleep.

"You, okay?"

He seemed so pleased with life, alive and well, like I hadn't seen him in a long time. Zadar did that, filled the hole in my brother in his heart, the role of a companion, a friend, a *father*.

That hole in my heart remained vacant.

"I'm fine. I just need to take a shower."

Anders frowned, disbelieving, but left me to privacy, and I noticed how similar his walk was to Zadar's as he exited my room. I never saw Anders as less than my blood relative, but at that moment, all I could think of was us as half-siblings, and that I was the half that didn't belong.

This is what I had dreamed of for years, a family with a happy Anders, a present Mother, and an alive father, yet I wasn't content. Maybe I was too hard to please, or maybe I asked for too much, but there was still something lost I needed to find.

I did end up taking a shower, which gave a perfect excuse for my wet hair when there was a knock on my door, followed by a solemn-looking Zadar.

"Mind if I come in?" he requested, forcing a smile that appeared much more convincing than when I faked an expression. I nodded, struggling to find words, and Zadar took a seat next to me on my bed. "I wanted tae apologize for earlier. I can imagine what ye're goin' through, and it's no pleasant. I meant tae tell ye in a mair gentle way, but as ye can see, a few things came up that changes that."

"All I want is honesty," I interrupted before he could continue on with his apology, when I was the one supposed to be saying sorry.

"And ye deserve it."

"Why Scotland?" I asked, testing if he meant his words, and there was no hesitation in his response.

"Ye'll be safe there. I've friends who'd dae anythin' tae keep the threat aff ye."

My focus remained on the hands nervously fiddling in my lap, unable to meet his stare or stop the bouncing of my leg.

"And what is the threat?"

"Ye really want tae ken?" He asked sensitively, and I wasn't truly sure what I wanted but nodded regardless. Zadar shifted to a more comfortable position on my bed, a silent preparation for a long conversation that I worried I wasn't ready for.

"This world's no what ye think it is. There are creatures hidin' behind human skin, and maist o' them are dangerous."

Shimmering scales and layered fins. Strangled cries and panicked words. Moonlit blue and violet. 'You are a siren, Ari.'

Zadar paused, his reasoning unknown, but I took it as my opportunity presented.

"Are you human, Zadar?"

My bluntness understandably caught him off guard, not expecting me to accept this easily, but after what occurred with Kiernan, I couldn't do anything but take his words seriously.

"No entirely," he responded, confusion prominent in his voice, and my second nod was a form of acceptance.

"Neither is Anders?" I guessed.

"Naw."

"Mother?"

"She's human," he barely had the answer out before he added, "I'm sorry, did I miss somethin'? Ye're takin' this... awfu' easy."

"What are you?" I deflected, never letting my eyes leave my lap.

"We're called kelpies," he reluctantly spoke, and I could sense his eyes boring into me, "Scottish water horses who serve the Queen o' Lochness."

"As in the Lochness Monster?"

"She's no a monster, and her name's Nessie," he clipped rather defensively, "She's got the gift tae see bits of the future, and sometimes, she passes it tae us."

I lifted my head, terror striking my chest as I faced him.

"You mean Anders..."

Zadar's knowing look said it all. "His dreams are real."

"He saw me die, Zadar. He cried about it for weeks," I nearly shouted, remembering all the nightmares he'd screamed about over the years, what sort of torture that would be on a child.

"I've seen it too, but it'll be awricht. The future can be changed, and yer murderer won't follow us intae Scotland. No unless he's wantin' tae die."

"What is he?"

Zadar almost seemed apologetic as he said, "A dragon."

The proper response would have been to laugh or roll my eyes, and dismiss the idea altogether, but I did none of that. I'd seen Anders' drawing, and these creatures were not something to take lightly.

"What do they look like?" I asked to always be on the lookout.

"Their human mask is... weaker than oors. Dragons cannae handle emotions- it makes their reactions a bit... strange."

'What does embarrassment feel like?' Lifeless eyes and forced smiles. 'What does happiness feel like?'

His voice slammed into me with painful force, memories of laughter and confusion alike echoing in my mind, and the room instantly felt too small.

"They've got keen hearin'. Ye cannae hide frae them, and they thrive off of the fear their victims gie aff."

Near to drowning and being pulled closer with motivated strength. 'Sing and I will hear you.'

I subtly began shaking my head, but Zadar didn't stop, watching with empathy.

"They dinnae look fully human either. Their faces are too perfect, too symmetrical, tryin' tae blend in wi' folk, but whit really gives them away is the harsh green o' their een."

My heart stopped altogether.

"What?" I breathed, knowing well what he said, and Zadar's look told me we were on the same page, simply a different section.

"Aye. The man that attacked ye was a dragon."

And Kiernan.

"You are lying!" I accused, yelling more at my thoughts than Zadar, but he didn't flinch.

"I dinnae have that ability as a kelpie," he claimed, overly calm in hopes of easing my tension, "It's a blessin' and a curse. In danger, I cannae lie tae get oot o' it, but on the bright side, ye ken everythin' I say is true."

I stood, regaining space that was closing in on me, gripping my shell as I paced.

He was wrong, I assured myself, feeling myself begin to crumble, and Zadar was there the next second to catch me.

"Hey, hey, I ken it's a lot tae take in, but ye're goin' tae be awricht," he soothed, accent calming and promising a better life, kneeling where I couldn't avoid his kind face, "Never forget tae breathe, Ari. It makes aw the difference when panic hits."

I attempted to heed his advice, but my breaths came out sharp and wrong, akin to Kiernan's when he was panicking, and all I could focus on was that moment.

"Is there anything else I should know?"

I waited for him to finish the truth, telling me how I was one of the creatures he spoke about, and all I wanted was honesty. Zadar surveyed me, and with a warm smile, he spoke, "No yet."

The same words Mother used for me when I begged for the truth, a shut-down, a rejection covered under the cloak of fake thoughtfulness, and I could sense the cry weighing down my throat.

"Could I be alone for a little while?" I asked, turning my head away.

Zadar headed for the exit immediately at the sound of my weakened voice, pausing briefly to inquire, "Are ye comin' doon for dinner?"

"Not hungry. I think I'll just go to bed," I declined, resorting to my bed.

"I love ye," he called, and I knew he meant it, even if he wasn't trapped to honesty, but I feared repeating it lest it come out a lie and cause more hurt. Pulling the sheets over my permanently chilled body, I rested facing the wall to avoid viewing disappointment.

"Goodnight, Zadar," I replied, and after a pause, he closed the door.

I sang for Kiernan, pushing on through the forest as I memorized the place that had become home to me. Zadar warned me not to wander the woods at night, and now I could understand that it was more than simple forest animals he feared, but I didn't plan on informing him of this final forest visit, just as he didn't intend to inform me that the skin I wore was only a human disguise. I wanted confirmation from Kiernan about several things, possibly get a hug goodbye, and then I would be off to Scotland, where I was safe. I'd miss the redwoods, and I'd miss Kiernan even more, the two companions I made over the last few months, but I had a chance to start over where I wouldn't need to sneak away to be with people who brought me joy.

It made Zadar happy; it made Anders happy; it even made Mother happy. Why didn't I feel the same?

My song was laced with shouts, nervous he wouldn't show, and our near-death experience would be our last encounter. I held on tighter to the large kitchen knife I'd brought with me, promising myself it wasn't for Kiernan. His brother was still out for me, and it was for my self-protection from him, even if Kiernan had been lying to my face since the day we met, even if Zadar was right and he wanted me dead, even if he was a...

No, it wasn't true.

And this knife definitely wasn't for him.

Ten minutes wasn't a long time, but my voice was becoming weaker along with my dwindling hope, and when a voice broke the silence, all my hope was smothered, along with my comfort.

"You know... you are kind of naive for a witch."

He wasn't hiding this time, standing confidently in the middle of my path, and I hoped to exhibit no fear as I pointed the knife at him with both hands despite the wild pounding of my heart.

"Where is Kiernan?" I demanded, albeit rather weakly, and the man hardly gave notice to my weapon as he neared.

"At home. As you should be," he informed, lightly pushing aside my blade, "Your kelpie friend won't be pleased when he finds you here. Should I leave a trail of blood to your body, or do you think throwing you back to the ocean and letting him go insane looking for you would be better?"

Tears of pure terror collected on my eyelashes, and I did my best to hide them, fighting to take away what he wanted. If his only goal was to murder me, he would have simply done it this morning, but he had a sick enjoyment in torment, I could see it in how illuminated green eyes lit ever brighter when my hands trembled.

"How do you know about Zadar?" I tried, taking the subject off of me and what he planned to do, merely to give myself time for an escape plan, and he gladly took the bait.

"My brother wasn't the only one stalking you for all these months," he spoke, as though it was common knowledge, while I subconsciously began to lose grip of my weapon.

"He what?" I willed my words to be calm, yet they still wobbled as I spoke, and his humorless chuckle seemed to shake branches.

"He didn't tell you? Kiernan's been tracking you since you started your job."

It would have hurt less to shove a blade through my stomach.

This was their plan all along, I realized too late, an elaborate scheme to eliminate my existence. All those wonderful moments I shared with Kiernan were games of deception, and I fell for every one of them, emotions of embarrassment, guilt, and hurt surging through me. In a blind rage, I swung, not looking as I plunged the knife into him, taking off the second I heard him grunt, blood-chilling fear quickly replacing anger. I didn't get five steps away before I was gripped by the collar of my shirt with incredible strength and thrown into the rugged bark of a fallen tree. A pathetic noise escaped me on the impact, momentarily paralyzed from the pain shooting through my spine.

"I'm not in the mood to chase you," he stated, unimpressed, and before I could process it, a knife was planted inches from my head, slicing a section of my hair and pinning it into the wood, the color of his blood and my curls blending. I looked at him, spotting the wound in his left shoulder, eyes wide in the realization that the blood could have been mine if the weapon had been aimed the slightest bit to the left.

"Please," I breathed, both of us knowing the beg for my life in that simple word.

He gave a cruel smile, kneeling in front of me and nearly burning the skin of my collarbone with his fingertips as he reached for my necklace.

"Sirens are rather fragile creatures, especially when it comes to fire," he spoke, lifting the charm still attached to my neck, "Their skin is quite susceptible to heat, and like any flammable substance, it only takes one flame to consume and destroy." His brows pulled together after he surveyed my shell, a look of recognition in his eyes, hardening his stare and tightening his jaw. He dropped my necklace with disdain, giving nothing away as he stood back up. "Not all my kind have the gift of fire, but luckily enough for us, I am an Ember."

"I want to live," I pleaded, feeling a single tear drop from my eyelashes, watching as his face contorted into something sinister.

"So did my sister," he bellowed, and when I was unable to react, his arms flew up in front of his face, hands fisted and wrists connected, before throwing them out in a swift motion to reveal a blood-red, scaled face.

Dragon.

I couldn't move, couldn't scream, couldn't think, frozen in a state of fear as my eyes fixed on the predator before me. Its head alone was longer than my entire body, its wings large enough to wrap around the widest redwood while every shade of fire painted its hide. The earth trembled beneath its steps, matching my violent tremors, exhorting dominance over the forest.

I tried desperately to get up, groaning pitifully with each attempt, but as I shifted the slightest movement, my leg was trapped under a palm with enough pressure to snap it in half. I feared that's what he planned to do when a talon slipped into the soft tissue of my leg, crippling me from going anywhere.

Spots danced in my vision while a scream shattered my eardrums, brain rushing too quickly to register the pained noise as my own. Other sounds lingered as well, rustling leaves, deep snarling, shallow breaths, but none of them compared to the maddening roar that shook the ground.

I didn't see how it changed, or the cause, but the heavy pressure on my leg lifted, replaced by cold air seeping in. I was crying, for how long I wasn't certain, but the tears trailing down my cheeks ached just as painfully as the wood digging into my back. Liquid slick and hot trickled from my leg, and it was an effort not to faint at the sight of the wound gaping just above my knee.

Red and black spots continued to quarrel in my vision as I struggled to keep my head upright, flared wings on the dots making me wonder how much of it was real and how much I was imagining. It was dark, the moonlight pale, the breeze cold, the fume metallic, and one at a time I felt my senses slip from me.

The last thing I saw was the red blood painted around me, and the green eyes of a beast rushing my way.

Part 2

*B*eautiful, sweet girl. What am I to do with you?

She laughed, spinning herself in circles with her face towards the sky, relishing in the rain, and the world seemed to respond to her sound. It wasn't a lie to say the forest was alive, whispering trees and taunting breeze, but every living thing awakened in her presence, flourishing in ways I'd never seen before. Lightning streaked across the sky in attempts to match her glow, the thunder rumbled as though to mimic the melodious noise, but it couldn't compare.

She was alive again, and nothing was more beautiful.

I would've been content to watch her like that for the rest of my life, but she paused to find me with those starlit eyes in the moonless night and asked me to dance with her.

She could've asked for the very essence of my living, and I would've found a way to give it to her, just to keep her happy a second longer. I wanted to hold her face, capture that smile forever, deprived of her joy after these last miserable days, focused on restraining instincts woven in my being when she was distressed. Sometimes they wanted me to pull her to me, others to shove her away, both too harsh for her.

She needed someone gentle, someone who could hold her when she was afraid rather than hurt her, the someone I didn't know how to be.

But she wanted to dance, and she never asked for much.

There was a rush of something in my chest as I neared her, a slight tingling in my hands as we touched, a constant reminder of how her very presence had changed me.

Because with her, I felt.

She made me happy, laughing and teasing until all I could think about was her smile.

She made me nervous, uncertain and paranoid she'd run away when I said the wrong thing.

She caused my anger, not at her, of course, but at Kell when he threatened her safety.

She caused my sadness, seeing her hurting and frightened, especially when I was the source of it.

Seeing her hurt was the worst of it, and I didn't wish to think of it, entirely emptying my brain of the guilt as I spun her, just to watch those crimson curls take air, hear that sweet giggle overtake the storm's rumbling. Her heart refused to rest, for once racing in exhilaration rather than terror, and even the life in her veins sounded like a song. I couldn't understand how I'd ever convinced myself she was human, not when even the minuscule things about her, the adorable crinkle around her eyes when she smiled, the entrancing way she traced her fingers over the shell when thinking, were pure magic. Droplets rolled off her skin like liquid diamonds, enhancing her light skin until it appeared iridescent, and suddenly, I didn't mind the rain. It still left me powerless, but it made no difference, not when being near her was my greatest weakness.

And I knew better than to let my guard down again, but the ability to touch her once more was distracting, and my hands were slipping to her wrist before I could fully recognize what I was doing, pinning them behind her as our dance came to a halt.

It was an intimate movement, one exploiting vulnerability, bringing our faces too close, our lips a breath's distance away from disaster, and something so wrong shouldn't have felt so right. I'd witnessed my parents dance in the same way as a child, *Patér* holding to his wife the way I held to her, it all occurring naturally. I didn't need to think when leading her into this movement, yet it took all my focus not to continue the action, finishing the dance as intended.

I felt the pulse in her wrist quicken beneath my palm, her cheeks deepening into the captivating shade of pink that provoked an emotion inside of me I had yet to figure out, but there was no scent of fear anywhere near her, and that only made it worse. Temptation had me lowering my eyes to her lips, considering risks that would ultimately prove fatal, and reality had me releasing her to create distance.

I fisted my hands at my sides, pinning the nagging desire to reach for her, fearing something my heart knew, even if my brain didn't understand it.

I was in love with Ari.

Chapter Sixteen

"What were you even *doing* out there? You hate California!" Kiernan's muffled voice seethed, and I buried my head further into my pillow to block it out. My eyes didn't open to see the time, but my limp body told me it was much too early to be waking up.

"I could ask you the same thing."

That voice, despite its calm, was even more unsettling than the angered shouts of Kiernan, hazy memories sparking recognition.

"I could also ask why you leave every morning before the sun rises and come back *well* after it sets, or why you refuse to talk to any of us, or why you have been attached to your alternate form so much that now your skin is beginning to stretch—"

"Don't act like you care, Kell," Kiernan interrupted, his words dark and pointed. An easy sigh was released, one I couldn't decipher the owner of as my brain half-heartedly retained the argument, stuck in a peculiar limbo between sleep and consciousness.

"You are right," he continued smoothly, "I don't care. The problems began when *you* started caring."

"So that gave you the right to follow me?"

I could feel the sheets then, comforter crumpling against my fingers in a physical effort to grasp reality.

"You and I saw the same thing the other night. You expect me not to attack it?"

"For the hundredth time! She is not an *it*! Ari is—"

"Oh, so you've named it now?" A taunt, I could hear it in his voice, sounding like *'Over here, little songbird.'*, and sleep was suddenly less appealing. "As your older brother, it is my responsibility to deal with the problems you are too weak to solve yourself."

"You tried to burn an innocent girl alive!"

"Problem. Solution."

I shot up, gripping the mattress warmed from my body to keep the room from spinning, shooting pain resounding up my leg. I bit back my scream, a whimper escaping in its place, and it took several breaths for my eyes to adjust to my surroundings.

It wasn't a large space, enough room for the bed and dresser facing the opposite corner, moonlight streaming in from the tall window on my left, door set to my right, and though the bed felt close to luxurious, the fact that it wasn't my own took all its comfort from me. My leg throbbed with every subtle movement, and glancing down, I found it partially wrapped, blood seeping out through the corners as though there hadn't been time to properly secure a bandage. Nausea teased my throat feeling the blood creep down my knee, hot, wet, sticky, and I remembered that same sensation as wood dug into my back and screams shredded my throat.

It clicked then, who I was with, who I *wasn't* with, and terror made my blood run cold.

"Somebody's awake."

My head whipped to the door, tracing the voice seeming to mock at my vulnerability.

Silent killers. Done this before. Going to die. Never told Anders goodbye.

Silence followed, my heartbeat providing the sole sound aching through thin walls. The panic set in next, memories and recognition pummeling my senses and stealing rationality. I whimpered when attempting to move, hating how the tiny noise sounded like shouts in the painful quiet. My legs wouldn't cooperate as I willed them to, and the pain was increasing by the second.

Can't run. Can't move. Can't find a way home.

"If it keeps this up much longer, I can't be held responsible for my actions."

"Can't believe I am actually saying this, but I agree with Kell," someone added, sounding strained and vaguely familiar.

"Kiernan, would you mind talking to her? I think we would all benefit from her composure," requested a voice I'd never heard, before footsteps neared.

Going to die. Shouldn't have left. Need to find Zadar.

Again, I tried to move, and my whole body tensed in agony, barely managing to shift to the edge of the bed when light from the opening door pierced the room, and I froze.

Kiernan entered gingerly, crumpled hair and vibrant eyes, but the sight of him, looking like a rich dream through the intruding light glowing behind him, I couldn't think of anything apart from the deceptive moments we shared, and his intentions to end my life.

"S-stay away from me!" I shouted, finding the strength to escape the bed and tumble into the wall. Kiernan was there in a second, reaching to help me stand, and I recoiled at the heat, more focused on breaking free from him than how I tumbled to the cold floorboards.

"Ari—"

"Don't come any closer!" I cried, pushing my palms against the floor to gain distance until my back was pinned in the corner. I continued to push away, hoping to disappear into the wall, yet my spine wouldn't allow it.

"Okay, okay," he consoled, arms extended my way as though I was a feral animal needing taming, "I'll stay over here."

He slowly lowered himself against the opposite wall, careful with each movement he made, holding my gaze with a regretful stare, and I feared the effect it had on me. His body was taut, bracing himself against the wall as though to keep from coming closer, a vein bulging out of his neck, and a day ago, I would have willingly traced my fingers across it until it went away. How happy I had been to ease his pain when his intention had only been to harm me, how easily I could fall back into it because I wanted to believe his lies.

I wanted to think there was someone who wanted me.

We stayed like that for a while, watching one another closely, him tracking my breathing while I waited for an attack that didn't come. There was a crease on his brow, eyes pleading apologies where words could not, his face lilting in an expression of sorrow. A face, I reminded myself, that displayed as a mask; beautiful, alluring, dangerous mask.

"Where am I?" I asked, surprised by the sudden evenness of my tone.

Kiernan waited a moment longer, another breath, another blink, another second to stare into those inhumane eyes and ponder my helpless state.

"My home," he answered, sounding just like the boy I'd counted the stars with, not my captor, not a murderer.

"Why am I here? What..." I swallowed, choking down tears, "What are you going to do to me?"

I was far from the first abduction in Crescent City, and I tried not to let my mind wonder about what happened to the victims, but now it was all I could think about. Gradually, I'd accepted the fact I was never going to see my family again, only regretting I hadn't apologized to Mother for our fight, or hugged Anders goodbye, or returned Zadar's affirmation. I was going to die, yet that wasn't what scared me the most. Kiernan knew much about me, things he and his brother could use to break me mentally before physically, and it only made sense they would. Why else had he spent all those mornings with me, leading me on with topics of myself that I'd so willingly given him, desperate for someone to care. It was foolish to believe he'd done it out of pure enjoyment.

"Please don't look at me like that," he spoke, with fragility and deceptive innocence, and I could feel my guard falling as it always had around him. My muscles strained as I forced it back up.

"Was it true you stalked me before we met?"

That caused him to drop his gaze, resting his eyelids and exhaling through his nose.

"I want to explain."

"Are you going to kill me?" I questioned, unwilling to hear the string of lies he'd formed for me. It hurt not to trust him, and seeing mock pain on his face only worsened the ache.

"No."

He'd hesitated, and that beat of silence was more answer than his own.

The tears were instant in their descent on my face, but my hands remained on the floor, nails biting into the wood beneath me.

"Why couldn't you have killed me sooner? Why did you..."

My voice failed, my chest tightening to force the words out, and Kiernan examined it all, thinking of ways he could use this new vulnerability.

"Why did you have to be so *kind*?"

There was a shift in his eyes, a breaking behind them that words couldn't express, and his voice sounded equally shattered as he spoke my name.

"Ari..."

It still affected me, how gently he used the letters, only when he said it, only when it was my name.

Kiernan sat up, careful in his movements to reach me, and it broke his trance on my mind, recognizing what was happening. I had admitted what his affection meant to me, and he planned to use it to his advantage, and my back flattened against the wall in a feeble attempt to escape.

"No... no, just do it quickly. I don't want it to hurt. Please," I begged, wanting him to be the one to end me over anyone else, yet I trembled as he brought his hand near my face, hovering over my brow. He was shaking, his hand quivering as though the weight of the world was on the tips of his fingers, hovering a whisper away from my face, and my stare locked on the abnormal twisting beneath his skin, watching as the creature behind the mask tried to claw its way out. I couldn't decide whether death or a thoughtful touch from him would hurt more.

"Look at my eyes."

I followed the command, concentration and green staring back at me, his pupils slitting to appear more animalistic.

Not human. Not human.

Zadar's warnings circled my thoughts, and more than ever, I wished he were here, knowing exactly what to say and do. But he was gone, and I was alone and scared with a creature who thrived off of fear and attempts to calm only increased panic.

"You are making this very difficult for me," he said through clenched teeth, his forehead creasing with tension, "Breathe. I need you to calm down."

I tried to obey, but the air around us was thick and difficult to consume, lodging in my throat and stealing the smallest amount of composure I managed to maintain. Kiernan brushed the hair from my eyes, his trembling fingers skimming above my brow, and in his touch was familiarity, loosening my lungs to accept oxygen, and I was comforted in the heat that gingerly touched my skin.

Kiernan's pupils dilated as I breathed, the tense lines on his face smoothing out, human mask fully intact once again, and his fingers brushed away my tears like they'd never been there as he whispered, "Why would I ever hurt you?"

Not a threat. Not a danger.

This, I decided, was so much worse than death, the lie of comfort he gave, yet I leaned into his touch, knowing it would be the last tender gesture I'd experience. With that belief, it was easy to give in to him, to let my heart pretend I mattered to someone—to him. Even if it was a lie, it hurt less.

There was a mutual understanding that things would not stay this way, that we could never again be those people running in the woods together, but we could have this moment. A moment to study the other, to search for the scars life left on us, revealed through the windows of the soul, no sounds, just us in the silence, until a voice came from behind the door.

"Have you broken its neck yet?"

My eyes blew wide, and his pupils slitted. My heart leaped in my chest, and his hand gripped my throat.

It was a reaction on reaction, a feeding of fear and pain in the briefest of moments, and my head was thrust back against the wall, his fingers digging into the pressure points beneath my jaw. I didn't fight him, knowing it was coming, and giving up on hope, Kiernan released me, jumping to his feet before stumbling into the dresser on the opposite wall, looking more frightened than I had. I watched many complicated emotions flash behind his eyes as he stared at my surrendered form, landing on rage as he turned to the door.

"What is *wrong* with you?" he shouted once out of the room, and I flinched at the uneasiness his anger caused me.

"It was quiet. I assumed that's how you got it to shut up," his brother answered, the only other voice I knew.

"Don't twist this. You wanted me to hurt her!"

"Stop. Both of you. Nothing is getting solved this way," someone demanded, and the room went quiet, "I don't want to hurt her. For Evelyn's sake, if no one else."

Evelyn. That was Mother's name, and the horrible thought that they might be after my whole family, after *Anders*, filled me with a new sense of dread, creating the motivation I needed to ignore the pain and shuffle to my feet.

"We aren't even sure that's her daughter."

"The girl looks just like her."

"And what about her father? Are we not going to talk about that sick—"

Voices both recognizable and unrecognizable came and went too quickly for me to process, but I froze at the mention of my father, wondering how these strangers knew him.

"We cannot jump to conclusions."

"I *saw* that necklace. That wretched *shell*. It was the same one we gave him in peace before he attacked Kaida."

"We don't know that."

"*I know* what *I saw*! And I have no particular loyalties to the woman. For all we know, Evelyn is dead."

I scanned the room, drawing my attention to anything but the conversation right outside my door, distracting myself with the things I could see.

Floor. Bed. Walls. Mirror. Ceiling. Nightstand. Light fixture. Dresser. Window...

Window.

"No one is dying tonight, Kell. I need some time to think," the unfamiliar voice informed, sparking life to my desperate heart.

One night. One hope. One chance to get out of here and warn my family. I stood taller, ignoring the pain shooting up my leg, staring at my only possible escape.

"So, we just let the witch stay the night like some honored guest?"

"Exactly."

Tuning everything else out, I took careful steps to the window, focusing on being nearly silent when unlocking it. Apart from a satisfying click, I was able to open the window without a sound, cool breeze feeling like a kiss of freedom against my face, and I braced myself to climb out. It was a slow and painful process, but I managed to slip out and land in a pile of unkempt grass, pausing long enough to register the continuing discussion and that they hadn't caught on to my intentions.

Then, with no concept of where I was or where to go, I headed straight for the thick of the forest.

Chapter Seventeen

Running was a challenge, but I managed to hobble along at a decent pace, grunting with almost every step. I hadn't taken the time to examine my wound or catch my breath, hadn't given thought to where I was going, prioritizing gaining distance above anything else.

Twisting stars and dim moonlight paved my path, dark and dire as it was. Ominous silence sang its song, my steps seeming to interrupt the woods' rest, but the image of my own home kept me going. For a minute, I could picture myself running to his room, dirt blending into freezing floorboards and thick trees as suffocating walls, but I never reached my brother, terrified screams just the distant wind. I almost made the mistake of shouting for him and drawing unwanted attention, but despite my brain, I reminded myself I was utterly alone, a reality that was both comforting and unsettling.

Don't speak. Keep going.

Unknown landmarks passed me one by one, forcing me deeper into my lost state, and while I searched for anything that could lead me home, the redwoods had never looked so foreign. Shadows cast haunting illusions, images of things I longed to see and feared hiding in the darkness, and the constant glances over my shoulder slowed my pace. Anders' wails lingered in the back of my mind, and I wanted to sing to tune them out, but they would hear me, and this would be all for nothing.

Don't listen. Keep going.

My heart wouldn't rest, nor would my paranoid thoughts, and my injured condition only added to my anxieties. Mentally, I warned myself about the importance of maintaining my composure, thinking of how easily they could track my fear, until the idea triggered a fresh panic. When I was certain I might vomit, I braced myself on a boulder, briefly, to take a couple of inefficient breaths, and as the relief refused to come, I pushed forward, deranged.

Don't fear. Keep going.

Gradually, my strides became shorter, my steps heavier, and I was gripping the woods for stability as the world began to warp in my vision. I dropped all my weight on a tree, holding on to the bark as my only support, biting back the sobs while regaining my breath. I wasn't safe yet, danger prickling at the back of my neck, but my leg gave me no choice in the matter. Another step meant collapsing, and if I fell, I wasn't confident I could stand again. My hand found the red-stained cloth, fingers dampening from the blood seeping through, and a new wave of nausea curdled my stomach. Already lightheaded and struggling to intake oxygen appropriately, I allowed my hand to inspect the injury rather than view the nasty sight. It was incredibly tender, a difficulty to remain silent when touched in the slightest, blood puddling on the pads of my fingers, meaning the wound was still fresh, and I hadn't been hostage for long. Zadar would come looking for me, that I could take solace in, but I doubted he even knew I was missing and wouldn't until morning, when it was time to leave and the broken-hearted girl hadn't come down from her room.

I would've given anything to be that girl now.

Removing my hand from my knee and pressing into the solid wood behind me, I traced my blood into the grooves of the bark until my fingers were wet with the tree's compact dew. I didn't know how great of hunters kelpies were and whether or not my motives were useless, but ripping out a chunk of my hair adjacent to strands sliced earlier that night and tangling them in the roots was the only aid I could offer him to find me. It was while tearing my sleeve to assign another tree that I heard it once more.

My brother's anguished cry.

It was near this time, however, too real to be a part of my overactive imaginings, and its call had me lose all sense.

"Anders?" I uttered, voice shaking along with my body as the prior refreshing breeze turned bitter and sank into my bones.

Silence responded, but that wasn't enough to ease my fright. I had to know he wasn't here for certain, that they hadn't taken him as well, that he was home, safe with both of his parents, and that the nightmares I created were nothing more than nightmares.

"Anders, is that you?" I tried, hoping for a response, and yet nothing.

Again, no sound, and it took several brutal seconds, but I was able to gain the strength needed to break from the trees, hobbling without support to where the noise occurred.

Something moved out of my peripheral vision, a jolt of fear shot through me, and a small grunt was made from behind a tree where the movement had come from. My focus was fixed in that direction, waiting for the shadows to mock me and whisper I was insane, but everything was deathly still and too quiet to be a joke. I joined the silence this time as I inched closer, stunned by what I found hiding.

It wasn't Anders, but it wasn't my imagination either. A boy looking not much younger than my brother, stood peering around the tree at me, just as I was taking in the sight of him. His back was to me, body subtly quivering from either chills or fear, but what caught my attention was the rope fastened around his back.

"Lemon curd," I breathed, dumbfounded by the trembling child in front of me.

He jolted upright at the sound of my voice, not bothering to glance behind him before breaking into a sprint.

"Wait!" I shouted, cutting myself off in fear of how unexpectedly loud I became, "I'm sorry. I didn't mean to scare you."

He kept running, and I was left standing uselessly against the tree. I could chase after him, promising aid and safety, but something in my gut told me that giving this boy freedom meant losing my own. Looking off to the path I created, I pondered how easy it would be to write off the interaction as a delusion from loss of blood and continue toward home, immediately shaming myself for letting the idea cross my mind. We'd both been kidnapped and managed to escape, terrified and hurt, but we didn't have to be alone.

He suddenly fell to his knees, groaning in a way that sounded just like Anders. Any idea of leaving him vanished entirely.

My head throbbed along with my leg, but I didn't allow that to deter me from advancing his way. The touch I gave to his arm was feather light, yet he recoiled as though I chucked a rock at him.

"It's okay. It's okay," I whispered, soothing him as I always had with Anders, but he wouldn't relax, heaving breaths too large for his lungs. Shadows played games across his skin, contorting in ways I knew weren't real. "I'm not going to hurt you."

Though his panicking, I worried he'd further harm himself and resorted to the only other alleviating method I knew.

It started as a hum, but before I could consider the consequences, my voice broke into soft songs, alleviating the tightness in my chest and the shallow air in his. The boy had yet to show his face, but the muscles in his back relaxed while the quivering in his hands held behind him eased. I sang a few moments more for both of our relief, and when it seemed we remembered how to breathe, I attempted conversation.

"My name is Ari. I was taken from my family, too, but I'm going to find them. Do you want to come with me?"

He slumped against the stump, doing nothing but consuming the plentiful oxygen surrounding us, his body limp, looking defeated rather than at ease.

"Are you all right with me untying your hands?" I asked, careful not to touch him without warning, encouraged when he subtly nodded.

Cautiously, I grasped the ropes, my fingers occasionally brushing his arm as I worked on the restraints, losing count of how many times he flinched. He was warm in the sense that any human was, but what made it unnatural was the weather that left my skin chilled hadn't affected him, though that wasn't a bad thing. Whoever tied him was obviously well-practiced in the act, looping it through holes that took me multiple tries to figure out. From what I could see, his wrists weren't raw or bloodied, meaning he, too, had not been hostage for long. I wondered if our captors abducted more than the news suggested, and perhaps foolishly, I wondered if we'd be the first to escape these silent killers.

"Are you injured anywhere?"

He shook his head, ducking away from my view when I tried to look at him.

"We are going to work through this together, all right?" I assured, pulling the final strand through while viewing it sliding off his arms and tumbling on the ground, "We'll find a way out of here, and get you back home. There's nothing to be—"

"What did you do?"

I jumped at the deep, sudden voice, whipping around too quickly for the shape I was in, being pinned by a glowing pair of emerald eyes. I was startled, naturally, unnerved as he lazily looked me over, but not afraid, and when his focus shifted to the boy, a surge of protectiveness came over me. I instinctively stepped in front of the child who stayed crumpled on the ground, blocking the predator from the weak. The man with no emotions merely stared at me, as though unsure what to think of the situation. He was difficult to make out in the dark, but I knew from his posture and the heaviness in his voice that I hadn't met this man before, yet the obvious relation to Kiernan made him not seem like a complete stranger.

"What did you do?" he asked a second time, speaking just as he did the first.

"I released him," I answered steadily, holding his stare like a challenge.

"No. What did you do to calm him?"

Of all the things I assumed he wanted from that question, the child's ease was the last on my list.

Kiernan and a boy I had seen at the party caught up with the man then, Kiernan appearing hesitant while the other's head was tilted in curiosity, and I stiffened under the scrutiny of the three of them.

"She sang to me," the child answered, coming out from behind my defensive stance, and in my shock that he could speak, I looked at him.

The moonlight was honest, showing his face so young and vulnerable while his eyes held that condemning, *painful* green. My heart panged with fear, and the kid winced in response, movement creeping under his skin which I now understood weren't shadows.

"Kell," the man addressed to the person I hadn't even noticed join the group, "Take Kaid home. *Walk* him home."

I watched as the boy left my side and took the hand of my almost murderer, youthful expression staring at me bright-eyed over his shoulder as he was reluctantly led away.

"What is your plan?" the man demanded, forcing my attention back to him, "Where will you go from here?"

I reached for the confidence and strength projected seconds ago, but it fled, disappearing along with the child I had believed to be in the same danger I was.

"I'd rather not say—"

"—that you don't know?" he finished for me, reading my thoughts aloud as though I wasn't doing everything in my power to conceal my intentions, and my lips parted in preparation for an answer I did not have.

"If you don't freeze out here, starvation will certainly do the job. That is..." he paused to pointedly glance at my leg, "assuming infection doesn't set in."

I swallowed, not wanting to admit how right he was, trapped even when I was free.

"You can keep running; I won't stop you. Or you can come back with us, where there is heat and a comfortable bed. The decision is entirely yours."

I made the mistake of glancing at Kiernan, his face a perfectly constructed mask of sympathy, and I had to lower my gaze before my heart yearned to make him smile.

"She's made her decision," the man announced, turning away from me.

"You aren't actually going to leave her out here, are you?" the other brother questioned, smiling like this was just some silly prank.

"Enjoy searching for your family in the wrong direction, Rowe," the eldest called over his shoulder, ignoring the question as he walked off. It was unsettling to hear him say my last name, sounding close to a threat, and I didn't want to imagine what they planned to do to my family in my absence.

"Wait," I surrendered, trapped in a hole they deceptively put me in that I couldn't get myself out of, "I can't walk that quickly."

Kiernan was heading in my direction before anyone could stop him, and we were intently watched as he lifted one of my arms over his shoulder while his other hand firmly held my waist.

"I've got you," he mumbled, but it seemed as though he was trying to say something else. I nodded, letting his warmth seep into my skin and dropping most of my weight on him, which he took without complication. Managing to step in synchronized movements with Kiernan, I glanced at the man once more, his expression cold and distant, and a harsh lump pressed against my throat. I held on to Kiernan tighter, assuring myself that Zadar was coming for me and that I needed to stay alive long enough to be found.

Don't cry. Just keep going.

Chapter Eighteen

The sun had barely begun to shine its beautiful colors by the time Kiernan and I returned to the house. I made sure to study it, the handle on the entrance, the layout of the living room, the back hall with closed doors, and the surprising lack of any locks. I would have taken the time needed to inspect the building's entirety, but Kiernan led me into the same room I escaped from and placed me on the bed.

"Get some rest," he insisted, leaving me in seclusion to discuss the recent events with his family.

That had been hours ago.

Anxiety kept me from sleeping, but there were several moments I dozed off, unable to resist the emotional and physical exhaustion. The last time I felt consciousness slip from me, I forced my eyes open, confusing life and wakefulness, and found complete silence.

There were no hushed voices or heavy footsteps, and I stood to make sure I was truly awake. While the room spun, I kept to my feet, surprised that I still couldn't hear anything outside of my room. With small, painful steps, I made it to my door, something crinkling under one of my feet, moving to find a small piece of paper with a note.

> *We went out so you have some privacy. There are clean clothes*
> *on the bathroom sink and food in the pantry. We won't be back*
> *until sunrise. Please don't run off again.*
> *-Kiernan*

Tapping my finger against the paper in contemplation, I noted his hand-writing, how the letters were curved carefully but not entirely developed, yet something about it was incredibly endearing, and I wiped the subconsciously forming smile from my face.

You are missing because of him.

It was ridiculous I had to remind myself of this.

I debated leaving immediately, taking my chances in the woods rather than finding out what they wanted from me, but my blood-soaked pants stole my attention before I could finish that thought. The wound above my left knee tingled unpleasantly at the attention, teasing the idea of infection that lingered in the back of my mind, mentally straining to set aside another unwanted thought.

Bracing my weight on the doorframe, I peeked outside the room for confirmation that I was alone and not being set up, and only after scrutinizing the house for a full minute did I step out. The floorboards were solid wood, along with thick logs walls, and in my previous need for escape, I hadn't appreciated the beauty of its interior. Intricate designs were carved where planks met glass, outlining the windows with spirals and shapes forming pointed tails and sharp wings. I could've spent hours fixating over the precision of each engraving, searching for hidden pictures throughout the whole cabin, but I didn't have time for that, not when they'd be back at sunrise, and had no way to gauge the time apart from the dusk's shiftings.

The windows provided a clear view of the redwoods surrounding on all sides, large trees encasing a large residence, and I was entirely out of place in the too-open space. The living room was exceptionally big in both width and height, suggesting that it was part of a two-story building, although it lacked a second floor. Three worn-out couches and coffee tables huddled in the corners, looking just as tiny and afraid as I felt, tall walls mocking their size. Attached to the lonely living area was a makeshift kitchen consisting of unreachable cabinets, an old oven beneath an even older stove, a sink I was surprised to find working, and a polished, wooden countertop matching the rest of the space. On the wall closer to the few bedrooms sat a fireplace encased in stone, stretching impressively up to the highest point of the ceiling, forming a grey chimney on top.

All on one side, three doors held the entrance to three different rooms, one in which I'd become quite familiar, the other a bathroom, and the last at the very end of the hall was a room haunted by shadows.

Exploring hadn't seemed like trespassing, but stepping into the cold, lifeless space felt identical to violating a sacred secret. Clothes, books, and other random objects piled the place, the moonlight exposing a thick layer of dust coating it all. The bed taking up most of the area was fit for royalty, a serpentine headboard hanging above the massive mattress, and deep velvet covers fit over top with luxurious pillows to match. There was something incredibly sad looming in its hollow, and I was about to leave when the portrait on the opposite wall stole my attention.

A family of seven was presented, all smiling, emerald-eyed, and beautiful in a way that suggested they weren't as human as they appeared. The father was blonde, standing proudly next to his wife with a hand on her shoulder, hair dark at the roots, with cascading golden waves curtaining her face, holding her youngest in her lap at an angle indicating he did not want to be there. A girl appearing no older than ten stood beside her mother, holding a toddler with the same world-holding eyes as Kiernan. Another young boy was crouched in front of them, while the final child stood beside his father.

I stared at the picture for longer than I liked, tilting my head to better view the reason it called to me, and while squinting my eyes and picking out the noticeable use of the color yellow, it clicked.

This was Mother's style of painting.

I tried to convince myself otherwise, but I remembered how one of my captors had mentioned her, and common sense prevailed. It hurt to see such a beautiful family portrait from an artist who cared nothing for her own.

She cares. You saw the way she looked at Zadar, how she looks at Anders. She cares deeply, just not for—

I shut it down, tearing my eyes from the painting to focus on anything else. I began to question the life I thought I knew: a stepfather I'd never been told of, not being human, Anders seeing the future, and Mother painting a family of murderers. It felt so wrong to not know any of it.

My headache returned as something flashed in a box catching my attention, and I was more than grateful for the interference. Advancing to gain a better view, I discovered the glint to be from gold outlining several seashells shattered into hundreds of pieces, looking much like my necklace, and an unnerving chill ran down my spine. I wasn't aware of its significance, but I grasped my shell out of habit, deciding it was likely best I remain oblivious, and left before I could see something else I was not meant to.

With every other area inspected, I hobbled to the bathroom, temporarily comforted by my seclusion. Sure enough, a grey sweater and brown shorts lay on the sink, appearing much too big for me, but I wasn't in a position to complain. Glancing briefly out one of the oversized windows in the living area, I found thick darkness staring back at me and decided cleaning out possible infection wasn't the worst idea.

Shower, then leave.

The water was bitterly cold, seeping into my skin and chilling my bones, stealing the relief I wished for. I hissed as the liquid ice ran over my wound, digging in with unforgiving claws and taking my blood with it. Over the last excruciating hours, it managed to crudely clot, though that didn't matter now as the gash reopened from movement and lack of cloth.

I hummed to distract myself from the pain while I washed my hair, hands trembling, eyes closing, lungs collapsing.

Crashing waves swallowing whole and keeping you down. No air. Legs forgetting how to function and water-muffled shouts. No air. Kiernan exhausted, still, and... giving up. He's giving up, and you are going to watch him die. Lose him just like Father.

The faucet abruptly silenced, the screeching memories along with it, and I hadn't realized my hand was on the shower nob until I blinked the tenacious ocean out of my eyes. Water dripped from my eyelashes, melding into phantom tears that fell into the bloodied pools at my feet. The view initiated a wave of dizziness to wash over me, a need to cough strangling in my throat, but nothing came.

No air. No air. No air!

Yet air was all around me, and I couldn't breathe, lungs craving something denser while my limbs became unimaginably heavy. It was nothing short of relief when a strangled cry broke through, choking me until I was sure I'd vomit, but that dissipated once I caught my breath, and I nearly slipped trying to escape the shower.

The clothes were warm and unmistakably Kiernan's, clean earth and burnt marshmallows overtaking all other smells, and I was ashamed of the lingering breaths I took to remind myself he was alive and well, despite what it meant for me. Pulling the sweater over my head felt close to accepting a cozy hug I so desperately needed, the shirt falling past my hips and devouring my arms whole. I fastened the pants together in the back with a spare hair tie, shorts supposed to fall directly below the knee, brushing the middle of my shins, just another thing in this house making me feel small and insignificant.

Using my old shirt, I wrapped it around my knee, wincing as I secured the knot and washed the rebellious blood from my hands. With this outfit, I could survive the weather for several days, but that was all the time I needed to find help, and it was hope instead of fear that caused my heart to beat a bit faster.

As if on cue, my stomach growled, ripping away my aspiration to force realism.

Eat, then leave.

I told myself this was the last distraction, that I wasn't delaying my journey any longer after I'd gotten food and water into my system, but wandering into the kitchen caused an abrupt change in plans. The sun's first beams began to pierce the darkness outside, and I realized that if I wished to eat, it would have to be on the go. Convincing myself that I had been going slowly because of my leg, and definitely *not* to see Kiernan again to make sure he was truly alright, I carefully climbed onto the countertop to reach the cabinets. Blindly, I grabbed what I could, pleased to find my hands clutching several packages of crackers and dried meat, and with that final factor accounted for, I was ready for my second escape.

That was until I heard the front door click open, and Kiernan stepped in alone, catching me red-handed taking their food.

He stared, a little taken aback, not at the arms filled with bags holding enough to last me a good week, but at the oversized clothes covering my still chilled body. I panicked, the contents slipping from my hold and tumbling to the floor, drawing his attention to the ground, and his subtle expression shifted.

"Weren't counting on me coming home yet?" he guessed with a sad smile, speaking as though it was a lighthearted joke, but neither of us laughed. I tensed as he neared, bracing myself for his scent and heat, unwilling to let it affect me this time, watching warily as he skipped right over the crackers and knelt to pick up the packaged meat. "Have you eaten yet?" he urged, slipping the food into my hand without question of my motives.

My fingers curled around the plastic, but my eyes stayed on his face, desperately searching for any cracks in his mask to prove my hopefulness wrong. But he met my gaze with the most vulnerable look, reminding me of how he looked up at me that first day in the tree, and I was tripping, melting, *falling* into something I wouldn't be able to get myself out of.

It terrified me.

I tried to run, reach normal ground and find safety in a place far from him, but in my staggering movements to get off the countertop, my old shirt slackened, slipping fresh blood down my leg. Almost like he knew the scent of my blood, Kiernan's eyes dropped to my wound, something ticking in his jaw before returning his sight to my face.

"Here, sit down," he instructed, offering the aid I needed to lower myself on the counter, legs dangling above drawers carrying various kitchen supplies. Once I was settled, Kiernan stepped into the bathroom, leaving me a clear view of the fully opened front door while I heard him rummaging through the cabinets down the hall. In my left hand was food he handed me directly, bloodied shirt in the right, and all it would take was a couple of seconds to make it outside and disappear. Kiernan wasn't going to stop me, I realized, as he took a suspiciously long time to find whatever he was looking for. My gut told me this was my last opportunity, yet I froze in the face of freedom, and when Kiernan came back around the corner, relief noticeable in the way his shoulder steadily relaxed, I didn't regret it.

Not yet anyway.

He brought a box of bandages and a damp cloth with him, hands hesitating over my leg before returning my stare.

"May I?"

I nodded, shivering as his skin brushed mine while he pushed the fabric up just enough to view the gash. The shorts were too baggy to put up a fight, but he still was slow with it, lest the material scrape against my wound and cause more discomfort. The blood was much more vibrant in the sun's light, and I had to shut my eyes to avoid nausea, my breath catching at the feel of a soft hand cupping the back of my knee, holding it in place to dab the warm cloth over red-stained skin.

"Where were you?" I asked, trying not to focus on the warmth behind my leg or the comfort the simple contact brought me.

"Hunting. We go almost every night," he spoke, his voice just as gentle as his touch while he finished soaking up the excess blood.

I hesitated to ask my next question, watching as his eyebrows furrowed in concentration on my leg, discarding the cloth to grab a random jar of honey.

"What..." I swallowed, my throat suddenly very dry, "What do you hunt?"

I gripped the counter, bracing for the weight of his words and the sting of my skin as he unscrewed the jar singlehandedly.

"Fish mostly. Though Kell prefers bears, and I'll join him occasionally."

"Not humans?"

Kiernan's tending halted, eyes pained when meeting mine, and I was all too aware of what creature hid behind that innocent gaze.

"No, Ari," he communicated clearly, staring at me as though it could prove his sincerity, "We do not kill humans."

"Then your family is not the reason people are going missing?"

The hand cupping the back of my leg twitched, but Kiernan's face gave nothing away.

"No," he repeated, lowering his gaze back to his work.

"But you know who the cause of it is?" I guessed, watching as he scooped some of the honey in his hand and pressed it to the wound, earning a sharp hiss from me.

"Sorry," he murmured, smoothing stinging honey over aching skin a bit more tentatively, "I have been told I am the worst at giving warnings."

"You've done this before?"

"Many times," he agreed, tone turning playful as he added, "Kaid's surprisingly clumsier than you."

An unanticipated laugh burst from my lungs, and he looked up at me, a genuine smile playing on his lips as the sunrise hues painted his face into an unforgettable portrait of perfection. My appearance must've changed as well because Kiernan's expression suddenly fell, staring at me with a clear and unexpected wanting in his gaze that made the room incredibly hot.

Something snapped then, electrifying like an all-consuming force taking over everything else apart from Kiernan and the unrestrained gravity pulling me toward him. He stepped impossibly closer, and I leaned forward, eyes locked on the emeralds that took their time picking out each minute detail of my face, at last resting on my lips.

"Ari..." he whispered like a precious secret, longing lingering on his tongue, and my name never sounded so beautiful. His thumb swept over the side of my calf in rhythmic motions, and before I could stop myself, my hand found its way to his cheek.

The tension in the room, the desire in his eyes, the tightening in my stomach—it all came to an end when voices neared.

Kiernan pulled away, keeping his face lowered while I sat up stiffly, feeling how flushed my cheeks had gotten. Figures passed by the windows, masks on yet looking far from human, and my hands gripped the counter once more as the reality of my situation returned to me.

"There she is!" a boy exclaimed, instantly bringing me back to the night of that wretched party, talking just as he did with all those girls surrounding him. He made a direct line to us, propping his elbows on the countertop and staring up at me with sparkling eyes. "How are you doing, pretty thing?"

Kiernan kept his focus on my wound, but I felt his hand beneath my knee tense, and I wasn't sure if the boy caught the subtle action as his focus fell on my leg.

"Really, Kell? Was that necessary?" he fussed to his brother, who had just entered the premises, earning him a glare with no remorse, "I do apologize for my brother's actions. He gets sour over the silliest things."

"Just because there is a girl here, Keagan, doesn't mean you need to act like you are all that and a bag of chips," Kiernan interjected rather tightly, unpacking the stick-on bandage large enough to fit over my entire injury.

"Hey, I haven't been allowed to talk to her, but now that we know we are keeping Miss Lemon Curd, I am getting to know her. It's called hospitality, Kiernan," he responded with a smile that looked surprisingly realistic.

"Miss Lemon Curd?" I spoke up, and the boy beamed at my reciprocation, making me question if that was the best idea from the mischievous glint in his eyes.

"It's only Kiernan's favorite little saying. He recites it all the time when he thinks we aren't listening." My heart didn't feel so heavy in that moment, and it took more effort not to smile than it did to hide my nervousness. "None of us knew where it came from until you said it to Kaid last night," he finished with a playful nudge at Kiernan with his elbow.

"Killian should've kept it a rule you couldn't talk to her," Kiernan muttered, and it was sort of comical to see him like this, shying away from my gaze, circling his fingers around the lining of the bandage over my leg, borderline embarrassed, something he claimed he couldn't feel.

"Somebody's crabby," the brother laughed, expression over-exaggerated and purposefully humorous, and I couldn't help the small grin that pulled at my lips. "Oh, look at that!" he cheered, gesturing to my face, which instantly washed away my light demeanor, "I got her to smile. Have *you*?" Another unserious jab at Kiernan and the final two members of the household stepped inside before this discussion went any further.

"Keagan, come sit down," the eldest commanded, standing in the living room, "Bring her in here too, Kiernan. We have some matters that need to be discussed."

"Can you walk okay?" Kiernan murmured after washing his hands clean of blood and honey, and though I nodded, he chose to support my left side while guiding me to the center couch, silently taking the seat beside mine, which became my sole comfort. I glanced around the room, finding five brothers present when the painting had suggested four, and the young girl was nowhere to be seen.

The eldest remained standing as the rest of us sat and waited for the discussion to begin. He was young himself, seeming to be in his early twenties, but how he held himself and spoke proved his mind to be much older. He cleared his throat, and I took a subtle breath, subconsciously huddling closer to Kiernan while preparing myself for the worst.

"Our last interaction was not ideal, and I'd like to start over," he claimed, tone flat but promising, bringing a hand to his chest as he stated, "My name is Killian."

"Don't give it our *names*!"

"That's Kell," he continued, disregarding the spiteful stare he was gifted, gesturing to the boy lounging freely on an otherwise empty couch, "That's Keagan."

"We've met before," the boy added with a snide grin, "She wanted to dance with me, and I was forced to turn her down. It was a sad evening for us both."

"She never wanted to dance with you," Kiernan intruded, "She didn't even want to be there."

I swallowed, pondering what other things he'd come to know about me in those months I hadn't known I was watched.

"Neither did you," he fought back, but his voice held no seriousness or actual care, "and yet you somehow managed to rope the mysterious siren-on-land that we were clearly told to stay away from onto the dance floor without complaint."

"*And this* is Kaid," the eldest continued, ending the argument as he gestured to the child crumpled next to his older brother, watching me warily. "And I'm sure you are familiar with Kiernan."

I was, perhaps more familiar than I should be, but apart from him and Kell, whose name and intimidating face I'd witnessed enough to be ingrained in my memory, I was already clueless about who the rest of them were.

"I'll make a deal with you, siren," the eldest started again, leaving no time to gather my thoughts.

"Ari," Kiernan grumbled with a pointed look at his brother.

"*Ari*," he corrected, his gaze shifting from Kiernan back to me, "Don't try to run away again, and we won't kill you."

The overly confident one choked on nothing in particular, clearly taken aback by the blunt statement as much as I had been, while Kell's face seemed to be formed into a permanent scowl.

"Awfully forward, aren't we, Killian?" he offered, smiling despite the situation.

"I'm only being upfront with the girl. I'm sure she would appreciate plain honesty."

"You are holding me hostage?" I asked, putting his statement to the test.

"No," Kiernan assured beside me, face scrunched at the unpleasant idea.

"So, then I can leave?"

"No," his older brother contended, and whatever Kiernan was about to say got lost in the shadow of his demand.

"How long?" I forced out before my mind could tell me I was talking too much, bringing too much attention to myself.

"How long *what*?" someone clipped, and I was too focused on my twiddling thumbs to see who. I swallowed, willing my voice to sound stronger as I tried again.

"How long am I to stay?"

It still sounded weak, but I gained enough confidence to look the eldest in the eye, waiting for an answer.

"Until we decide what to do with you."

'*What to do with you.*'

Like some untamed animal, a problem without a solution.

I blew out a breath, tucking my hands in Kiernan's long sleeves to hide the tremor in them, though I knew they all sensed my uneasiness; it practically made the air electrified with tension.

"Whatever crime you believe I committed, I promise you I did not do. I never wanted to harm anyone or break anything you care for. It was only a few days ago I found out I'm..." I swallowed, still unable to verbalize it, "not entirely human, but I have lived my whole life as one. I'm not the danger you think I am."

They all stared at me in rigid silence, and I began wishing I had never opened my mouth, convinced that they were mutually planning my demise.

"I believe her," the youngest, whom I sang to in the forest, piped up, "She helped me."

He stayed mainly hidden behind Kell, but the youthful curiosity was visible in his expression, and all I could see was Anders.

"I'll stay under one condition," I announced, wistfully looking at the nervous child, thinking of how devastated my poor brother would be when I didn't come home, but at least he could be safe, "Leave my family out of this."

The overconfident one laughed at that, drawing my thoughts to him, "Your family was never—"

"Agreed," the eldest affirmed, jabbing his elbow into the other to promptly end his statement.

"I mean it," I reiterated, holding his stare, "They are never to be involved or hurt in any way, even after I am gone."

My abductor lowered himself in order to see me eye to eye, his expression set in a promise.

"You have my word. No harm will come to your family so long as you stay with us."

That was it; that was the best I could do, so I nodded, accepting my fate and hoping he would keep to his word.

With that deal secured, the man stood, turning toward Kiernan to instruct I be brought to my room, mumbling something about the necessity my kind has for sleep, and Kiernan obeyed.

"It'll be okay," he assured me as he closed my blinds, blocking out the sun and enveloping me in darkness, "This place grows on you after a while."

I didn't respond, and he watched me for a moment, wishing to speak of something else, but after a glimpse of the hopelessness overcoming my expression and fear creeping back into my heart, he swallowed the words. He left me alone with one last pained look, the door clicking shut behind him.

Closed doors; can't stand to be near you.

Chapter Nineteen

I didn't leave the room. I didn't eat. I didn't sleep. I didn't even speak.

For three days, I stayed secluded, exhausted, and starving, but I did nothing to change my state. I was terrified to make a noise lest I draw attention to myself and give reason for them to change their minds about my well-being, fearing to breathe at times when they were close enough to the door to hear their exchange. Discussion of me was the most common, along with the varying topics of conversation held by those who had known each other for years, but never a joke, a laugh, a yell. Nothing but cool, indifferent, *emotionless* words.

They left every night, or at least I assumed from the stillness that came over the house after the sun's setting, though that didn't explain the quiet shuffles made right outside my door in random moments of the silence.

Kiernan was the only one to enter the room, bringing soup once a day and taking away the untouched bowl from the previous day. I'd pretend to be asleep each time, knowing it was so much easier to refuse his ruses when I couldn't see him, fighting manipulation with blindness, and apart from the water he brought with the food, I received nothing from him.

I was never to see my family again, something I believed to have accepted, but in the looming darkness of my new room, I realized I had given up on them instead. Mother likely wouldn't have known I was gone unless someone told her, though I doubted she'd care regardless. I promised myself that Zadar was searching for me, uncovering the leads I left for him, that I had done *one* useful thing, but as each day passed, my confidence lessened. After all, why would he come? Where was he when his son was a baby, and a child was the only one caring for him? Where was he when his wife forgot the world around her? Where was he when Anders and I needed a supportive parent? Where was he all the birthdays, holidays, and firsts in life?

I wasn't his child. He wasn't my father. There were no loyalties.

I feared for Anders, though, my closest friend, my little brother, my wonderful sunshine. I thought of him most, how his smile brightened the room, lighting up the dark places my mind was dragging me to. He'd cry when I didn't return, likely haunted by the force of my unresolved disappearance, just as the other families who lost their loved ones to the Silent Killer, and I could only hope his dreams would be forgiving.

It was a constant battle to keep my eyes open, a challenge I often lost, but even when my body was resting, my brain was awake and alert, producing wild hallucinations. Kiernan was in the center of it all, in the forest, on the beach, tangled in the crowded dance floor, too close, too hot, and I relished in it much too easily. And when he entered my room, steaming bowl in hand, looking like a dream meant for eternal rest, I forgot to act asleep. I longed to take it back, lie down, and pretend my heart didn't pick up after acknowledging his presence, but the damage was already done, and all I could do was pull my knees to my chest and timidly watch him. He watched me back, circling around the bed to set the bowl on the nightstand, and, with some diffidence, he joined me on the mattress.

"You haven't come out of your room in days," he voiced, steadily tugging the sheets away from my face, "I've given you food, but you haven't touched it. You have a bed and yet look exhausted. I don't understand."

It was silly to think I could hide from him by burrowing deeper into his own clothes on my body, yet I did it anyway, eyes burning in the aroma of smoke. Kiernan sighed into the silence, situating himself more comfortably to face me, and I feared he intended to stay until he got a response. I knew I should've closed my eyes or looked away at the very least, to withstand the emotional manipulation, but I was entranced by that sad gleam on his face, a mirror of my own expression, added with the burning light of desperation.

"What is it you need?" he murmured, brows drawn, sounding like a request and desire all at once.

The question hurt in the most beautiful way, pain laced with care and hope for recovery, and I pondered enabling that healing. I didn't allow myself much, but if there was ever a time I'd forgive my stupidity, it was now.

Forgetting all the lies and hurt he caused, lowering my guard if only for a minute, I curled into his chest, slipping my hands through his arms, and reached up to grip his shoulders. He was my last lifeline in the sea of eternity, and though it wasn't wise to be this close to someone who could kill so easily, I couldn't let him go.

Kiernan's body went rigid, but all I felt was a rejuvenating rush of heat press into me, melting the frozen weight crushing my ribs. It wasn't until my fingers dug into his shirt, savoring the sensation of its soft texture, that he relaxed and enveloped me in a solid embrace that tightened when my despairing clutch on him didn't stop the tremors traveling across my limbs.

"I'm so scared, Kiernan," I whispered with the same sincerity I'd used in the woods when I foolishly told everything I knew about my life.

"I know," he murmured, lips pressing into my hair, tangling the words there, "and I won't let anything happen to you."

He sounded like he meant it, *felt* like he meant it, bringing the covers over us to wrap me in his security, and allowing another act I promised never to do, I began to cry. Kiernan didn't hesitate to draw me closer, mumbling things I couldn't hear over my sharp breaths, but it was simply soothing to feel his speech rumble through him.

Warm. Wanted. Safe.

I let it all out through shuddering sobs, the poorly hidden terror, the pent-up anger, the creeping depression, knowing that once I let go of him, the moment would be over, and I would never allow myself to enter that state of vulnerability in his presence again. It was a goodbye to my family and the life I knew, an understanding that things were never going to be the same again, a release of internal ache. His fingers ran along my spine, loosening the knots and tension until nothing was left to fight against him. I fell wholly into his embrace, sighing deeply into his skin and intaking his scent. This close, I could feel his heart pounding heavily, even as mine eased, and the sound of something so *human* sparked the tiniest flame of assurance inside me, but it was all the light I needed to ward off the darkness.

My grip eased, thinking that things could possibly get better after all, and Kiernan misinterpreted the action as a wish to separate, and I had to force down the pitiful protest as he sat me back up straight. My chills were gone, but Kiernan wrapped the comforter around my shoulders regardless, hands lingering around the blanket's edge longer than necessary. The crease in his brow was gone, replaced by the relieved gaze complimenting every soft feature of his face.

"Could you do something for me now?" He asked, unhanding the sheet to wipe away a remaining tear, and I had to stop myself from leaning into the tender touch. Kiernan was already leaning past me to grab the fresh bowl of soup before I could respond, placing it into my untucked hands and watching me expectantly.

My eyes fell from his to the coffee-colored liquid, warming my palms before finding him again, murmuring, "I'm not hungry."

The lie had barely left my mouth when my stomach growled, betraying any unlikely hopes to fool him, and Kiernan tilted his head, the slightest smile playing on his lips.

"I'm not leaving until you eat," he persisted, and I reluctantly took a bite.

It could've been that I was starving, but as my mouth was hit with the abundant flavors of mushroom stew, I was sure I'd never tasted anything better. Kiernan was smiling fully at me then, startlingly beautiful when pleased, and I could almost hear the river babbling again while we splashed one another, laughter echoing in the distance. I blinked the memory away, trying to pretend my mouth wasn't watering for more food as I pressed the bowl into his abdomen, worried about whatever meaningful memory might surface next if he stayed longer, and with a gentle push back, Kiernan added, "All of it."

"Why are you doing this?" I asked, unable to conceal the suspicion in my tone.

"Eat, and I'll tell you."

He was incredibly stubborn when he wanted to be, and without much choice, I consumed another spoonful, internally relishing in its savor.

"This may come as a shock, but you'll die without food," he teased in answer, grinning like this was another one of the games he'd created in the woods to brighten my mood, and as I swallowed a mouthful of soup, it was very clear he was winning.

"Why do you care?"

He gave a pointed look to the bowl, and after I took another influenced bite, Kiernan's tone reverted to serious.

"This wasn't how things were meant to happen. You weren't supposed to end up here. Kell wasn't supposed to intervene," he said, glancing at my slow-healing leg, and I continued eating absentmindedly as he went on. "You were never supposed to meet me. Although I can't blame anyone for that but myself. In all fairness, you weren't supposed to be a siren, either."

"That's why you followed me?" I asked, going back to my meal once the question left my mouth, and Kiernan tracked the movement, offering a solemn nod.

"I rarely go by the trails. It's easier to avoid humans altogether, but I felt drawn to Crescent City that day, and it just so happened to be your first week on the job. I think a part of me knew as soon as I spotted you walking very cautiously on the paths that you weren't all you appeared to be, but the logical side of me wouldn't let the thought go further. Sure, you had their eyes and nearly entrancing aura, but sirens can't leave the ocean, and you were obviously on land. I told my brothers about you, which I now see was a mistake, and Kell was ready to track you down then and there. My family is... *sensitive* when it comes to the topic of sirens, but I was able to temporarily convince them you weren't a danger, though Kell didn't settle long without proof. I thought if I got to know you, I'd find something to end the suspicions, and things got out of hand," he groaned, a clear apology in his eyes as he promised, "I never wanted to hurt you, Ari."

I lowered my stare to the nearly empty bowl, hands tensing around its fading warmth, bracing myself for the reality I refused to accept.

"So, it's true then?" You're a..."

"Monster?"

I blinked at his words, lowering the spoon back into the bowl with a gentle clink I gave no notice to.

"Dragon," I corrected, struggling to force the title out, and Kiernan released a displeased huff.

"Yes."

It was something I already knew, despite what I told myself, yet the confirmations sent chills down my spine.

"Can you... control it?" I tried, but the ease he granted me began to slip.

"Sometimes," he answered, attempting to read the expression on my face unknown to even me. My mind flashed to my first night here, his hand around my neck, my breath gone, how a spilt second was all the time needed to change everything, and my fear is what dictated his shiftings. He'd been as close to me as he was now, speaking with the same softness, and I had to distract myself from how easily it could change into violence.

"I have a different question."

"Nope. Eat," he insisted, the light coming back to his face, just as happy with the topic change as I was.

"I've finished it," I argued, handing him the container grown cold from lack of substance.

Kiernan leaned past me a second time to take hold of the untouched food from yesterday, and with less reluctance, I accepted the bowl. Some of the effect was lost in the lack of heat, but the taste remained exquisite, satisfying my stomach before satisfying my curiosities. I made a point of consuming spoonfuls before asking something new, to which Kiernan would give his approving look, comically persistent, and if I weren't so exhausted, I would've laughed.

"I saw a box of shells like mine shattered in the other room. What are they for?"

His brows drew together, but I couldn't discern the expression that briefly flashed across his face.

"How do you know about that?"

"I don't see your bowl of soup," I remarked, surprised by my own ease of tone. Kiernan gladly accepted the challenge I hadn't meant to set, taking the food from my hands and bringing it to his mouth for a generous sip.

"There," he settled, handing me back the contents, "Now answer my question."

"I... searched your house when you were gone," I muttered, dumbfounded by his sudden boldness, and before I could process it, he was enjoying another gulp of *my* soup.

"What were you looking for?"

"N-nothing," I responded weakly, earning a smirk from him.

"Come on, Ari. I didn't lie to you."

"I'm not lying. I only wanted an understanding of my surroundings."

He reached for my bowl once again, but I held it back.

"You are avoiding my question."

Kiernan sighed, giving in to my request.

"My parents collected seashells and lined them in gold to trade the sirens for their song, but that was years ago."

"Why—"

But my inquiry died when the food was unexpectedly stolen from me and hurriedly consumed.

"Looks like you are out of questions," Kiernan announced, picking up both dishes and standing from the mattress, bed groaning in protest.

"But I still have so many things to ask you," I fussed, displeased with how he cheated when I was finally getting the answers I'd desired, but Kiernan didn't seem to mind the abrupt end.

"After you get rest," he agreed, talking to the exit.

"Don't you have something else to ask me?" I questioned, honoring the rules the creator of the game refused to follow.

"I guess you will just have to owe me for now," he responded from the doorway with a smile, and when he closed it, I wasn't frightened any longer. Lying back down, I pondered everything I learned and experienced, my mind clearer when it wasn't focused on the pain in my stomach, but that hadn't changed the drowsiness from exhaustion.

I dozed, but I didn't sleep.

It was a rough night, one filled with tossing and turning, limbs tangling in sheets that provided consoling warmth one moment, then unbreathable heat the next. I'd become restless in the long hours after Kiernan left, and I hated how I was a shadow of the person I knew in his absence. Dark thoughts hiding in the back of my head made their appearance each time I closed my eyes, thoughts of my family facing my grave, learning to grieve a girl gone but not dead. It would be easier, however, for them to believe I was murdered and eventually move on rather than forever worry about what happened to me. Yet, that didn't stop the painful twist in my heart at the thought that my death was more satisfactory than the stress of locating my existence. Anders would likely be the only one to cry at my funeral.

It spiraled more rapidly than I could control, and when the moon reached its peak in the night, I'd forgotten all sense of comfort. My lungs began to hurt next, demanding more than air until I decided to get a drink of water, giving my uncomfortable limbs a use.

I stood from the bed, and though much of the pain in my leg had subsided, the initial use of my muscles sent a shock through my body, a new kind of ache settling in my wound. The room subtly spun as I made it to my door, twisting the handle with a grip strong enough to readjust my balance, stepping into the dark of the hollowed cabin, instantly tripping.

"Ouch," he mumbled without any real emotion, and my heart leaped painfully in my chest at the sound.

"Kiernan!" I shouted in a hushed tone, embarrassment and surprise from my foot jabbing into his leg causing me to sound urgent, "What are you doing here?"

It took a moment for my eyes to adapt, but I was able to pick out his form sitting against the wall, one leg outstretched and the other bent beneath an arm draped across it, head leaning on the door's frame.

"Resting," he put simply, but I couldn't get over the idea of how uncomfortable the floor looked.

"Right outside my door? There are couches just a few feet away."

He looked up at me incredulously.

"Is everything alright? It's not like you to leave your room," Kiernan asked, deflecting my question, trying to set my brain on a different path.

"I just wanted some water," I responded, and when it was clear he wasn't going to answer my question, I walked to the kitchen.

Kiernan's eyes followed my less-than-graceful limp to the sink, silently inspecting the cup I chose to drink from and which hand I used to turn on the faucet, gauging how long of a breath I took in between sips. I never saw him looking at me, but I could feel it, the intensity heating my skin, pretending to be unaware as I placed the cup in the sink and headed to my room. Head lifted and focus set on my door, I planned to walk by him indifferently, yet my body tensed as I neared, and I jumped when his hand gripped my fingers, shooting electricity through my entire body. His hold on me had a demand I was not used to from him, firm, unlike the times we had danced. He didn't speak until I lowered my gaze to him, finding his stare on my hand, and I wondered if he was thinking back to our first meeting as well.

"Let me take you outside tomorrow," he rushed out, hold tightening the slightest, sights shifting between my knuckles, "You can continue to hate me. You can curse the day we met. You tell me all the ways I've hurt you. Scream. Cry. Hit me, if you'd like. I don't care. Just..." His eyes were prickling with emotion: strong, raw, *real* emotion, "just let me see you alive again."

He looked into my eyes then, and I was overwhelmed with the feeling burning behind them, dying leaves catching fire in the forest of his stare, and the smoke prickled at my sight.

This wasn't a request; it was a plea.

I nodded, afraid of what I'd say if I spoke, and only then did he loosen his hold, not releasing me but giving me the freedom to pull away. His throat bobbed as I moved, separating our touch to enter my room, and while closing the door, I witnessed him stare at his hand as though he'd held the world and chose to let it go.

I curled into bed, my body craving rest, my mind racing, Kiernan remaining deathly silent outside my door.

Still, I didn't sleep.

The shades did their best to divert the sun, but my room was layered with a thin sheet of light every morning regardless, and the room didn't spin as much when I arose. Happenings outside of my door were nearly silent, but not still enough to convince me of my seclusion.

The boy from the party sat on the couch against the far wall, getting a direct view of me opening my door, and he perked up.

"Miss Lemon Curd!" he cheered, all smiles and confident posture, running a hand through his hair before patting the seat next to him, "Come sit."

There was an initial hesitation, but assuming Kiernan was likely just around the corner, I obliged.

"It's wonderful to see your lovely face. Why haven't you shown it sooner?" he asked, and my sight dropped to my fingers fidgeting with my necklace, wildly uncomfortable with small talk.

"Didn't feel like it," I mumbled where even I couldn't hear myself, but that encouraged him to lean in closer.

"So, you are saying I make you nervous?"

His eyes sparkled with mischief, and I sat up straighter, glancing around the *very* empty room while clearing my throat.

"Where is everyone else?" I asked, avoiding eye contact, and I startled when he laughed.

"Relax, Love. I mean you no harm," he answered with a mock expression of innocence, "Kiernan's finishing up his shower, and the others are outside."

"Why aren't you with them?"

He shrugged, leaning back on the couch to rest his head, perfectly trimmed dark hair flopping to the side.

"Didn't feel like it," he answered smugly, and I glanced at him then, finding glowing jade fixating on my face, a pinched appearance on his, with a dangerous beauty that attracted many, looking similar to the first time I met him, as he hadn't known what to do with the situation.

"Kaid smiles now. Five times, actually, since you sang to him," he spoke, eyes narrowing to pick out something in mine, "He's never done that before."

The door opened then, and my sudden enthusiasm sank when I recognized the sound coming from the front door rather than the bathroom. The eldest entered first, looking as lifeless as any living person could, and while his eyes remained dead, his brows shot up when spotting me seated on the couch rather than cooped in the bedroom.

"Morning, Rowe," he called, dull and casual as though our last conversation hadn't involved a threat on my life.

Kell walked in next, and I made a point not to view the heated glare he always gave me, my attention catching on the child outside, peering in through one of the many oversized windows. The youngest bashfully smiled through the glass, adding a timid wave that I was quick to reciprocate.

"Six," the boy next to me mumbled, but I barely heard him, focused on the warmth in my chest as I watched the youngest. A part of me wanted to give him a hug, closing my eyes and imagining he was Anders, while the other reminded me there was a reason he was kept outside.

"How does your leg feel today?" the boy started again, and I tried not to think about how quiet everything became in anticipation of my answer.

"Keagan, would you leave the poor girl be?" the eldest called dully.

"Right, because staring at her in silence is so much better," he quipped, peering obviously at Kell, whose focus hadn't left me since the minute he stepped into the house, muscles stiffening in preparation to fight as he sat on the couch across from me.

"She's shy," Kiernan spoke up, eyeing how his brother leaned in to talk with me, "She needs her space."

I hadn't heard him leave the bathroom, and a familiar rush ran through me as we locked eyes, amethysts meeting emeralds. His hair was wet, onyx waves clinging to his sculpted face, flashing me back to the night on the beach where he almost died, but the light in his expression promised he was okay, that he made it out just fine, and he'd never looked more handsome.

"Forgive me if I am a little excited to see someone besides your sorry faces for once," the boy quipped, his voice lacking any seriousness, diverting me from my daze but not completely pulling me out of it.

Arms folding warm around you. Secure and gentle. Wrapped in warmth. 'I won't let anything happen to you.'

I chose to believe him, despite the warning my brain screamed, and it was better than slowly being driven to insanity from paranoia. Having decided this, I turned back to the boy, confidently answering, "My injury is getting better. Thank you for asking... um..." I racked my brain for his name, pressured by all the attention on me, stunned silence created by my joining in casual conversation, "Killian?"

"Keagan, Love," he rectified, beaming from such a response, "and I am delighted to hear that."

"Would you like breakfast, Ari?" Kiernan asked, already making his way to the kitchen, his steps seeming lighter than usual. The eldest slipped by him, walking to the front door and joining the youngest outside without so much as another look my way.

"We are out of eggs again?" Kiernan huffed, closing the pantry unsatisfied, "Keagan, would you mind taking the money we made from selling the fish this week, and buy Ari some food while she and I are out?"

"Where do you think you are going with it?" Kell spoke for the first time that morning, cold and haunting as I remembered, and I wished he would've stayed quiet.

"In the forest. Not very far," he recited easily, coming my way and offering a hand to help me to my feet.

Kell and I stood at the same time.

"Killian doesn't want it leaving," he stated, tone and posture challenging his younger brother.

"I will be with her the whole time," Kiernan informed, meeting his glare head-on, and while I was incredibly uncomfortable with the tension, Keagan acted as though this was a regular occurrence.

"Are you sure that is the safest idea given how it reacts to our kind?" he contemptuously mulled over, hard stare shifting to me, and all I could see were the sharp edges of cut emeralds and the poisons in various plants, "Animals fear, just like anything that senses their death approach, but you..." he took a step a forward, and I matched it with a step away, deadly dance in motion, "You feel so much. Practically drip with emotion... with *fear*."

"Back off, Kell," Kiernan demanded, and it wasn't a challenge anymore; it was a threat.

"You can't tell me you don't enjoy the scent of terror on it."

I couldn't decide what made me more unsettled: the way Kell looked at me, or how Kiernan didn't argue with him.

"It frightens so easily, too." Kell advanced nearer, his lips twisting into a grin that was anything but pleasant when I stumbled back, and Kiernan stepped in his path.

"I said *back off*."

"Why should I? You've gotten to do whatever you wanted with it. Why can't I simply...?" My wrist was suddenly on fire, burning as a scorching hand clamped on it.

My heart spiked with a jolt of fear, and Kiernan snapped.

The blow was clean and swift, one I would've missed if I blinked at the wrong time, and the room went deafeningly silent as the phantom flames on my arm died. Kell held his head in the direction of the impact, eyebrows lifted in the same surprise that was apparent on my face, my palm hiding my gaping expression. Keagan's hand also covered his mouth, not in shock, I noticed from the sparkle of intrigue in his eyes, but to keep from laughing. Kiernan's eyes went wide, his hand flexing while he struggled to comprehend what he'd done, and the other curled protectively around me behind him as his older brother slowly faced us once more. Kell dragged his thumb over his lip, glimpsing the blood, then brutally locking eyes with me, spitefully, as though I'd been the one to throw the punch.

I lost my breath.

"Come on," Kiernan urged, fully placing his hand on the small of my back to guide me out of the house and away from the nearly fatal game I hadn't meant to start.

Kell's eyes strained on me, but he didn't advance further. "You win this one, siren."

"Don't listen to him," Kiernan mumbled, keeping his head forward while opening the door and refusing to look back when closing it. When we were several feet away, masked in the shadow of trees that looked normal-sized next to the cabin, the stiffness in his back eased, and I felt the safety to speak.

"I'm sorry. I'm pretty sure that was my fault," I tried, but Kiernan shook his head.

"Don't apologize. Kell was asking for it."

His face was set in pure irritation, and I decided my noiselessness was necessary at the moment.

We walked through the woods in silence, stepping into the memories we had before when we were nothing more than a boy and a girl who enjoyed one another's company, no creatures, no danger, no fear, just us and the trees. It was strange, however, to have the roles reversed with family issues, and I wished I could've comforted him as he had me, but I wasn't able to get a read on him. The hand he'd placed on my back to lead me away now fisted in my shirt, subconsciously, I presumed, along with the briskness of his steps I struggled to match with my injured leg.

He was angry, that was obvious, but how he felt it was what left me puzzled.

"I wouldn't worry about Kell, though," Kiernan started, lost in thought as I had been, "Despite his big talk, he won't do anything against Killian's instructions. Kell's much too loyal, and I believe Killian might like you."

His expression had softened, pacing slowed, and the hand gripping the back of my shirt fell to his side.

"Like me?"

I was too concentrated on Kiernan's demeanor to see the ground in front of me, and he pulled me out of the path leading into the thick of the brush, pondering his response.

"Like isn't the right word for it. None of us *like* anything, but I do think what you did for Kaid the other night stood out to him."

"Kaid... the young one?"

"Are you calling me old?" he smiled, and my heart tumbled at his brilliance, missing his joke entirely, "Yes, Kaid is the youngest. He's doing very well for an eleven-year-old."

"What do you mean?" Kiernan looked at me thoughtfully, easing his stride even more.

"It's... difficult, being what we are," he chose his words carefully, avoiding certain titles to evade triggering emotions in me that he could act on, "and learning how to contain it, especially at a young age. Most can't control shifting until teen years, and even then, you don't always succeed," he explained, examining the knuckles he used to punch his brother.

"Is that the reason Kaid was tied up in the woods that night?" Kiernan's lips were pursed as he nodded.

"We need our arms in front of our faces to change, so when they are kept behind us, we are trapped to the alternate form."

Alternate form. Not human mask.

"It hurts but is extremely effective," he finished, and I'd finally built up enough request to sit, which he agreed to instantly, settling us on the surface of a nearby rock large enough to contain us both.

"And your other brother?" I urged, hoping he'd open up fully as I had with him.

"Keagan? He's a hopeless flirt," Kiernan groaned, "It's how he copes, I know it, but sometimes his act is almost believable. He struggles the most out of all of us with the seclusion, the biggest people person out there. "

"I don't know," I countered, "Maddie is like a social ostrich."

He laughed, and my heart tumbled again.

"Ostrich?"

I shrugged, my arm accidentally bumping against his, unable to hide my smile.

"It's bigger than a butterfly."

"Of course. How could I forget Maddie? Didn't she invite you to that party as well?"

My grin disappeared, reminded of how there'd always been a pair of eyes on me. "Is there anything about me you don't know?"

Still, the question came out like a joke, playful and light, and Kiernan gave me an apologetic smile.

"Why you ended up going to that party."

It took a second to remember my reasoning, and I began fidgeting with my necklace during the recollection.

"Anders convinced me to go," I told, my tone growing solemn, but I kept my smirk, concentrating on the gold of my shell glistening in the sun, "He said I was acting like a lemon curd, and I would not stand for such scrutiny." A lump pushed into my throat, and I knew I needed to change the topic. "Why did you go?"

Kiernan had lost his smile when I glanced back at him, appearing apologetic, but he graciously didn't bring the subject up.

"Maddie invited Keagan while we were out getting supplies, and he pestered Killian to let him go until he gave in. Kell and I were there to make sure nothing went wrong, and it was safe to say neither of us wanted to be there." My eyelids grew heavy as he spoke, the gentleness of spring soothing me to long-awaited sleep, and my head lulled, involuntarily finding Kiernan's shoulder, and it was too heavy and too tiring to lift. He didn't voice disapproval either, steadying himself so my head didn't sink uncomfortably.

"Kiernan?"

"Hm?"

"What is... a gap... a gap in tea?" I tried, finishing with a yawn.

"*Agapiti?*"

"Yeah. That's the word. What is *Agapiti?*"

His suspicion was shown in not just his tone but how his fingers questioningly brushed the hair from my face.

"Why do you ask?"

"You whispered it when you were half asleep the night we went stargazing," I said, my words beginning to slur together, eyes falling shut.

"I did?"

I hummed in affirmation, and there was a pause long enough that I almost slipped into unconsciousness, "It means dear friend in Greek."

Kiernan didn't feel like a friend anymore, and I wasn't awake enough to discern why, but I didn't really care. He was close, and in my sluggish brain, I knew that was all I wanted.

I felt slightly damp hair sweep across my forehead, a warm weight lying on my skull, and I couldn't bring myself to pull away.

At last, I fell asleep.

Chapter Twenty

The thunder was loud and scary. I pushed my blanket into my ears, but I could still hear the rain hitting the window. Daddy was out there. What if he got hurt?

Lightning struck right next to the house. I screamed, and my door opened a few minutes later.

"Are ye awricht, Hen?" a man asked.

It was Mommy's friend. I liked him. He could do neat tricks.

"Why does the sky sound angry?" I worried.

Zadar sat on my bed and smiled.

"The sky's no angry, only sad. Storms are the earth's way o' cryin' sympathy on the world."

"Daddy doesn't like it when I cry. He says I shouldn't do it just like I shouldn't sing."

Zadar looked disappointed.

"Never be feart tae cry, Ariella. Tears arenae a sign o'weakness; they're proof ye ken how tae be strong. There's healin' in them."

"What do the sky's tears heal?"

"Monie things, Lass. Without rain, the grass wouldnae be green, animals would hae nae water tae drink, and we'd hae nae strawberries."

My mouth fell open.

"But I love strawberries!" I fussed, and Zadar chuckled.

"Then it's a guid thing we've got rain, eh? Even if it's a wee bit loud at times?"

"But why does it have to be scary?"

"Most things in life are. Even bonnie things like love and care. There's nae greater way tae show love than tae lay doon yer life for the ones ye cherish, and nae greater truer proof o' care than the sorrow others feel when yer gone."

Those were big words, but I tried to understand. I stared up at him thoughtfully.

"Do you think I will ever die for someone I love, Zadar?"

He looked down on me. There was water in his eyes.

"I hope it never comes tae that."

Thunder banged outside my window, jolting me from a dream that felt all too real, and I glanced down at my hands to make sure they weren't those of a four-year-old. My cheeks were chilled as I rubbed my palm over my face, washing away the strange surfacing of emotions the vision gave me, choosing to push back the window's curtains and watch the storm rather than give it another thought. The rain came down in sheets, piling on tree limbs and dripping from leaves in mesmerizing intervals, and I desperately wished to touch it.

I clicked the window open, reaching a hand to feel nature's tears, and I was comforted by the idea that life carried on despite a single person's situation. The sun was beginning to set, marking the heavy clouds in a thick violet, and I questioned how long I'd been asleep. The last thing I remembered was talking with Kiernan, discussing things that were all a blur to me now, but I recalled the pure exhaustion that took over, and there was no bed nearby. I tried to contain the embarrassment, thinking of how I'd fallen asleep on him, quickly turning into the question of how I woke up in my room.

He must've carried me all the way back.

The sky painted its watery patterns on my palm, and I watched as the drops soaked into my skin, soothing my fingers until their trembling ceased. Curiously, I stretched further, leaning over the windowsill until the sky reached up to my elbow, and I giggled as the tickling droplets ran down my arm.

"Wait!" Kiernan urged, causing me to jump from the unexpected noise, and twisting around to see his anxious expression, I tilted my head in question. His grip on the door handle loosened, along with the muscles in his shoulders, as he took a moment to ease his whole demeanor. "Sorry. I thought you were trying to..."

Leave, I pieced together from the way he studied me and the open window, but he shook his head instead, ending his unfinished sentence with a "Never mind."

I stood silently, unable to decide whether I should apologize, thank him for things that were still hazy in my memory, or go back to pretending I didn't want him near every second that went by.

"I'm sorry," I opted, awkwardly holding my wet arm, "I wanted to look at the rain."

Kiernan's face softened, eyes tracking every movement I made as he always did, and his focus rested on the water dripping from my fingertips.

"Would you like to go out in it?"

My brows drew together, knowing I wouldn't be able to leave the cabin without him.

"I thought you hated the rain," I posed, holding my arm tighter as he closed in, shutting the window behind me.

"I've never been in a storm with someone who appreciates them. Maybe you could change my mind," he suggested close enough to sense the fire embedded in his skin, a smile lilting.

New game. Make Kiernan like the rain.

I lit up in excitement, grabbing his hand with both of mine and tugging him along in a race to make it outside, and his easy laugh only encouraged me more. It only lasted a second, though, reaching my doorway and stumbling back into Kiernan with a sharp hitch of my breath.

Four large, dangerously powerful beasts stared at me, green piercing the darkness engulfing the cabin.

Keagan was the first to react, barely catching the light-green creature before he was human again, abnormally attractive and charismatic as usual in a cream shirt and dark pants. The eldest followed immediately behind his brother, and I watched as massive tan wings encircled his form, the covering of scales shifting into the covering of clothes, hiding the transformation until the wings morphed into arms, unmasking the face of a man carrying the lives of too many.

I was very familiar with that expression.

The dragon with burning red scales made no move to change his state, and in the darkness, I was thrown back into the memory of that same beast hovering over me, talon slicing into my leg as I screamed.

"He's scaring her," Keagan murmured, nodding to the smaller dark grey dragon crowded near the dying embers of the fireplace, trembling and trying to hide in his wings, but he couldn't remain still, something I believed to be my increasing panic's fault.

"*Kell*," the eldest demanded, and after another beat of painful tension, the flame-colored dragon shifted into the ridged, muscular form of the second eldest, dark clothes to match his hair and glower. Kell held my stare, challenging me to remember who he truly was and what he could do, as though it wasn't already burned into my brain. I dropped my gaze, listening to Kell's ignorant huff and the struggling shuffles by the fire subside, but my heart still raced.

I had known what they were, had seen some of them without the mask even, yet it didn't prepare me for the wave of dread at the sight of them changed and all in the same room, which now felt appropriately sized.

"Rain, remember?" Kiernan whispered in my ear, tickling the sensitive skin with his breath, "You were so excited."

His hand steadily slid down my arm, interlacing his fingers with mine in a silent request to lead him again. He was moving too slowly and precisely to be anything less than intentional, and while his distraction captured my full attention, striving to suppress the shivers he was sending down my spine rather than run away, it captured everyone else's attention as well. None of his family said a word, and I refused to look at their faces but could feel them staring at him, at me, at *us*, and after witnessing him carry me inside just this morning, I didn't want to imagine what they were thinking.

I kept my head down as I walked, an ashamed blush rising over my face, and I wished for the rain to wash away the horror. Kiernan was the one who kept our hands together despite me initiating our steps past the aching silence, and when the rain hit my face, my first reaction was to exhale deeply. All my worries melted, dropping to the ground to meld in mud, and I took a few more breaths before opening my eyes. It was night, and the moon was gone, but the darkness added to the serenity of it all, sky brilliantly glowing up as lightning flashed across it.

"How could anyone hate this?" I mumbled, but I knew he could hear me, trying not to overthink it when his hand fell from mine.

"We can't shift when wet. We are creatures of air, and water breaks every rule of that. It's not so much a hate for rain as it is a hate for weakness."

He started walking, and I followed close behind, noting how little the trees did in blocking this weather. After some time, he stopped at an open valley, free of anything that could hinder the droplet's fall, and I was running into the center of it without another thought. My lungs had stopped aching, my head had stopped hurting, and I'd forgotten entirely about my injury as I twirled around and around, facing the sky with closed eyes and relishing in the tears kissing my face. I searched for Kiernan, finding him leaning against an outer tree, grinning at my solo dance as though there was nothing more precious to him.

"Dance with me!" I shouted over the rain, over the thunder, over the pounding in my heart. I stretched my hand to him, elated when he met me halfway, pulling my stumbling, deranged form to him with incredible strength. My quiet giggles sang with the thunder, my feet sliding through muddied puddles in rhythm to the music of the storm. The steps were second nature, falling in the soft waltz made gentler with his thoughtful movement, holding me close to him like he was worried I'd hurt myself without his support.

One. Two. Three. Four.

I'd done this enough times with Anders that counting wasn't a requirement, yet it made the moment feel more special, savoring each second I had with Kiernan, remembering the last time we'd danced, when my biggest fear had been if Anders was going to be okay. He would now, my agreement with dragons securing his safety, but deep down, there was a part of me that knew I'd always worry for him. The world didn't tend to be forgiving, especially to those with a kind heart. I found that out the hard way.

Back. Left. Forward. Right.

Kiernan chuckled along with me, and everything I once thought beautiful seemed pathetic next to his smile, forest paling in comparison to the intensity of his eyes. It was the only time I was jealous of my mother for her ability to capture scenes in her mind and paint them permanently on a canvas. A portrait was certainly a thing he belonged on as the water seemed to glow over his face, reflecting the tan of his skin and enhancing every perfect curve of his face, and I never wanted to forget the sight.

'Only with you.'

I hadn't known someone could be so intoxicated with joy, but it prickled every fiber of my being and I forgot there was evil in the world. I recalled our every interaction as we continued dancing in the rain, each gentle touch, light-hearted joke, easy smile, lively laugh, heavy conversation, and look filled with promises. I thought of how he gazed at me with such wonder and adoration when I was happy, and the deepening sorrow that overcame him in the absence of my joyfulness, and that made me pause to ponder whether he truly did care about me or if I'd succumbed to my own delusions.

'Stay with me, Agapití.'

His eyes were hazed over in thought as well, holding me as he did the night we met, and that persistent butterfly wing hooked on a nerve, pulling out the desires I wouldn't let myself feel.

I wanted to be his. I wanted to be selfish. I wanted to be the reason he smiled every day. I wanted to stay with him until the world came to an end. I would...

I would lay down my life for him.

"Look at you keeping steadily to your feet," he teased with a playful scrunch of his nose, and this time, I didn't ignore the strange flip my stomach made.

"I have been practicing," I responded, releasing his shoulder to spin outward and back in, perfecting each action and allowing my hair to flail around me to show off.

"Practicing? With whom?" he questioned smiling, though he didn't look as proud as I would've expected, like there were words he wished to say stuck on his tongue.

"Anders. He's almost my height now."

My brother had been thrilled to hear I'd learned a new dance that day I came home from the redwoods, careful to leave out the information of where I'd gotten the unique waltz from. It was the perfect distraction from the dark things swirling in his mind, giggling as we fell over each other, trying to figure out the patterns, switching the pace when the song on the radio changed. The memory was soothing against my brain, and it didn't hurt to think of him, grinning as I brought my focus back to Kiernan, whose face was pinched with concern as he listened. "When my leg is completely healed, I'll have to teach you the dance I used to do with Mother."

"Is your leg bothering you now?" he asked, slowing the dance until we were simply swaying back and forth while he maintained most of my weight.

"No, there's just a lot of jumping and skipping that I'm not quite up for. It's more of a group dance, anyway. In fact, I dare to say you are going easier on me now than you did while teaching," I purposely lilted my tone at the end, hoping he'd pick up on the ruse in it.

"Is that a complaint? My leadings not enough for you?"

My sigh was far from genuine, the disappointed shake of my head entirely unnecessary, and I was barely able to hold back my smile while watching his grow in intrigue.

"It's truly offensive, Turner, to sway with me when I am clearly now a professional dancer," I played, delighting in the way his eyes sparkled with determination.

Then I was suddenly falling, shouting with unexpected pleasure as Kiernan dropped me into a dip that had the length of my hair surfing the mud, lowering himself until his mouth was to my ear.

"Then keep up with me, Rowe."

The world was upright for less than a second before it was spinning, forest blurring and twisting in my vision, but I planted my feet into the soft ground before he could make me lose my stance, offering no time as I was pulled back into movement. His steps formed a square, yet we started circling around the wood, and I began to lose sense of any shape as we weaved through the trees. He was flawless in the grace he used, back straight, stride swift, hand steady against my waist, chuckling as I did my best to follow. He spun me in tight triplets, and I had to grip his shirt to keep from slipping, laughing so hard I could barely breathe, though if I were being honest with myself, I hadn't breathed better in days.

Lightning streaked across the sky, and the storm paid no heed to our little competition, soaking our clothes until everything felt heavy, but that didn't hinder the dance in the slightest. It was unfair that he dictated it all, purposefully making me dizzy in hopes I'd crash, injustice sparking me to take the lead for the briefest moment, releasing one side of him to lift my arm up and make him duck under it, standing on the tips of my toes to reach over his tall figure. It wasn't a traditional action, but Kiernan followed with a bright smile, and all proper moves of classic dancing fell away after that, remaining close and in the same rhythm, but moving however we were charmed.

Kiernan mainly pulled, and I constantly pushed, both of us laughing, neither thinking, and before I could register how it happened, my arms were suddenly restrained behind me, firmly pinning my wrist with both his powerful hands, leaving me vulnerable and entirely at his mercy, face to face. My breath caught, his mouth a whisper away from mine, and I should've been terrified to be trapped in this helpless position with a creature much stronger than myself, but as the pounding of my heart in my ears overcame the thunder, I recognized it wasn't out of fear.

Kiernan's eyes were as wide as mine, and I could see my feelings reflecting in his stare, could feel the brutal flush overtaking my body, and though I couldn't read the thoughts behind that gape, I wished more than anything to see. Neither of us moved or dared to breathe, tense in the yearning for something more, yet it didn't come, and when Kiernan at least freed me from his commanding hold, his hands fisted at his sides, muttering, "Let's go back."

Kiernan refused to look at me or even allow his hand in my direction as we returned to the cabin, knuckles white from the strength he used to contain his anger. I wished to know what I had done to upset him so greatly, but he didn't appear in the mood for conversation, enabling the continuing storm to occupy the silence. It was, at least, a relief to find his family human-looking, and after being given another pair of Kiernan's clothes, I shut myself in the bathroom.

It took time to free the mud from my hair, and by the time I was finished changing into clean, warm clothes, the rain against the windows had ceased, leaving the uneasy stillness to stifle the house. Kiernan was waiting for me once I exited, fresh bandages in hand, waiting for an approving nod, which I gave gratefully, before bringing me to the kitchen stool and beginning his work on my wound.

"It's still not healed?" Keagan asked curiously, surveying the injury that was mending at an abnormally rapid pace, swelling gone along with the excessive bleeding.

"No," Kiernan coolly spoke, "humans recover slower."

"Good thing it's not a human," Kell grumbled, and Kiernan ignored him completely.

"Just cry for her and save her the pain," Keagan urged, flicking a hand through the air.

"That's impossible, and you know it," he reminded the same in the same flat tone, and his brother's smirk was directed at both of us.

"Is it, Kier?"

Kiernan ignored Keagan this time, and the guilt that I'd irritated him climbed in my throat, watching him place the new bandage. He'd been gentle and cautious the last time in fear of harming me, but now he was slow and careful as to touch me little as possible, and I tried not to focus on how that curled painfully in my chest.

"What good would crying do?" I echoed to distract myself, glancing at Kiernan, but the answer came from Keagan.

"Wow, he really has told you nothing, has he?" Keagan tisked his tongue, viewing his older brother with a disappointed look, though his eyes still smiled, "There is a healing power unlike any other in dragon tears. They can mend all injuries, rejuvenate all scars, and end pain."

"They are also a myth," Kiernan finished, closing down the conversation with the last press on my bandage. "I'll be back in a little while," he announced to me as he stood, and I watched him head to the bathroom, my throat itching to talk with him, but he needed his space, and I needed to be fine with that.

Static rang in my ear, shaking my attention from Kiernan to the other room.

The eldest, *Killian,* I reminded myself, was in the living room, messing with the struggling radio on one of the couches, but no matter what he did, Killian was only able to get every other sentence in.

"Ten-year-old Abigail Parker... missing as of this morning... her distressed family..." the eldest sighed and shut it off, placing his head in his hand, and for once, he didn't seem quite so impassive.

"Are you okay?" I asked timidly, walking up to him, and he lifted his head, staring at me with that same silent discussion behind his eyes that I'd known from Kiernan.

"No," he answered unashamedly, no expression on his face, no pain in his features, no life in his words, just straight, brutal honesty, "and I don't think I ever will be."

His words were depressing, but his tone suggested otherwise, a genuine acceptance of the life he had soothing his voice.

"You want something," he observed, eyes flicking to the seat across from him, then back to me, "Sit."

Willing my nerves to remain calm, I sat as he instructed, slipping my hands into Kiernan's sleeves before mumbling, "You said you know my mother."

"I did. Things were good back when she lived here."

I blinked at him.

"Mother lived here?"

"You both did. I don't expect you to remember it, you were only a baby, and I've forgotten most of it because I was a child."

"How did that happen?" I asked, dumbfounded, and Killian set the radio aside, crossing his tanned, muscular arms over his chest as he leaned into the couch.

"My parents found your mother in the wreckage of the tsunami that struck the northern part of California, and they took her in. It was only supposed to be a temporary thing, but Evelyn quickly became close with *Mitér...* my mother, I mean, and after they both found out they were pregnant, my mother offered to help yours since she had no one else."

"Did Mother know who you truly were?"

He hesitated with that question.

"Humans aren't supposed to know about us. We do it for their sanity and our peace, and any human who discovers the secret is to, by law, be promptly eliminated." I flinched. "So, while we did not *tell* her what we were, I do believe she had her suspicions. Your mother was a very clever woman, and judging how you are here, it is clear we were not her first interaction with the mythical existence."

"If things were fine, then why did she leave?"

"That has always been a mystery to me. When my sister was murdered by a siren, and your mother went missing the very next day, we all assumed you and she both would be his next victims, but now I can see we were wrong."

"And the painting?"

His expression didn't change, but something in his body language shifted, though it was too subtle for me to notice.

"Please stay out of that room."

"I'm headed to the store," Keagan announced loudly, unaware of the conversation he'd just interrupted, standing by the open door as damp air seeped through, glimpsing at me to add, "Is there anything you would like me to get you?"

I smiled a bit, thinking of the wonders the rain allowed, and while turning to him, I was pleased with how easily casual conversation was becoming.

"Strawberries, please."

Chapter Twenty-One

"**W**hat in the world does Jack need *fifty* apples for?" Keagan exclaimed, lying on the couch while tossing a palm-sized rock he'd gotten from the woods aimlessly in the air.

"It's a word problem, Keagan," Killian grumbled without any real bite, focusing more on Kaid, who was trying to decipher how many apples Jack would have left if he ate four. I'd been sitting on the couch to the far left of them for an hour, quietly observing the lessons the oldest taught the youngest, occasionally glancing out the window to spot Kiernan speaking with Kell. They were both solemn, and I could only imagine it was a discussion about the accidental strike to the face that transpired just two days ago, an event I still cringed at when it'd make an unwanted appearance in my memories, but guilt had constantly been pressing on my chest from more than that. Kiernan still barely looked in my direction, speaking to me solely when necessary, and the distance he kept was far from discreet. It got to my head more than it should've, replaying every interaction from the previous day, with and without rain alike, losing sleep hoping to understand what I'd done wrong.

"Sounds like an addiction to me," Keagan murmured, snatching the stone mid-air to chuck it again.

"Forty-six," Kaid answered after a long moment of consideration, smiling proudly when Killian nodded approvingly, and I caught the way Keagan noticed his brother's grin, adding another tally to the record.

"Good. Now, write it down," Killian instructed, eyeing the piece of paper Kaid carried on his lap.

I noted how far behind he was academically for a boy his age, the stern concentration on his face as he worked to form the letters, Killian observing over Kaid's shoulder. I pondered how long the eldest had been playing the role of teacher and parent, remembering the days when Anders was struggling in school, and I did the same for him.

The front door opened, and I was taken aback when Kiernan made direct eye contact with me, but there was something very different about the way he looked this time. It was no longer a battle behind his eyes but a full war, and I'd become the white flag he wasn't sure if he'd take, yet it was difficult to dismiss the hope burning through it.

"Do you want to go out?" he asked, and that, too, didn't sound quite right, the sharpened twisting beneath his skin stronger than I had seen before. After the last fiasco, the Turner's determined to keep to their masks when I was near, which made things simpler for everyone involved, but his was slipping, and I wasn't the only one to notice it.

"When was the last time you shifted?" Killian questioned, setting aside the papers he had Kaid write on. Kiernan's stare faltered after a few blinks, and the bizarre pulsing eased when he turned his sight from me.

"I'm fine."

"Five days ago," Kell interjected, stepping in behind Kiernan from outside.

"As I said," he reiterated firmly, "I'm fine."

"What's stopping you?" Kaid questioned, followed by an easy laugh from Keagan, who had paused his game of toss.

"He's bashful," he announced, giving an indicated nod to me with a head hanging upside down over the furniture's arm.

"Kiernan, why don't you stay inside today?" Killian said in a tone that suggested he had no choice.

"Ari needs to get out of the house," he argued, and I was about to deny the claim when Killian came up with his own solution.

"Keagan can take her."

Instantaneously, the couch Keagan lay on became unoccupied, jumping to his feet with enthusiasm that could've bounced off the walls.

"That is a terrible idea," Kiernan shut it down immediately, but he wasn't Killian, nor did he have the final say.

"Oh, come on, Kier. It will be fun. You can watch my pet for the day," Keagan encouraged, handing Kiernan the rock he'd been throwing around mindlessly, "and I'll watch yours."

Keagan grinned at the dark indignation that grew over Kiernan's face, evidently getting the reaction he was searching for, and as Kiernan opened his mouth to start a new quarrel, Killian cut in.

"You are not remaining in your alternate form any longer today. You've pushed it too far. The decision is yours whether you want her to stay or go, but you are staying."

Kiernan's eyes skipped over me as he closed in on Keagan, avoiding viewing how I felt about the situation, which was probably for the best; I wasn't confident with either option.

"Don't you dare try anything on her." His threat was hushed but not enough for me to miss his words, and the boy smiled brightly, folding his hands behind his back to give a mock bow.

"My dear brother, I would never *dream* of such a thing," he spoke, catching my eyes and offering a playful wink that could mean more than one thing before lending me his arm in a gentlemanly manner, "Come, Love. Let's see how you do around heights."

"Where are we going?" I questioned hesitantly, following loosely behind the boy who could change at any moment and tear me apart.

"You'll see," he assured, stepping seamlessly over rocks and roots, walking as though the trail he created was cleared and not covered in ferns reaching my knees. Evidence of the previous day's downpour was everywhere, causing my mud-covered boots to slide unpleasantly over the slick grass, and the what should have been warm thought of how Kiernan would have laughed at me, felt cold to my heart.

I glanced behind me continually, hoping I might find Kiernan trailing behind us, changing his mind about letting me go. He promised he wouldn't let anything happen to me, but he wasn't here now, and we'd been walking for a while.

"This is your problem," Keagan called, noting my searchings and the obvious distance between us, "Always looking for a way out or a place to run." He stopped walking, and I did the same, pausing several feet away from him. "You are much too alluring to be walking around this scared. It's not healthy for anyone involved. Luckily for us, I happen to have the antidote."

Can't handle fear. Plans to kill you. Kiernan won't come. Doesn't want to see you.

"*Trust*," he asserted before my thoughts could spiral further, like he could taste the panic in the air and wanted to spit it out, flashing a charming smile for good measure, "I am trusting you not to enchant me, and you can trust me not to end you where you stand."

"You abducted me and threatened my life. I have more reasons to distrust you than not."

"But we've kept our word, have we not? Your family remains untouched, and no harm has come to you."

I gave him a blank stare, lifting the baggy pant leg far enough to see the bandage beneath it, and he had the audacity to grin.

"We don't include Kell in our agreements."

Again, another wink at me, and I considered how often he must have worn this mask to be this convincing, because beneath the sly smiles and mischievous eyes, I knew he was just as dead on the inside as the rest of them.

Keagan continued on his path, but I stayed where I was, viewing how he climbed a slick knoll with terrific mastery, gripping one of the upturned roots of a redwood, and bent over the edge to offer me his hand. Still, I didn't move.

"We are almost there, Beautiful," he urged, waggling his fingers of his free hand at me, "Just a little farther. It'll be worth it, I promise."

I took one last glance behind me, shaming my disappointment to find no one there, before feeling the regular human warmth of Keagan's hand as he pulled me over the sharp hill. He kept me at his side this time, backing up when I tried to create distance between us, avoiding eye contact at the very least. He chuckled but said nothing, and after a few more moments of silence, I finally spoke up.

"Is that the ocean?" I asked, perking up at the sound reminiscent of home, desperate for that sense of familiarity.

"Indeed, it is," Keagan affirmed, leading me closer to the sounds until I could see the waves rolling in, "Welcome to Secret Beach."

The beach was far below us, masses of foam washing on the shore, piling over sand darkened from its dissipation. Rock formations jutted from its waters, large enough to carry its own trees, minuscule compared to the woods at my back. Seagulls cried in the distance, the scent of salt filling my nose, and if I closed my eyes, I could picture myself at Pebble Beach once more, the ocean in front of me, my house behind me, and Father's voice singing his woeful lullaby.

"Why is it a secret?" I asked, choosing to keep my eyes open rather than long for things I'd never regain.

"No one else knows about it. Not even the sirens."

I wasn't sure if he was looking at me or the view, but Keagan paused a second, as though expecting a certain reaction in his words, but I simply memorized the sea's patterns.

"It's safe here," he claimed, yet I struggled to find safety in a place hidden from the rest of the world with a creature more lethal than anything the ocean could conceal.

"Why did you bring me?"

"Well, my lemon curd, someone likes questions," he playfully mocked, gently bumping me with an elbow that didn't carry the spark of heat I would've expected. He laughed when I didn't, fearing the moment I left my guard down would be the moment he struck, and my cries for help would be useless in this place echoing solitude. "I want to show you the world up there," Keagan clarified, indicating the sky, a different shade of blue from the sea, clouds appearing just as bubbly as the foam.

"How?"

My entire body locked up when a hand was placed over my shoulder, sight tracking where his other pointed to the landscape's edge, dirt and stone overlooking the ocean.

"You see that cliff over there?" he questioned from behind, and I swallowed, realizing where he was going with this.

"You want me to jump?"

His quiet laugh was the first time his amusement sounded unnatural, on the verge of threatening, causing the hairs on the back of my neck to stand, and his hand tightened around my shoulder on instinct. Keagan took a few steps back then, fingers stiff as they removed themselves from me, like they wanted to dig into my skin until something snapped beneath them, but the confident smile he wore covered the urge behind his eyes.

"I want you to trust that I'll catch you."

Something was very different in the way he stared, all the charm and comfort of his human persona relinquishing, and I told myself if I could get control of my heart rate, he would go back to normal. Taking a steady step away from him and closer to the shore, I cautiously murmured, "What if I don't jump?"

There was an edge in his smirk, a wild flash in his eyes, and then a dragon was in front of me.

I stumbled back, losing the tight grip on my fear I'd been fighting to hold, and I made the mistake of searching for the best place to run. He was gone before I could register how it happened, an eerie silence taking his place, and it appeared the only sanctuary was that of the water, much too far below us. Seeing the beast was terrifying, but losing sight of him in a place I couldn't escape was even worse.

"Keagan," I called, his name aching in my throat, and I clutched my shell as though it could help my voice carry. The ocean was calling for me, a hum that bristled under my skin, but the pounding in my ears overcame the sound. "Keagan—"

There was a whack against a nearby tree, my head jerking in its direction, catching the ferns swaying from the earlier impact before his voice carried over the wind, echoing, "What is it you are afraid of?"

My eyes skipped past the ground, studying the bending of the branches and twisting in the leaves far above me, hoping to spot the creature that made the giant trees seem normal.

"Where are you?" I demanded, though it had no power behind it, and the jolt in my bones at the sound of talons scraping wood further proved my weakness.

"Answer the question," he ordered from some unseen location, carrying the strength I lacked, "What are you afraid of?"

"You," I forced out, and the wind seemed to shift at the word.

"Why?"

I turned sharply in the direction of his voice, my focus straining on him as though I could pin him there, but he was the portrait of ease, loose and free from any bonds but his own, leaning in his alternate form against a stump with head tilted in question.

"Why are you scared of me?" Keagan reiterated, smirk returning to prove his current control over himself, but the distance he maintained didn't go unnoticed.

"Because I am going to die."

"Wrong."

I blinked, and he was gone again, enabling the creeping dread in my lungs to return, crushing the oxygen until it felt like suffocation. Suddenly, I was back in the redwoods I knew, being taunted and lured under the title of witch, and I was with no knife to fight back. Powerful hunter and vulnerable prey, it only ever ended one way.

"Stop," I begged as the trees began to narrow in my vision, tunneling out my surroundings as the ocean's call became louder.

"You have to learn how to calm down, Rowe."

A branch snapped just above my head, and I jumped away from it falling near me, terrified yet stimulated as I finally glimpsed the beast.

"Stop!"

"Not until you do."

He shifted long enough to speak, transforming in and out of this true form as easily as breathing, remnants of his hide visible in his false skin in random blotches. Keagan was the color of grass in the meadow on a bright summer day, slimmer than the bulky form of Kell, and when he moved, it was with a mesmerizing grace, slipping through the forest like it was smooth silk, ignoring all rules of gravity. The scales that embedded his thick skin reminded me of a snake, intricate and resilient, used to blend in with the surrounding earth.

"Keep talking, Ari," he urged when the terror increased, sounding a bit more cautious as he voiced, "Why are you scared?"

"You threatened me!" I shouted like a cry for help, and his answering was that of easy chuckles floating in the breeze.

"Let's not start accusing, Love. I *strongly implied*, but that is not the answer I am looking for."

He paused in the center of his self-made trail, appearing insignificant in the large brush without the wings and tail, keeping my unblinking sight on him as I took several backward steps toward the sea, and Keagan followed the movement.

"Why are you doing this?"

My throat felt weak, but my voice sounded in my ears as though I'd been screaming.

"You won't find the solution if you can't even identify the problem. So, we will continue this game until you either discover the root of your fear or instead choose to jump off the cliff and allow me to show you the marvel of dragons."

I shook my head, gluing my eyes to him, continuing to back away even as my boots crunched against rock.

"Neither will happen," I assured, causing Keagan to cock his head and grin dark hair falling just above his right eye, advancing without missing a beat.

"And why is that? You can't tell me you have never wondered what it is like to fly."

He smiled as I backed to the edge, trapped above dangerous waves and in front of something more lethal. It was clear Keagan was enjoying this, and why wouldn't he? I was a ball of emotions for him to feed from.

We watched one another a moment longer, and it was obvious I wouldn't be taking that final step, he brought his arms to his face to change once more.

I panicked.

It was an instinct, a defensive reaction that forced my voice into song, singing lyrics my brain hadn't had time to process, and ever so slowly, Keagan lowered his hands. His body unraveled at my sound, making him the helpless one in a strange turn of events, and only when his head drooped did I bring it to an end.

He was silent for several long seconds, barely moving or breathing while fixating on a patch of grass in front of him, but the waves behind me responded, crashing and wading to form their own song, and I wondered, in the release my chest had, if I truly was as defenseless as I believed myself to be.

"You are afraid of being alone for a lifetime," Keagan uttered, his eyes wide with realization, and from the shock in his expression, I couldn't decipher whether he was speaking to me or himself.

I was fearful of that, among many things, but that wasn't the root of it. No, he hadn't been talking to me.

I watched as he lowered himself to the ground, his body appearing too heavy to carry as he shrank, and the painful solemnity that overcame his usual vibrant face was more unsettling than anything. I surveyed him warily, hesitant to lower my guard, but it was clear whatever I'd done ripped his armor from him, and he couldn't even bring himself to look at me as he quietly asked, "Could you, maybe, sing again?"

The hurt in his tone shattered the trepidation I had for him, and it was without thought or hesitation that I answered his request.

Keagan hadn't spoken a word to me after I finished my song, nor did he push the matter of flight again, providing a long, silent walk back to the cabin. His focus kept to the ground as mine did to him, pondering my mistakes as I had with Kiernan. I wanted to speak up on several occasions, but the words died in my throat each time, worried but not fearful as I had been.

The cabin was free of dragons as Keagan brought me back, remaining in the doorway while I stepped into the home lit by the late afternoon rays. Keagan gave me one more smile before transforming and flying away, a smile that was darker and defeated compared to his others, but it looked more genuine, more like a person who learned how to smile in the storms rather than going through life jovial because the sun was out.

"What did you do to him?" Killian questioned, but it wasn't harsh or firm as one would assume from a protective older brother, curiosity laced with something else I couldn't discern, like he'd expected this to happen. He was sitting in the exact place I last saw him, papers plain and used alike scattered over his lap and couch while the youngest prioritized one sheet. Kaid had paused his work when Keagan and I returned, silently observing it all with the calm interest the man beside him exhorted. Kiernan and Kell were nowhere in sight.

My stare honed to the window, where the green dragon had been seconds ago, once again running through the memories, subtly shaking my head before answering, "I don't know."

Chapter Twenty-Two

I didn't sleep much that night, and judging from the shuffles outside of my door, I knew Kiernan didn't either. He was still avoiding me, still not giving a reason for the distance between us, and apart from the pain it caused my heart, I feared he was beginning to care less about what happened to me. I wanted to believe that wasn't the case, wanted to *trust* that Kiernan meant it when he promised me safety, but it was unlikely when I hadn't seen him for who he truly was, and I was walking to my door before I could change my mind. The sound of its opening was quieter than the silence that followed, holding the handle while steadied breaths were examined in the darkness.

"I want to see you," I spoke, yet my eyes remained glued to the ground, even as I heard him shift to stand.

"I'm right here," he answered, and his voice was different, calm and affectionate, the prior strain in his tone lost. I lifted my eyes to his and found the nostalgia in them, the stare of someone who promised the impossible. It felt wrong to hold so much power in a gaze that faked human resemblance, though I supposed it made me a hypocrite to think such things.

"The real you," I countered, ignoring the way my heart quickened at the realization of what I was asking.

His brows lowered, offsetting the calm in his expression, but I determined to hold strong, even if everything inside me felt weak.

"Ari, I don't think—"

"I'm not afraid anymore," I broke in, hoping he didn't notice how my fist clutched the door handle tighter, emotions more than uncertainty surging through me, "Not of you."

He stepped away, his reasoning unknown to me, and I did it again, displaying my debarred weakness as I reached for him. There was a second of panic, a second I believed he'd disappear like Keagan had if I didn't catch him in time, but he stayed, and it was all I could hope for. His hand was what I now clutched, and I wanted to be the one to let go and disappear, prove I didn't need him, that my mind could rest without his presence, but it was getting harder to convince myself by the day.

"Are you sure?" he asked, analyzing our joined hands as if they didn't make sense, and I could sense the colors of roses blooming across my face.

No, I wasn't sure. I wasn't sure if I could handle it, if I wouldn't run away screaming, if I would ever look at him the same again.

"Yes."

He hesitated as though he could feel the uncertainty in the little heartbeat in the tips of my fingers, but he didn't let go, gently rubbing his thumb over the back of my hand until my heart calmed, while his stare held there.

"Okay," he surrendered, leading me outside despite the privacy we had in the cabin.

It was night, the breeze gentle, and my eyes were too focused on the ground to notice the lighter blue of the beginning rays of the sunrise painted across the sky. Kiernan's hand fell from mine, and my fingers curled around my other arm, stifling the desire to be touched. The forest air was too calming, too quiet, too peaceful for the anxious twisting in my stomach like it wished to coax my guard down, but I could hear every shifting sound Kiernan made, and I hadn't realized my eyes were closed until I wanted to go back into the cabin and couldn't find my way.

There was a moment we didn't move or breathe, and when a pointed exhale blew the stray strands of my hair from my face, telling me he was ready, I recognized I wasn't. I kept my eyes sealed shut, pushing down the rising dread and the overpowering presence looming over my fragile frame, but I promised myself not to show vulnerability around him again, and where I failed once that night, I determined not to let it slip through a second time.

I opened my eyes.

Four massive paws were the first to command my attention, dark and domineering, talons sharp enough to slice me open in an easy movement. I didn't allow the thought to circulate as I forced my eyes upward, tracking the strong limbs and powerful chest, his stomach solid black while the rest of him was dusted with a deep purple that harnessed a glow from the moonlight. His wings seemed to match the pattern of the rest of him, but he kept them tucked tightly to his body, and though it didn't help in making me not feel like the smallest thing on the planet, he wasn't as threatening. Still, I struggled to crane my head up further, my sight stuck on the complexity of each scale embedded over his shoulders and neck, and how they appeared just as sharp as the talons that were too close to me. My limbs were stuck in a state of dread, cowering from the sheer power the creature's presence inflicted in the air, making it almost too thick to breathe in, and when my breath came out shallow, he lowered his head to find my eyes.

Even covered in scales and horns, even dark enough to blend with the night, even too large to capture in one look, even though he appeared the furthest thing from human, I could see the questioning look on his face, the same expression he wore when something bad would happen and he feared I'd break, but now I could feel myself beginning to mend.

Because it was him.

I knew those eyes anywhere.

They were on the dance floor, curious. They were in the woods, smiling. They were in the ocean, panicked. They were in the sky, sparkling.

The same eyes I saw rushing toward me before I lost consciousness.

They were bigger now, splitting the darkness, and I could pick out every emerald tree in the jeweled forest of his irises, casting shadows of jade and sage around the pupils, which enlarged the longer I stared.

His mouth was closed, hiding the pointed teeth I didn't allow myself to consider, his nostrils casually flaring with each exhale, warming the already heated air. The horns perfectly symmetrical on top of his head were the same color of darkened shadow that showed over his stomach, encasing his excessive warmth.

He looked like the night sky, violet flecks that would make the most mesmerizing of galaxies jealous, and I couldn't remember how I once believed there was anything dangerous about him.

"You are beautiful," I breathed, reaching to touch the scales between penetrating life-filled eyes. He leaned forward, meeting my hand halfway, eyes closing when my fingers brushed against his brow. A deep, rumbling trill echoed in his throat, resonating in the hollow of my bones, and my heart nearly beat out of my chest, not in fear but in awe.

His tail was cautious as it inched its way to me, as if it were its own being with its own fear of how I'd react, but the face in front of me was too entrancing to divert from, and I barely noticed the thing brush the hair from my shoulder.

But I did recognize as it skimmed down my back, feeling like a warm hand that knew exactly where to touch to release the tension in my body, and I sucked in a breath when the heat curled around my stomach, hoisting my feet from the ground. Instinct kicked in then, and my hands gripped the tail lifting me, my legs close to burning as they were placed upon his back, just beneath the fire caged inside of him. The spikes lining his spine down to his tail flattened against the rest of him to avoid stabbing me, and I gripped one with stiff fingers in fear of slipping off. At his height, I was sure to break something by falling.

"What are you doing?" I asked tentatively, watching the wings unfastened from his side, sizing up to his full strength. "Kiernan?"

There was a soft growl in response, one that I felt more than heard, and then his wings were in motion without another sound. I held tighter to him as I felt the hold of gravity loosening around me and the desire to scream mixing with the demand to be released lodged in my throat. The air pressed onto my body, forcing me down, and I clung to Kiernan as my only safety net. When I found my voice, it came out desperate, and if he noticed my protest, he didn't let it show, bringing us mid-air before I could regain my breath. I tried to close my eyes and wish it all away, but that just made it worse, gaining more speed by the second until my long hair was battered against the wind, blocking my line of vision and blinding me from all surroundings, and I was *slipping*.

Then it all stopped.

The breeze was no longer an attack but a soothing touch, crisp but not cold, and the chaotic world suddenly fell silent. It took a second for me to pry a stiff hand from him to tuck my hair from my eyes, another to lift my head, blinking from the unexpected light. The shy sun scarcely peeked from behind the horizon of trees, casting the sky in a myriad of pinks and purples and oranges. It looked like a scene out of one of Mother's paintings, yellow taking up most of the sky through golden rays of sunshine. I subconsciously reached for the colors, imagining they were the delicate hands she'd use to bring portraits to life, to let her know I was alive, because deep down, there was the smallest part of my heart that, despite everything, believed she cared for me.

I hadn't seen Kiernan's head turn to glimpse at me until his neck was moving his face forward, and my hands fell back to his pelt at the tickling sensation of us ascending. He continued climbing the sky, breaking every law of physics to walk on the wind, halting when the clouds were close enough to touch, and Kiernan peered around at me. His eyes flicked upward with an expectant expression over his majestic face as though he planned for me to do just that. Initially hesitant, I let go of him to straighten to my full height, reaching for the sunrise's pools with both of my hands.

I felt nothing, and I wasn't sure why I assumed to sense contact with evaporated air running through my fingers, but I was slightly disappointed, wondering if that's how Mother felt about me.

Descension started then, a slow, gradual process that Kiernan took more ease with than takeoff, and I mourned the loss of the sky's closeness. Glancing at the ground far below us, I noted his wings, the sheer strength and control in them, cutting into the air with an authority that suggested he controlled the wind's direction, and even those ended in sharp points at their tips. Every part of him was lethal and dangerous, yet he carried me with such softness I forgot to be frightened.

We glided for a while longer, and I drank in the scenery I could see for miles. From this height, the forest didn't appear so daunting, treetops dotting the ground, looking like its own unique pasture, and in the far distance on my left, I could make out the faint blues of a shoreline. There was a peace about the early morning that calmed my anxious mind, soaking in lungfuls of fresh oxygen, thinking of nothing apart from the beauty of the world, that was until Kiernan's tail wrapped around me again and plopped on the branch of a random tree.

I shouted in a mixture of displeasure and alarm as I hugged the thick branch, observing the treacherous distance my body was from the ground. I heard Kiernan laughing, and I tracked the noise, spotting him by the roots, grinning up at me, and I was surprisingly startled at the sight of him in human skin.

"I never took you as one to be afraid of flying," he chucked, and I shifted to better see him.

"Let me down," I demanded inside of a nervous laugh, clutching the surrounding branches for dear life.

"Why?" he baited, and I could finally understand it, the unnatural spark in his eyes, the animalistic gleam in the green, even if his smile was far from the features of a dragon.

"Because I am going to fall."

"No, you won't."

My legs were tense, my back pressed into the damp bark, bracing for the wood beneath me to snap.

"What is this about?"

My insistency was stronger the second time around, but Kiernan casually sauntered around as though content to leave me dangling for the remainder of the day.

"I'm surprised you haven't recognized it yet."

"Recognized what?" I questioned, allowing my sight to leave him in search of the answers to his vague statements. Then, without a word or really any sound of indication, he was in front of me, effortlessly balancing on the outer part of the branch, and it startled me enough to lose my own stability. Kiernan reflexively caught me around my waist, a hand on either side, bracing my tense body against the tree, and my heart started racing.

"See? What did I tell you? No falling."

But his hands didn't leave my sides, holding me against the damp bark while very little air separated us, and though I tried not to think about the effect his touch had on me, I couldn't stop the heat rising up my neck and blossoming over my cheeks. I waited for him to react as he normally did, to back away and stare at me strangely, but he instead smiled as he studied my pinkened features, and I told myself I was imagining the fingers pressing slightly deeper into my waist, the heat seeping through the hoodie he gifted me and landing on my skin, only adding to the redness on my face.

"That way," he mumbled, one hand leaving my side to hook a finger under my chin to gently lead my focus in the proper direction, and my eyes fixed on it, widened in realization.

"You brought me to the tree?"

You brought me this close to home?

"*Our* tree," he corrected, taking a step back but still observing my face, "And I thought you might appreciate some familiar sights."

I liked the sound of that.

Our tree. *Our* place. *Our* memories.

It had officially been a week since I was taken, but I'd felt like years since I last saw this side of the redwoods, and a cracked part of my heart healed in the moment.

Kiernan dropped out of the tree before I could respond, transformed before I could blink, and I was being dragged along with him before I could register how it happened. Once I was dropped on the tree in the center of so many wonderful interactions, it clicked why he wouldn't allow me to be on the ground. I finally knew where I was, and he couldn't risk me running, as though I stood a chance against him, but there was a part of me that still wanted to try.

Kiernan changed again, landing on the branches with enough force to shake the whole tree.

"You have to stop doing that," I shouted, grabbing hold of a new branch to evade gravity's clutch.

"But it's fun to see you flustered," he prodded, and I detested how my face flushed all over at his words, involuntarily giving him exactly what he wanted.

"You are a pest."

Yet I smiled as I said it, grateful he pushed aside enough irritation I'd brought him to tease freely again.

"*Pest*," he pondered, "Keagan would like that word, though he tends to gravitate to the statement 'broken in the brains'. Kell's favorite is 'disappointment'." His expression fell briefly, and I panicked that he was reverting to the closed-off countenance he had when upset.

"Whose idea was it to give all of you 'k' names?" I questioned teasingly as though it was the silliest concept when Anders and I were no different, and he smiled once more, only it was sadder, reminding me of Keagan's hurt-ridden grin.

"My parents. They always liked sharing things. Even had the same first letter for their cover names to blend in. Jared and Joanna," he murmured it like the beginning of a tragic song, his eyes far off, "Those weren't their real names, of course. Chioni and Ouania were names that didn't fit for a young, new couple in Oregon."

I thought of the portrait, the room that wasn't meant to be seen, how such a beautiful family could be covered in a layer of dust yet never forgotten.

"What happened to them?" I asked, and it was such a surreal feeling to know that less than a few months ago, we were in this same tree talking about my parents, back when I couldn't understand why he kept so silent about his own life.

"They were banished," he told, raking his sight over the blooming spring ground.

"Banished? From where?"

"Agrond." He tried to smile, but it was the farthest thing from real. "The land of the dragons. I haven't been there myself, but I've been told it's beautiful. 'Paradise', *Patér* used to call it."

"*Patér?*"

"It's Greek for father, as is *Mitér* for mother. I never got used to the English titles, especially since they attempted to fit as much of our native language into our vocabulary while ensuring we could speak with the humans. It's hard to remember much of them: I was only a kid when they died, but I know they always considered Agrond to be their real home despite being taken from it."

"What for?"

"They fell in love," he spoke softly, and I realized I'd diverted the topic that bothered him to one that he ached to remember a little too late, "They managed to keep their relationship hidden, even eloping in secret, but pregnancy is not so easily disguised. *Mitér* refused to reveal who she had been with to keep *Patér* safe, and as far as everyone else knew, she was expecting without promising herself to another. Marriage is sacred in my culture, and without any witnesses, she was to be punished for a law she didn't break. She would've gladly taken it on her own to secure their future, but *Patér* wouldn't stand for it, so they revealed themselves and were banished to the human realm to live the rest of their days in hiding."

He paused, like he wanted to catch his breath but had no need for one, and I took it as an opportunity to indulge my curiosities.

"What was so horrible about them being together?"

"He was an ember, and she was a serpent, and it doesn't matter that we are the same creatures who bleed the same blood; it is forbidden for Embers and Serpents to be involved romantically."

"Why?"

"Power. Why else? Only Embers can reproduce Embers, and the mixing of the two creates *weaker links.*" He rolled his eyes. "Or so they say. Dragons and sirens have been feuding for longer than anyone can remember, and the fire breathers are bred for war. Serpents get overlooked despite being the primary reason that the island is bountiful, simply because they can't burn the world down. I pity the Embers, though. Serpents tend to find that special, deep connection with a partner because no one is after them. Rarely do Embers get that, either marrying for lust or benefits."

"Aren't you an Ember?" I asked, thinking of the heat he always put off, wondering why he spoke of them as though they were creatures he barely knew, and the chuckle he gave lacked humor.

"I'm a weak link, me and all my brothers, though if you wanted to fit us into categories, Kell and I are the only embers. The rest of my siblings are serpents, and that was including Kaida."

I noted his use of the word *was* and treaded my next question cautiously.

"Kaida... your sister?"

Kiernan faced me with a puzzled stare.

"You know about her?"

"Killian mentioned you had a sister, but the conversation didn't go very far."

He turned back to the nature glowing in the rising sun; eyebrows raised in surprise.

"Killian rarely talks about Kaida," he stated in a lowered tone, a whisper to himself, readjusting his voice as he started a new story, "My parents grew up with the understanding that sirens were dangerous, so when they first met one after their banishment, they were wary of her, to say the least. Adrielle, however, was just as lost and alone as they were, and it wasn't long before the three became close. She would sing to them almost daily, and they paid her in hand-painted, golden shells. The exchange lasted multiple years, and it was the first time in centuries that a dragon and a siren befriended one another. This was all before I was born, but Killian will bring her up at certain moments, reminding us there is a little good in everything. She was the reason Kaida, Killian, and Kell were so trusting when a new siren appeared, so excited to make another friend in this world where you can't form relationships with locals for their safety, and they got too close." He slouched onto the branch, and I copied the movement, watching as his brows knit together as he spoke, "My only sister was murdered that day. They were just kids, not much older than Kaid is now. Killian and Kell almost didn't make it back, shouting as they told my parents all that happened, and *Patér* wanted to go back to Agrond right then to inform them of the siren attack and appeal to be brought back for the safety of his young family, but *Mitér* talked him out of it. We stayed hidden in the cabin, far from the seashore, protected for almost six more years, until another interaction nearly got me killed, and *Patér* was set in his decision to appeal to the king of Agrond. The problem was returning after banishment had been punishable by execution. Still, *Patér* was confident he could talk through it, and I remember how *Mitér* pleaded with him, saying if he went, he'd never come back. She was right. *Mitér* was *always* right.

"She wasn't like herself after his death, and once she found out she was expecting Kaid, she gave all her dwindling energy to him, only lasting a few minutes longer after his birth. Killian was twelve, Kell was ten, I was eight, Keagan was six, Kaid was a newborn, and we were completely alone in a place destined to destroy us. I honestly don't know how we made it this far."

There was no hiding the horror on my face, imagining the fear and loss they felt as children, and I was grateful Kiernan's focus was on everything but me.

"I didn't grieve them," he whispered, his eyes glassy as though it still haunted him, "I didn't know how."

My heart broke at the defeat in his tone, and I placed my hand on top of his, offering the only comfort I could. He gladly accepted the touch, flipping his hand and pressing our palms together, mine swallowed whole as his fingers curled around the contact.

"It messed Killian up, and mental scars like that never leave you, but he has been able to heal from it," his voice fell even quieter as he said, "Kell hasn't."

There was a moment of mutual silence, and I determined to let it last as long as he needed, keeping a close eye on him while his sight scanned over our hands, flicking up to my necklace.

"Kell thinks your father killed Kaida," he spoke, and my hand turned tense with the need to grab my shell, but Kiernan securely kept it in his warmth.

"And what do you think?" I asked warily, searching for any shifts in his expression. There were none.

"I try not to think of it at all."

"Do you ever think of living in Agrond?" I hoped to shift the subject off the accusations of my father, a man I loved dearly, who was gentle as he sang with me, and I couldn't picture him assaulting innocent children.

"More than you would assume. I counter the idea with the understanding that I would be separated from most of my brothers, and that helps the dream seem less appealing."

"Why would you be separated?"

"There is a clear hierarchy system that determines your place and role there, depending on your classification. Embers in the palace dictate everything, while serpents are forced to follow and keep to the outer land."

I scowled.

"That's not right. How has it not started a revolt?"

"There isn't a care for it. We don't *feel* as you do. There is loyalty, protection, desire, and fear. Nothing else."

"But you were happy."

"What?"

He shot me that puzzled look again, and it had me overthinking the few things I thought I'd discerned about him.

"Back when we were at the river, you told me you felt happiness," I clarified, grateful when his features softened in comprehension.

"You sang, Ari. There is a tremendous amount of power in your voice, and I'm not sure how you did it, but you have begun to heal a part of me that was very broken. I'm surprised how much you don't understand about yourself. I originally thought you were lying to me when you said you couldn't swim, but you were being honest. A siren that can't swim. How is that possible?"

"I was told my father drowned in a boating accident, and I've feared the water ever since. I never wanted to experience the terror of needing to breathe when you can't, though I suppose that isn't something I need to worry about anymore." I shoved down the memories of the waves pulling me down, him falling unconscious beside me, yet breaths came easier than ever, and my legs were stronger adjoined. "I've been lied to my whole life."

"And I've lived in a lie all of mine," he chuckled that fake laugh again, "Turner isn't even my real name. It's just another cover-up to avoid suspicion."

My head tilted to the side as though the altered view could help me get a better perception of their elaborate attempts to go unnoticed.

"It's not humans you are trying to hide from, is it?"

Kiernan shook his head.

"Sirens lurk on the beaches near Crescent City."

"Why are they there?"

"I don't know, but it's been that way for over a decade."

I didn't understand it, but I wanted to, thinking that I could feel closer to my father with the more answers I had about him.

"Will you tell me about the sirens, Kiernan?"

"No."

It was a quick shutdown, one that left me momentarily stunned.

"Why not?"

"Because I don't want you to change," he admitted openly, refusing to meet my stare, "Your heart is still soft, and if it were ever to be corrupted by the evil of your kind, you would become unrecognizable."

I tried not to think too deeply about what he meant, but I couldn't ignore the twinge of hurt in my chest at his presumptions.

"You think I would hurt somebody?"

"No," he answered, and I could tell he meant it, or at least wanted to, "But you could. If you ever had the desire, you could do terrible things to a person, and the sickest part is you can make them think they want it."

Nausea twisted in my stomach, shuttering unpleasantly throughout my entire body, and I pulled my hand from his.

"If sirens are such horrid creatures, why do you live near them?"

He frowned a little, but it wasn't enough for me to question, noticing how his hand flexed the smallest amount.

"We are far enough away that it's very unlikely that they even know we are here, and besides, the cabin is the home *Patér* built. I can't bring myself to leave the only thing I have left from him, and I know my brothers couldn't either. He placed us here on purpose; the redwoods seemed like the best place in this world for dragons to hide. Did you know even the trees here are fire-resistant?"

I perked up at the chance to show off the knowledge Zadar taught me, pushing past the strange miss I had for him.

"I did, actually. The bark holds too much water to burn. I learned that during training."

He smirked, and I barely caught it from the side of his profile as he remained focused on his hand.

"Nerd," he mumbled, at last sliding his gaze to me, and my mouth dropped in mock offense.

"Okay, mister let-me-give-you-a-full-length-backstory-on-every-single-constellation-in-the-sky."

"You were uneducated. What else was I supposed to do?"

I laughed brightly, and Kiernan's smile lit his entire face, grabbing my wrist to steady my balance, keeping me from falling out of the tree as I freely giggled.

"Ari."

"Yes?" I responded, startled by the sudden seriousness in his expression, and I swallowed the laugh that had built a second ago at the feel of his fingers pressing slightly deeper into my pulse.

"Thank you."

It could've been for many different things. A thank you for seeing him. A thank you for listening. A thank you for understanding. A thank you for staying.

I guessed it was a little of everything, and the sincerity in his eyes put me at a loss for words.

"My family will be wondering where you are. We should probably head back," he informed before I could find my voice, releasing my wrist to climb down, "And one more thing," he called from the tree's base, "Maybe don't mention where we were to Killian. Or Kell, for that matter. I don't think they'd approve if they knew I brought you back to California."

I nodded and watched as he shifted, the dark beast glorious in the daylight, ready to carry me back to my welcoming prison, and I could sense the opportunities slipping from me.

I could've let my necklace slip from me and fall into a pile of moss below. I could've broken branches at angles too odd to miss. I could've scraped my nails against the wood until it left marks. I could've done so many things to give evidence that I was out there, alive, looking for help.

But I didn't.

Chapter Twenty-Three

"**D**o the trick! Do the trick!" I clapped.

Zadar laughed, turning into the friendly horse. It was big and strong and snorted when you touched its nose. I giggled as it neighed against my hand, and Mommy laughed too. She was so pretty when she laughed.

But Mommy didn't smile long. A lot of things distracted her, and right then, it was something outside.

Zadar turned back.

"He's callin' for me," Mommy said. She was staring out the window. I didn't like the look on her face.

"I'll see tae her," Zadar said. He had the same look. Mommy shook her head.

"I dinnae want tae see him ony mair. I'm feart o' Avam. He killed—"

"Noo's no the time, Evie," Zadar stopped Mommy. He cupped one of my ears to block out sounds. "No the time."

Mommy's arms were crossed tightly around her. She looked like she might cry, but she stepped outside where I couldn't see. Maybe she wanted to be sad by herself. I wanted that sometimes.

I turned to Zadar. He was staring at her through the window. I tugged at his hand.

"Is Mommy okay?"

"She'll be fine," he told, and my little ears were too oblivious to catch the whispered, "one day."

I woke up feeling incredibly cold.

"Is something... burning?" I questioned as I opened the door to my room.

It was the middle of the night, a light shower ran along the darkened windows, and every one of the Turners was planted in the living room by the heatless fireplace, everyone apart from Kiernan, that was, whose presence I sensed beside my doorframe the moment I stepped out.

It may have been a silly question to ask a house full of dragons, but the extra scent layered the air, seeping into my room, and the trauma of ruining food in the past pulled me from my sleep. Keagan was the only one to respond, jumping from the couch with a sharp, "Shoot—"

My eyes followed him to the kitchen, analyzing his brisk movements, the light coming back to his face, light that now confronted the small flames inside the oven. I still wasn't sure what my voice had done to him, but after the conversation I had with Kiernan hours ago, learning I had power but unsure of the danger in it, I decided the absence of singing would be best for everyone.

"Your voice is our little secret, okay? Don't share it with anyone else."

If only I'd listened to Father, I likely wouldn't have ended up in this mess. I miss him so much.

Keagan pulled the pan from the oven with his bare hands, blowing out the barely emerging fire to reveal the charcoaled substance, the same color as the dark grey tin holding it.

"So much for a midnight snack," he huffed, staring at his ruined creation with a disappointed frown.

"It's three in the morning," Kell argued from across the room, and I noticed him carefully blow into his hand, catching the tiny blaze in his palm, letting it dance across his fingers. I blinked in fascination, and he caught my stare with a challenging one of his own.

"Kiernan, would you mind opening the windows?" Killian instructed in the form of a question as his focus stayed on Kaid, concentratedly writing the words his older brother instructed, and Kiernan stood from where he sat, towering over me from my left.

"Who thought it was a good idea to let Keagan into the kitchen in the first place?" he complained, and the scowl Keagan formed made me smile. He looked back to normal, almost enough to allow me to forget the image of him crumpled in the forest as despair swam in the mossy pools of his eyes. Almost.

"There's nothing else to do in this boring house," Keagan grunted, struggling to get the rock of what I thought was supposed to be bread out of the container. Kell flicked the miniature blaze into the open fireplace with clear precision, the logs inside bursting into flames at an unnatural pace, and the direct eye contact he made with me was more intimidating than anything. He was itching for a fight, likely payback for the punch I hadn't meant to initiate, and I recalled our last one-on-one quarrel ending with a knife wound in his shoulder and a gash in my leg. Though he was completely healed and I nearly the same, the last thing I wanted was a fresh injury, so I dropped my gaze and turned back to my room until I was told otherwise.

"Come look at this, Ari," Kiernan beckoned, holding open a window that should've been too big to maneuver, but he maintained it with little effort as the trapped smoke escaped into the rain, and I wondered if his strength didn't shift to match human even when he was in his alternate form.

By now, I should've been used to being watched, but I felt every single eye on me as I walked past the large space, tracking, waiting, bracing for me to move unnaturally or do the wrong thing, as though I was the one who could transform into a lethal beast, and I made sure to keep my focus on Kiernan to distract my growing unease.

He smiled as I approached, opening the window a little farther to give me a clear view of the light storm, creating little pools throughout the forest floor. I focused on the puddles, imagining being tiny enough to swim in them, splashing and giggling as the rain soaked into my hair.

"Do fairies exist, too?" I asked while stretching my arm outside to feel the sky's tears warm against my palm, and Kiernan reached to do the same.

Does like the rain.

I inwardly congratulated my small success.

"Yes, but in a world far from this one. I don't think they could survive here," Kiernan confirmed, and I pictured a world where they could survive, mushroom houses and moss plains, wondering what they would think of redwoods, a place where *I* felt entirely too small. "Every creature that you have heard of in those fairy tale stories lives in their own realm, but they are real."

"Except unicorns," Keagan added, and I had forgotten Kiernan and I weren't alone for a moment, his voice jolting my attention, "As if that wasn't obvious. Horses with long horns that eat rainbows or whatever they do." He shook his head, smiling that smile he easily charmed others with. "Humans are so silly."

My laugh caught them off guard.

"So, dragons are not impossible to believe, but unicorns are where you draw the line?"

"At least we can *fly*," he argued, and I laughed once more.

"But it doesn't make sense," Kaid's voice broke in, and it took longer than it should've for me to realize he was talking to Killian and not joining our conversation, "I can't get it."

I peered over at them sitting on the couch while pulling my hand from the rain and wiping it across my borrowed clothes, seeing the youngest's face scrunched in confusion, as Killian patiently leaned over him to see the paper Kaid held.

"That's a 'd', Kaid. It's supposed to be a 'b'," he corrected gently, and Kaid only appeared more perplexed.

"But they are the same. One is just turned around."

Before I could talk myself out of it, I began walking to them, leaving Kiernan on his own at the window and Keagan still fighting the burnt bread in the dish. It was a mistake to glance at Kell as I passed, yet I fell prey to the hope that he was distracted by something else for once, but he was *always* watching me, and this time was no different. There was a part of me that softened to his burning hate, knowing every traumatic thing that happened to him at such a young age, but I knew I wouldn't necessarily be the politest to anyone I believed wanted to harm Anders. I just needed him to see I wasn't a threat.

I stopped in front of Killian and Kaid.

"But they are two different letter—" Killian broke off his statement, both of them glancing up at me in unison so perfectly it looked unsettling, and I sensed the nerves building under their intense stares.

"May I help?" I offered, trying to keep my hand still as it itched to hold my necklace.

Killian's face, as usual, revealed nothing, while Kaid's was hesitant and a bit fearful, and I kept a tight seal on my emotions despite how tense the air became. The older glanced at the younger; the decision passed in silence, and after a second, Kaid scooted to make room for me beside him. Killian remained quiet, but it was clear he wasn't sure about his brother's invite from how he warily watched me. I was careful with my movements, conscious of the fact Kaid was triggered more easily than the rest of them, and the last time we were this close, his hands were tied, keeping him from transforming. That wasn't the case anymore.

I slowly shifted the paper in my direction, painfully aware of how heavily I was being monitored, and I spoke clearly enough for them all to hear as I put the pencil into motion.

"I had a younger brother back at my old home." I hated saying it in the past tense, like he was some distant memory I fought to remember, though that was the furthest thing from my truth. "He struggled with his d's and b's, too. I used to work with him for hours after school."

I shaped the letter b on the paper, extending for the writing to create other lines around it, and Kaid cocked his head as he watched.

"It wasn't until I showed him this little trick that he finally got it," I continued, adding eyes to the simple sketch and making sure the drawing appeared happy, "B is the first letter in the word boy, right?"

Kaid nodded, and I gifted him back the paper.

"Well, using that letter, you can draw a boy's face. See how it makes up the side of his head and one eye?"

He blinked at the picture a few times as though I'd presented this grand optical illusion, and I found behind the dullness in his expression, Killian was slightly amused. I handed Kaid his pencil, and he eagerly took it, not waiting for instruction to begin drawing.

"There you go," I encouraged, smiling as he drew a face of his own with the letter, his eyes sparkling with excitement as he looked up at me for approval, "Try it a couple more times."

"How is Evelyn?"

Killian's sudden question completely derailed my train of thought, and I had to remove my attention from Kaid's work to understand his words.

"She's... not like she used to be," I responded with drawn brows, wondering how discussion of Mother came about. I looked to Kiernan, the only comfort I still had, as I talked about such an uncomfortable topic. His eyes were set on Kell, that silent discussion wading behind them, and I hadn't noticed how truly endearing it was with his face set that way. "Were you close to her?"

"She was *theía* to me."

"A what?"

"Aunt. Sorry. I'm not used to translating names into English."

"You speak Greek?"

"When I find the excuse to, but there isn't much of a point here. It's the language of the dragons, and we are far from our kind. *Mitér* didn't get very far in teaching me, but I could carry on a discussion if the opportunity ever presented itself. I've done my best to pass it on, but as you can see," a short glance to the boy sat between us, "English is a hardship on its own."

Kiernan was looking at me now, and I couldn't read his expression, but it wasn't a quiet debate as he had with Kell, which I also couldn't tell was a good thing or not. The cabin was free from smoke, but he kept the window open, and everyone was too concentrated on the conversation between Killian and me to care; even Keagan paused his battle with the bread to listen.

"Does she still paint?" Killian continued, bringing my focus back to him instead of his brother by the window I'd unknowingly been staring at, "Your mother?"

It was a struggle not to scoff.

"It's all she ever does anymore," I answered as politely as I could, but the words still tasted bitter in my mouth.

"Does she still sing?"

I shook my head, unable to recall the sound, as I was desperate for faded memories of the old her.

"Mother is deaf."

"Deaf?" He questioned, the briefest flicker of concern moving behind his dull mask. "How did that happen?"

I shook my head again, opening my mouth before pausing in confusion, rushing through my memories for the answer.

"I... I don't remember," I admitted after recalling childhood in a few seconds.

There was Mother with her hearing, alive and joyful; then there was Mother without her hearing, hollow and distant; but no matter how long I stared at the floor in concentration, I couldn't find how those two instances crossed. It should've been something I knew off the top of my head, maybe even something to keep me up at night, but it was simply... missing, a hole in my memories that couldn't be patched. I wanted to blame it on my unreliable age to retain information such as that, but it was different from the fuzzy recollections of a child. It was just blank, and I questioned how I had never thought of it sooner.

There was the gentlest poke on my arm, and Kaid rested his accomplishment on my lap, not quite brave enough to face me, but the small, proud smile he formed was noticeable.

"Could you... help me with this, too?" Kaid questioned tentatively, and I was still trying to piece my understanding together as he placed arithmetic sheets in front of me, which I graciously accepted. Killian stood to aid Keagan, silently entrusting me with the youngest, feeling like the softest hand of approval over my shoulder, and I dared a glance at Kell. His eyes were softer than I'd ever seen them when observing Kaid before catching me, reverting back to hard and unchanging, and I may have imagined it, but it appeared almost forced.

I focused back on Kaid, and as we began work, everything else faded into the background. I didn't hear talking in the kitchen, or Keagan fitfully throwing the whole pan in the garbage, or the rain cease, I just drew more pictures to help Kaid count and told myself that he was Anders, and I was home, and my life was no longer in constant danger.

It wasn't very effective, especially when Killian pulled Kaid from the studies, claiming the storm had passed and it was time to hunt. Again, I was alone with Kiernan in a home much too large for two people pretending to be human.

"That was kind of you to help Kaid," Kiernan offered, claiming the empty seat next to him while I was forced back into the reality I'd never escape from.

"Kaid reminds me of my brother," I answered, feeling the need to cry, but reminding myself I promised not to unless I was alone, so instead, all that came out was a constricted, "I love Anders so much."

Kiernan went quiet, but I could feel his eyes on me, could see his remorseful expression in my mind, yet his next words were the furthest from what I would've expected.

"What does love feel like?"

I turned to him, taken aback and put into silence, willing myself to understand the sincerity in his eyes. It wasn't ridiculous for him to ask, but how long it took me to find my voice was.

"I never saw love as a feeling. I always believed it to be more of a promise."

The kind of undying devotion a parent shares with their child.

"Can you describe it?"

I glanced down at my hands, only to see the pale skin that Mother and I shared, as my fingers began to tremble. She told me she loved me, but that was years ago, and I wasn't sure what I believed about my childhood anymore.

"No," I voiced, unable to release the invisible clutch on my throat, "I cannot."

She never loved you. Never deserved it. Weren't good enough. Failed her. Failed Anders. Couldn't help him. Caused him fear. Failed Father. Can't obey. Can't listen. Can't be loved.

It happened again, the sensation of losing all control, tripping, melting, falling into places I didn't want to go, things I didn't want to feel, and it was so much darker this time. I couldn't see or scream for help, caged in a world of black, heavy in ways that didn't make sense, and Kiernan caught me just before I fell under.

His hands are on you. He's holding you still. Not falling. He cares. He cares. Why does he care? Doesn't make sense. He should let you fall. He won't. Why won't he? Almost like he wants you. Almost like he lov—

"...Ari! Ari, are you *listening* to me? Can you hear me?"

I could then, the worry in his tone, the increasing volume, and my throat ached to echo back.

"I'm sorry," I rasped, but it didn't relieve the desire, as though words were not what I wished to free. Kiernan was holding my shoulders, and I was crying, two things that took longer than necessary to process. "I don't know what happened."

"You stopped talking and... breathing. There was nothing in your eyes. I've never seen you like that before," he informed, like he was trying to piece together a reasonable conclusion, and while his voice maintained concern, his touch stayed.

"I'm sorry," I repeated, desperate to move closer to him, sounding just as hopeless as I had when I locked myself in that room, but this time, Kiernan didn't have to ask me what I needed. He leaned back on the couch and drew me with him without restraint, near enough that I could feel his steadying breaths and sinking into his heat, new, fresh tears spilled down my cheeks.

"What is this feeling?" he asked, sinking his fingers into my hair and bringing my forehead to rest against the side of his neck.

"Hurt," I choked, "It's like an open wound in your heart being pelted over and over until you think the ache will never go away."

That one was easy enough to describe.

"Does it go away?" he asked, stroking my hair, the fire in his fingertips occasionally brushing the side of my face, warming nerves under my skin that prickled sweetly at his touch.

"I don't know."

I hated how weak my voice sounded; I hated how I was everything I promised myself not to be, hating mostly that I wanted to stay like this forever.

"Who hurt you, Ari?"

I attempted to shake my head, but all it accomplished was burying myself deeper into his hold.

"It doesn't matter."

"Does she know how she hurt you?" he questioned next, proving his understanding to get me to open up, but I could feel my body shutting down in every area.

"I'm exhausted," I murmured, deflecting his persistence while my eyes fell closed.

"Because of your nightmares?"

"You know?" I whispered, but of course he did. There was nothing about me hidden from him.

"Your heart rate will pick up at random points in the night, and your breathing becomes shallower when you first wake."

"You can... hear all of that?"

"Yes. Even now, your heart is beating like it does when you are resting."

My mind attempted to understand his words, but his pulse was in my ear, sweet and calming, easing statements out of me that I lacked the sense to control.

"Kiernan," I spoke his name, and it felt different on my tongue, and some loopy part of my brain wanted to repeat it over and over again.

"Ari?" he responded, his voice soothing my mind further, putting away painful memories and protecting me from unwanted dreams.

"Please don't leave," I begged, consciousness slipping from my head to my fingertips curling into his shirt. I wasn't worried about his disappearing physically, after all, Mother lived in the same house where I saw her almost daily, but she wasn't truly *there*.

"I won't," he whispered, "I promise."

I think he knew what I was asking, and my heart believed him.

I fell asleep feeling incredibly warm.

Chapter Twenty-Four

S moke tickled my nose, but it wasn't like the air had been when food was burning; this was sweet and delicate, tainted with warm memories unlocking in my barely conscious mind.

Bandaging your wound. Wrapping you in a blanket. Stealing your soup. Carrying you in a dance. Never letting you fall. Always careful. Always warm.

All the memories smelled just like this moment, and I wanted to curl into it with the heat beneath me, soaking it into every fiber of my being until I was permanently stained with the scent, forever encased in the thought that I was wanted.

My head tingled pleasantly at the feel of fingers softly combing through my hair, gingerly touching my scalp to avoid rustling me awake, but with every second passing, I became more aware of where I was and with whom. My hand was fisted around his shirt like it normally did my necklace, while the weight of his free hand rested over the middle of my back, thumb tracing the indentation in my spine. He must've sensed my consciousness returning, the generous touches fading as though something so meaningful would be unwanted in my wake.

It still felt like a dream even as I opened my eyes, the sound of his heart pressed over my ear, steady and secure.

He stayed.

The rest of the night, he stayed with me, warding off the loneliness and silencing the aching whispers. My mind was quiet when he was around, even from the first time we met, his presence overcame crippling thoughts, and subconsciously, I always knew I was safe when with him, despite not always knowing why.

My head was heavy when attempting to lift it, groggily glancing around the empty living room. The light cascading through the generous windows told me it was close to midday, that I had entirely overslept, and Kiernan and I were still alone. Normally, I would have scolded myself for resting so long, but my muscles groaned in thanks, drowning exhaustion slowly relinquishing its weighty claws, and as my sight turned to Kiernan, whose head lay over the couch's arm, I couldn't bring myself to regret it.

Lemon curd, he is beautiful.

A strand of hair had fallen into his line of view, a small detail that made the rest of his perfect features seem the tiniest bit more human, simpler for my sluggish brain to comprehend, yet still in awe. His eyes held the same contentment I felt throughout my entire body, masking his countenance into a blissful calm, yet as I studied how the sunbeams fit his completion, his heartbeat quickened under my palm. Even the pounding in his chest was gentle against my hand, each movement careful enough to nearly convince me that the skin I wore was made of the most delicate glass.

Without my own permission, I was moving, repositioning until I was closer to his face, balancing my weight on one arm, enabling the other to reach for him. Kiernan didn't blink as my fingertips grazed his brow, brushing the stray hair away from his eyes, holding my stare with enough intensity to enact a heated shade of red to blossom over my skin.

I wanted him to never stop holding me, touching me, looking at me like *that*, like I was something, like I was *everything*.

Slowly, my hand brushed down the side of his face, and I was guilty of the way I savored every touch, my vision dancing over tightening brows, warm cheeks, pointed nose, curved lips...

His lips.

I couldn't tear my focus from them. They were something I seemed to miss in the grandeur of his eyes, and before I could stop the thought, I wondered if they were as soft as they looked. When my eyes found his again, the contentment in vibrant green was gone, replaced by an unspoken desire that I, too, experienced deep in my chest, shutting out everything else around me. Kiernan's hand tangled in my hair, lowering my head until my forehead rested on his, and I could hear the grounding intakes of oxygen he drew. His eyes fell shut, and mine did the same, trapping me in the divine oblivion that allowed me to shun the part of me that screamed to run away, the rapidly diminishing part that still held the smallest ounce of fear for him.

"Kiernan," I whispered, my throat aching to voice more, but my breath caught as he slightly tilted his head to the side, brushing his nose against mine. He hummed back, not in answer to me but in reaction to how his name sounded in my breathy tones, desperate to express everything I felt about him.

"I—"

The front door opened.

I was worried I hurt Kiernan by how aggressively I shoved away from his chest, but his mask of indifference was up in an instant, leaving no signs of what just happened, though it didn't matter; I wasn't fast enough.

Killian caught the briefest sight of his brother and the deadly monster they thought I could be dangerously close to crossing a line, and the painful blush that stained my features did nothing to aid the situation.

I arranged my hair to fall over my back, fixing the strands Kiernan held mere heartbeats ago, my hand skimming over my neck and shocking my fingers at the sensation of a water-like substance lingering there, but I was too flustered to give it attention. My back was too stiff, my skin too flushed, and I knew I shouldn't have glimpsed Killian, but the silence ached, and the presumed scrutiny tugged at my nerves, forcing me to look his way. Killian's gaze was questioning and edged in a clear suspicion while glancing me over, hardening slightly when shifting to his brother, an expectant stare to which Kiernan met shamelessly, almost daring him to say something.

"I'm telling you, Kell, he's out there, and if we go searching together like a wonderful, *unified* family, we're bound to find him," Keagan's voice cut in as he entered the house, piercing through the tension like a hot iron to snow, "Killian agrees with me."

"I do what?" Killian prompted, eyeing Kiernan a second longer before turning to the boy who knew just what to say when things got too quiet, and I could've sighed in relief from the way the heaviness in the room lifted.

"Agree that we should go looking for Sasquatch."

"Not this again," the eldest grumbled, moving past Kiernan and me to the kitchen, where I struggled to get a read on him.

"*Patér* believed in him. You, of all people, should remember how diligently he searched."

Keagan lifted his head higher, straightening his shoulders while a hand came to his chest as he vowed, "I must carry on the legacy of our bloodline."

I watched Killian disappointedly shake his head as he grabbed something from the pantry, Kell and Kaid coming into view.

"Keagan, *Patér* told us that to keep us busy during the day to give *Mitér* a break." It was almost startling to hear Kell speak in normal tones that didn't lead to threats on my life, but he paid no heed to the couch I shared with Kiernan, which meant he didn't witness what Killian did, and my odds of burning to death significantly decreased. "There is no ridiculously tall and hairy creature hiding in these woods."

"You think that because you are broken in the brains," Keagan snipped.

Kiernan immediately gave me a knowing look, and I tried my best to keep my laughter down, but a quiet giggle escaped, drawing attention from the kitchen.

Kiernan smiled at me. I smiled at him. Killian watched us both.

"I say if he wants to traipse around the forest looking for a storybook character, then let him. The house will be quieter while he's gone," Kiernan joined, ignoring Killian's analyzing gaze entirely as he attempted not to chuckle at Keagan's irked expression

"You don't think Bigfoot is real?" I questioned, hoping to attain his nonchalance, but the sound of my voice gripped the notice of an otherwise preoccupied room, and I forgot how to distract the hands fiddling with my shell.

"You do?" Kiernan questioned, and if he would just stop *smiling* at me like that, maybe I could convince myself this electric twinge he put in my heart when he faced me was some strange form of anxiety. I stood, creating distance from him before prior unwarranted actions could get the better of me, masking my cowardice in siding with his younger brother.

"I didn't before I met you. Now I think I'd believe anything," I argued, standing next to Keagan, whose brows were lifted in surprise at my participation, "Even someone who finds unicorns ridiculous."

"I knew I liked you," the all-too-excited boy murmured to me, bumping me with an elbow, but my focus remained on the boy still grinning at me, making me wish for things I shouldn't be longing for.

"You do realize what you are saying, right?" Kiernan prompted, and it took all my sheer willpower not to see who was still watching us, scrutinizing our behavior.

"You do realize that Sasquatch was living here first, right?" I mocked his words with a grin, and I could see the moment something shifted behind his eyes, animalistic in the way it was set.

It was a new challenge, a new game, a new excuse for me to get out of the house and straighten my thoughts.

"All right then. Prove me wrong."

"I will," I assured, crossing my arms and lifting my head, "Keagan knows where we will look."

"I do..." Keagan agreed, though the hesitance in his tone gave me pause, "But we can't get there on foot."

"Then it's a good thing the rain hasn't returned," I settled, turning to Keagan, who smiled before shifting.

More than just Killian watched as I faced the dragon before me without fear.

"Prepare yourself, for these are the things mankind was never meant to see," Keagan readied, fingers tightening around the plant hovering above the softened ground. I leaned in when he pushed away the fern, revealing a massive track in the mud, and I bit my lip to hold back the laugh clogging my throat.

"Keagan..." I started, stopping when my amusement came through my voice, pressing two fingers to my mouth to cover my smile.

"What?" he demanded, brows drawn, "It's a print of a *big foot*."

"From a *bear*."

Keagan crossed his arms.

"Sasquatch would be very offended to hear such accusations."

I couldn't hold in my laughter any longer, giggles tumbling out, and the genuine look of shock on Keagan's face only added to the comedy.

"Oh, so this is funny to you now?" he fussed, but I could hear the struggle in his voice to hold down chuckles, "You know, I don't appreciate your fickleness. You told me you believed me."

"I did... still do but thought you had a valid lead."

"I'd like to see you find something more *valid*," he pitted, eyes narrowing and reminding me of the snake-like beast that brought me here, but the sparkle in them proved the behavior to be playful.

"Okay," I agreed, starting on a new path, "I'll take this side, and you take that one?"

"Deal."

And with that, I was aimlessly walking, searching for something I doubted existed the longer time went on, in hopes of distracting myself from something that was *very* real. I spun the chain around my neck in a fidget, unresponsive to the way it felt damp moving across my fingers. My eyes skipped across the misty wood, looking for an escape from a reality I hadn't allowed myself to accept, but it was no use. Everything reminded me of him.

The ground was uneven, like the ground I chased him on in our exhilarating game of tag. The wind pressed into the trees like my back into the bark as he kept me from falling, breeze tangling in the branches as his hand did in my hair while I rested on him. Droplets clinging to the environment of the old storm plummeted to the soft dirt, creating new showers, calm enough not to limit the dragon with me but sweet enough to bring me back to the dance I shared with him in the pouring rain. And the stupid, wonderful, life-filled greens were impossible to miss in every plant in this never-ending forest.

Lost in memories that I recalled too much detail from, I almost tripped off a cliff hidden by the ferns, throwing my arms out to aid balance. I stared at the ground far beneath the grass I stood upon, judging how long a fall it would be before I hit the earth. Pondering the pain that would spread through my limbs on impact should've made me back away, but it was the first thought I had that didn't involve Kiernan, and I eagerly welcomed it.

"Hey, Keagan!"

The boy I no longer feared lifted his attention from the ground he focused on, finding me across the stretch of forest, smiling daringly.

"I trust you!" I shouted, then tipped off the edge, catching the shortest sight of panicked eyes and green wings as I fell. The feeling of my stomach tangling in my throat lasted a total of three seconds before the shirt Kiernan gave me just a day prior was punctured by sharp talons, barely missing my skin. I was dropped to the ground rather spitefully, and I rolled on my back, chuckling breathlessly while damp grass tickled me through the torn patches of the oversized top I wore.

"*Never* do that again," Keagan ordered with an unsettled tremor in his voice, running a hand through his ruffled hair.

"Why?" I prodded, still laughing at the pale tint that had overcome his tan face.

"Kier would kill me if I brought you back broken."

My heart tumbled, immediately failing my mission to forget him for longer than five seconds, but Keagan thankfully missed how my expression abruptly dropped, continuing with, "I doubt he will be happy about me ripping his shirt."

"You told me to jump off a cliff," I argued, clearing my throat and throwing my smile back on, desperate to deter the conversation.

"*Last time*, I was prepared to catch you," he corrected, shooting me a glare while he cooled his features.

"You caught me just fine."

"*Just barely*, I think you mean."

"I thought it was fun," I added with a shrug, grinning the same way he always had when messing with me, "But I'll be sure to give you more of a heads-up next time."

"You lemon..."

"Go on," I prompted, prepared for another mocking of my saying, and Keagan shook his head.

"Nope. Just lemon. You know, tiny and constantly sour. Fits you perfectly."

"Strong words coming from an apricot," I fired back, and Keagan's mouth fell open, a surprised laugh escaping, and it may have been that my head was still not cleared, but the sound seemed to resemble Kiernan's perfectly.

"*Language*," he reprimanded, chuckling but attempting to appear offended as he did, plopping himself down at the base of a redwood facing me. "Okay, but can we at least agree Killian is an orange?"

I wasn't exactly sure how we got on such a random topic or even what half of it meant, but I was happy with it. I assumed most conversations with friends were similar to that.

"Only if you agree that Kaid is a blueberry," I said, but what I left out was how my little brother loved the fruit, and the resemblance helped soothe an inner ache.

Keagan nodded approvingly. "Yes, I could see that. Kell's like a grape."

"Grape*fruit*," I countered, and the finger Keagan had placed over his chin in contemplation pointed directly at me.

"*Yes*! That's exactly it."

I swallowed and hoped my voice gave nothing away as I spoke his name.

"Kiernan?"

"Hands down, an avocado."

"Is that even a fruit?"

"Exactly."

"What?" I questioned, utterly confused, but managing to find the fun in it.

"Kier is a fruit but thinks he's a vegetable, and Mr. Orange doesn't like that very much. They'll argue sometimes, but it's nothing like the fights he and Mr. Grapefruit will get into." Something flashed behind his eyes, an emotion too quick for me to identify, the rest of his features settled into ease, "Kiernan is the most rebellious out of us all. When he thinks something is right, it doesn't matter what anyone says; he won't change his mind. When we were younger, he was convinced the stars were the sun's tears trapped in the sky after it set. He was so confident about it at the age of six that he persuaded me." I was able to identify the new light that came to his eyes, a clear flicker of admiration, a brightness I'd witnessed Anders give me once or twice, a want for approval from the older. "Back then, he'd argue about the sky, but now he disputes about sirens, and I fear I may be siding with him again. Though, I don't see Kell staying content with how things are going." I looked down at my lap, fiddling with my hands, and Keagan's tone lifted, bumping me with his arm as he confidently stated, "Mr. Apricot, on the other hand... he's perfect. Can do no wrong."

"The charred bread told me otherwise," I reminded not so gently, glancing at him with a prodding smile.

"It was supposed to be a cake," he grumbled, "It's not my fault I was never taught how to cook."

"So, who taught you how to be such a shameless flirt?"

"No one, Love. That just comes naturally," he answered with a wink, and I rolled my eyes. "Everything wonderful about me comes naturally. It's really a shame I couldn't talk to you at the party. I'm sure we would've gotten along well."

"I wouldn't have wanted to distract you from the group of girls hoping to experience the *natural ability* you had for kissing at midnight," I mocked, trying not to think of the headache that evening had been.

"Oh, I would be an excellent kisser..." he agreed, giving an awkward pause before finishing, "that is, if I ever got the chance to."

"All this flirting you've done with girls and never at any time kissed one?"

"Killian has a very strict *'look but don't touch'* policy when it comes to humans," he explained as he plucked at shorter plants outlining his long legs, "It's to keep everyone safe, I understand that, but it doesn't stop the desires. I guess that makes me selfish: to want more than this sad, secluded, *safe* life we have. It's truly pathetic the amount of time I've spent thinking through every possibility, every scenario in which I find a way to settle down with a human girl who could handle me, the actual me, and I haven't found one that didn't end in tragedy. I can't form attachments with people. None of us can. Not here," he flicked a strand of grass between his fingers, unamused and unpleased, before flicking his gaze to me, "You really opened my eyes to that, you know. It was something I always knew, but it didn't truly hit me until after I heard you sing. I will never have the privilege of loving someone."

'You are afraid of being alone for a lifetime.'

I pictured him crumpling to the ground, broken and despaired, voicing fears of his own while on the hunt for mine, and guilt clutched my throat.

"I'm sorry, Keagan. I didn't mean to hurt you."

"Things have to hurt before they can heal," he stated, giving one of those smiles that revealed the pain creased in the corners, "It may ache, but at least I can *feel* it. I'm not empty anymore, and I have you to thank for that."

"Do your brothers know?"

"Killian does. He tends to know things before someone is able to figure it out themselves," I swallowed, trying not to let my mind wander to the conclusions the eldest was drawing about me and Kiernan. "But I doubt the rest have picked up on anything. Despite my charms and great sense of humor, I am not the main attention. Kaid is. Along with Kell, when he is especially aggravated with something, which happens more than not."

"You will find someone," I promised, but the words didn't weigh in the air the same as I felt them in my chest, and although Keagan's smile was kind, his eyes held disbelief.

"Your positivity is admirable, Ari."

"I mean it, *Agapiti*," I pressed, hoping to present my gravity through a language personal to him, but the sharp, puzzled look he sent me had me rethinking that idea.

"Why would you call me that?" he demanded, his brows drawn downward in a disconcerting stare.

"Because you are my friend," I answered, thinking he may not reciprocate the feeling, and Keagan's responding chuckle wasn't the reassurance I hoped it'd be.

"Ari, unless you would like to be more than friends, I wouldn't suggest using that terminology."

"Did I use the wrong word? I'm sorry. Still trying to figure out this whole Greek thing."

Keagan tilted his head, amusement lining his facial features as he quizzed, "What do you think *Apapití* means?"

"Friend. That's what Kiernan told me," I fumbled in answer, worried I'd done something offensive, and Keagan's smirk only grew, beautiful face lighting up in entertainment.

"Did he call you that?" he questioned rather smugly.

"Yes, but he wasn't really conscious—" Keagan laughed, bright and full, interrupting my thought process. "What is so funny?"

"*Agapití* does not mean friend, Ari."

"Won't you explain it then?"

"That," he stated, standing from the tree's base, "is not for me to tell you. Come on. We have a Bigfoot to find."

He offered his hand, and I took it, allowing him to bring me to my feet. Once I was stable, Keagan looked at me for a long moment, and I didn't feel the need to shrink away, not when his eyes carried warmth.

"Oh, Mr. Avocado, what have you gotten yourself into?" he mumbled to himself, chuckling as he did, but I couldn't miss the smallest lilt of worry in his voice.

Chapter Twenty-Five

Mommy was screaming.

I didn't like the sound. It scared me.

I tripped running down the stairs, but she didn't see. She was crying in her room. Zadar was there, which was strange. Mommy didn't say he was coming for a visit again.

"I've tae see him! Ye dinnae understand!" Mommy yelled, "He's in ma heid! Callin', singin', demandin' I follow him! It only stops when I see him! I've tae see him! He cannae be gone, Zadar! He cannae be deid!" She started coughing like I did when I ate too fast, and I wanted to pat her on the back like she always did for me, but Zadar reached her first.

"Evie? Evie, listen tae me. Ye're in shock, awricht? We'll sort this oot, but ye've tae breathe!"

He was very close to her. It looked like he was going to give Mommy a hug, but she backed away.

"He told me he was comin' back! He promised it would only hurt a wee while! It hurts! It hurts *terrible*! I need him tae make it *stop*!"

"Mommy?"

Mommy and Zadar didn't know I was there until I said something. I wanted her to be happy again, but when she looked at me, she didn't smile.

"Whit am I supposed tae dae aboot her?" I didn't know why, but it hurt to hear her say that. Mommy kept looking at me, but I wasn't the one she was talking to. "I can barely be a mother as it is. How am I meant tae be a single parent? I dinnae even ken how tae tell her…"

I hadn't heard Mommy call herself 'mother' before. Maybe she would like it better if I said that instead.

"Let me talk tae her. Ye just take a second tae calm yersel, awricht?"

Mother didn't nod. Her eyes were too big for the rest of her face. I was grateful when Zadar lowered himself to my height, so I didn't have to see the tears anymore.

"Why is she crying?" I asked.

"Ariella... yer father..." Zadar paused, and I could hear Mother breathing loudly, "he's gone."

I blinked, confused. "I know, but he will be back soon. He said so."

Daddy told me he was going on a trip a while ago. I was sad I couldn't go with him, but he said it wasn't going to be a fun trip, so I couldn't be too sad. Then, he gave me a pretty shell to look at whenever I missed him. I carried it with me everywhere.

Zadar looked sad, and I wanted to show him my shell so he could be happy, too, but he lowered my hand when I tried.

"Naw... Lass, he's no comin' back."

Mother picked something up. Her hands were shaking.

"Why not?" I asked Zadar, but I watched Mother. I couldn't see what she was holding, but it had a point at the end. Zadar gently took my hand.

"Because he's deid."

Mother shoved the object into her head. It was one of her drawing pencils. She screamed again.

Zadar stood and ran to her.

Blood was everywhere.

I was scared.

The door was shut in my face.

I woke up.

Sick was too kind a word to describe the twisting in my stomach, a hole in my memory seamed together, and I felt every excruciating puncture of the stitches.

Mother deafened herself—mother deafened herself, and the last thing she heard was her own scream.

A cold sweat trickled down my back, coating my skin in chilling shock and heated discomfort, and I couldn't decide whether I wanted to shove the sheets off me or pull them closer. I sipped at the air as though it could suffice the water my lungs craved, trying not to think how real the blood on her hands looked, how her anguish echoed in my mind like a forgotten memory, or how I was shut out for the first time.

Closed doors; can't let you see.

The door I now faced was one used to keep me in rather than force out, but I felt no different from the helpless little girl in my surreal dreams. The wood crumpled my new, untorn shirt as I slid down the closed entrance, gathering my limbs into a tight ball in hopes of keeping myself from falling apart, and while leaning my head against the frame, I caught the slight shift from the other side.

"Can't sleep?" Kiernan asked, voice quiet but not a whisper, and simply hearing him speak, knowing I wasn't alone, helped me to reject the tears that wished to spill.

"No," I admitted, resting my eyelids only to open them when Mother's pained face became too apparent, changing the subject when my ears began to ache as I imagined them being pieced through, "Do you ever sleep?"

Kiernan's chuckle was muffled by our separation.

"I do, just not as much as you. You humans love your sleep."

I could hear the grin in his words, provoking me to form my own. I held on to the thought of him smiling, no longer distant and evasive, desperate to avoid another ache grinding in my ribcage.

Since Keagan and I returned from our escapade, Kiernan had resorted to avoiding me in looks as well as nearness, just as he had after we danced in the rain and were closer than ever. I hadn't known it to be possible to be even closer to someone until this morning, when we shared a couch too small for the both of us to sleep on, and it was clear to me now that I was the problem.

You make him uncomfortable. Doesn't want to hold you. Doesn't want to have you.

Doesn't want you.

But when I thought back to how carefully he touched me, how his heart raced, how he brought me closer, the accusations lost their fierceness. I slipped my fingers under the slim opening beneath the door, because when it came down to it, I was selfish and just wanted to be touched by him once more. There was a moment when the coolness of chilled floorboards sank into my palms, then divine, intoxicating heat brushed against my knuckles, resting over my hand, and I was too slow to catch the contented sigh that fell from my lips. It was quiet and barely audible to my ears, but I knew Kiernan heard it, just as he could hear the very beat of my heart, and his fingers curled around mine in reply.

"Do you want to talk about it?" Kiernan nearly whispered, and something coiled in my stomach at those words, a reaction to the same question I asked

Anders nearly every night for almost thirteen years. It wasn't until now that I understood why my brother went so many nights without wishing to discuss his nightmares, and while I didn't want to speak of the horrors my subconscious witnessed, I did want a distraction. I wanted to ask Kiernan to dance with me until my legs numbed in exhaustion and my head fell limp on his chest or simply lay with him and count his breaths until I'd forgotten what I'd been upset over in the first place, but both of those required him near me, touching me, and I couldn't handle him distancing himself further from the interaction.

"Could we go stargazing again?" I asked, knowing it was an activity he wouldn't choose to avoid, something we could do together through separation. Kiernan's hand released mine as he shuffled to his feet, clicking the door open, and I scurried to face him. I suddenly felt very shy seeing him, his head tilted in doubt, eyes illuminated in the darkness, an unrecognizable emotion bleeding from the green.

"You'd be willing to do that?"

"Why wouldn't I?" I questioned back, but Kiernan looked unsure as he held the door, debating whether to let me out or not. It was difficult for me to picture him grinning when he stared as though he expected me to change my mind, but I didn't intend to, and I think he could see that. "I wasn't able to count all the stars last time."

"So, you admit it?" The faintest phantom of a smile played on his lips. "It's impossible."

"I already told you I don't like that word."

"Doesn't change anything."

"It could."

"No, Ari. It can't."

He pinned me with a stare I hadn't seen from him, stern and bordering on harshness, and it felt too personal to still be talking about the night sky.

"Why not?" I inquired, hoping to catch the heavy discussion behind his eyes, but he dropped my gaze before I could read the answers I searched for.

"Someone will get hurt," he explained in a heavy tone, his hands clenching into fists, and it took everything in me not to reach for him.

"Kiernan," I called instead, and he thankfully responded with his attention, "I want to see the stars."

Immediately, he snapped back into cool indifference, the mask he wore when he needed to keep his feelings hidden, and I hated how it stole all the light from his face. Kiernan didn't argue with me, though, stepping out of the entrance and allowing me to pass and head for the front door.

It was a cloudless night, the sky dusted in glittering jewels, and I didn't get the chance to take it in as I was swept from my feet by a large tail and placed on the dark dragon's back. I tried asking where he was taking us, but the response I got was one I couldn't understand: a soft growl that I felt pressed beneath me, and it wasn't until familiar woods came into view that I recognized where we were.

Kiernan had mentioned that our tree was the best place to view the stars, and while cautiously being placed on solid ground, my eyes glued to the sky, I realized how right he was. The tree stood in the center of a small patch of forest free of redwoods, displaying the heavens in all its grandeur, and the constellations came alive the longer I stared.

"What is it you are looking for?" Kiernan questioned, sitting on the ground closer to me than I thought he would've, close enough to feel the heat spill off his skin.

"A way to forget."

Kiernan went suddenly silent, but I could *feel* him analyzing me, as if he were looking for something as well. I began counting the planets, if only to keep my thoughts from racing over things I couldn't control, change, or have.

"What do you see?"

He sounded nearer, and the attempt to control the way my heart picked up in pace was useless. He didn't sound as he did in the cabin, hardened and quieted; he sounded curious, hopeful, desiring.

"Stories," I told, keeping my sight upward, knowing if he appeared as wishful as his voice led me to believe, I would convince myself that what almost happened that morning was real and wanted. "So many of them written in the stars."

My tone was far off. The pictures in the sky seemed to blur together, forming one great tale that I would've read if not for the nearly undetectable tug on one of my curls capturing my attention. A strand of my hair slipped through Kiernan's fingers as I turned my head, finding his expression just as surprised as mine, his focus staying on the hand that held a crimson curl as though he had no intention of the action.

"Sing, please. Before I do something irrational."

Stuttering at first, I complied, projecting the first melody that came to mind, and as Kiernan closed his eyes, I went back to exploring the sky. My voice was unsure as I sang, worried something was wrong, adding a quiver that shouldn't have been there. The song was supposed to help him gain control, but the longer I sang, the closer he moved toward me until we were at last touching, and it didn't feel like he wanted to control himself. His hand slid up my arm, slowly, leaving a trail of electric sparks over my skin that sent a shiver down my spine and broke my voice off. I was prepared for him to pull away then, and for the blood rushing to my head to ease, but he stayed, just as he promised he would, leaving me to fumble for reality on my own.

"Don't stop," he whispered over the shell of my ear, lips dangerously close to touching my skin, "It's beautiful, *Agapití.*"

He spoke the title like a sacred promise, soft but full of meaning, entwined with secret yearning, and I forgot the sound of my own name replaying the title in my mind. The song continued on a softer note, but I was barely able to recognize it as my own, while my ears prioritized the soft noise of his breaths tickling the hairs on the back of my neck. His fingers traced over my throat, touching the power held in my voice, before trailing farther up, brushing my jaw, lifting my chin, and with one tentative movement, my sound was put to an end.

Kiernan kissed me.

Chapter Twenty-Six

Kiernan's lips were gentle, questioning, as they pressed to my mouth, wanting me to respond, waiting for me to pull away while I forgot how to breathe. Everything I had been thinking dissolved into an insignificant haze of disarray, and with no thought, my head lifted upward, following the overwhelmingly gentle touch with blind, implicit longing. His hand, steady and grounding, set over my stomach, an action generated to push me away as it strained on my middle, yet did nothing more than press the heat through my crumpled shirt that seeped into my skin.

A cascade of butterflies erupted inside me, fighting to break free and kiss the palm pressed over my abdomen, their wings following the touch even as it trailed over my side and flattened over my back, drawing me closer. Kiernan leaned forward the slightest amount, and I fell back on my elbows, penetrating the soft ground as my fingers dug into the silky grass.

He kissed me like a whisper, a desperate secret, a caress of tender words against my mouth, and the longer he spoke his silent wishes, the more desirous they sounded. The forest was perhaps too quiet, as though afraid to interrupt such a vulnerable moment, afraid to reveal who was watching, but the pounding of both our hearts overrode any other sounds, including the alarms in my mind warning how dangerous this was.

He was warm and inviting, wanting and careful, and his spare hand was brushed down the side of my face, knuckles sweeping over my flushed cheek, fingers stroking my jaw once, twice, three times before...

Gone.

My breathing shouldn't have been labored, not when I barely moved, but my lungs couldn't claim enough air as Kiernan separated his lips from mine, remaining close enough to blind me with the earnest green staring back.

"I'm sorry," Kiernan whispered, his eyes focused on my mouth like he intended to kiss me again, and just when I thought he might, his head dropped to my shoulder, resting as heavily as his words when murmuring, "I shouldn't have done that."

He didn't let go of me, though, his hand fisting into my shirt while he breathed me in, struggling to satisfy his lungs as I did.

"I can't keep doing this," Kiernan started again, using a hopeless tone I hadn't known from him as I felt the tickling sensation of his eyelashes brushing against my neck, "Acting like you aren't on my mind endlessly. Pretending that I don't *feel* this way. It's raw, it's real, it's utterly consuming, and I don't know how to handle it. You're driving me *insane*." His voice dragged as though something deep inside of him was tearing apart, his lips grazing my collarbone, and when my uneven breathing hitched, something in him snapped. He was up in less than a second, scrambling to get away from me.

I was whipped back into reality too quickly, and when the weight in my limbs pinning me to the ground seemed to ease, I forced myself to my feet, wiping the dirt from my arms. Kiernan eyed my movements like a frightened deer sensing danger, only I wasn't the predator. It was clear he was afraid of himself, *stumbling* back when I attempted to close the plentiful distance between us.

Kiernan doesn't stumble.

"It would be best if you stay away."

He wasn't going to hurt me as his tone suggested, not when he seemed so wounded himself, yet I struggled to believe he didn't want me nearby. His body was tense, as though it took all his muscles just to keep him in place; his eyes taking me in like he hoped to permanently memorize my being as if it were his last chance, and I was suddenly worried about what he planned to do.

"Kiernan, I—"

"Please, Ari, let me go first," he requested, and with some remorse, I closed my mouth. He sighed, tossing his gaze to the ground, his hands in tight fists at his side, and I now considered that it might not have been an act of anger this entire time. "I figured it out."

"What do you mean?" I pressed, growing more uneasy by the second, and I knew Kiernan could sense it. A vein twisted wrong in his neck.

"The feeling of love," his tone dipped as did my stomach, "It's something I knew, but never understood. Not until now."

He met my gaze, then, and it was electric. I hadn't known it was possible to carry the amount of emotion Kiernan was exhibiting in one deep, earnest look, and heat poured from my skin in reaction.

"It's the feeling of dancing with you in rain too heavy to think of anything else, yet wanting the world to be quiet so I could catch your laugh while almost slipping in the mud. It's the reward of seeing the light come back to your face after you close yourself off from everything else when I create a new competition. It's listening to you count every star in the galaxy and still wishing there were more, just to hear your voice because I can't get it out of my head, and I never want to.

"And I tried to stay away, so many times I tried, but I couldn't. I kept coming back. Again and again, I kept coming back to you, waiting for you in the early hours at this tree, preparing myself for the day when you'd figure it all out and I'd never see you again. But day after day, you kept coming back, too, and it became harder to watch you leave the longer I was with you. I told myself when you inevitably ran from me, screaming in terror, I wouldn't chase you, but I tell myself the same thing now, and I'm not sure how much I believe it. I don't understand why I need to be near you, like I can't feel *alive* unless you are around, but everything about you draws me in. It's your hair. Your eyes. Your smile. Your skin. Your scent. It's how you move, talk, laugh, *breathe*— "

But I couldn't breathe, not with him confessing like this, not when it strangely sounded like a grievous goodbye.

"It's how your heart flutters when something excites you, or how you always manage to be gentle even when your surrounding circumstances are far from kind. You touch me, and I forget everything I know about myself. You say my name, and it's like you give it meaning when there wasn't any before. You have healed me in ways I can't even explain. I'm *happy* for the first time in my life. That is all because of you, and I can't... *I can't—*"

Kiernan cut himself off, running a stiff hand through his hair while trying to gather his composure, shaking his head as he went on.

"The thought of anything happening to you ruins me. I am so terribly afraid of losing you that the measures I've pondered taking to ensure your safety are reckless at best." He laughed cruelly, the joy in it dead and unsettling enough to send a chill down my spine. "Ironic, isn't it? The things I would do to protect you could harm you further? That is not a life you deserve. I terrify you now as it is."

"How could you think that?" I whispered, sounding smaller than I felt, and his expression softened slightly in response to my voice.

"I almost killed you on your first night here. I let my guard down for one second and nearly crushed your throat. I saw the horror in your eyes, and you think you can convince me my presence doesn't frighten you? You don't think I notice how you flinch if I move too quickly? Your heart beats quicker when I enter the room. You can hardly pry your fingers from your necklace," he stated, eyeing the shell I hadn't realized I was clutching. I kept shaking my head, hoping to express how misunderstood it all was, but only shallow exhales escaped as I tried to argue.

"If I am right, and this is how it feels to be loved, I never want to feel anything else," he said too sternly, words full of meaning turning sour from the wariness in his tone, "If this is what love feels like, then I never want it to stop, and that is a very dangerous thing, Ariella."

He'd never called me by my real name before. It was only ever Ari, or Rowe, or *Agapití.*

I didn't like this.

Neither did I like how his features sharpened, appearing more beast than man, his voice unnervingly steady as he spoke once more.

"Which is why I am giving you this one chance. Leave."

The heat pouring from my skin was gone in an instant, replaced by a dreadful cold that plucked out the butterflies' wings in my stomach.

"What?"

"Go home. Go to Scotland. I don't care, just get away from me, from all of this, and do it now. Because if you don't, I am never going to let you go."

I should've retreated as soon as the words left his mouth, ran until I was found and helped to safety. I knew where I was after all; I could trace my way back to the trails without a second thought, but the wind discouraged the idea as the breeze became suddenly frigid, the grass biting at my ankle as I took a step back, and my heart crumbled at the thought of leaving him.

Kiernan's face was set, his posture tall and stiff as though to scare me off, but his eyes were telling me something entirely different. They were broken emeralds doing everything they could to piece themselves back together, a wall of moss trying to disguise an ancient monument. *"Stay,"* they pleaded, *"Stay with me, Agapití."*

And I would.

Kiernan's countenance shifted when I stepped closer.

"What are you doing?" he demanded, but I ignored the edge in his tone, focusing on the despairing way it cracked, "Why aren't you running?"

"What if I don't want to?"

Kiernan blinked, surprised, as though he'd never considered that response, and he froze in place as I carefully advanced toward him.

"Don't do this," he pleaded, but I was already taking another step, "You are making a mistake."

I shook my head again, and his expression dropped, his defense crumbling, leaving him maskless so that the broken beast was impossible to miss behind that penetrating stare as I reached him.

"You'll get hurt," he whispered, vulnerability coursing through every part of him, yet he didn't touch me.

"That's okay," I assured, lifting a hand to his arm, tentatively wrapping my fingers around the inside of his elbow, physically feeling his muscles tense, but he did nothing to stop it.

"I'm not *human*."

"Neither am I."

My thumb soothingly rubbed over his arm, and drawing his eyebrows together in intense concern, Kiernan's attention dropped to the contact, tracking the movement as he admitted, "I can't always control it."

As if on cue, the uncomfortable pulsations returned to his face, trapped scales pushing just above the corner of his jaw, and without permission, I swept attentive fingers over the spot, cupping his cheek with my palm.

"Then let me help you," I softly provided, guiding his focus to my face, "Just don't force me to leave."

I didn't know where it came from, the sudden surge of confidence to release his arm and grab the collar of his shirt to pull his mouth back to mine, yet the immediate response of Kiernan's lips ignited a new strength in every one of my limbs, despite the way he held my waist making me feel weak in my knees.

It was my turn to tell him how I felt, to whisper inaudible declarations that my heart carried for far too long, and Kiernan eagerly accepted each word. My arms found their way around his neck while his hands traveled up my back, leaving sparks of warmth shooting down my spine, and as I melted into him, I felt how perfectly we fit together. He deepened the kiss, no longer distancing himself as he pressed me to him, holding me as he warned he would, with no intention of letting me go, though I couldn't understand why that would be unwanted. A life encased in his arms, wrapped in the security he brought, seemed like a life I'd never be deserving of, yet Kiernan planted kiss after kiss as though it'd never be enough for me.

He abruptly pulled back enough to laugh, breathy and deep like his head had been underwater his entire life, and he finally found air.

"I love you, Ari," he professed, relief and elation outpouring through heavy exhales as his forehead rested on mine, "I love you so much."

I wanted to reciprocate his declaration, tell him how I hadn't allowed myself to picture him saying those words in fear of the effect they'd have on me, but he was kissing me again before I could even regain my breath, and the effect was stronger than I could ever have imagined. My heart wouldn't calm, nor would the dizzying feeling of blood rushing to my head, and despite thinking every sense of cold in my body had vacated, I'd shiver with new chills each time his fingers brushed over my skin. For a simple moment, I forgot what pain was, or fear, or hurt, or any other sensation that wasn't this erratic, powerful intoxication Kiernan was presently giving me. His skin pulsed under my hands, the dragon beneath his false form desperate to reach for me, adding a new layer of heat to him that burned passionately with each touch.

Then his hands were in my hair, gently tugging in the strands like it was a toy he always wanted to play with, and it made me want to laugh, but I lost that the moment his fingers grazed the back of my neck. Kiernan untangled himself from me suddenly, a furrow in his brow caused my countenance to switch within a second.

"What's wrong?" I asked, still breathless, but Kiernan's eyes only narrowed in response. His hand found its way through my hair to press over my nape before once more pulling away to examine his fingers.

"Your neck. It's..." he started, circling around me and brushing my hair to the side, "No."

The sudden dread filling his denial prickled at my nerves, and I quickly spun to face him, meeting a state of panic, disbelief, and... fear.

"It can't be true. No. No, please *no*," he murmured, each word more anxious than the last, and when he tried to get another look, I caught his hand.

"What's *wrong*?" I tried a second time, but he was no better than the first, locked in speechlessness as that silent war waged behind his eyes, "Kiernan, talk to me!"

"Just… don't say anything for a little while, yeah?" he fumbled in answer, his hand instinctively holding tighter to the touch I shared with him, "We need to find Killian. Stay close to me."

Kiernan didn't wait for me to finish before he transformed and hoisted me onto his back. Anxiety was curling in my stomach, gnawing at my bones, and I hugged tighter to Kiernan as we flew, clamping my eyes shut. I felt the rumble in his powerful form before I heard it—the majestic roar of a dragon, the mighty call for their kind that could be heard from miles away.

Kiernan kept me close to him after we landed in a part of the woods I was unfamiliar with, tucked under a wing as though every living thing was out for me, and it wasn't until three dragons appeared, tan, grey, and green, that Kiernan shifted. Even in his alternate form, he kept me pressed to him, holding my hand, glancing twice around the forest, and he wasn't the only one doing double-takes. Killian's eyes fell on our adjoined hands, then flicked to Kiernan's face with an entirely parental look.

"We talked about this not even a full day ago," he reprimanded, and Kiernan brushed him off completely.

"We have something more urgent to discuss," he stated, then, with a glance at Keagan and Kaid, he added, "First, we should probably find somewhere private."

"The first thing you should do is separate them, Killian," Kell interjected, emerging from the shadows, "It has its claws deep in Kiernan, and he can't be trusted."

I felt Kiernan go tense, rigid, because now that his brother was here, I doubted he'd get to speak freely on a matter that was clear he needed to discuss, and I couldn't help the way I shuffled closer to Kiernan.

"I don't know what you are talking about, but it is really not the time," he argued tightly, gifting Kell a sharp glare before facing Killian.

"Don't you, though? Something about 'leave' and 'go home' and 'it's not safe for you here'?" he chuckled darkly, locking eyes with me to announce, "Foolish as my poor, gullible brother is, I was hoping you'd taken his advice. I had such a nice parting gift for you." Tiny flames danced over his fingertips, and all the color drained from my face.

"Calm down, Ari," Kiernan warned in a whisper, but all I could think about was what would've happened if I'd left as Kiernan requested.

"Kiernan?" Killian broke in, "You tried to take her back home?"

"Oh, that's not even the best part," Kell stated before Kiernan could, "Why don't you tell us *all* what you discovered about your precious little mind-stealer?"

"You had no right to follow me, Kell!" Kiernan shouted, slipping from my hold to close some distance between the two of them.

"If you weren't so *reckless*, I wouldn't have to," he bit back, the sarcasm wiped away to form cool anger. He stepped nearer, unafraid to challenge his brother, and while Kiernan saw the action as a desire to meet head-on, I only noticed how Kell was now closer to me than Kiernan was.

"What is this about?" Killian interrupted before they could argue further, and Kell didn't miss a beat in answering.

"The witch is the one prophesied."

The air went cold and stale, the wind tasted rotten with tension, and my throat became incredibly dry.

"The *Dákry?*" Kaid spoke up, his voice cracking in fear, but more than that, he sounded hurt.

"She's not," Kiernan insisted, "There has to be some explanation."

"He is enchanted," Kell spoke plainly, looking past everyone and only to Killian, who had fallen eerily silent.

"I'm not *enchanted—*"

"It has now overtaken his mind so that he is helpless to its seduction. I saw them. Kiernan had no control," Kell went on, still only facing Killian.

My eyes blew wide, horror bleeding into my expression.

"No, I—"

"*Don't—*" Kell's interruption was more than just vocal as his hand clamped around my neck, "use your voice."

I couldn't use my voice, neither could I *breathe*, and my attempts to remove his grasp were feeble against his strength.

"*Get your hands off of her,*" Kiernan demanded, his voice darker than I had ever heard it before. He moved to attack his brother, but Keagan grabbed his arm, holding him back and keeping him from transforming, eyes wide and panicked as he stared at me before flicking his attention to the eldest.

"Killian, make him stop," he pleaded, and it took me too long to realize he was asking about Kell, even though he fought Kiernan as he spoke. Keagan's physique was deceptive, the strength of a dragon hidden in a lean, toned human body, keeping up with Kiernan's untamed power. Though it was clear one was stronger, Kiernan, not wanting to hurt his younger brother in his need to reach me, wouldn't be contained for much longer.

"We let the *Dákry* into our home. Our minds are likely no longer our own," Kell contented, undeterred by how my throat felt as though it were closing up.

They all looked to Killian, like soldiers waiting for instruction, but he appeared just as lost, and I was getting lightheaded.

"Does she have the symbol?"

Kell released my throat and kicked me to the floor in front of Killian, gripping me by my hair so that my neck and the droplet of unmoving water there were exposed for all of them to see, but all I could think about was how I was still unable to breathe. The eldest took a long look at me while I tried to gasp, but there wasn't enough liquid in the air.

"I'm so sorry, Ariella," he whispered to me, though it was apparent everyone else could hear, Keagan bristling in the blacking-out corner of my vision.

"Killian... no." Keagan's tone was soft, but nothing short of distraught, and it didn't go unnoticed how his grip on Kiernan loosened.

"You know what the prophecy says. We have no choice," Killian settled, and that was it; there was to be no more discussion.

I was going to die.

Guilt as I had never seen before bled through every feature of Killian's face, his eyes begging for forgiveness in mine before shifting to Kell and giving the smallest nod.

My heart dropped in terrorizing devastation, throbbing painfully in my stomach, and each one of them reacted to it. I missed most of the responses, except for Kell, who snatched the back of my neck with enough force to snap my bones, and how Kiernan's features twisted into something feral. I barely had time to blink before there was a dark, dangerous, *angry* beast in front of me, throwing Kell to the side, and with another blink, a boy was standing over my crumpled form, one leg on either side.

"*No one* touches her," Kiernan threatened, and though the world was spinning, trees dancing together in unparalleled rhythms, I was starting to catch my breath as blunt sticks protruded into my stomach.

"Can't you see what's happening? It's pitting you against us. We are family, Kiernan."

I heard Kell's voice, but it sounded so far away, my mind confusing consciousness through the parts of me begging to sleep.

"I can do it myself, Kiernan, if that would help you. I know how to make it painless. She won't feel a thing."

Killian, too, was far away, but he didn't sound as strong as Kell did.

"*No one touches her.*"

Kiernan was undeniably close, his voice deep enough to be a growl, and that frightening noise was enough to awaken me.

"This is bigger than any of us, and you know it. I wanted to keep her alive, believe me, I did, but this has to do with our entire *race*. We have no other *choice*," Killian repeated, the emphasis of the situation evident in his voice, but Kiernan didn't move a muscle from his protective stance over me, hands fisted, ready to fight, and Killian sighed, defeat in his tone as he spoke, "Hold him down, Kell."

My eyes were still bleary, a strand of hair had fallen over them I felt too exhausted to move, but I managed to find Kell stalking toward us from several feet away, though he froze in place when Kiernan shouted.

"I claim *peirasmós*!"

They *all* froze in place.

"None of you can harm her until it is finalized," Kiernan informed, though it didn't seem like he needed to. The silence wasn't one of confusion but rather understanding, a dreaded, painful understanding.

"It can be rejected," Killian contended, sounding tired and worn from so many years of leading, "You have no upper hand in this."

"That's why I am enacting it to Kell," Kiernan announced, and all heads turned in his direction, "You win, and you can do whatever you want to her. I won't say a word."

My chest began to swell, the ground constricting as I lay on my stomach, and it didn't matter how much oxygen I was inhaling; it wasn't enough.

"And if you win?"

"Ari goes home unharmed."

"Don't go through with this," Killian insisted, worry tainting his demand because the power was shifting.

"Whatever I want?" Kell smiled, but it wasn't one of joy, twisting upward cruelly that entirely changed his cool, handsome face.

"*Kell.*"

It was a command, and Killian was never disobeyed, but at this moment, he wasn't in charge, and Kell looked bloodthirsty.

"Whatever you want," Kiernan promised, and I tried reaching for his leg, tried to get him to stop whatever this was, but my energy was giving out.

"Kier..."

Keagan was holding Kaid together near the base of a tree, close to falling apart himself, and the shake in his voice fed the black abyss crinkling around my sight. Keagan, the boy who laughed in serious situations, who rolled his eyes over threats and never showed an ounce of fear, was *terrified*.

"I accept."

"Then it is done."

There were no relieved sighs, no noises of protest, just harsh, brutal silence.

Kiernan was on his knees the next second, holding my hands that were trembling, staring into my eyes that were blinking out of a daze.

"Tell me you are okay," he pleaded, tucking that rebellious strand of hair behind my ear, and he was so warm. I just wanted to rest my head in his palm and slip out of consciousness, but he was quickly torn away, my sole comfort shredded with it.

"If I don't get to touch her, neither do you," Kell asserted, hand firmly gripped over Kiernan's shoulder.

"She could be hurt," Kiernan fought, his eyes skimming over me, but Kell wouldn't let him near.

"You have to win to coddle it."

"I never established the time."

"Which is exactly why I am. The gorge. Now," Kell instructed, and while I heard several shuffles from shifting and wings flapping from flight, my head hurt too much to look. I attempted to sit, teetering a bit, but two hands grasped my shoulders as I began to slump, drawing me up to my feet and forcing my limbs into working.

"Are you okay?" Keagan asked, but it didn't sound right. He wasn't smiling, or teasing, or winking; he was concerned.

"What is happening?" I questioned instead, glancing around to find everyone else gone.

"Kiernan challenged Kell. They are going to fight in primary form until one of them submits."

I blinked, suddenly very awake.

"What happens if no one submits?" I asked, a new sickness clawing up my throat.

Keagan didn't answer.

Chapter Twenty-Seven

The gorge matched the vastness of the redwood forest, a crack in the earth that I was surprised to have never seen before. Upturned roots and moss-ridden stones paved the walls to this pit of the unknown, and from this angle in the sky, it appeared endlessly deep. Keagan, with hesitation, obliged when I requested to follow everyone else, my head still spinning from lack of oxygen. I struggled to put the recent events in order, piecing them together in a way that made sense, though I strived for understanding as we flew, second-guessing my decision to come when we arrived, and I wasn't the only one.

"Take her to the cabin," Killian instructed after Keagan landed and tentatively placed me on the ground, careful as though still unsure of the danger I was, "She shouldn't be here."

"She has the right to stay," he argued, and I was trying to move past them, hoping to better see the gaping land, but Killian stepped in my way.

"Kiernan needs to focus."

"I don't think he's ever been more focused," Keagan offered, regarding the boy whose eyes held enough determination to defeat impossibility, and I followed his line of sight.

Kiernan and Kell stood on opposite ends of the ravine's opening, watching, waiting, preparing for something I didn't want to imagine. They remained in their alternate forms, facing each other, and though no words were said, a silent conversation was being held across the vast distance. I wished for them to nod and mutually back away, coming to an understanding that whatever this was didn't need to happen, but neither of them withdrew, staring as they braced for the other to make the first move. Kiernan's face was as tense as the rest of him, but as his eyes shifted, something in him unwound, softening as his sight raked over me, and if he'd held my gaze a second more, maybe I could convince him to come back from the edge. He looked away too quickly, however, his decision set, and I grew sick with anxiety.

"There has to be some way to stop this," I begged, though unsure who I was speaking to, and as if I had only been talking to myself, there was no response.

Then they fell.

Ignoring the few shouts of my name calling me back, I ran to the crater's edge, peering over the sharp cliff to find two barely visible dragons at the bottom. They attacked in brutal, quick movements, though most of it was difficult to perceive in the dim light. The moon was hiding behind the clouds, afraid to watch as two brothers tore each other apart, or maybe he was confiscating his light to keep me from seeing the chaos, like he knew I couldn't handle it, but that didn't stop me from trying. Screeches and roars echoed off the jagged forest walls, rocks tumbling down in its command, and I couldn't decipher which sounds were Kiernan's. My legs gave out then, forcing me to my knees and much too close to toppling over the edge, and I didn't know what to do with my hands, whether to cover my mouth in shock, grip my shell, or perhaps block out the horrifying noises beneath me by flattening them over my ears.

I felt it before I saw it: a flash of light, a whisper of flames, teasing to melt my skin from an uncertain distance. It was Kiernan who used fire first, lighting up the ravine as well as the night, presenting a concise view of the damage, and I debated if shielding my eyes might be the best use for my hands. I wasn't able to catch much in the quick shed of light apart from torn dirt and scraped stones on the gorge's floor, the creatures moving too swiftly for me to discern, but I caught the unmistakable glistening of light from the reflection of liquid.

Dark, hot, thick liquid.

Kiernan was bleeding.

If Kell had been, too, the color of his scales disguised it well enough. Another spout of fire brightened the night, this time coming from Kell, and tears began to tint my vision, blurring everything until it was all just marks of color.

Red and black.

Black and red.

Blood and night. Wounded and afraid. Spots dancing in your vision. Wood digging into your back. Pain shooting down your leg. Screaming didn't help. Crying didn't help. He tried to kill you. He will kill you. Kiernan is going to get hurt, and Kell is going to break every part of you. One by one. Screaming won't help. Crying won't help. Kiernan can't help.

I could feel the bruises forming on my neck from earlier, painting my skin in blue, and purple, and murderous intent. There was only one reason Kell agreed to this bloodied brawl, a cause with enough justification to willingly harm his own family. It wasn't enough for him to kill me; Kell wanted it to hurt.

He wanted revenge.

A soft whimper directed my attention from the battle below for just a second, Kaid curling into himself, trying to hide under his wings, clearly reacting to my panic. Killian was observing over the edge while glancing around, his arms folded over his chest to assume a casual posture, but his shoulders were rigid, fingers digging into his skin each time an attack was made. Keagan was closer to me than the rest of them dared, yet it was obvious the distance he kept derived from uncertainty. Neither of them noticed the youngest's struggles, distracted by the fight and unprepared to aid the situation above ground.

Calm down. Calm down. Calm down.

I could almost feel Kiernan whispering the words to my ear, promising not to let anything happen to me, just as I had promised to stay, and though it was insufficient, I forced my lungs to accept mouthfuls of air until I became lightheaded. My hands found their way to the grass, splaying my fingers out against the damp strands, focusing on the chilling sensation over my sweltering skin. My eyes fell closed, listening to the pounding of my heart over the inhumane screeches, prioritizing each throbbing beat and imagining it slowing, easing, calming—

"ARI, GET BACK!"

Keagan's voice shattered my thoughts, and as I opened my eyes in alarm, they fixed on the two dragons battling in the air, hovering over the gorge's opening. I did my best to scramble away, thrusting my hands in motion to push back as they dug into the dirt, but Keagan was there, pulling me up by my arms when I wasn't fast enough. Kell landed on the patch of grass where I'd been mere heartbeats ago with his back to the ground, Kiernan over top of him, talons digging into Kell's chest and roaring into his face with a demand Kell dismissed with one brutal move. I barely had time to blink before his teeth were barred into Kiernan's front leg, refusing to loosen even as Kiernan released the talons from his chest. Kiernan bellowed in pain, using his wings in an attempt to break free of Kell's hold, but it wasn't until he brought his other arm up, slashing pointed claws against Kell's face, that he escaped into the air. Kell rubbed at his eyes, and I momentarily wondered if Kiernan blinded him, but he blinked them open, revealing a deep laceration right through his brow and over his snout, his sight impaired from the blood spilling into it. In the time it took for Kell to refocus, Kiernan attempted to land, groaning as his wounded leg met the ground, unable to regain his footing before Kell was up again, ambushing from behind. They collapsed together, Kiernan unable to hold himself up, and the impact had me stumbling to stay upright myself. Kiernan was closer now, and I could almost pick out every gaping injury, every minor cut, every drop of blood the color of fire dripping from his stained scales, and every new wound Kell created as he tore into Kiernan's back. Ripping, and breaking, and biting made Kiernan go limp, his magnificent body crumpling into a pile of broken hope, and I felt like screaming, tearing them apart with my voice, but my lungs could only offer a tortured cry.

Kiernan's attention snapped to me immediately, hurt in his eyes as though my sound pained him more than the physical torment he was enduring, and he opened his mouth as he always had to comfort me, but the noise that escaped him was anguished and small, shattering at its core. I felt my entire body tense, buckling as though prepared to snap in half.

Kell gave no reaction or remorse to Kiernan's cry as he continued inflicting pain, waiting for him to give in and place my fate in his hands, but Kiernan kept to an aching silence, eyes clinging to my petrified being as though the sight of me could keep him strong forever when the rest of him was crumbling down.

"He's not submitting," Killian spoke tightly, and though the words were only meant for himself, it was the first thing someone had said in what felt like hours.

"He's not *breathing*!" I yelled, angry and terrified all at once, and I didn't realize Keagan was still holding on to me until I tried to run to Kiernan. "Let me *go—*"

"There is nothing you can do," Keagan sympathetically assured, unfazed by how I yanked my arms in an attempt to escape his hold.

"He's going to die if this keeps going!"

My panic was growing, and Kell fed off of it, striking harsher

"STOP IT!" I screamed because Kiernan wasn't going to tell him to stop, and this couldn't continue. He wasn't moving, the strength he salvaged dying, and his eyes turned glassy, beginning to close. "NO—"

"Kell!" Killian cut in, and the red dragon halted instantly, "That's enough!"

"Look at me," Keagan commanded abruptly, spinning me around to face him, but I was straining to see Killian, trying to understand why he was walking to

Kell and Kiernan and what was happening next, "Do you remember Secret Beach?"

"Is Kiernan—"

"Answer the question!" he shouted, shaking me by the shoulders until I met his eyes, and I was startled by the sudden seriousness in his face.

"Y-yes."

"It's to the far left of us. Run in that direction, and don't stop until you are in the ocean. You hear me?"

Keagan released me, and I froze, trying to process this too quickly, blinking like an idiot.

"What are you—?"

Killian said something I missed, but I turned to find Kell moving off of a very still, dark dragon, eyes narrowing on me, Kiernan's blood and his own covering his face, and I then understood why Keagan told me to run.

Kell won.

Chapter Twenty-Eight

I ran.

I wasn't fast enough; I knew it. I should've fled sooner; I knew it. I couldn't escape him; I knew it.

But I ran, nonetheless.

There was a stabbing pain in my chest from not breathing properly, but that was nothing compared to the painful beating of my heart, pulsating as though to break from my ribcage and escape my inevitable fate. I pumped my feeble legs as far as I physically could, shoving plants out of my path and blinking water out of my vision as I ran against the wind while flashes of Kell's sharp teeth baring into Kiernan did their best to distract me from my one chance of survival.

Make it to the ocean; that's all I had to do. As long as I was in the water, a place where dragons were forced to shift and unable to breathe, I would be protected from Kell. I didn't allow myself to think of the possibilities if I were caught, because Keagan was right. Secret Beach was near, and I could see it just over the hill.

A powerful roar shook the ground.

I couldn't tell if it was angry or hurt, but I stumbled into a tree at its booming, grateful to grip the wood and push forward rather than gather myself from the ground. The hairs on the back of my neck stood as I sensed a presence behind me, moving swifter and faster than my human legs could manage, but the ocean was in sight, and I couldn't afford to glance back. I gripped roots and rocks with a newfound determination in my climb, and where the stones crumbled beneath my hands, slitting one of my palms open, the roots held firm, providing a lifeline for me to hoist myself up with.

Adrenaline had overtaken my body, rushing through my blood as it believed we could make it to safety, and within several shallow breaths, I made it to the cliff's edge and jumped without a second thought. Falling didn't offer the exhilarating high that it did when I was with Keagan, anticipation curling in my stomach rather than the gleeful rush tingling my nerves, wishing to grasp gravity with my bare hands and force me down further. I braced myself for the freezing shock of the water, preparing my mind for the unruly loss of my legs after submersion, and I wasn't ready for the weight of my body to yank against the base of my arms as I was caught in the air, talons barely missing my skin but unafraid to clamp down until I thought my bones might snap.

I screamed, wide eyes taking in the ocean falling away as I was carried into the sky and thrown on the top of a large rock formation overlooking the sea. I grunted as my body hit the rough surface, rolling over multiple times from impact, and despite the ache it caused everywhere, I forced myself back on my feet, stumbling in a run to retreat the beast behind me, focus set on freedom off the rock's side.

"*Ari...*"

I froze in place.

Kiernan's voice was wounded and desperate, reaching for me over the ocean's mist when his arms could not, almost strangled as it broke at the end.

I spun around, afraid that my brain was playing tricks on me, that my ears were letting me hear what I wanted as a final gift before I was tortured to death, but Kiernan was there, and I quickly realized that though he sounded weak, it was only through strength that he called for me. He was crumpled on the rock, lying on his side so that he was facing me, arm outstretched in my direction. His brows were drawn tightly together, his other arm wrapped around his abdomen, and it wasn't until he mouthed the word "*please*" to me that I noticed the major cut over his bottom lip.

I was running again, but it wasn't to the ocean, my knees feeling like they would fracture as I fell to his side, scanning him over with frantic eyes.

"Oh, Kiernan," I whispered, guilt gnawing at my throat, wanting to hold him and kiss his scars until he forgot he was even in pain, but all I could do was watch him struggle to breathe. I was careful when peeling back the blood-soaked layer of his shirt, exposing his open wounds to the night air, my hand falling away instantly to cover my mouth, and if my heart was cracking before, it shattered into pieces at the massacred state of his back.

"Don't look at it, Ari," Kiernan grunted, jaw tight and eyes clamped shut, "You don't do well with blood."

"You are hurt," I argued, suddenly feeling very sick, not because of the blood, but because he was put into this pain for me, and the guilt was closing around my throat. "Tell me how to help. Please."

"I'll be fine. I don't take as long to heal," he spoke through clenched teeth as though that fixed the problem, and my eyes fell back to his injuries. Obvious lacerations were made, the teeth marks visible in punctured holes through his skin, and the blood wouldn't stop rushing out of him. Kiernan was strong; I knew that for a long time, but even the strongest of people bled out without proper support, and my panicked mind acted before I could consider the consequences. With no cloth or bandages to aid me, my hands rested over his back, careful but steady as they created pressure over a laceration in the middle of his spine, and I felt his muscles go taut under my touch.

"Gosh, you are cold," he hissed, and I pulled away in an instant, worried I'd only hurt him more, professing numerous apologies, and after a few slow, heavy breaths, Kiernan murmured, "No, no. It's good... Distracts."

His eyes remained closed, incredible discomfort creasing his forehead as his brows knitted together, and all I desired to do was take his pain. Tentatively, I placed both of my hands on his back, orange-red blood oozing through my fingers, making me suddenly lightheaded as I felt his torn skin, unable to stop my eyes from filling. Beneath all the blood, Kiernan's skin was hot, scorching my touch and burning the cut I'd gotten deep in my palm, but his shoulders were relaxing, and I imagined his blood slowing, less eager to leave his body. I managed a sharp glance over my shoulder, bracing to run and somehow take Kiernan with me the minute something emerged from the forest, but the stillness of the woods only mocked me for my distress.

"He's not coming."

Kiernan's voice startled me, and I turned back to him with a jolt, analyzing his weakened features as he noticed my tensing through heavy eyelids, "I tore Kell's wing before chasing after you. He'll have to heal before he can get to us."

I swallowed, allowing that information to ease my panic, though it did little for the part of me concerned for Kiernan's life. He had subconsciously rolled closer, better enabling me to reach for all of his scars, and I took my time cooling his skin, hoping above all else that I brought a semblance of relief.

"You shouldn't have done that," I stated, the growing lump in my throat straining my speech, "He almost killed you."

"It was the only way I could ensure you lived a just a moment longer, and I don't regret it for a second," he stated as firmly as he could, slumping from the effort to speak as he added, "And Kell wouldn't kill me because, despite it all, we are family. I knew he'd take the bait, and I was pretty confident he'd win it, too, but you are alive, and that is all that matters."

"That doesn't change the fact that your own brother ripped you to shreds."

"Yeah, well, Kell is stubborn, and I've never been one for fighting. Not like this. I guess you've brought something new out in me."

His hand brushed my arm, clearly meaning to hold on to me, but he was too exhausted, and the brief touch was enough to make me shiver. I moved my hands up to his shoulder blades, bracing for him to tense at the contact, but I only felt his muscles unwind beneath my palms, the harsh states of his frame at last relaxing, calming so much so that his chest stopped moving up and down, and the jolt of sudden fear shot through my entire body.

"Kiernan? Kiernan, hey, look at me, please? Keep your eyes open," I begged, and he complied with much effort, dimmed emeralds gazing at me through slitted lids. I nodded, turning back to his injuries, to the blood and peeled skin, trying my best to put him back together, and I wasn't sure if I was speaking to him or myself as I mumbled, "You are going to be okay. You are going to be okay. You—"

"You are breathtaking," he murmured, and I felt my cheeks go pink, tears tumbling down them, finding difficulty meeting his gaze even as I felt his all over me, "I always thought you were the closest a human could come to looking like an angel." My sight shifted to his face then, and it didn't feel fair to be cared for this intensely, not when it was so blatantly undeserved.

"Don't... don't do that."

"Do what? Admire you?" He smiled, but it held half the brightness it normally did. "You can't take that from me. I have a lot to say that I've held back, and to make me keep quiet after confessing I love you is just cruel."

I tried not to let it distract me, the way my stomach flipped as he repeated those three delicate words he'd professed earlier that night, attempting to blink the tears away and refocus my vision on the imminent issues at hand.

"You need to preserve your energy."

"So, I'm allowed to say how angelic you are after I'm healed?"

I half laughed despite myself and our situation, baffled how he could think of anything apart from his survival, especially over something that wouldn't normally be said even in good conditions.

"Yes, after you stop bleeding to death, you can tell me how my eyes look like the stars," I joked, shaking my head incredulously, but I was smiling, my heart lightening the slightest because his words were sounding less labored.

"Every part of you rivals the stars, *Agapití*."

My hands stilled.

His eyes had fallen shut again, but I couldn't bring myself to reprimand him as I studied his face. Evidence of pain had escaped his expression, an overcoming tranquility painting his features, and I felt as though I could breathe again at the sight.

His skin began to mend itself, healing beneath my fingertips, and I was convinced I'd imagined how the blood retracted back into his wounds, slipping away from my hands as easily as if I'd washed them, leaving them bare apart from the cut of my own. Kiernan was sitting up before I could finish watching the lacerations tie themselves back together, the teeth marks filling in on their own, leaving dim scars in their place, and I instinctively grabbed for him as though he might topple over.

"How did you..."

"As I said," Kiernan chuckled, loosening my grip on him, "I don't take long to heal."

I only stared at him, unable to find words worthy of being spoken, tears still dripping from my eyelashes, but Kiernan weighed the air with words full of meaning before I could process that he was okay now, no longer in pain or anguish.

"Did you mean what you said?" he asked, sweetly brushing the tears from my face, "That you didn't want to leave?"

"I didn't want to leave you, Kiernan," I assured, the warmth of his hand over my cheek grounding me, thumb sweeping under my eye, clearing my thoughts, but he frowned, pulling away.

"And now? After all of this? You've changed your mind?"

"No," I whispered as though it were a death sentence, and even if it were, I'd gladly take it after everything he'd gone through for me. Kiernan was searching my face again, thoughts and decisions warring behind those life-filled eyes, and I felt worthy of speaking once more.

"What are you thinking?" I asked, gently combing back the hair concealing a dark bruise over his forehead, lightly tracing over the purpled edge until the color rejuvenated into the deep tan of his skin. He didn't answer, fixating my face with enough intensity to make my knees buckle, and I was grateful to be seated. I was unable to read his gaze, and when he refused to look away, I was unable to hold it, my eyes dropping and landing on his mouth, the gash over his bottom lip. My hand fell from his forehead, moving to brush a careful touch over the split until it healed and enabled him to smile without strain, but Kiernan caught my hand before I could, catching a glimpse of the blood in my palm.

"Do you trust me?" he asked, and I could feel the severity in his tone, reminding me of the last time he'd asked me that, when everything I thought I knew about myself came tumbling down. But Kiernan was honest, providing me the truth when no one else would, and the truth was the most essential component of trust.

"Yes."

Using his thumbs to carefully splay my hand open, uncovering my injury to the biting air, Kiernan surveyed it a moment, taking in every detail. Then he lowered his head to my palm, brushing his lips once over my wound before pressing a secured kiss in the same place, holding there for several breathless seconds. His lip was fully healed when he pulled away, leaving no trace of blood over his mouth, and I glanced at my hand, finding the slit slowly closing.

"I need you to look at me, Ari, or this won't work."

I obeyed, nearly blinded by the green piercing deeply into my vision as though reaching for my very being through a single look, and it took everything in me not to shrink away from its heat.

"What are you doing?" I asked as one of his hands came to cup the back of my head, bringing my forehead to his in a tender manner, his other hand pressing into my wounded one.

"I am giving you my *týpos*. It's a gift rarely given from our kind, one which permanently ties me to you in a connection deeper than humans can feel. And it happens through the transferring of blood," a gentle squeeze to my hand, "along with the press of my vision."

It was said that eyes were the window to the soul, and I could almost feel mine being pulled toward him, tied to him, and nothing had ever felt more secure.

"My hand, it's burning," I stated, an unknown heat hotter than Kiernan's hand over mine, melting the skin around my wound.

"It's sealing. You won't be hurt, I promise. Don't look away from my eyes," he instructed, and I trusted him, never tearing my sight from him even as the burning turned to tingling until it went numb. In his eyes were more care and love than I'd ever seen, and I would've been content to stare into those eyes for eternity. They no longer were eyes simply filled with life; they were filled with *my* life, securing my fate, mapping out my future, and it was all painted green.

"Done," he announced, closing his eyes, and I did the same, readjusting my sight, but the green stayed, and Kiernan didn't let go of me. "May I kiss you?"

Some exhausted part of my brain assumed it was a step in the gift he was giving me, and I nodded rather than kissing him myself, but when his lips pressed to mine, it was so easy to forget everything that hurt to remember. Each touch he gave me was overly careful, a question I wasn't sure how to answer, and after a light show of love that wrapped heavily over my heart, Kiernan released me.

I blinked a few times, setting my world back into view, and Kiernan watched in concern as my hand came to my head while I voiced my lack of understanding.

"What is it?"

"Your eyes will glow green when you are near someone who has the intention to harm you. For dragons, it's a symbol," he explained, pressing a kiss to my right cheek, "For others, it's a warning," continuing, he moved to the left side of my face, gifting me a kiss to that cheek, "But for me, it's a reminder," I removed my hand from my head, and his lips found that exact spot, "And for you," one kiss so gently to my mouth it almost didn't feel real, "it's a promise."

"A promise for what?" I whispered, delighting in how close he was, that normal volumes were unnecessary, and from the sparkle in his eyes, I could tell he enjoyed it too.

"That you will forever be under my protection."

"Forever?"

"When I said I wouldn't let you go, that is something I meant."

Yet he still held that hesitance in his tone, the preparation for me to run away, as though that would ever be something I wanted.

"What about Kell?" I inquired, understanding that nothing was quite that easy, but Kiernan remained incredibly soft as though I made everything too difficult.

"Kell won't be able to hurt you now, not without gravely harming me and everything we stand for." A kiss to my temple, a whisper in my ear, "You are safe, *Agapití*."

"*Agapití*," I shaped the word around my lips, looking up at him to ask, "What does it mean?"

"It's a term of endearment in my language," he admitted, not even trying to back himself up for his previous statement of the title, "*Patér* used to call *Mitér* that all the time. I'm not sure what it meant to him when he said it, but for me, when I say *Agapití*, it means my life, my world, my everything."

It all ached so beautifully to be wanted so strongly, a comprehension that there is a person who would choose to cherish me, and though I didn't understand it, I never wanted to lose it.

I never wanted to lose *him*.

"What should I call you?" I tried, wishing I could hide the blush creeping up my neck, but it didn't appear to bother him any longer.

"Just hearing my name on your lips is enough to make me feel as though I'm someone who matters. I need nothing more."

I smiled, leaning in to softly touch my lips to his cheek, speaking barely in a whisper by his ear, "I love you, Kiernan Turner, and—"

"Kallías," he stated, face dripping in adoration as he tipped his head to see me, "My name is Kallías."

"Kiernan Kallías," I corrected, loving the way the syllables played on my tongue, and the glow of pleasure in his eyes was nothing short of captivating.

"Say it again."

"I love you, Kiernan Kallías."

"*Lemon curd*, your voice," he whispered, planting another kiss on my lips, but it was over too quickly, like he was afraid to touch me as he had before, "It's going to be the death of me."

I went rigid, mind swirling around thoughts I didn't fully understand, but the mere idea of Kiernan's death being my doing drained all sense of pleasure from me.

"Don't say that."

"Okay," he chuckled, and only when he smiled could I see the little, white scar resting on the side of his lower lip, "Then you are my reason for living, Ari."

Chapter Twenty-Nine

"**L**ook who decided to show up," Kell announced as Kiernan and I entered the cabin, his tone far from welcoming, stare honing in on me, "Didn't expect to ever see you again. I thought Kiernan would've hidden you in a hollowed tree by now."

"We had an agreement," Kiernan admitted harshly, not sparing a glance at the rest of his brothers located throughout the room.

"So we did," Kell voiced while repositioning himself on the couch, getting to his feet, and standing taller than the others, and I shrank away. "A shame, really. I was looking forward to hunting you down," he spoke as though he was truly disappointed, like I was just another animal he could devour.

Kiernan had warned me this would happen back on the rock, that Kell would attempt to harm me at first, but it would all end up fine. He'd made everything sound easy and achievable that I hadn't thought to worry until he flew us back.

"Don't be afraid," he'd said, *"He'll be wanting that. Look him straight in the eyes and prove he doesn't scare you."*

And I'd nodded, foolishly confident when it was just the two of us, but seeing Kell once more after witnessing everything he'd done to Kiernan was a difficulty I wasn't prepared for. My eyes cast on the ground, I heard Kell step forward, and my back pressed into Kiernan, trying to retreat. One gentle brush down my side, a movement too subtle for anyone else to notice, yet much was communicated through such a seemingly insignificant touch Kiernan gave.

"You can have her," Kiernan offered, taking a step back from me, removing the fraying confidence I had, and I desperately wanted to hide behind him.

There was a moment of silence, a heartbeat of painful anticipation in which no one moved, and I didn't look up. My eyes began to hurt, a strange sensation close to burning that nearly had them watering, and it only worsened as Kell spoke very near to me.

"Kaid should leave."

"Don't hurt her," the youngest spoke up, and I wished to glimpse him, to see if his expression matched the anxiety of his voice, but the blazing in my sight wouldn't allow it, "She hasn't done anything wrong."

"The fact you believe that further proves my point that it has manipulated itself into our lives, and we have simply *let* it," Kell responded tightly, but it was kinder than the responses he'd given to everyone else.

"Just make it quick," Killian cut in when Kaid tried to argue, though the remorse was evident in his tone, "The girl has suffered enough."

"Don't tell me all of you are falling for this innocent facade!" Kell snapped, scanning the room, anticipating his confirmation.

"There is no facade," Keagan answered, sparing me a glance as I did to him, and what was an apologetic stare slowly shifted to confusion the longer he watched.

Kell laughed cruelly, and I felt myself lock up, bracing for him to strike.

"Tell them how you do it," he demanded, and I didn't have to see him to know the words were directed at me, "Tell them how you have corrupted their minds with your enchantments. Tell them how you planned to murder us in our sleep."

I flinched, shaking my head, wishing to blink away the fire, but that was nothing compared to the hit across my face, sending me to the ground.

"Tell them!" he yelled over me, but it was too loud, my face throbbing, and Kiernan looked like he was about to attack for a second time, "Tell them, or your voice box is the first thing to go!"

"I-I didn't... I... no—" I stammered, striving to get Kiernan's attention, but he was fixated on Kell, and I couldn't handle another fight, couldn't handle him getting *hurt*.

A foot was to my stomach then, crushing my organs as a bleat of pain broke from my voice, and Kiernan was advancing before I could protest.

"*Kiernan*," Killian warned, stepping in his way, "We've already had one fight tonight. Do not do this again."

"Look into her eyes!" Kiernan commanded but stayed where he was, and if my body hadn't been aching, I would've felt comforted.

"Why? So, it can brainwash me as it did you? I don't think so. You had your chance to keep the witch, and you lost."

"Kell..." Keagan cautioned, sight fixed over my face with an expression between shock and relief and coated in realization, but Kell was distracted with Kiernan.

"Maybe after I rid this wretched earth of it, you will open your eyes and recognize it's using you!"

"Kell!"

"*What?*" Kell shouted, directing to Keagan, and the entire room shifted as he spoke.

"She has his *týpos.*"

Kiernan visibly calmed, Killian stepped away from him, and Kaid's mouth fell to the floor.

Kell's attention shot back to me, and I did meet his eyes, but mine were blanketed in the fear I assured Kiernan I wouldn't show.

"You didn't," Kell tried, eyes piercing enough to add to my ache as he stared at me like I'd stabbed him.

"I did," Kiernan assured, but it wasn't a matter of triumph; it was a cool reality that numbed the senses. Kiernan kneeled by my side, aiding me as I gathered myself together, and I couldn't handle being looked at like I was a monster, momentarily hiding my face in his chest as his hand carefully shielded my head.

"No... no, I *will not* let another member of this family be taken by one of them!" Kell determined, and I felt Kiernan's hold tighten around me when footsteps neared, the reaction causing me to turn back to those watching us.

"It's too late," Killian interceded, disappointment and worry prominent in his features, "They are tied. If you kill her, it will result in Kiernan's death, just as it did for *Mitér.*"

"What have you done?" Kell was back to shouting, and it was the closest I'd seen him to being afraid, "Where is the loyalty? Where is the protection for *our* kind? You've doomed our entire race!"

Kiernan didn't respond, holding me by my waist as we stood, and our closeness only angered Kell further.

"Look me in my eyes and tell me there isn't one insignificant part of you that believes it will destroy us," he ordered, leveling Kiernan with a look that shattered my broken composure, but Kiernan met his stare with an eerie calm.

"I love her."

Those three words solidified their fears.

The atmosphere seemed to stiffen, nearly suffocating with unsolicited tension, and Killian turned away in affliction. It wasn't fear, I then realized, that I witnessed in Kell's eyes; it was hurt that went deeper than normal pain, a wound only inflicted personally, and it was evident in his voice as he declared gruffly, "Then we are all to die."

Kell shot me one last hard stare, a look that spoke, *'This is the last time you win, witch.'* before making his way to the cabin's door.

Then he was gone.

Kiernan's hold on me loosened, but that was the only thing that eased. Keagan plopped on one of the vacant couches, running his hands through his hair, focusing on nothing but the floor. Kaid's frightened eyes shifted from each of his brothers, careful not to linger long on me. Killian was so still I couldn't determine if he was breathing while staring blankly at the wall. I stole a glance out the window, searching for Kell, but he wasn't there, and the sun's first beams of light were touching the stars, kissing the moon goodbye.

"I should have seen it sooner," Killian mumbled suddenly, gripping all of our attention, "The information laid out for me."

The *Dákry*, a creature of wind and sea,
Will wake the one who sleeps in the Loch Ness deep.
One dead. One lost. One liar.

A ruin to worlds of old,
The power is in the voice she'll hold,
and break the winged beasts of fire.

At the point of youth,
She will receive the tide's call,
Reforming all souls for her desire.

A deliverance for those kept to the sea,
The cause for what was to be,
But the mark of the ocean's cry will not disguise her.

Killian's eyes flicked to me, sharp and determinedly slanted, and Kiernan's arm was around my shoulders instantly, pulling me closer to him. "A creature of wind and sea. A siren from the land and ocean. She matches the description."

"Prophecies can be misunderstood. It has happened before," Kiernan reminded, eyes narrowing as though sensing a new threat, and Killian pinched the bridge of his nose.

"What was there to misunderstand?" he sighed, sounding so very *tired*, "She has the mark of the *Dákry*. She fits the prophecy. And you know firsthand the power of her voice. It only makes sense."

"The term youth is broad," Keagan reasoned, tearing another hand through his hair, "It's possible we still have plenty of time before she receives anything."

"The word it was translated from Greek is *éphebos* which refers to the age of eighteen," Killian informed.

"When do you turn eighteen, Ari?" Kiernan asked gently, quieter since we were near to each other.

I opened my mouth only to shut it. Time had lost all its sense for me since being taken. I hadn't even seen a clock in what felt like weeks, and the weather was too fickle to allow me to guess what month we were in.

"Less than two days," Killian answered when I couldn't, "April 11th. She was born a month before Keagan was."

"So, what do we do?" Kaid asked, and I hated how lost he sounded.

"We need to prepare," Killian replied firmly, no longer thinking heavily, his decision set and plan created.

"We need to rest," Kiernan argued, "It has been a long night for us all."

No one fought him on that understanding, and though I was filled with questions, Kiernan ushered me to my room. He closed the door behind us, and though it did little for privacy for a house of dragons with excellent hearing, it was nice to be alone with him again. I sat on my bed, replaying the many moments one night held, my mind stuck on the prophecy, hearing the verses Father used to sing to me in the foretelling, creating a new desire for answers, but those weren't questions I could ask Kiernan.

"Do you believe those things Killian said? That I'm meant to..." I trailed off, my voice wobbling, and he stepped into my line of vision, smile warm and revealing that little scar.

"I've believed in the *Dákry* for years," he admitted softly, reaching for a scarlet lock of my hair, running his fingers over it before tucking it behind my ear, "But I believe in Ariella Rowe more." Then he kissed the top of my head and whispered, "Sleep, *Agapití*. I'm right outside your door if you need anything."

I watched him leave with a bizarre sense of remorse, longing for him to stay with me, but the door was closed, and it felt as though we were meant to be separated. Instead, I burrowed myself into the blankets, and knowing he could hear me, I softly spoke the three words that'd been the reasoning for such pain.

"I love you."

Chapter Thirty

Kiernan was in his primary form, curled around himself on the floor as an animal would, wrapped in a deep sleep. It nearly startled me to see the massive creature beside my door, not blocking the way but outlining it as though wishing to be as near to me as possible. He didn't hear as I exited my room, nor did he stir as I approached him, and I wondered if all dragon senses deadened when resting. My limbs were heavy, dragging as I softly stepped, a heaviness in my heart and murkiness in my brain trying to tie me to gravity. I'd woken up feeling more exhausted than I had when falling asleep, despite the long hours I spent in unconsciousness, though it strangely seemed like I'd been awake the whole time, sensing what was to come, dreading the evening closing in on us, the sun beginning to set just outside the windows.

I was to turn eighteen in just a few hours.

There were days in the past when I'd looked forward to this moment, aspiring older age would fix my problems, and maybe if Mother didn't see me as a child any longer, we could start a new relationship. The cries of her not wanting to be a mother lingered in the back of my mind, along with the image of her harming herself, and it suddenly made sense why she hated me.

She knew what you were. Never told you. Closed the doors. Hid you from the world. Monster needing to be caged. Never hurt anyone. Die alone. That would be good.

A tail flicked at my hair, tossing crimson curls over my face, and after I cleared my vision, I was met with large, green eyes staring at me, reflecting concern.

No. Can't die. He needs you.

Kiernan's head was tilted in question, sensing my anxiety, and my previous thoughts of dragons unaware during sleep were proven false. I placed myself on the floor beside him, resting my head on his arm, the one that'd been remarkably wounded for me, and my body dropped as I sighed, leaning into his heat. He dropped his head, gently nuzzling me until I was against his stomach, cradled in his warmth, and I had the sudden urge to cry. I fiddled with my necklace to stifle the desire, and Kiernan propped his hand over his arm, observing my movements, softly grumbling when I refused to answer his concerns. The necklace fell from my hands, but that didn't stop me from deterring to his chest, wings, paws, anything that wasn't his eyes.

"I didn't mean to wake you," I apologized, running my fingers over the ridges of his scales, careful as they dipped into scars. Kiernan responded with a contented hum, his tail coiling around my ankle in a manner that made me feel secure, and though it was the furthest thing from what I deserved, I allowed myself to find solace in the touch.

It was an accident, meeting his stare, something so natural to me it almost felt instinctual, and I broke instantly under that look of care embedded in his eyes. I hid my face in my hands, hoping the tears would stop with enough pressure over my eyes, but it did nothing to help, and Kiernan was shifting, his tail releasing its hold on me so his arms could.

"Talk to me," he whispered, tucking my head under his chin, and I took in the clean scent of the woods on his skin.

"I don't want this," I whimpered, hating how pathetic it sounded, holding on to him just as tightly as he held me, "I don't want to be in a prophecy. I don't want your family to be torn apart because of me. I won't want to hurt anyone."

"You won't."

"That's not what Killian said."

"Killian says a lot of things," he confirmed, smoothing my hair, and it was a dangerous thing how easily I could be convinced of anything he said when he was touching me. I pushed away.

"Kiernan, I need you to promise me something," I pleaded, wiping my eyes and swallowing the lump in my throat, "Promise that you will kill me if the time ever comes."

Kiernan's countenance shifted from worry to alarm.

"You can't be serious."

I crossed my arms over my chest, folding in on myself, sight cast down to avoid the look of impairment I knew he would have.

"A lot happened last night, and most of it is uncertain to me, but there are several things I know. You nearly died, your relationship with your family is crumbling, I am destined to kill all of you, and from my understanding, you've given me this protection that interferes with others causing me harm, but..." I lifted my sight, and I was right; he looked perfectly dejected, "can you?"

"Ari," he tried, reaching for me, and I broke from the contact despite the painful twist it inflicted on my heart.

"Can you hurt me?" I repeated, determined to have his response.

His arms fell to his sides, flexing into fists as I had witnessed many times prior, and it felt like I was losing him rather than receiving his help.

"According to the law, because it's my *týpos*, yes, I could. But—"

"And you would live? Even if I died," I pressed, recalling Killian's caution to Kell over hurting me, needing to understand the extent that we were tied.

"Yes," he answered steadily, composing himself as though this conversation was appalling to him, "But you must understand that it was buried in me to keep you safe even before all of this, and now, if someone so much as looked at you the wrong way, I want to kill them. It doesn't matter who it is, and it doesn't exclude myself."

I exhaled sharply and dug my fingers into my arms.

"I want to believe that everything will be okay, but I'm always going to be afraid if I don't have that security of someone else being there to stop me."

He watched me for a moment.

"I promise."

My brows drew downward.

"You don't mean it."

"Not in the slightest."

"Kiernan—"

"You don't understand what you are asking of me!" he exclaimed, the earnest state of his voice startled me, "I am a dragon. My entire being is made for loyalty and protection, and even thinking of harming you destroys everything I am! If it's the words you want, I will give them to you, but I could never promise to kill you in any sense of honesty."

"Then take it back!" I pleaded, matching his tone, "Whatever this guard you put over me, this marking that keeps your kind from defending from their prophesied ending, take it back so someone can do it for you."

Kiernan was shaken, his forming argument dying on his tongue, staring at me like I'd spoken his worst fears.

"I can't," he stated, but it was hollow of the emotion his voice carried seconds ago, "It is permanent."

"What are you going to do if the prophecy is right?"

"Killian is back," he dismissed the idea as though his brothers' return could fix any of this, and I was left with no solution and a greater dread pitting in my stomach.

"Good evening, you two," Keagan cheered, entering first, Kaid and Killian following after.

Kell was nowhere to be found.

"How are we feeling?" I missed Keagan's question, noticing how Killian's features were neutralized, stepping into the cabin with an exaggerated focus, refusing to acknowledge me as he walked past Kiernan and me to the supply closet at my back. "Well, I am wonderful, thank you for asking. It's incredible what a day of sleep will do for you."

"You all slept outside?" I asked, focusing my attention on someone who clearly wanted it.

"I'm sure this house feels very spacious to you, Love, but when four dragons try to rest in the same room, it gets pretty cramped," he explained in that teasing tone of his, finishing with a wink, and for a split second, I smiled.

"Killian... what are those for?" Kiernan questioned suspiciously, and the nearness of his voice told me he'd moved close to me while both distracted, as if I was a force field he couldn't combat.

"We don't know what to expect," Killian answered, closing the closet door with several long lines of rope in his arms, the same kind I'd found around Kaid's wrist that night I attempted to escape, "Sirens' gifts are a formidable thing, and she may very well become dangerous after tonight. The best we can do is restrain her. There is a cave that feeds into the ocean a good distance from here, and I think that would be the ideal place to contain her as she ages."

"You plan to tie her to a *rock*?" He seethed, and I threaded my arm through his, worried a new battle was starting with a different brother.

"I do," he answered unapologetically, and the nonchalance of it only upset Kiernan further.

"Careful, Kier. Your possessiveness is showing," Keagan taunted, and it was comforting to see him smirking again, even at Kiernan's expense. It gave me hope that things could go back to normal.

"He just gave his *týpos* away. His protective nature will be stronger than normal for a while," Killian explained, speaking as though none of what occurred the previous night affected him, his cool and collected mask pasted on, indifferent haze in his eyes when turning to me, "Rowe."

"Yes?" I answered, sounding altogether very tiny, feeling even smaller under Killian's scrutiny.

"What would you prefer to do?"

They were all looking at me, and while Kiernan's skin was abnormally hot under my touch as I continued to hold his arm, he said nothing. I glanced at the remaining four of them, attention straining on Kaid neither smiling nor apathetic, the boy too young to mask what he was feeling, and the emotions set in his face were too strong.

"Use the ropes."

"There you have it," Killian announced, shifting focus to Kiernan and leveling him with a look, "The decision was hers. We leave now."

I watched the stars the whole flight. They weren't as bright as they'd been the night before, shining proudly as Kiernan and I gazed at them, or perhaps that was simply my perception. The world itself seemed to glow when he first kissed me.

We were in the air longer than I was used to, moving farther than their normal range, and as I spotted the hollowed cliff attached to the ocean, I didn't ask how they found it in the first place, not speaking at all unless deeming it necessary. "Sea Lion Caves," I heard Killian call them after we landed, though I didn't see any of the animals around the area and decided that was probably for the best. I hadn't been told the time, but judging how Killian and Keagan hurriedly worked together to tie the ropes around the center rock I was placed on, I assumed we were nearing midnight. My wrists were bound separately in attempts to give me a fraction of freedom, while my ankles were tied together to uncomplicate things when I inevitably lost my legs. Kiernan was extremely displeased with the entire process.

"Let me stay with her," he pleaded as they readied to fly out, but Killian was unmovable.

"The tide is coming in. You will drown, Kiernan."

"Go," I insisted, "I'll be fine."

I didn't want him near, not if there was a possibility I could hurt him, and after a bit more resistance, Kiernan left, joining his brothers on the top of the grassy cliff. I was alone but didn't despise it, comforted by water and unbreakable rocks being the closest things in reach, secure in the way my limbs were pinned. I stared at the cave's ceiling for some time, examining the different formations throughout the whole space.

The tide began to wash in, splashing against the rocks and dotting droplets over my face. It was deafeningly loud, the sound of waves colliding echoing through the cave, the water chilling as it lapped around my ankles, rushing over my waist and coming up to my neck until it, at last, overtook my head.

I was drowning and breathing. I was screaming and silent. I was distraught and comforted. I was human and siren.

But under the current, the ocean whispered over the mark at the back of my neck, flowing a different sort of air into my chest, and my lungs greedily consumed liquid oxygen. My eyes readjusted to the water, taking in the sea's power from beneath the tide, and with no one drowning or a desperate need for air, contentment greeted me peacefully. My legs were gone, a brilliant tail replacing them, and I examined the blue and violet hues of the scales, moonlight reflecting to give it an entrancing glow. I traced my fingers over the cold, smooth ridges and was slightly surprised to find them almost ticklish. My hair floated around my face, and the waves seemed to play with it just as the wind had, and I found the two to be very similar. The ocean was gentle and warm, so quiet, caressing me into relaxation, and all too easily, I fell under a spell, closing my eyes and accepting the visions.

I remembered the world feeling too big. I didn't remember being six. I remembered running to Mother's room. I didn't remember waking up. I remembered trying to get the baby to stop crying. I didn't remember crying. I remembered fearing he would wake Mother. I didn't remember Mother was deaf. I remembered lifting the baby into my arms. I didn't remember Mother's bed creaking as someone stood. I remembered feeling warm. I didn't remember being hugged. I remembered whispering, "I can't do this." I didn't remember him answering, "You shouldn't have to." I remembered the baby being taken from me. I didn't remember heading back to bed. I remembered not having a father. I didn't remember gaining a new one.

But I did remember, one by one, the memories reforming my past into the truth.

I remembered Mother remarrying. I remembered not raising Anders alone.

I remembered Zadar most of all, his kind smile, his caring nature, and the days he left, leaving me in charge until he returned. Sometimes, it was weeks, other times, it was months, but he always came back. As though a veil had been lifted from my eyes, I remembered all the places that fit in my life, the gaps in my memories that I could never make sense of. He was the one who sat in the empty seat. He was the one who put that present under the tree for me for Christmas. He was the reason Anders was conquering his nightmares. He was my friend. He was my dad.

And I remembered the day I began forgetting.

"Yer mother's worried," Zadar had said, a crease in his brow telling me he was nervous himself, "Her mind's no... sound, and I fear it'll only get worse the longer she frets aboot ye."

"She worries about me?" I'd questioned, wondering if we spoke of the distant woman who knew nothing more than how to hold me at arm's length, and Zadar had nodded like he understood my confusion.

"I knen it may be hard tae see just noo, but she cares for ye deeply, and efter yer father's death, she cannae bear the thocht o' losin' ye. It's fear that it is keeping her frae tryin' tae reach ye. Ye're someone verra special, Ari, and once the world kens ye're here, ye'll be no safe. When ye're eighteen, ye'll be able tae defend yersel, but that's six year awa', and there are folk oot there who'd dae anythin' tae get tae ye while ye're vulnerable."

"What would anybody want *me* for?"

"It depends. Some for guid, others for evil, and those who'd rather see ye deid." I'd felt myself pale, recoiling a step, and Zadar's gaze was remorseful.

"Why has Mother said nothing of this?"

"She doesnae want ye tae ken. In her mind, if ye're ignorant o' it, danger winnae come seekin' ye. Which is whit I wanted tae speak tae ye aboot," Zadar hesitated, taking the seat on the couch, and I could tell the matter was serious from his posture, "There are mony worlds outside of this one, and ye're no a bairn ony mair. I ken ye've realized I'm no exactly normal, and that's where the problem lies." I'd known Zadar wasn't completely as he presented himself to be from the mysterious amount of time he spent away. He had this strange ability to talk with Mother without words yet took the time to teach me and little Anders sign language. "The mythical realm's what she's wantin' tae protect ye frae, at least till ye're auld enough tae handle it, but that involves removin' everythin' ye ken o' that world... includin' me."

"Mother wants me to forget you exist?" I'd questioned, and it felt so wrong to say.

"Aye," Zadar answered, appearing just as displeased.

"But how?"

"I've the ability tae... alter a human's mind tae make them believe things that arenae real, and for ye, I'd erase masel from yer memories so it'd feel as though I was never here at aw."

I'd thought over his words, understanding how strongly I didn't want this, but Mother hadn't smiled at me in years, and I would do anything to get her back.

"You really think this will help her?"

"She asked for it specifically," Zadar answered, and I nodded, recognizing the truth in his words.

"Okay. I will do it," I complied, and he tried to smile, but it came out wrong.

"Ye'll no remember me, but that disnae mean I'll no be here. I'm no abandonin' ye."

"I know," I assured, beginning to fidget with the shell tucked in my pocket, "You will come let me remember one day, won't you?"

"I will. Ye'll no stay like this forever; that's my promise to ye. Noo, look intae ma een."

I'd obeyed, meeting his ocean stare, sensing key memories being washed away, drowning until the day I could learn to swim strong enough and save them.

"I love you, Dad," I said in a temporary goodbye, and Zadar's eyes began to water as he smiled one of those sad smiles.

"I love ye too."

It was finally that day, bringing it all back to the surface, and I remembered everything.

Someone was shouting my name over and over, but they were far away, and I couldn't see. I did my best to follow the sound, quickening my blind run as the familiar voice became more frantic, deepening my scavenge into past thoughts, and I spotted a light in the distance. The closer I got to the brightness, the less I could see, but I kept walking until I was blinded, and the voice was near my face.

"Ari. Ari, can you hear me? Open your eyes. Look at me."

I pried my eyelids open and was shocked to find it easy to see, meeting the stare of a boy.

He was rugged and handsome, with a sturdy jaw and full brows, hair a pale blonde, and sea-deep eyes glittering like liquid sapphires.

"Who are you?" I whispered, longing to understand this person I hadn't met yet, strangely feeling as though I'd known him all my life. The man appeared younger when he smiled, close to my age, dimples in his cheeks, and when answering my question, he leaned in dangerously close.

"Yer mate."

The atmosphere began to shift, the light surrounding the boy diminishing, blonde hair fading to black, ocean blue evolving into forest green, and I knew that face.

"Kiernan," I rasped, trying to identify where the other man had gone.

"She's awake!" Kiernan shouted over the waves to his brothers, lifting my spinning head to lay it on his chest, "Are you alright? You weren't responding."

"I'm fine," I drawled, continuing to glance around the cave, "Just fell asleep."

Keagan stepped into view, carrying the wet ropes, glancing at me with concern, while I stared back in confusion.

"Why did you untie me?"

"I didn't," Kiernan answered before Keagan could, and I briefly wondered if the ocean-eyed stranger had been the one to release me, "She's frigid, Killian," Kiernan informed, but I didn't feel cold at all, not with him holding me. Killian used the back of his hand to touch the side of my neck and rest over my forehead as a mother would check for signs of sickness.

"Let's get her back to the cabin. We can discuss things there," Killian instructed, but I barely heard it, closing my eyes, nuzzling into Kiernan's warmth, and doing my best not to forget the handsome stranger as I had forgotten so many other things in my past.

Chapter Thirty-One

"You fell asleep?" Killian interrogated, standing while the rest of us sat on the couches, Kiernan close to me and doing his best to warm my chilled skin, holding the hands he claimed were frozen, but I didn't feel cold at all, nodding to Killian's doubts, "Nothing else happened? For *five* hours?"

"It was that long?" I questioned back, glancing out the window to see any implication of time in the sky, but it was just as pitch black as it had been when we left. I couldn't decipher whether Killian assumed I was lying or if he was simply displeased by the lack of events I'd recalled, but he looked at me strangely.

"You don't feel any different?" Killian asked at the same time Keagan pondered, rather jokingly, "There wasn't any magical water explosion or something?"

"No," I answered, but it was an honesty to Keagan. The holes in my childhood were filled, and where I once felt hurt and confused, I felt hope for the family I always desired, but that wasn't something I could admit, not when, despite everything, I was still their hostage.

"This doesn't make sense. The prophecy was clear. The *Dákry* would accept her call once she turned eighteen," Killian impatiently explained, a balance of frustration and determination.

"I think the ability to sleep underwater is pretty neato."

"Keagan," Killian reprimanded, and the boy shrugged with a smirk.

"Are we confident in the clarity of her calling?" Kiernan pondered, dropping my warmed hands and shifting to hold me from behind, and though I tried not to let its effect be noticeable, the heat against my back gave me goosebumps. "A calling could be interpreted as something other than an evil power. All the prophecy *plainly* stated was that, if the course of the future was to be changed, it needed to happen before she turned eighteen, not that she gains some dark force."

"You mean to tell me *this* girl is supposed to tear us down? Just as she is? I've seen young elk with more lethal qualities than her."

I flinched. It was entirely involuntary, and I shouldn't have been hurt that Killian didn't possibly see me as a threat, but it felt like a disappointment, and I'd had that impression enough without his opinions. Kiernan propped his chin on my shoulder, more silent communication through insignificant touches, and the cool ache began to simmer away.

"What if the prophecy is just wrong?" Kaid joined, and it was obvious he only wanted to help, watching how Killian stressed, but no one agreed with him.

"Or maybe..." Killian drawled, examining me for a long moment, "maybe she is not the *Dákry*." I held his stare, wanting him to believe that, even if my visions of Zadar proved otherwise, "For now, keeping distance from her until we have a full understanding of the situation is our best option," Killian instructed, taking notice to Kiernan, whose head still nestled over my shoulder, arms encircling my waist, then sighed, "I need to clear my head."

We watched him leave with sealed lips and scrambled minds. The sun was rising, and because of the previous two nights, I didn't notice the ruined mess my sleep schedule had become.

It was too silent, the room filled with musty, unanswered questions, and I was the source of it all.

Problem without a solution. A nightmare. A curse. A monster.

"Stop it," Kiernan whispered, and I felt it more than I heard it, a soft stroke of words on the side of my neck, stirring the butterflies in my stomach. I focused on the feel of him calmly breathing against me, the steady sound, and it was the only thing keeping me anchored when my thoughts wanted to spiral and guilt attempted to reside in my chest. My heart spiked when he took a sharp intake of air, hands brushing over my abdomen as he let go of me to stand.

"We can worry about this later," he said, walking to the radio and turning it on. Lively, upbeat music poured from the speaker, easing the tense silence. "*Dákry* or not, it's Ari's eighteenth birthday. Let's celebrate."

"Celebrate how?" Keagan piped up, sounding very excited for a distraction, and Kiernan nodded to me, smiling wickedly.

"She has a new dance to teach us."

"What?" I stammered and was promptly drowned out by Keagan's enthusiastic voice, practically leaping from his seat.

"Dancing? Count me in. How does it go, Beautiful?"

"Wait, no," I protested, but that did little to stop them.

"You said it was for a group. Here is your group," Kiernan offered, taking both my hands in his and bringing me to my feet.

"But Killian—"

"Such a little rule follower," Keagan sighed, shaking his head in a disappointed manner, as if my very being wasn't potentially life-threatening.

"Killian's not here," Kiernan reminded slyly, and I almost giggled at the sneaky expression he wore, if it could even be called that.

"Spoken like a true older sibling! Now then, you were saying?" Keagan clapped, rubbing his hands together and waiting for directions.

"We need at least four people," I explained, shutting the idea down until a shy voice ruined my final attempts.

"Can I join?" Kaid requested, sounding so hopeful to be included, and Kiernan turned back to me with raised eyebrows.

"Any other excuses?" he prompted, a challenging lilt in his tone, and I caved. "Take my hands."

Kiernan and Keagan complied, holding a hand on either side of me, and Kaid quickly caught on, connecting our small circle on the other end. I began leading them while adding small instructions, and in a matter of seconds, the group was effortlessly spinning in unison, unfazed as we shifted to the other direction, hopping back around until we were in our original placement. I broke it off then, turning to my right, and they all three watched as I faced Kiernan, skipping in place with proper footwork before reaching for both of Kiernan's hands and spinning in a circle the two of us created, informing Keagan and Kaid to do the same, and pure chaos ensued afterward. The movement of singularly dancing around one another, forming incomplete figure eights, was used to rearrange participants, ensuring a new partner each time, but while the explanation was understood, the follow-through was a disaster. Keagan attempted to gracefully weave through, but Kaid's pace was quicker, and I got caught in the crossfire.

I hadn't heard such lively, contagious laughter condensed in a single room in a very long time.

Keagan was cackling on the floor, Kiernan sounding just like him as he helped Kaid up, who couldn't stop giggling himself, and I was bent over, holding my aching stomach while trying to regain my hysterical breath.

We still didn't get that part correctly the second time, or third, but it was almost more fun through the mistakes made than the way I had it perfectly practiced. We all took turns spinning each other, laughing when there was a collision, and I began to think Keagan was bumping into me on purpose. The music was pulsing through my veins, demanding a way out, a release that my body would find as a refuge, and Kiernan could sense it as he took my hands, pulling me slightly closer while we spun.

"Sing, Ari," he encouraged, beaming like nothing could make him happier, and I couldn't refuse him anything when his eyes were sparkling. My voice accompanied the song blaring on the radio, harmonizing with the tune and creating my own ridiculous lyrics when I didn't know the words, and while I expected Kaid at the very least to stop dancing and stare at me in concern as he had many times before, the boy only jumped higher, seemingly excited. Smiles widened as I carried the song around the room, my lungs expanding more easily despite how out of breath I was becoming, lost in the exhilarating understanding that I'd been dancing with dragons.

After a moment of twirling with Kaid, laughing through my singing as he giggled, my dizzying sight caught a figure looming by the door, and I froze in place.

Killian was observing us, for how long, I was uncertain, but I braced myself for a proper reprimanding. There was a painful longing in his eyes, a broken happiness as he watched his younger brothers smiling lightheartedly, and his focus shifted to me, my body stiffening. Unexpectedly, Killian's head dipped slightly, offering me a small nod that conveyed more than I assumed he could express, heading then to the seclusion of his parents' old room, a place rarely visited.

"Ari, you're my partner this time around. Stop slacking," Keagan jokingly scolded, and if he was aware of the interaction, he did not let it show. Keagan easily swept me back into the dance, and it was easier to forget about any prophecies when I was looked at as someone who mattered.

Song after song shuffled through the crackling radio, our tempo changing to match the beat, and my breathing became too heavy to join the lyrics, but that did not hinder me from dancing. I could already feel the soreness in my legs, moving in ways I hadn't since I was a child, dancing in the kitchen with Mother, but Kiernan was there, pulling me from my negative thoughts once more as we joined hands.

"Come with me," he mouthed, leading me to the door, the music masking our exit, enabling Keagan and Kaid to continue uninterrupted.

The new rays of daylight were blinding, and I lost sight of Kiernan initially, that was until a dragon pounced from my poor field of vision, wrapping a tail around my waist and tossing me into a redwood.

"Stop *doing that*!" I scolded wide-eyed, gripping the tree for stability, but he was chuckling, and I couldn't stay mad when he was happy.

"I want to talk about last night."

"I thought we were going to worry about that later," I reminded him of his own words, hoping he'd simply forgotten he'd said as much and would drop the topic, but things were never that easy.

"Yeah, except, there is something you aren't telling me," he responded, and I blinked, causing him to smile as though I'd just proved his point, "You are terrible at hiding how you feel. Even without my senses, I can see the emotions plastered on your face."

"Oh," I exhaled, grinning sheepishly while better supporting myself over a branch to descend, and Kiernan was suddenly there, scandalously close, blocking my way and covering the places my hands rested with his own, pinning my arms in place.

"I'm not letting you down until you give me honesty," he promised, tracking the heat rushing up my neck, reading into the redness of my face, and I realized just how much of an open book I was to him. "I'm waiting." But he was too near, his little grin too distracting, and I couldn't think properly.

"I got my memories back," I spewed with my brain on autopilot, and graciously, Kiernan leaned back, giving a perplexed look, anticipating elaboration, "My stepfather, Zadar, the kelpie I was with in Crescent City, he removed all of my memories of him in my life because Mother asked him to."

"Why would she wish for that?"

"She wanted to shelter me from the mythical realm because she knew who I was. Zadar did, too, but he didn't say specifics, saying I was someone special that people would come for once they knew I existed."

Kiernan studied my face, and I couldn't read into his expression, so I attempted to change the subject before he discovered something I may not have even known yet.

"Where did the prophecy of the *Dákry* come from?"

"All prophecies come from kelpies."

Kelpies who only spoke in truth, as if I had any question in my mind about whether they were lies.

Kiernan answered too easily, swapping between both of my eyes for more answers, and just when I was about to deflect to another topic, he squinted at me.

"That's not all, is it?" It wasn't a question.

I hesitated.

"I saw someone," I stated slowly, dropping my eyes from his, "It was only a vision like everything else, but he looked so real. He might've been a kelpie. I didn't know him, but... but I think I am supposed to? I've been trying to piece it together for a while now."

"Did you talk to him?"

"Briefly. I tried to get his name, but all he said was that I..."

"You what?"

I wetted my lips, glancing back to him.

"He said I was his mate."

Kiernan's brows lowered.

"Sounds like kelpie ridiculousness, but that doesn't make sense. Kelpies can't have mates. They don't have romantic desires."

"But Zadar married my mother. He's the reason I have a brother. How can you explain that?"

"I can't. In fact, it's... strange that happened. Something's not lining up," Kiernan answered, no longer looking at me but eyeing a fern below us suspiciously, "I know you care for him because of the role he has played in your family, but I wouldn't trust it. Kelpies can bend feeling to their advantage, and that is something to always be cautious of."

"Zadar wouldn't manipulate me," I argued, and that drew Kiernan's attention back to me.

"Hasn't he already?"

I wasn't sure what Kiernan was seeing on my face now, but I knew it wasn't pleasant. I wanted to defend Zadar, but I was still learning of different creatures, and Kiernan already had all of his information gathered. I searched for the fern Kiernan stared at, mumbling, "Do you think Kell will be coming back soon?"

Kiernan jumped out of the tree, pulling me with him, and though I didn't feel stable, I was grateful to be on the ground.

"*That* is something we *will* worry about later," he announced, a refreshing life returning to his voice, "I don't want to discuss anything more today that isn't about you and the many wonderful years you have ahead of you."

I was happy with that decision, and Kiernan's hands came to cup my face, his eyes falling to my lips for a split second, but he didn't advance further, instead smiling as he said, *"eithe zeses polla ete, Agapití."*

Chapter Thirty-Two

"Evie!" Zadar called, "Evie, why dinnae ye come doon the stairs?"

Mother didn't respond. Zadar kept forgetting. I did, too. She stopped hearing our calls a week ago, and in that time, I gained a new father. It was strange seeing Zadar this long. He'd normally left by now, but he was here, cooking us a classic Scottish breakfast while Mother painted in the room that eventually became Anders'. I liked having him around. Zadar kept the house from being silent.

"Evie? Is everythin' awri—"

He stopped, recognition setting in, and he was getting better, just as I was. It was going to take time to get used to a deaf family member. Zadar sighed, setting down the tongs he used to flip the bacon, his displeasure with himself evident on his face, and I didn't like it when he looked sad.

"Why do you call Mother 'Evie'?" I asked, taking a seat at the table and staring up at him. Zadar was very tall.

"Because she's special tae me, and I wanted tae gie her a special name," he answered, sitting in the chair across from me. Most of his sadness had been washed from his eyes.

"Can you give me a special name too?"

Zadar smiled at me.

"I've already got one. Ari. D'ye like it?"

My face lit up.

"It sounds just like hers!" I cheered, nodding fast. Zadar chuckled.

"Well, Ari, would ye mind keepin' an ee on the food while I go get yer mother?"

I nodded again. I loved to help. The pan was too high for me to reach, but I wasn't going to let Zadar down. He left, and I stared at the sizzling food. Mother would be happy to eat today. She liked the strange-looking sausage

Zadar made. My hand played with the shell in my pocket while waiting for them. I worried the tomatoes were going to burn, but Zadar was back in time to save them. I smiled when they entered the kitchen, excited to have three members at our table. Zadar pulled out Mother's chair, and she touched his arm to say thank you, but he stopped moving suddenly, and his eyes got really blue.

"Whit d'ye see?" Mother questioned while taking a better hold of Zadar's arm. She forgot she was deaf at times, too, speaking nearly flawlessly despite not hearing herself. Zadar snapped out of his trance at the sound of her voice, facing his wife with a wondering expression.

They did that sometimes, talk with their eyes, but they suddenly appeared excited, and I felt left out.

"What is it?" I asked, touching Mother's arm to get her to speak with me instead of Zadar, and I was happy to see her smiling again. She was so pretty when she smiled.

"I'm goin' tae have a baby," she said, but her voice was really quiet. I looked at her, confused, but excited that she was happy.

"I want to see a baby," I answered, searching for it near Mother, and she held my hand. She hadn't done that since Father died.

"I have a baby in my tummy," she clarified, her voice even smaller than before. I was scared she would lose it forever.

"What's her name?"

"We dinnae ken if it's a boy or a girl."

"Maybe it's a girl," I answered, and Mother laughed. I loved her laugh.

"Do ye want a sister or a brother?" Zadar joined, taking the food from the stove and placing it on the table. Eggs and mushrooms sat in front of me.

"I want a sister."

"But ye'll love it if it's a brother," he gently persuaded, Mother reading his lips, the joy still in her eyes.

"No, I want a sister," I answered honestly, and it made Zadar laugh. He sat to my right, Mother across from him, the dark sausage and tomatoes in front of her.

"Evie and Ari. Ma two lassies," Zadar stated warmly, squeezing both my hand and Mother's.

"Maybe three girls soon!" I exclaimed, liking the idea of having a baby the longer I thought about it.

"Maybe," he chuckled.

"What are you thinking about?" Kiernan questioned, taking the seat next to me, and I had to blink at him multiple times to bring him into view, along with my life at the present. I'd zoned out while staring at the woods through the window, recalling memories I couldn't before as I watched Keagan and Kaid chase each other in the sky.

Anders and I nearly shared the same birthday, a small amount of time separating the two, and it had been two days since I turned eighteen.

Today was Anders' golden birthday.

"Ari?"

'Ari. D'ye like it?' Zadar's voice echoed in my mind, and I could almost feel his presence with me, my family so close yet so far.

"I have to go back," I blurted, and that grabbed Killian's attention from across the room as Kiernan's face twisted into confusion.

"What are you talking about?"

"Anders turns thirteen today. We always spent our birthdays together. He's going to be broken-hearted more than he already is. They need to know I am alive!"

"I agree," Killian added unexpectedly, "Go home, Ari."

"Really?" I questioned, never imagining those words would escape him, and Kiernan seemed equally surprised.

"You've proven to be the opposite of what I assumed. We have no right to keep you here," Killian explained, and there was something in his eyes as he said it, something hidden too well for me to discern, but his expression was almost softer.

I hopped up from the couch, eyes wide and heart filled with anticipation, grabbing Kiernan's arm to yank him to his feet.

"I get to go home!" I shouted, squeezing his muscles under my palm in anticipation, "I'm going home!"

"Hold on a minute," he gently insisted, grabbing my wrist, "What about us? You can't just leave like that."

"Coming down to her well-being and your selfish wants, you would choose for her to stay?" Killian proposed before I could respond, but he didn't know about all the promises we made about just that, that Kiernan was justified in his concerns when I assured him I wanted to stay, but I doubted saying that would change anything. Killian was watching him carefully, assessing his response, and I sensed this was more a test for Kiernan, but he seemed to pick up on the same idea, sighing before caving.

"Okay. Let's get you home."

"My lemon curd, I didn't think you would be *this* excited to leave me," he chucked, observing how I bounced as we stood at the edge of the redwoods, overlooking the beach and my neighborhood.

"I will be back soon, don't worry," I promised, stepping on my tiptoes to kiss him without warning, and I loved the surprised delight it brought to his face, "You'll know where to find me."

"Our tree?"

"Our tree."

Kiernan appeared as though he had more to say, and I felt the strain in his hands that he fought to pull me back to him, but he let me go, and I ran to the little orange door.

My heart was racing, and after days of being in fear, I relished in the sensation deriving from excitement. I pictured Anders' face when he saw me alive, the joy and relief that would wash over him, or Zadar's as I confessed to remembering everything. Mother had done all of this to keep me safe; surely I'd see her smile as she had so many times in the past.

I was entirely breathless once I reached my driveway, my smile wild and unconfined because I could finally see him. Anders, my little brother, my sunshine, visible through the front window, sitting at the table with a grin nearly as large as mine. Zadar stepped into view, placing a firm but loving hand over his son's shoulder, and the look he gave Anders reminded me of the expression he wore when gifting me a nickname.

Then Mother appeared.

I was mere steps away from the door, a few seconds away from reopening the life I'd dreamed of, but I was suddenly frozen, an unseen force halting me by the window. Mother was carrying a cake in her hands; one freshly baked enough that she still had blue frosting on her apron. It was a fever dream watching her set the cake on the table in front of Anders, planting a kiss on his head, beaming a smile that replenished me with nostalgia, signing to him as I'd imagined her doing for the last thirteen years, and it suddenly felt as though I was intruding on such a special moment.

Slowly, my smile receded, my limbs jittery with excitement, now falling limp and useless. Rocks were tumbling down my throat, scraping as they went, blocking my airways and landing in my stomach, weighing my body down. I was sinking into the ground that had always felt stable in the past, cold as it was, and the world around me seemed to darken the deeper I descended.

They thought I was dead, and they were laughing. I was gone, and their life was finally complete. They were the picture-perfect family, and I was the piece that didn't belong.

The doors were closed, and they were happy.

My legs were backing away from the window, looking to run from this constriction building in my chest, but I wasn't fast enough. Swallowing harshly reminded me that my throat wasn't collapsing, sprinting that my knees hadn't given out, finding Kiernan that I wasn't completely abandoned.

He hadn't left yet, wanting to ensure that I made it inside safely, but my brain was too scattered to understand the reasoning, only seeing the moonlight in my world that was losing its sunshine, and Kiernan met me halfway on the beach.

"What's wrong?" he asked, instinctively bringing me into his embrace, and something was breaking inside me, something I didn't know how to put back together.

"Could we go back, please?" I whispered, knowing that if I spoke any louder, my voice would crack, my strength with it, and I couldn't fall apart as I was inwardly.

"Yeah... sure," Kiernan responded, the confusion prominent in his tone, and when I failed to elaborate, he shifted and carried me away. I never let go of him, hands clinging to his scales with more energy than my wilting body had to offer, panicking that he'd disappear too, that he would find someone else who made him smile brighter, and my head drooped onto his powerful form. Still, I did not answer the unspoken questions stuffing the air after landing, wordlessly walking to the cabin door while Kiernan reinstated his human mask behind me.

"She's back!" Kaid cheered, but I couldn't bring myself to look at him, and though I kept my sight on the floor, I felt the room shift from excitement to concern as I stepped into the threshold. It was worse, I realized, to be disregarded by the ones I thought loved me rather than caring for someone I knew didn't because the latter didn't make me feel like a fool. I was a fool, though, to ever assume peace would come from my living. Anders had enough monsters to deal with in his mind; he didn't need a sister, too.

Keagan was the first to break the growing silence, and I wish he hadn't, asking the one question that tore down impenetrable walls, drawing a match to a forest of dry grass.

"Are you okay?"

Then I crumpled to the floor and sobbed.

Chapter Thirty-Three

K aid had been the first to react, getting on his knees to hug me, and his empathy felt too much like Anders'. It must've been his first time witnessing such an emotion, seeing an ache in invisible wounds so blatantly through cries of despair, and he only held on to me tighter. Keagan inched closer, but Kiernan made it to me first, never seeming to leave my side, and as they both rested on the ground, I found myself being comforted by three dragons. Killian stayed where he was, watching the tender exchange, and though he didn't join, his eyes softened.

No one questioned why I'd fallen apart so suddenly, and they didn't have to. The information was easy enough to piece together.

"You are welcome to stay as long as you like," Killian offered with a gentleness in his tone that had the same effect on my heart as though he'd given me a hug, and while I tried to express my gratitude, my breaths were too shaky, "Keagan. Kaid. Let's give her some space."

Rather reluctantly, the two stood, following the eldest as he left the cabin and flew off, leaving Kiernan and me alone in the middle of the floor.

"Would touch be good or bad for you right now, *Agapiti*?" he asked, keeping his distance but ensuring I wasn't alone.

"Good," I whispered, sighing as I was pulled into an enveloping warmth, and Kiernan seemed just as pleased to hold me, his fingers moving up and down my spine as they did anytime he wanted me to relax, "Always good."

"What happened, Ari?" he asked sincerely, and despite wanting nothing more than to take in the burning scent of wood on his skin and forget all but him, Anders' brilliant smile appeared in the darkness of my closing eyes.

"They are happy," I answered softly, my melancholy tone offsetting my words, and I didn't fault Kiernan for the confusion that twisted his features.

"Isn't that what you want?"

"Yes."

My voice was distant, in no hurry to ever return, and I didn't mind it so much as the concern knitting Kiernan's eyebrows. He lifted my chin, studying my face in order to read my expression, wiping the slowing tears from my cheeks as they fell.

"Stop closing yourself off," Kiernan pleaded, "You are hurting. Tell me why."

"Mother didn't let me leave the house most of my life. That family is all I've ever known," I tried to open up, but it was only ripping a gaping wound, sharp memories and harsh understanding prodding at my sensitive flesh, "And even then, I didn't know fully. I've wanted a father for years, and the moment I found out I had one all along, I see how happy they are without me." I choked on the air, pressing into Kiernan, desperate for him to take the cold away. "They all think I'm dead, and I've never witnessed such... relief."

Relief.

That's what it'd been, the ease that floated in that room. I wasn't upset with them; how could I be? I was a burden they carried for far too long.

Should've left sooner. Selfish to be alive. Never see them again. Let them live happily.

My limbs were too heavy again, and I was too drained to hold myself up, dropping onto Kiernan.

"Okay," he gently announced, scooping my numb body into his arms and lifting me from the ground, "Let's get you to bed."

"I don't want them to ever find out I'm alive, Kiernan," I whispered, almost in a plea, as though he planned to tell them, my head resting over his shoulder and my message near his ear.

"Ari," he soothed, laying me down over a bed that felt far too big to occupy alone, kneeling at the edge to meet my gaze, "You are hurting. Don't make decisions like that right now."

"I'm sorry," I answered, relishing in the warm touch of his fingertips sweeping over my brow, "You're right. I'm overreacting."

"You are not overreacting. I'm the middle child of five brothers. I know what it's like to be overlooked. How do you think I was able to sneak away every day to see you?" He offered a tiny grin, sympathetic yet breathtaking in its glow, his eyes illuminated in the darkness, and my brain was too tired to keep from impulsively speaking the things that entered my mind.

"You are beautiful," I mumbled, staring at his magnificent features through bleary eyes, but that didn't hinder me from seeing his brave face melt away. I wouldn't have thought a small cluster of words could impact a person as strong and lethal as Kiernan, but it did, folding onto the side of the bed with his chin under his crossed arms, a softness coming to his eyes as his pupils enlarged, reminding me of a hopeful puppy. I giggled slightly, committing his expression of deep and whole affection to memory so I wouldn't forget I still mattered to someone, and as if that look weren't enough, he acted on it.

Kiernan kissed me slowly, taking his time as his hands found their way to my face, delighting in the feeling of my lips on his as though there was no better place we needed to be than in each other's company, and I supposed we didn't, not anymore. His scent flooded my mind with every wonderful moment we shared, each challenge, each tease, each touch, and it was a comfort to have such a distraction. The butterflies in my stomach were still grieving as my heart was, but for him, they took on a new life. Dragon's senses were something I would never experience fully, but for just a moment, if only for a holding of breath, I felt him. There was such adoration and desire to protect, to lighten and crush my heart all at once, crippling yet overpowering, and this need to be closer to him had me inching to the edge of the bed, using a hand to cup the back of his neck while his touch slid down to my waist. Every movement from our lips to my fingers slipping into his hair, to the shapes he drew over the small of my back, were grounding and precise, and he was the only thing keeping me from spiraling. My hand came to his chest, one of his withdrawing from my waist to rest on top of the contact before he pulled back, and it took everything in me not to kiss each symmetrical curve and edge of his face, to see if he could feel the love I felt as I did for him, but our foreheads were pressed together, and I needed to catch my breath.

"I shouldn't keep doing that to you," he murmured close enough to my mouth to feel like a taunt.

"Doing what?" I asked, but the words formed involuntarily; every thought of my mind intoxicated by each point of contact we shared, how much he communicated through simple touches.

"Kissing you without warning."

He moved farther away then, and my world was able to come back into focus, even as it strained over the hand pressed against mine, my palm soaking in the power of his heat as I watched him curiously.

"Is that why you kept asking? You wanted to give me a heads-up?" I giggled, and his thumb began rubbing over the back of my hand.

"I'm still trying to figure all of this out. Balancing emotions when you haven't had them your entire life is no small task, and the feelings I have for you are only getting stronger. My biggest fear is doing something that would give you a reason to be afraid of me. I have to remind myself often how breakable you are and how easily I could hurt you without thinking. I can't seem to understand why you would choose this... choose me. It doesn't make sense, and quite honestly, I'm still waiting for you to run away."

"Kiernan," I eased, running a comforting hand through his hair, scolding myself for not doing so sooner after realizing how soft it truly was, "You are the best thing that has ever happened to me. I love you, and you shouldn't be afraid I'd change my mind on that. I know you'd never hurt me, and even if you did, the last thing I'd do is run. I'm yours. Kiss me whenever you feel like it."

"That is a dangerous thing to say," he warned, but it was only teasing, the easy nature revealing the reassurance my words brought him, and I played along.

"Maybe I like dangerous."

"You can't handle being put in a tree."

"I said danger. Not heights."

Kiernan chuckled, closing his eyes and leaning into my hand as it continued to lightly comb his hair before resting his head on the bedside, allowing me to graze my fingers over his neck.

"I love how cold you are," Kiernan sighed contentedly, "There is nothing more soothing than your touch."

"Do dragons get overheated?"

"No, you just feel nice, and since I'm not dying anymore, I can compliment you however I want," he reminded me of our little agreement back on the rock when he'd nearly bled out, and I'd done everything in my power to keep him awake.

"Within reason," I countered, and Kiernan leaned in close with a wide, playful grin on his face.

"Everything I say about you is very reasonable."

I was about to argue, but he was a step ahead of me, pressing a hushing kiss to my lips before a word could be uttered.

"We can debate later. You need rest."

He stood, and my brain must've remained on autopilot because I was speaking out not of my own accord, a quick rush of panic that he was leaving.

"Kiernan."

"Yes, *Agapiti?*"

I thought of different meanings that the title had, how incredibly intimate he made it sound coming from his lips, and it gave me the confidence to continue.

"You don't have to leave," I offered, perhaps too quietly, moving to give him space to lie, and his eyes fixated on the open spot. Kiernan was tentative in nearly everything he did for me, and now I understood it was a concern for my comfort, but he didn't have to worry when I offered the idea myself. My intentions were pure, as I knew his would be, resting together, wrapped in each other's closeness as we had on the couch days ago, yet he still hesitated.

"I would love to share a bed with you, Ari, and I like to think I will someday, but I can't now."

His wording left me confused, and if he simply didn't want to be near me while I made my best attempts to sleep, I would've accepted it, but that wasn't what he suggested.

"Why?"

"In my culture, a bed is not shared until the wedding night. We sleep on the floor or outside before we meet our partner. After the agreement of marriage, the groom will form the frame using the roots of the ground as a gift to the bride, and the more detailed the frame, the larger the display of affection. Marriage is sacred to my kind, and this is a symbol of it. Believe me, this doesn't come from a lack of wanting, but from a desire to respect you."

I closed my mouth, unwilling to argue a point that was sentimental to him, yet I hated not having him near. No one had chosen to stay with me until him, and nothing frightened me more than losing the connection we were forming.

"I'm not leaving you, Ari," Kiernan assured, reading the uncertainty in my eyes, "Forever, remember?"

"Forever," I echoed, hoping to sound understanding even if my heart struggled to believe him, that he would be the one to change his mind, decide I was not worth the burden and leave, but the kiss he placed on my head was tender, his whisper in my ear a promise.

"Sleep well, my beautiful sun tear."

I had no dreams, my mind dark as though blocking out the beautiful memories of my past, memories that would ache to see now. When I woke, my numb limbs were still aching, telling me I hadn't slept for nearly long enough, and I quickly became restless attempting to fall back to sleep, brain running through recent events until I was inspired with an idea. Ignoring my displeased body, I got out of my bed and entered the lightless atmosphere of the living room.

Kiernan, as I expected, was right outside my door in his primary form, his head propped on one of his arms, eyes far from tired, and upon seeing me, he shifted.

"What are you doing awake? It's the middle of the night," he questioned, head tilted, making him appear dragon-like despite wearing his human mask.

"Good. Your brothers won't be back for a while still," I answered, recalling the many times they returned from hunting at sunrise.

Making my way to the kitchen, I read through the mental recipe from the large cookbook of my memory, sorting the needed items. In the last several years, since I didn't have school to occupy me and the daytime hours in Crescent City were very lonely, I'd taken to cooking and memorization to pass the time, and it appeared to be paying off now.

"Could you light the fireplace? I can't find anything like this," I requested, and rather perplexed, Kiernan complied, brightening the area near the couches, but it did little for the kitchen across the large, open space connecting the two.

"What is this for?" he prodded, watching me rummage through the cabinets until I retrieved a large bowl.

"Expressing my gratitude. Now, where is the flour?"

Kiernan had to help me reach the things on the top shelves because this house, I was sure, could make Sasquatch appear small, and I didn't particularly feel like climbing on the countertops to collect ingredients.

I spent hours making the pastries, Kiernan standing by my side with a small flame cupped into his palm, shedding light onto my immediate line of sight until I'd move too quickly for him and he'd crush the fire in his hand in fear of accidentally burning me, then assessing I was fine, he breathed sparks into his hand to create a new light. He was never close enough to risk causing harm, but the sheer sincerity of concern on his face when I squeezed by him to reach for a utensil across the counter never ceased to make me laugh. Distracted by the entertainment Kiernan unintentionally created and the idea that his eyes seemed to be gaining more color by the day, the food was baked, the sun had risen, and the brothers were home in quick progression.

"What is the glorious smell?" Keagan inquired the moment he stepped inside, and before I could respond, Kaid spotted the dish cooling on the stove.

"Cinnamon rolls!" he exclaimed, eagerly rushing into the kitchen, and something clicked instinctually inside of me, seeing him reach for the dish freshly removed from the oven.

"They are hot, Anders! You'll burn—"

Kaid respectfully waited for me to finish, penetrating me with those innocent green eyes, but there was already a cinnamon roll in his hand, steam rolling off of it, and I remembered he was a dragon meant to handle the heat and not my brother, who had given himself a second-degree burn years ago in eagerness to taste my baking.

"Sorry," I sighed, collecting my composure and recognition, and I could sense the sympathetic gazes landing over me. It was quiet for a second, the patience they offered undeserved, and I wouldn't allow myself to cry, no matter how much my throat tightened. "I wanted to thank you," I started slowly, bracing my hands on the counter behind me to keep them from fidgeting with my necklace as I viewed them individually, "for yesterday."

Kiernan, head high, was eyeing Killian, a tiny smirk on his face that revealed his pride in me, as though baking was an unparalleled accomplishment.

"She made them from scratch," he bragged, and the way he spoke made me feel like the most magnificent thing to walk the earth.

Killian seemed to consume even the smallest of details involving the situation, the homemade treat, the cleaned state of the kitchen, my holding back tears, and Kiernan's hand resting supportively over my shoulder before staring at me.

"I'm sorry, Ariella."

"What?" I voiced, not prepared for that response, and I was suddenly afraid he'd changed his mind, apologizing for needing to send me back home, but Killian continued before I could ask any more questions.

"I misjudged you greatly. You have been good to our family. I can't recall the last time I saw my brothers pleased in living," he stated, glancing in the direction of Keagan and Kaid, though his attention primarily focused on the younger, "Thank you. You have my respect."

I was stunned, unsure how to respond, but the gift of Killian's respect was one I assumed was rarely given, and Kiernan gave me a gentle squeeze on my shoulder in gratification.

"Yeah, I guess you have mine too," Keagan offered, waving a hand in the air holding a cinnamon roll, "but that's only because of the sugar. You left and didn't even say goodbye."

"You are right. I'm sorry."

"Just don't do it again," he reprimanded playfully, a twinkling in his eyes that was too prominent to be mischievous, "You are the only friend I have outside of my family. It would be very disappointing to never see you again."

Kaid was there next, wrapping his arms around me in a hug much different from the last, and I wasted no time reciprocating the action.

"You are like the sister I never met," he spoke softly, fragile and honest, "They named me after her, but I never got to see her. I want to believe she is just like you."

If it were possible for a heart to melt away and fall into the stomach, mine did in that minute. I held Kaid tighter to me, and I didn't pretend it was Anders responding this time, because to him, I was dead, and there was a different little brother who needed me more.

It wasn't more than five seconds after Kaid let me go that I was hugged from behind, the scent of smoky wood and burning marshmallows surrounding the air around me.

"I'm so proud of you, *Agapití*," Kiernan whispered into my hair, placing a kiss on the side of my head before his lips found the shell of my ear, "I love you. Have I told you that today?"

"You two are sickening, you know that?" Keagan called from the living room, and I hadn't even noticed them leave the kitchen.

"He's just jealous," he murmured, nuzzling the side of my ear, lips smiling against the corner of my jaw.

Kiernan didn't understand how right he was, and a prick of guilt greeted my heart, realizing how insensitive I was being to Keagan's pain. I moved from Kiernan's touch, doing my best to be subtle about it, finding the lid to the container, giving myself something to do.

"Would you like any more cinnamon rolls, Keagan?" I asked, trying not to look at the bemused stare I knew Kiernan was giving me, finding his younger brother lounging freely over one of the couches.

"I'm okay, Ari," he responded, offering a smile that didn't reach his eyes, and we both knew he wasn't talking about food, "I've gone many years without sweets. I can wait."

"Good," I announced, bringing my hands together in a satisfying clap, "Because I am making chicken and dumplings for dinner."

Chapter Thirty-Four

Killian was gone most of the day, to where and for what reason he never revealed, but Kaid asked if I could help him with school in his brother's absence. Happily obliging, it was the closest I'd been to returning to my normal life, aiding Kaid and making meals, minus the air of loneliness I'd known as Kiernan and Keagan remained present. They didn't question Killian's leave, and while I didn't verbalize it, I had the sudden fear he would disappear as Kell did, becoming the cause for another broken relationship, but he was back by dinner time, requesting Kiernan's help carrying in a new addition to the cabin.

"I thought that if we are having meals as a family, a table would prove beneficial," he explained after situating the carefully crafted piece of wood in the empty space between the kitchen and living room.

"You made that? Just today?" I questioned, baffled, noting the smoothed surfaces and detailed carvings over the sides.

"It's not impressive seeing as *Patér* created this place almost single-handedly, but I attempt to follow his footsteps in carpentry."

"This is amazing, Killian!" I argued, running my fingers along the wood, still damp and a fresh color of red.

He smiled, and I had to stop myself from staring. Life came to his face, painting him younger and revealing how handsome his features truly were, and I wondered how rarely he was complimented.

"How did you do it?"

"Knocked a tree down and carved a table and chairs from it," he explained, making me rethink how strong they were to break apart a redwood so meticulously.

"Chairs?" I echoed just as Keagan walked in with two heavy, wooden seats, a bit darker shade than the table they were placed at, Kiernan carrying in the same amount behind him. The set was complete once Keagan brought in the last two, and I observed how perfectly the furniture fit the room, counting the available six places for a household of five.

"Kell will be back," Killian answered the question before I even thought to form one, "It's not his character to desert us." Yet his smile was gone, and an unsure gleam in his expression made the confident Killian appear more hopeful than anything.

The timer I set for the meal rang, announcing dinner was ready, and after accepting the bowls of chicken and dumplings I passed out, the brothers claimed their seats. I took the chair between Kiernan and Keagan, Kaid sitting across from me, and Killian to his right. The seat across from Kiernan was empty and entirely out of place, a hole in a neatly stitched seam, and it hurt to remind me of Zadar.

"This is wonderful, Ari. Thank you," Killian offered, and I hadn't realized I was zoning out until I heard his voice.

"Of course," I responded, taking an admittedly tasteful bite myself, "It's still not as good as that stew I had after first getting here. Who made that?"

"I did," Killian continued

"Just full of hidden talents?"

"I fill in where it's needed," Killian chuckled, glancing down, attempting to hide his gratitude for my sentiment.

Kiernan was quiet by my side, but his approval was present through how tenderly he touched me. His knuckles swept over the back of my hand once, barely feeling the heat of his skin before it was gone, and the manner was almost a question, a request.

I caught his hand before it could retreat fully, bringing our interlaced fingers to my lap while my free hand traced careful shapes over his knuckles, following the outline of his veins, and the effect it had on Kiernan was visible.

"It's so nice to have homemade food again. Hunting gets tasteless after a while," Keagan started, and Kaid nodded in agreement.

"You could learn to cook," Killian suggested.

"You all know I have tried."

"Rest in peace, little loaf of bread," I mumbled in mock sorrow, moving the hand I used to trace Kiernan's skin to pick up my spoon and continue eating, making sure to keep his hand in my grasp.

"It was *cake*! I wouldn't go near trying to make bread after the stunt Kier pulled."

"Oh?" I asked, brows lifted in question as I turned to Kiernan, who was trying to eat in peace, and his eyes flashed to Keagan in a challenging stare.

"Don't," he threatened, but all that did was entice him and me further.

"Do," I insisted, excitedly facing Keagan, and he shrugged in fake acceptance.

"Can't disappoint the lady," he settled, his smile growing mischievous, "You know the difference between baking powder and flour? Yeah, well, somebody else didn't. Neither did he let the dough rise. He stuck that sucker in the oven and just assumed the hot mess would magically turn into bread after *four hours of baking*."

"The result was... memorable," Killian agreed, struggling to keep his laughter down as I did.

"I was Kaid's age," he grumbled, the only person at the table unamused, and his mild frustration made it more comical to me.

"I wouldn't have made a mistake like that," Kaid defended.

"At least I can tell right from left," Kiernan responded evenly, pointedly glancing at Keagan before taking another bite of food.

Keagan lifted his arm and presented Kiernan the back of his fisted hand, brows lifted and lips a thin line.

"Keagan!" Killian scolded, and apart from myself, Kaid was the only one visibly confused.

"What does that mean?" he spoke up, and Kiernan laughed.

"Yeah, Keagan. Why don't you tell us what that means?"

"You know," he answered snidely.

"I don't," I spoke up, too curious by Killian's reaction to let it go.

"We can't disappoint the lady now, can we?" Kiernan mocked, and while he was sent a glare, Kiernan kept his eyes from me as Keagan spoke.

"Basically, I demonstrated the lack of effect Kier has on me because my hands are still in front of me, and my power is intact."

'It's an offensive gesture," Killian put plainly, shooting Keagan a look that was entirely parental, and I tried to imagine Mother using that expression in my growing up.

"I bet you don't even know which hand you used," Kiernan muttered tauntingly, taking my thoughts from my broken childhood, helping me in my goal to one day forget it all.

"Can you really not differentiate the two?" I questioned in honest sincerity, and Keagan responded with equal genuineness.

"It's hard."

"Keagan was dropped on his head as a baby," Kiernan clarified as though it summed everything up.

"He was not," Killian argued, attempting not to chuckle as he shook his head disapprovingly.

"He had to have been at some point while we weren't looking. It's the only explanation."

"You were still newly awake when Keagan was a baby. There wasn't much you were seeing anyway."

"Newly awake?" I questioned, and Kiernan turned to me in answering.

"Dragons are born in alternate form, and for the first year of our life, we are in an unresponsive state of deep sleep. When we do open our eyes, we imprint the first person we see."

"So, you are like birds?"

"That's a bold statement," Keagan murmured, his eyes on his bowl as he ate.

"I wouldn't go so far as to compare us to birds, but in a way, I can see where you are coming from," Killian tried.

"You can fly, your first year of living is no more responsive than if you were inside an egg, and when you hatch, you imprint. Sounds like duck behavior to me."

"Sure, but ducks are stupid," Keagan noted, and I really should've kept quiet, but I was getting far too comfortable.

"Which hand am I holding up, Apricot?" I baited, lifting my right arm, and Kaid choked on his water. Kiernan blurted out a laugh, Keagan's mouth fell open in shock, and Killian gave me that look I'd seen from Kiernan when we challenged each other.

"Careful, Rowe. If I didn't know any better, I might've assumed you wanted to debate with me," he warned, but the competitive gleam in his eyes was almost inviting.

"Well, if your ideals are incorrect, it might do you well," I prodded, and it was so surreal to see Killian smile, like the recovery of a loved one after being told they wouldn't make it.

"Keagan," he announced, "Go get the cards."

"Oh, she's in for it now," Keagan laughed, jumping from his seat and disappearing into the forbidden room while Kaid politely took our empty bowls to the sink. Once the table was cleared and Keagan was back with a deck of cards, hand-painted and diamond-shaped, nothing like the playing cards I'd known, the rules began.

"This is the game of deception, defeat, and domination," Keagan introduced dramatically, and Kiernan lightheartedly rolled his eyes while Kaid fed off his brother's excitement.

"It's more of an opinions hash out than a game," Kiernan leaned in to whisper, though everyone around us could hear him perfectly.

"Killian is undefeated," Kaid joined, and once again, Killian grinned.

"Gold stands for two coins, and silver stands for one. Fire can melt both gold and silver, but water can diffuse fire, therefore leaving the metal's point to stand. Fire and water together can make an obsidian card, which cannot be revoked and has the equivalent of gold. A diamond's worth is ten coins and cannot be overtaken. Whichever side has the most coins at the end of the round, wins the argument," Keagan explained, dealing us three cards face down each.

"Fire tops gold and silver. Water tops fire. Obsidian tops both, and diamond tops them all. Got it. So, it's a fancy version of rock, paper, scissors with stakes?" I clarified, letting go of Kiernan's hand to view what I'd been dealt.

"What is rock, paper, scissors?" Keagan questioned, sounding just like Kiernan had when he asked me what tag was, and I responded the same, shaking my head with a smile.

"Never mind."

"All right, practice round. Here is my argument," Keagan started, placing down one golden and two silver cards, "Pineapple belongs on pizza."

"Pineapple shouldn't be warm," Kaid asserted, laying down two golds and a fire to combat a silver of Keagan's.

"Pineapple should be warm," Killian contended, wiping Kaid's score clean with two fires and a water to bring back Keagan's loss.

They turned to me then, waiting for my stand, and I hoped I was doing something right when I showed my three silver cards, voicing, "I like it. It makes the pizza sweet."

"I choose to fold," Kiernan announced, setting his cards on the table face down and handing us the win, and Keagan wasted no time gathering the cards to shuffle them.

"I did it," I cheered, happy with myself for no apparent reason.

"Yes, but Killian was on your side," Keagan reminded, dealing everyone new cards, "Let's see you try to win against him. State your argument."

"Dragons are large birds with scales," I declared, setting the bar with a high coin count containing two golds and a silver.

Killian responded first, dropping a fire and water to make obsidian, along with an extra fire to melt my silver, "Ducks tend to hide from predators rather than fight them."

"They don't mate for life," Keagan added, placing a silver and two fires to cancel out the rest of my gold, leaving me with no coins and no way to combat.

"Ducks waddle when happy. I find that very relatable," Kiernan stated, placing three waters to defuse all the fires pitted against me, and it was such a blatant lie that I couldn't help but laugh.

"You little backstabber," Keagan growled, not sharing in my amusement or enjoying the fact that they were now losing.

"She has him wrapped around her finger. There is nothing we can do about it. Kaid, it is all on you," Killian answered, and all eyes fell on the youngest.

"They molt," he defended, revealing a perfect hand of three gold cards, sealing their win. Keagan's cheer was perhaps too enthusiastic, high-fiving Killian and Kaid in their victory, but I wasn't done getting under his skin.

"But instinctual behavior can't rely on chance," I complained, "This is about facts."

"Nope. The game has decided," Keagan answered shortly, leaning back proudly in his seat.

"I guess that's fair. Now that I think about it, you are more like lizards anyway," I prompted just for the reaction, sparking a new debate in which only Kiernan jokingly defended me, but the losing argument didn't matter to me. We were spending time together, laughing over a heated game after a warm supper, and there were no doors around us to close.

I was home.

Chapter Thirty-Five

Life was becoming simple, and it was the most beautiful thing.

I'd stopped counting the days and began enjoying them for their priceless moments. Singing regularly while cooking and doing chores, no one cowered from my voice, rather listening intently as though I was something worth hushing over. The brothers had changed drastically, full of so much life and emotion that I'd nearly forgotten how they were in the past. Killian smiled frequently, which took some getting used to, and Kaid started talking more. Keagan laughed just as much as he teased, and it became Kiernan's mission to make me feel more loved than I did the previous day. He was always whispering compliments in my ear, touching me as he did so until my stomach was nothing more than a cage of excited butterflies and I'd forgotten how to function properly. Kiernan found enjoyment in my flustering, along with acting innocent when I confronted him for distracting me from different activities, but it only ever ended with him staring at me like there was nothing more precious to him, and me silently thanking every star that he managed to find something in me worth cherishing.

Dinner was my favorite. It guaranteed us together, laughing around the table like problems couldn't reach us, and I began to think the redwoods were a dome of protection from the dangers of the outside world. I found dragons had a strong fondness for meat, but salmon especially, which I'd supposed made sense with how much they fished. They sold most of their catch, but I assumed some of the profit was enjoyed. On the few days they went out, I stayed at the cabin, hoping, in time, I'd forget what it was like outside the forest, remaining dead to the rest of the world, and it was only when the ocean called to me that I struggled.

Its pull was getting stronger, and at times, when it felt like the air was too thin and my lungs were unsatisfied, I'd politely excuse myself from whatever situation and take a shower. I didn't tell Kiernan what the sea whispered to me, the longing melody of the waves and the mighty roar of the tide, not when things were calm, and they had nothing to worry about.

Living at last felt like a gift, and we were all content... well, almost all of us were content.

"Keagan, no," Killian answered as he stepped inside the cabin from spending the evening hunting, his tone indicating that this wasn't his first time responding. I was lying on one of the couches, face in a book I had discovered while cleaning, but the story was entirely in Greek, taking away the relaxing fulfillment of reading and replacing it with a determination to understand the language. Kaid sat quietly across the room from me, studying as well, finishing up his homework for the day.

"Come *on*. It's just in Brookings, and the girl who invited me was so cute!" Keagan begged, following Killian around as though he held on to all hope in a place of despair.

"The last time you went to a party, there was almost a scene. We can't afford that kind of carelessness."

"Yeah, but look at what we gained from it," Keagan offered, gesturing to my oblivious state on the couch, squinting as though that could aid me in reading a language far from my understanding, and I blinked up at both of them when the younger laughed, "Who knows? Maybe I will get to be the one who brings home a girl this time."

"That is exactly what I am afraid of. Kell's gone, I have to watch Kaid, and you are too much for Kiernan to handle on his own," Killian discouraged, but Keagan was persistent.

"Ari could go."

"Hm?" I perked up at the sound of my name, realizing I should've been paying more attention to the conversation at hand.

"She is arguably the safest person I could be with. I mean, if the girl wanted to, she could take over the minds of an entire room with one song."

"Absolutely not. Ari hates parties," Kiernan defended as he emerged from the bathroom, taking on the role of disappointing so I didn't have to, while he dabbed a towel over hair wet from his shower. Keagan could successfully hide his dismay from his brothers because they didn't know to look for it, but I noticed how his shoulders slightly slumped, the bounce in his stride slacking. Parties were his one escape, his one chance to pretend to live a normal human life, and while I didn't understand how he saw that as a luxury, I couldn't take it from him.

"I think it would be fun," I admitted, even if the thought of entering another crowded, loud space after becoming accustomed to the quiet life of the forest had knots of anxiety tying my stomach.

"What?" Kiernan quipped at the same time Keagan exclaimed, "You do?"

"Sure," I agreed, setting the book down, "I have you guys this time, so I won't be nervous, and a night of dancing doesn't sound like something you'd turn down, Kiernan."

Kiernan's stare was uncertain as he watched me, waiting for my explanation to continue, but he was too far away for me to touch and silently communicate how I wanted this, instead giving him a tiny, reassuring grin and hoping that was enough. Keagan laughed in victory, clapping his hands together once, and I silently took credit for the excitement that had returned to his form.

"The lemon has spoken. We leave at five," he announced, glancing at me with gratitude dancing in his eyes as he winked.

Brookings, as it turned out, was not far from where we lived. We flew to the edge of the redwoods, and then, to avoid the attention two massive dragons would draw, we walked the rest of the way. The town reminded me of my old home, its quaintness, and the surrounding of the sea, a sea that was humming my name, and though I wouldn't admit it aloud, I missed Crescent City.

Keagan held the door for me, and if I weren't so anxious to follow, I would've frozen at the entrance. This party wasn't like Maddie's, though it had its similarities: loud music, flashing lights, and chaotic dancing, but this place was much bigger, designed to hold entertainment rather than cramming people into a house. There wasn't much of a theme apart from finding enjoyment, no countdown to midnight broadcast on the wall, which stupidly relieved a small amount of pressure on me, yet there also wasn't anywhere to tell the time, as if this place didn't sleep.

The people, however, were the worst of it, crowding every corner and edge and looking very unapologetic about it. The ages were concerningly varied, with rules seemingly nonexistent, as I spotted someone painting on the wall, and a few people appeared to be there for that very reason.

Kiernan's hand was on the small of my back, and I'd never felt so protected by such a light touch.

"You two enjoy your time dancing together, staring into each other's eyes, or whatever it is you do. Don't worry about me one bit," Keagan prefaced, peering over the crowd as though he already knew everyone and was in search of his friend group, and I didn't doubt he'd have one after tonight, though uncertain how many of them would be his gender. Charismatic Keagan, with his beautiful facial structure, dark hair, and bright eyes, was a threat to any other man hoping to gain a date here.

"That makes me worry about you," Kiernan contended, but Keagan was already gone, disappearing into the crowd and gaining attention like rapid wildfire.

"He will be fine. Come on," I laughed softly, taking his hand and hoping he didn't feel mine shaking as I moved us to the dance floor.

I did my best not to look anyone else in the eyes, but it felt like I was being stared at, whispered about in the far corners of the poorly lit building. The sudden fear of being recognized flooded me with a new sense of unease, that the news of a girl missing for weeks and finally found would be relayed for all to know.

"We can leave at any point," Kiernan assured, his hand smoothing down my side as his other carried mine in the near-waltz position I was growing familiar with, "No one is forcing you to be here."

"No, this is fun," I disagreed, striving to mean it, loosening my muscles and focusing only on Kiernan and the slow dance he led, allowing the music in my veins to fall into the blaring songs.

"Sure," he chuckled, not buying my words as he lifted his arm to twirl me, "At least you talk to me now."

My brows knit together, knotting my expression in a questioning look that Kiernan couldn't view until I'd stopped spinning. "I talk to you all the time."

"Not when we first met."

I thought back to our first: the first time I saw him, the first time he touched me, the first time my mind was quiet. My world had shifted to align uneven plains, my life gaining more color to its dark hallways, and I hadn't known how to process it, his very being rendering me speechless.

"I don't think you understand just how mesmerizing you are."

"Mesmerizing?" he repeated, the amusement reflecting in his radiant eyes, "Well, whatever it is you saw in me made my job to search you easier. You didn't question a thing."

"What do you mean?"

"Why do you think I danced with you that night?"

"Because you wanted to?" I guessed, but no other answer made sense in my brain, and Kiernan softly laughed as though there was an essential factor I had missed.

"You were a very curious thing to me, Ari, but I didn't know how to want. There wasn't much I could gather from watching you far up in the trees, and when I sensed you at that New Year's party, I took the opportunity to get closer."

"Sensed me?"

"Your fear, it was impossible to ignore. I never saw you. It was too crowded and loud to even spot Keagan at times, but I felt your panic from across the room, and I believe that's what impulsed me to go up to you." He slowed the dance even more, breaking the rhythmic rules of the music, drowning us out from unwanted ears, "I can't explain how, but I knew it was you even before I could see your frightened face, and when I reached for you, and you looked at me..." My hands rested on his chest while his dropped to my waist, supporting my middle as we swayed to the beat of our hearts, and he lowered his voice to continue, "Siren or not, I knew you were harmless. Perhaps too entrancing for a human, but being pretty doesn't make you dangerous."

"Then why did you dance with me?" I prompted with equal quiet, adding a layer of intimacy that allowed me to forget the commotion surrounding us.

"As I said, I was curious, and selfishly, I wanted to know what you felt like." One hand then moved to brush the side of my jaw, as though all the other times he touched me weren't enough of an answer for him, fingers gliding down my neck, and my breath hitched as his heat landed over my collarbone, his eyes following the lines he traced along the structure. "I've always wondered if human skin was truly similar to the covering we use, but for you, it was different. It wasn't enough to know how you felt; I needed to know *why*: why you were so cold, why you shivered when I touched you, why your face reddened when I studied you too long."

Heat flooded my body, and his sight was intent on a flush he seemed to cause on command, like he had yet to figure it out.

"I thought you said you didn't know how to want," I whispered, gradually losing myself as I had the crowd around me, because whether he knew it or not, he was pulling me closer, and I couldn't think straight with the sweet haze of his scent wrapped around my mind.

"Not before you. I didn't even know how to smile before you. Keagan was always the one who learned how to blend in with the humans anytime needed. I tried to pattern my behavior after the mannerisms I'd seen him use with girls, which was the furthest thing from natural for me, but I eventually got you to join me in the forest, and the more time I spent with you, I realized I didn't need to pretend. You kept coming back to the tree, and it was much easier to find what I was searching for."

"What was it?"

"Fins..." I felt the easy motion of knuckles brush down my spine, any sense of cold leaving my body in tingling chills, "and webs," delicate fire traced the outline of my hand, following each dip and trailing up the tips of my fingers, and before I knew how, I was falling, dipped with an arm bracing my arched back. Kiernan's large hand cradled the entire back of my head, and lowering his mouth to my neck, he whispered, "and gills." His heart was pounding under my palm, igniting the desire to lean forward the slightest amount and feel his lips press beneath my jaw, but I was hauled to my feet too quickly, slightly dizzy, but Kiernan wasn't watching me.

"Hold on," he instructed, untangling himself from me while his attention fixated on something behind, "I will be right back."

Kiernan's aggravated sigh was answer enough for what he was doing, but my eyes still followed him to Keagan and the group of girls surrounding his brother. I wasn't near enough to make out all the details, but it appeared Keagan was getting a little too close with a pretty blonde, and while the party boy did not appreciate Kiernan's reprimands, none of the girls complained. Half of them had turned away from Keagan altogether, staring at Kiernan with a longing in their eyes, and something dark and unpleasant stirred in my chest as so many fawned over him while I stood alone and awkward on the dance floor. A far too bold brunette seductively ran her hand down Kiernan's arm, and in that split second, I found murder to be extremely agreeable.

"I think the lemon curd not," I muttered under my breath, marching my way through the crowd, anger seizing my limbs, and though Kiernan ripped his arm away and eyed the girl with distaste, justice had not ensued. The multitude gave no heed to my attempts to slip past them, dancing or talking without a care who else was near, and I should've paid more attention to whom I was passing.

"Isabella?"

He held the inside of my elbow, an instinctual grab as I tripped into him, and if I hadn't been restrained, I would've run away, pretending not to hear the voice I barely knew, acting as though I was never spotted, but it was too late for that chance.

"Jason?" I voiced, staring at him in surprise as he did the same to me. His hair was still in that unfortunate shape of the mullet, his eyes the same dark shade of brown, but the rest of his features seemed very different to me, so unmistakably... human, and I hadn't noticed they had a certain look until after spending time only with dragons and their false attempts to mirror that human appearance. "What are you doing here?"

"How are *you* here? You were pronounced dead weeks ago," he asserted, releasing me with his hand, but his gaze kept me trapped, "You and Heather's disappearance is the reason my family moved to Brookings."

"And Maddie? Is she..."

"She's fine. Still in Crescent City and is going to *flip out* when she finds out you are alive. What happened to you?"

I huffed, pushing the hair from my eyes, scrambling for a way to get out of answering.

"It's a long story, but listen, it is important no one knows I am here."

His stare of bafflement shifted into one of worry, purposefully glancing around before turning back to me with a lowered voice.

"Are you... running from something?"

"No, it's just... really complicated. I need everyone to believe I am dead."

His face was unsure, reading into each of my nervous habits like they could tell him the deeper things going on.

"You sure you aren't in danger?"

"I'm fine—"

I was interrupted by a warm mouth to mine, hot hands around my waist, moving me to face him and press closer, and since I was so accustomed to how he felt, I didn't push away. It wasn't like any other kiss Kiernan had given me before, soft and gentle, careful with every action, tenderly speaking his affection; it was intense and domineering, escalating too quickly, ending far too soon, leaving me dazed and struggling to process such an unannounced passion. I'd forgotten where we were, surrounded by people at a party, forgetting our reasoning for being here and even my name, but Kiernan wasn't lost in the slightest, staring directly at Jason after he pulled away.

"You heard her," Kiernan asserted, watching him expectantly, "She isn't looking for help."

I blinked back into focus, noticing Jason's eyes darting between us, landing longer on me as if waiting for a signal that Kiernan was the danger he assumed, and while he wasn't necessarily wrong in his ideas, he wasn't right either. I gave him a sheepish grin, leaning into Kiernan behind me, hoping Jason could see my contentment, that he would drop this interaction and keep my reappearance a secret, but he was just a little too suspicious to rest in that comforting hope. He didn't say a word, not with Kiernan tracking his every movement, and after a long moment of uncomfortable silence and the two sharing a stern look, Jason returned to the crowd.

"Go get a haircut," he murmured, glaring at the back of Jason's head as he pulled me to the front of himself.

"What was that for?"

"Keeping any ideas away. I don't share," he put plainly, and if it weren't for the worrying nausea that lined my throat, I would've laughed at his blatant jealousy. Trying to resume our interrupted dance, Kiernan took my hand, losing it almost immediately as I grabbed his shirt, wishing the room would stop spinning. "*Agapiti?*"

"People... too many—"

Too many that could notice me. Too many that Jason could tell. Too many ways the truth could get back to my family.

Kiernan cautiously led me off the dance floor and to a secluded corner, bringing me a chair which I accepted gratefully.

"What did he say to you?" he guessed, clearly only managing to pick up the very end of Jason's and my conversation.

"They can't find out, Kiernan," I whispered, panic rising at the thought of ruining their joyful lives a second time as I clutched my necklace, "This was a mistake."

"I'll go get Keagan."

"No, please don't. I just need water."

My lungs screamed for it, and there was a refreshments table just across the room.

Kiernan left at once, and I buried my face in my palms, swallowing profusely as I sipped at the air, trying to trick my body into accepting oxygen. The music was increasing in volume, banging against the drums in my ears, vibrations shaking the base, and I didn't understand why no one was turning it down, chatter growing louder to overcome the noise. Paranoia was creeping in, morphing the surrounding voices into those of people I knew, Mother's old singing, Anders' contagious laugh, Zadar's strong accent, and it was only a matter of time until I began hallucinating them, haunted by the mere idea of my old family. It was pathetic, and I hated myself for not being able to move on.

"Party not treatin' you well, lil' lady?' A gruff voice asked, sounding much older than the rest of the attendees.

"We could take you someplace better," A different voice questioned, and my head lifted from my hands to see two men hovering over me. One seemed to be in his late twenties, eyes black and heartless, offsetting the harsh pale of his skin, his companion a good decade older, and I wasn't able to discern any of his features past his unkempt beard.

"Not talkative, are ya?" the bearded one asked, taking a step closer, and my eyes began to burn, drawing the other's attention.

"Look at that. Her eyes change colors," he said, touching my face, not understanding the warning it posed, and I flinched away.

"Please don't," I requested with a pleasantness I hoped they would respect.

"Pretty and polite? What a find. It's a shame to see you lonely," he said sympathetically, but his dark eyes revealed the fortune he saw in my solitude, and I had the sudden desire to scream for Kiernan, but my lungs still weren't even processing air properly. "Why don't you come with us? Your headache won't get any better with this music."

"No, thank you," I answered as evenly as my voice would allow, standing to discreetly excuse myself, which earned a firm hand to clasp my shoulder.

"Fresh air would do ya good," the bearded man offered, but it felt like the furthest thing from my benefit.

My other arm was gripped next, and I realized too late how much they overpowered me, terror overcoming my body because they weren't letting go. I frantically searched for Kiernan in the hoards of bodies, and was so grateful for his abnormal height when I managed to spot him across the room. He was scouring for me as well, senses enhanced by my panic, and when he found me, his eyes darkened. I lost sight of him being tugged to the exit, my unwillingness ignored, and while Kiernan had to make it through a crowd of difficult partiers, he wasn't the only dragon here familiar with the scent of fear.

"HEY!"

Keagan's demanding exclamation did its job, grabbing my new captor's attention along with half of the room.

"This is a nice party. We wouldn't want to cause a scene and ruin it all now, would we? Kindly let the girl go," Keagan extended through a smile that held no warmth, and it was the first time I saw him struggle to keep contained, snakelike formations dancing under his skin, but the two men didn't understand its severity, or that Keagan was something to be feared. "Sorry, that came out too friendly," he chuckled darkly, and the sound sent chills down my spine, "I'm afraid I didn't make myself clear. Get your repulsive, brittle hands off of her, or you will discover all the unnatural angles at which the bones in the human fingers can be snapped."

That gave them pause.

"And who are you? Her *boyfriend?*"

The words were a mock, looking Keagan up and down like he was nothing, even if the provocation dwindled in confidence.

"Her brother," he corrected, "and you should be grateful it's that way. I am being much more gracious than her boyfriend will be."

"Take her to the car," the younger of the two instructed, "I'll deal with this."

But he barely had the sentence out when Keagan acted, taking the arm that pulled me and crushing it with his bare hand.

The snap of bone echoed over the pounding music, followed by the man's scream and collective gasps from the groups watching, and the hold on me slackened as his arm fell from me, folding the wrong way. Then, for good measure, Keagan punched the other in the face, most definitely breaking his nose, his shouts of pain adding to the layered commotion.

"*Beat it,*" he snarled, his tone promising more violence if his warning went unheeded, and the two scurried off and out the door instantly.

Keagan spun on me after they were gone, and I caught the briefest glimpse of his slitted pupils and slightly morphed face, trying to shift, but his handsome, normal features returned, softening when seeing my fear-paralyzed state.

"What is your problem? You are supposed to be keeping *me* out of trouble. Not the other way around."

My mouth was open, but nothing came out, eyes wide as I absentmindedly rubbed my wrist where the hand that was so easily snapped in half gripped me. Kiernan was there then, looking even more terrifying than Keagan had. Despite how long it felt, the whole interaction was no longer than a minute, making Kiernan's return from across the room very impressive, posing as human while pushing past people to avoid suspicion.

"Where did they go?" he demanded, and hearing him use that tone was like listening to a different person, deep and horrifying, the closest a human could be to sounding dragon, but Keagan waved him off unfazed.

"I already took care of it."

"Not nearly enough. They *touched* her."

The words came out close to a growl, and Keagan and I could both see his mask slipping.

"Kier, *Kier*," Keagan warned, putting a hand on Kiernan when he tried to walk out the door, "there are people around," he mumbled tightly, glancing at the room full of humans who'd become fully invested in our private situation.

"Not outside," Kiernan argued, and with the predatory look in his eyes, I didn't want to imagine what he planned to do to them. I'd finally snapped out of my shocked state enough to carefully take his hand that was burning up.

"I'm okay, Kiernan," I assured, smoothing a free hand down the scales that tried to claw out, his heat terribly powerful when worked up, preparing to burn down whatever bothered him. He was even angrier than he'd been with Kell, but he wasn't looking at me, sight set on the exit, calculating the most agreeable possibilities, and I cupped his cheek, bringing his eyes to my face, whispering, "I'm okay." His pupils enlarged, his muscles loosened, and now that almost the entire party had turned their focus to us, there wouldn't be any escaping scrutiny.

"Let's just go back home," Keagan sighed, "You two are the worst babysitters."

The trip home felt longer than it had going, and that included Kiernan setting me down a good distance from the cabin before shifting himself, and Keagan leaving us behind.

"What are you doing?" I questioned, and he threaded his fingers through mine.

"Walking the rest of the way. I want to talk to you," he responded, sounding like a disappointed parent, and Zadar appeared in my mind before Mother did.

"I'm sorry. I didn't mean for any of that to happen—"

"Why did we go to that party?" he diverted, focusing on my expression, and when I went to answer, he saw right through it, "Don't you dare say it's because you wanted to."

I huffed.

"Keagan needs—"

"I knew it," he groaned, running a hand over his face, "You shouldn't encourage him. It's going to get us all in trouble."

"You shouldn't discourage him. He looks up to you, Kiernan."

His gaze lowered, swallowing harshly as though he knew it, and it burdened him.

"Keagan tends to bend the rules when there is something he really wants, and we can't afford that right now."

"Didn't your brothers say the same thing to you about me?"

"That's different, Ari. What happened with us—"

His head lifted like a deer sensing danger, his sight fixating on home, and his abrupt behavior change had me on high alert.

"What's wrong?"

"He's home," Kiernan mumbled, more to himself than me, letting go of my hand to run towards the cabin. I took off after him, but he was so much faster, making it inside before I could even reach the doors, yet when I did, I halted. Through the window, barely visible by the dimming fireplace light, was the man who wanted nothing more than to see me dead.

Kell was back.

Chapter Thirty-Six

Maybe I should've run and disappeared in the forest, maybe I should've followed Kiernan into the cabin and stayed close to his side, but I did neither, frozen in place as the overgrown grass seemed to encircle my boots, keeping me from moving forward.

Kell was home, and none of them appeared relieved.

The discussion held behind the closed walls and open windows was serious, the firelight revealing the brothers' rigid posture, whether from anxiety or anticipation. I knew joining now would be an intrusion, but Kiernan had gone painfully still, his expression closed off, and if I could only touch him, I might be able to understand what was stressing him. Shoving aside the fear of reuniting with my near murderer, I broke from the forest's hold, heading for the cabin's entrance, thinking only of Kiernan and how I was safe with him.

"...which doesn't explain how you are still alive? We were banished! Going to Agrond is under penalty of death for us!"

It was rare to hear Killian yell, and it caused me to hesitate, fingers lingering over the door handle and ears open to the discussion just beyond.

"Our *parents* were banished," Kell contended, his dark voice bringing back dreadful remembrances, and I willed the tremor in my legs to subside, "We ourselves have broken no laws and own the right to claim our residence with our kind."

"I cannot believe you took that risk!" Killian continued, and it was a clear reprimand, one I assumed Kell would take with little value.

"How soon are we able to leave?" Keagan joined, the excitement in his tone prominent enough for me to picture the light in his expression, even as I stared at the wooden door masked in the gloom of night.

"Now," Kell responded, and I couldn't stall any longer, forcing my arm into submission as I pushed through the opening.

"Leave?"

My voice was small, the word quiet, but it managed to take all the attention from the room. Kell's eyes flicked to me just as Kiernan extended his arm, shielding my form and detaining me from moving any closer. Keagan wordlessly shifted his position as well, stepping in line with Kell's direct path to me, and I could hardly see the older past the two brothers' tall, protective stance. Kell didn't acknowledge them, centering on me with a look that was deep, yet lacking in the hate I'd seen burn so passionately before, now cool and contemplative, refusing to break eye contact first. The tension grew along with the silence, but it radiated from Kiernan and Keagan rather than Kell, Kaid watching anxiously while Killian assessed the situation, no doubt ready to step in if needed. But Kell was the most composed out of everyone, and my eyes weren't burning.

"You are all leaving?" I spoke up, and I couldn't tell if that made things better or worse.

"Kell has secured us safe passage to Agrond," Kiernan answered, tilting his head in my direction but keeping his eyes on Kell, waiting for him to move wrong and attack.

"How? I thought you were never allowed to return."

"I have spoken with *Basileús* Draco, our leader and Agrond's ruler, and he has promised us sanctuary as a result of our parents' passing," Kell responded, acknowledging my confusion, my worries, my presence, and I didn't know how to react.

"We should take her with us," Kiernan offered, but it sounded like less of a suggestion than it did a decision.

"Do you hear yourself?" Killian instantly responded, evidently prepared for the subject, "Bringing a siren into the dragon realm? She'll be dead before we even make it through the caves."

"Ari has my *typós*. No one will do a thing to her without my permission."

"She's the *Dákry*, though," Keagan added, surveying the topic with genuine concern, "The moment that information gets out, all of Agrond will be after her."

"Then we won't let it get out," Kiernan bit impatiently, "Ari is good at disguising herself, and most of them have never seen a siren anyway. This is entirely feasible."

"Kiernan is right."

Of all the people to agree, Kell was the last person I would've assumed, and the surprised shift in the room told me I wasn't the only one taken aback.

"With her being the *Dákry*, sirens and kelpies are going to hunt her down to fulfill their little prophecies. Ari would be in no more danger there than she is here. We are not the only ones I mentioned to his lordship. He took a particular liking to bringing the girl, and I am confident he'd accept our *human* companion just as he accepts any of us."

Her. Ari. Not it. Not witch.

Something changed in his trip to Agrond, something influential enough to soften his perspective of me, and while I was sparked with a flame of hope, Kiernan did not seem as convinced.

"Why go through all of this trouble for her?"

"It's not for her, believe me. It's for you," Kell answered evenly, unsurprised by the suspicion, "Because, whether I like it or not, I know you won't go anywhere without her, and I want you to come home with us."

Kiernan didn't respond, but his hand gradually fell away from me, and the action said more than words could.

"It's too dangerous," Killian persisted when the tension had eased.

"Killian," Kiernan started again, stepping closer to his brother to speak in a lower volume, "I have made my impression. You know I can't leave her."

"You made a reckless decision based on feelings alone," Killian corrected, "It was you who put your claim on a siren, not us. We shouldn't have to be punished, and either should she." My lips parted in preparation to disagree, but Killian graciously lifted his hand in silence, continuing on to Kiernan, "You are almost twenty and are fully capable of staying on your own, but your brothers and I are escaping from this exile. I will give you the remaining evening to make your decision. We leave at first light, with or without you."

"Killian, that's not fair to do," Keagan put gently, the concern knitting Kaid's brows portraying his mutual feelings, but the eldest only had his sights on Kiernan.

"If you truly want to keep her safe, then Ari must stay here."

It was Killian's final word, which meant the matter was settled, and no one was to question it.

"Walk with me?" I requested, taking Kiernan's hand and bringing him outside, and it may have been that the night's heavy darkness impaired my sight, but Kell almost appeared pleased by the action. There was much he still had to say; I could feel it in the stiff way he walked, but Kiernan reluctantly followed me into the woods and privacy.

The ultimatum was jarring for both of us, and attempting to think it through outside of my own selfish desires, I forced, "You need to go, Kiernan. You belong with them."

He was silent, the kind that was painful, felt in the nerves beneath my skin, and I leveled my voice to push the point further.

"This is the moment you have always wanted. Take it."

Leaves crunched under our feet, his long strides forcing me to step twice as fast, creating mismatched footprints over the bustling, windblown grass, but no words were formed.

"I *want* you to go."

"I'm not leaving you," he put plainly and abruptly, sounding as adamant as Killian had.

"You are meant to be with your kind, Kiernan. Including your family."

"I'm not leaving you," he repeated with more persistence, and I pulled him to a stop.

"You were the one who told me not to make rash decisions when you are hurting."

"This isn't rash," he argued, "and when I said that you had no other place to go. I'm torn because I don't know where to go."

'Both. Balance it. I wasn't going to abandon you after I went back, and neither will you."

"It's not that simple!"

"It could be!" I fought, desperate to shed a positive light on this, "You could come visit me and still live with them."

"Kell was gone for a week, but to him, it was only a day. Time works differently across realms, and having one of us experiencing life at a different pace than the other could be consequential. That is a risk I am not willing to take with you."

He was shutting me down, and I had to remind myself it wasn't the same as shutting me out, that Kiernan wasn't Mother, that there was an easy solution we were missing. My composure was failing, my breaths coming in faster, and Kiernan took note of it, sighing as he raked a hand through his hair.

"Where would you even go?" he asked, giving me a chance to be heard, analyzing how I fidgeted.

"I can stay here."

"Alone? In the woods? You could die out here, and no one would even know!"

"Wouldn't be any different than what people already think," I murmured to myself, momentarily forgetting how well he could hear.

"Not *helping*."

"All right then, I'll go back to Crescent City."

"To your family? I thought we established you never wanted them to see you again."

"You were right. I was hurting and shouldn't have been making decisions like that then. I've had more time to think about it, and maybe I was wrong. Maybe they still miss me," I lied, their content expressions prominent in my memories, but I only needed to fool Kiernan, and his mind was so conflicted that he seemed to be buying into the possibility.

"You promised to stay, and I promised never to leave you," he reminded, bringing up a point he knew I couldn't combat, and I was gradually understanding his mind wasn't going to be changed, no matter what I said.

"But you let me go!" I also reminded, not yet done trying, "I had the chance to go back to Crescent City, and you let me take it! Why should it be any different when you finally have the opportunity to go to your home?"

"Because I thought you would be safe there, and after what happened tonight, I..." Kiernan stopped himself, closing his eyes and taking a large breath before refocusing on me and distressingly voicing, "You could've been seriously hurt at that party, and I don't know if I would've made it to you in time if Keagan hadn't stepped in. How am I supposed to keep you safe if we aren't even in the same *realm*?"

I pursed my lips, knowing all of his stress wouldn't have existed if I'd stayed out of his life, that he would've already been gone in his own world if it weren't for me, and I needed to fix it.

"You can't stay here alone," I tried one last time, touching the heated skin of his arm, feeling as the dragon beneath drew toward the contact through twisting veins.

"Neither can you," he expressed, his mask crumbling, and though his features stayed the same, he lost his human air, "If I were to leave, and something happened to you, I would never forgive myself. I'm struggling to do that now."

I couldn't truly pull him into a hug, not when bringing us closer resulted in me moving to him, but I initiated the embrace, wrapping my arms around his middle and hoping he could feel my concern for him. Kiernan's response was immediate, leaning into my hold as though I was the one who could melt the world with a single breath, resting his cheek on my head, and I listened to his heartbeat slow.

"Please, just let me do this, Ari," he pleaded, and coming to terms with his stubbornness, I nodded. I felt the understanding settle over him, the heavy reality that he'd have to learn how to manage this life as the sole dragon, and I was only now realizing how much of an open book he was to me as well.

Chapter Thirty-Seven

I didn't want to say goodbye.

I hadn't gotten the opportunity with Anders, and now, Kaid hugging me tightly, I wondered if it would've been easier to lose that chance once more.

"Come on, Kaid. It's time to go," Killian intervened, placing a comforting hand on the boy's shoulder, and Kaid complied reluctantly. I kissed the top of his head, and though he smiled, it looked too sad to be associated with joy. Killian led him off, gifting me a grateful nod in farewell. "I wish you the best, Ariella."

"You too," I echoed, grinning to portray my mutual gratitude.

Kiernan was incredibly quiet, remarkably calm as he stood by my side, doing nothing more than watching his brothers prepare to leave, and I knew it was a front to keep himself from breaking.

"Have fun taking care of my brother," Keagan bid sarcastically, poking my arm until I faced him, "He gets needy after a while. Then again, you are sort of needy yourself, so you should be fine."

I slapped him, and he laughed, tugging me into a hug and sneaking a quick kiss on my cheek before jumping away, escaping the second playful hit.

Kell's expression was blank, but his stare was intent on me as I laughed with Keagan, and I knew better than to give him a goodbye any closer than ten feet away. I offered a small wave, which he, unsurprisingly, did not reciprocate, bringing his wrists up over his face before throwing them back, unveiling the fire-red beast beneath like unzipping a jacket. Killian and Kaid followed suit, tan and grey dragons appearing, their slender serpentine bodies overshadowed by Kell's powerful ember form.

"Tell Sasquatch I said hello when you find him!" Keagan called with a wink that promised to meet again, and I desperately wanted to believe that, watching as his flirtatious expression was covered in moss-colored scales to match his burning eyes.

Then the four of them flew away, disappearing behind a cliff, reaching the places I couldn't follow, and it took me a concerning amount of time to realize Kiernan was no longer by my side.

I tracked my way from Secret Beach back to the cabin, finding the place eerily still, and I hadn't determined why it felt so off until I noticed the door to his parents' room open.

"Kiernan?"

My footsteps to the doorway were light, my tone questioning, searching for how best to aid.

"Love?" I tried again.

He stood unmoving, facing the portrait Mother painted of his family years ago, with a look in his eyes I'd never witnessed.

Grief.

"Would you like me to stay or leave?" I conversed tenderly, fearing to have already ruined a fragile moment with my callings.

"Stay," he answered, and the rawness in his voice was enough to prove his pain over old wounds, but the fresh ache was displayed through his tiny, "Please."

I neared him to embrace his strong form, holding him from behind as my cheek rested on his back, slowing my breathing to match his. Nothing I could say would change the sadness he experienced staring at a photo where half of the memories were dead and the other half now gone, allowing touch to speak for me where words could not.

I love you. I'm so sorry this has happened. You deserve only happiness. My darling. My forever. My moonlight.

Kiernan's response was mutual, silent but meaningful as the hidden beast inside him pushed against his mask to touch me, and my fingers followed the path of moving scales created across the muscles of his abdomen.

"I wonder what they'd think if they knew everything that has happened," he spoke softly, staring at the family he lost, the gentle rumble of his voice echoing through my body, and I affectionately kissed his back.

"They would be proud of you, Kiernan," I assured, convinced any parent would feel pleased in life with a child as wonderful as him, but the dragon sank back into the human skin, and Kiernan faced me.

"I'm not so sure about that," he disagreed graciously, and it hurt to see how honestly he said, "But I am confident they would've loved you."

An unexpected sadness overcame me then, longing to have known them as he had, to see whose smile he had and where he got his personality from. It didn't seem right that two magnificent people were taken from this world when there were so many others unfit to continue living, but life had a cruel way of shaping events, and I found myself missing my father alongside Kiernan's parents.

Now, out of my hold, Kiernan freely moved to the bed that consumed the large room, respectfully wiping away the dust, and I quickly joined.

"It's all so intricate," I mused, letting my fingers brush over the carving on the headboard, the complicated divots holding years of neglect in the form of wood.

"He loved her greatly," Kiernan agreed as if our statements were the same thing, and I could see him cracking inside and how he struggled against it. I acted, in need to help him, placing my hand on his, drawing the attention to me and the present before I lost him in the past.

"Come on. It is time to improve your character," I teased, hoping he could see the wish to distract him bleeding through my eyes, and with some strain, Kiernan smiled playfully.

"Is that so?" he chuckled, gratefully accepting my offer, following as I dragged him along by the hand.

"Yep."

"And how do you plan on doing that?"

"I'm going to give you a lesson in bread baking."

I loved him so much.

His tongue just barely peeked out at the side of his mouth while he kneaded the dough, not focusing on putting enough pressure as he rolled it out, but rather concentrating so that his hand didn't press through the countertop, smashing the workplace to pieces. There were multiple reasons Kiernan struggled in the kitchen, one of them being that his powerful ember strength and tiny measuring utensils did not favor each other, and watching him battle the overflowing ingredients while he mixed in a too-small bowl had been more than entertaining for me.

Flour had gotten in his hair at some point along the way, speckling the onyx waves with flecks of white, messy and deeply charming, and I took my time admiring him.

"You want a turn?" Kiernan voiced, taking his eyes off the uncooked bread long enough to side-glance me with a curious smile, no doubt feeling my sight on him.

"No, you got it," I encouraged, unapologetically observing every concerted movement he made, and Kiernan chuckled.

"Is my baking *mesmerizing* to you?" he played, and I broke fixation on him, a subtle shade of embarrassment layering my face, recalling how frequently he tricked me into saying things I never wanted to leave my mind.

"Don't flatter yourself," I chided, rubbing the back of my neck absentmind-edly for the fifth time in the last hour. It was the first occasion my hair was up in weeks, well, most of my hair, as the strand Kell had cut the night of my abduction refused to fit into the messy bun atop my head, exposing my neck that was normally shielded by the layers of crimson curls. My marking was visible, and I had caught myself touching it without thinking, my subconscious hoping to wipe water away, but it stayed, dotting my hand with miniature symbols.

"Apparently, I don't have to. You do it for me."

I rolled my eyes, unable to contain the stupid grin pulling at my lips as I brought out a clean bowl from the cabinet.

"All right, fine. I'll take over," I grumbled lightly, scooting him out of the way to set the bowl by the dough before folding it into a ball. Kiernan lifted his flour-covered hands in surrender, waiting until I had the dough settled to rise and a cloth over the bowl before he made his move.

I blinked as I was tapped on the nose, dusting the tip in white and causing me to sneeze as some of the powder tumbled into my airway.

"Why did you do that?" I asked, wiping the flour off my face.

"How long does it need to rise?" Kiernan deflected, indicating the bowl on the counter, and that only confused me more.

"An hour?"

"Perfect," he gleefully expressed, pressing another finger to my nose until it carried more flour than before.

"What are you doing?" I laughed, batting him away.

"You weren't messy enough."

"Oh, I see how it is," I declared, placing my open palms over the mess-ridden countertop, both of us laughing as I attempted to smack him on the arm just as he tried to interweave it into my hair. I shoved him away, leaving white handprints on his shirt, and he grasped my wrist before I could flee, pulling me to his chest and encasing me in his arms. This was not a hug, no matter that we'd assumed this same position before, because he was wiping his arms down the back of my shirt, and mine were pinned between us.

"Cheater!" I scolded, trying my hardest to wiggle out of his embrace, but he held tighter, his head dipping so that his lips toyed with my ear as he answered identically to the first time I'd reprimanded him for playing unfairly.

"Not necessarily."

I pinched him hard, my fingers barely reaching his skin from the way he trapped my hands, but his hold slackened when the pain registered, and I was running to the other side of the table before he could restrain me again.

"You lemon curd," he muttered, rubbing at the skin I'd squeezed on his lower stomach, and I giggled challengingly. He held eye contact with me as he redusted his arms in flour, tracking my movements from across the table, assessing the best course of action, and I never thought I would have found enjoyment in being hunted by a dragon.

I was careful to mirror his movements to keep our distance, stepping to the right when he did, running to the left as he had, gathering the messy counter's contents as I passed. Scraps of dough and various ingredients were thrown and dodged, dirtying the cabin more than us, and I recalled the same elation I experienced when splashing him in the stream months ago.

Despite my valiant efforts, Kiernan was winning, and in a blind need to be victorious, I grabbed the whole container of flour and tossed it at him, scattering the contents across his face, and when he stopped reciprocating, staring at me darkly, I knew I had gone too far.

"I'm sorry!" I shouted, dropping the container just as he charged at me, and my attempts to escape him didn't get me far when his tail coiled around my middle, shrieking as he lifted me off the ground and watched me dangle helplessly in the air. Being eye-to-eye with any other beast would've paralyzed me with fear, but this was Kiernan, and he wasn't truly upset, no matter how much irritation he feigned.

"I love you," I reminded in hopes of gaining leverage, smiling sheepishly for good measure.

He exhaled sharply through his nostrils, sending flour flying in the air, landing over my whole body, and I coughed through the dust storm it caused. He set me down in the corner, and I wiped my eyes, blinking the alternate Kiernan into focus, his face free of the substance which covered mine, and I scrambled to my feet.

"It was an accident," I insisted, pleading for mercy with a stupid smile on my face, but Kiernan advanced.

"Was it?" he pondered, the teasing barely slipping out through his tone. I nodded, shrinking into the wall as his looming presence trapped me, even if there was plenty of space for me to slip away. I was right where I wanted to be, and Kiernan began chuckling again.

"What?" I prodded, dusting off my arms, and he was still closing in on me.

"I have you pinned, and you aren't afraid in the slightest."

"You could never scare me."

"I wouldn't say that just yet. I still have revenge to inflict."

"Covering me in flour wasn't enough for you?"

"Definitely not. You need something cruel," he whispered, kissing my right cheek, "and terrible," he continued, kissing my left before taking in all of my face, "and if you would stop distracting me with your pretty little color change, then you could see just how terrifying I am."

"It's called blushing, Darling," I clarified with a giggle, slightly breathless from trying to free myself, finally understanding his fascination. His skin was different, accustomed to the power of heat, and the reddening that came from flustering was impossible for him to attain.

"Do it again," he said excitedly, his eyes growing slightly when focusing on me intently.

"That's not how it works," I argued, but even as I said it, my body was counteracting my words, the heat building in my chest, waiting for the proper release.

"Then how can we make it work?"

I pressed my lips together and shook my head, choosing to match his stubbornness.

"Well then," he drawled, his hands suddenly on my waist, lazily dragging over my sides, "I guess I'll have to figure it out on my own."

I tried to suppress my shiver, lowering my face to hide the obvious effect he had on me, but his face dipped in time, forcing his mouth to mine before I could stop it. I caved almost instantly, unable to resist him when he claimed the air I consumed, helpless to how he lifted the kiss, giving him a perfect view of my face when he pulled away.

"There it is," he grinned in victory, and I felt the color blotching my features.

"It doesn't count. You didn't ask," I retorted, reinstating rules I'd abolished prior, but this was a new game, and I needed to win something.

"You are right. My deepest apologies. Let me try that again."

But he didn't go for my lips, moving closer until I could feel the heat radiating from his body, his head dipping just beneath my chin, and I went suddenly taut.

"Ari," Kiernan mumbled, his voice running through me, his words melting the sensitive parts of my neck, "May I kiss you?"

My breath caught, and I needed to stop focusing on the hand moving against my side to find my lungs, which took more effort than I wished. Kiernan's lips grazed my skin as he patiently waited, taunting me with what could be if I gave permission.

"Yes," I at last exhaled, falling back into forgetting everything I was and knew, just to think of him.

It was almost painful how lightly his lips pressed into the side of my neck, trailing up to the corner of my jaw, tracing the hollow of my throat, sweet, tender, steady, contrasting with the aggression of my heart. I knew he was listening to my pounding pulse, not needing his superior hearing to find the sound when it was already so loud. His hands tightened around my waist in response, and when he kissed the pressure point tucked under the edge of my jawline, he lingered there, relishing in the response he'd gotten from this gentle act of affection.

After all, that was why he was doing this, to make me blush, but I was convinced my cheeks were painted with red instead of pink, burning rather than warming.

Every part of me was hot, the tips of my ears, the line of my spine, the backs of my knees, and it was evident he enjoyed how I melted, kissing over the places he'd already been, slower this time, and more precise as though he found the most delicate spots and want to intently focus on them.

I now understood what Kiernan meant when he said it was dangerous to let him kiss me whenever he wanted, because no one person should have that much power over another, nor should they be allowed to simply take it away when the effects were so devastating. He could've asked me anything in that regretful moment his lips left my skin, and the only answer my voice would've been able to utter was his name, which I doubted he'd find issue in.

"You should blush for me more often," he murmured, observing my flustered state with a pleased expression, and I forced myself to think straight rather than get lost in the thought of how gentle he was or how mesmerizing his face could be when smiling like that.

"Kiss me more, and I will," I posed, setting it as a challenge, and either way, I was going to win this one.

"We both know I don't need to kiss you to make you blush, *Agapití*," he twisted my statement around, smirking in a way that blossomed little butterflies in my stomach. "I don't even have to touch you." His hands left my waist, bracing his forearms against the wall on either side of my face, encasing himself as my only view and forcing me back into the headspace that thought of nothing but him. "Though I suppose I wouldn't complain doing either if needed. With your permission, of course."

"Of course," I echoed back in a mock, and his smile faded the longer he searched my eyes, diversion over and reality still settling in.

"We can make this work, Ari. Just you and me," he spoke like an unfaltering promise, and I could see the possibilities he hoped for when he used that tone. "The redwoods are our world."

I liked that idea. We were two people separated from our families, longing to build a life together, and I couldn't picture anything more wonderful than one day starting our own family to join our plan for forever. Kiernan tried to brush the flour from my cheek, the powder clinging to my skin, taking notice of how tightly it clung to me before acknowledging the fact that it was spread throughout nearly every surface of this spacious cabin.

"You go get a shower, and I will start cleaning up. We can finish baking afterward," he instructed, and it seemed like the most feasible plan, accepting a new set of his clothes and heading to the bathroom.

Closing the door behind me, I readied to remove the shirt, my hand holding the collar as my eyes caught my reflection, dancing over the imprints from where his lips had been, missing patches of flour dotting my neck that'd been entirely white, and my skin was hit with another wave of heat. I shook my head as I tried not to smile, seeing just how right he was.

Kiernan didn't even need to be in the same room with me to make me blush.

Chapter Thirty-Eight

Kiernan was acting differently.

He wasn't shifting any longer, as though making the transformation cost him too much, and the toll it took on him to stay in his alternate form was visible. The majestic air about him gradually dissipated, turning his features painfully human, and I hated how he pretended not to notice. His eyes were dimmer, his skin distressingly hot and near tearing as the dragon fought for freedom, and he was constantly near me. I'd grown accustomed to Kiernan's unabating presence, but in the days we were alone; it felt more intense, a necessity rather than a pleasure, like I was the only thing giving him energy, and it was beginning to scare me.

I encouraged him to go outside while I slept, hoping nature would bring back the part of him I couldn't seem to find, but he was glued to my doorway to the point I thought he might stay in my room with me. I then tried walking the woods myself, finally freeing him from the enclosed cabin, but he didn't shift or listen as the wind begged for him to fly, refusing to leave my side while we carried easy conversation during our stroll, and once I caught him *yawning*.

"When was the last time you slept?" I asked, he startled by the mention of an action so foreign to him, and he, again, pretended his behavior was entirely normal.

"When was your birthday, again?"

"Kiernan!" I scolded, hauling to a stop, and as though we were attached by an invisible chain, Kiernan froze beside me. "I know you don't sleep as much as I do, but that doesn't mean you can just go without it."

"I've had a lot to think over."

"Lay down," I directed in a tone sturdy enough to be a demand, and the unwavering nature of my voice managed to surprise and confuse him simultaneously.

"We are in the middle of the forest."

"And the trees want you to rest just as much as I do."

"Ah, so you are a tree whisperer now?"

He was smiling, but it didn't reach his eyes, flooding me with memories of when he was broken and void of emotion, and I couldn't handle him reverting.

"I learned from the best," I answered lightly, reluctant to show my worry as I pointedly glanced to the ground, expectant in my gaze when it returned to him. Kiernan lowered himself onto a patch of moss in submission, and I mirrored the action, sitting cross-legged behind him before lowering his head into my lap. His body went still as I held the sides of his face, staring up at me while I attempted to block the sun from his sight. I was sure to wear a warm smile so that when he closed his eyes, the last thing he would see was my pleasant, content expression, a gentle reminder that we were safe, and it was okay to relax.

"What are you doing?" He questioned softly, barely a whisper, and I responded with equal quiet, carefully rubbing his temples.

"Putting your mind to rest until you fall asleep."

My hands ran through his hair, savoring the soft sensation of the dark waves, and Kiernan's pleasure was apparent when his eyes fell shut, words barely forming in quiet mumbles.

"You are good at this."

"I've had plenty of practice," I giggled, bending down to gently kiss his lips, and after the tenseness of his body loosened slightly, I took my window of opportunity to ease his heart with the lullaby I sang to Anders.

I witnessed the exact moment when consciousness slipped from him, his whole-body cooling at my touch, easing into my voice as I soothed him. His head drooped to the side, allowing me to brush at the back of his scalp, grazing gentle fingers at his neck, but I enjoyed outlining his face the most. Tracing the edge of his jaw, the curve of his cheekbones, smoothing out the creases in his brows, brushing away the thin line of his mouth, and if it hadn't affected my singing, I would've softly kissed every part I touched.

The familiar shape of the words I used to sing to my brother every night reawakened the levity I experienced while singing, the same desire to project my voice until it stretched across all of the redwoods, but for now, I shoved the urge down, voicing softly the lullaby of my childhood, tracking the rise and fall of his chest. His breaths had deepened and slowed, the plenteous forest oxygen weighing heavily in his lungs, and I took comfort in his vulnerability.

Once reaching the end of the lullaby, I began again, remaining in the loop until his rest was fulfilled, and it didn't matter to me that it could've been hours. The sun was gentle against my skin, the wind still as melodic sounds escaped my mouth, and in the distance, I could hear the roaring waves of Secret Beach, calling me more pressingly than it had in days. In the distance, a strange echo in warped tones harmonized in the stillness of the brush, and when my singing paused, a second voice continued on. I sat up, attentive to the imitation of words in perfect unison to my song, a song I'd only ever heard my father sing, and a burning need to find the voice ignited in my chest.

Kiernan shifted slightly, softly groaning in protest at the absence of my sound, his subconscious searching for its source of ease, but he didn't open his eyes.

"Do you hear that?" I whispered as though my words could scare away the new, beautiful utterances that had taken the air, but Kiernan was finally lost in sleep, and the last thing I wanted to do was wake him when he desperately needed the rest.

"I'll be right back," I gently assured into his ear, placing a gentle kiss on his temple before carefully resituating him off my lap and onto the soft patch of grass beneath me.

The lovely sound reflected the breeze and twisted around through the trees, and my heart began to race, suddenly afraid to lose the voice and the secrets it contained. I began stumbling over myself, sight set on the horizon and beach ahead rather than the fern-hidden stones in front of me, but I didn't feel the pain as my legs were scraped up against broken branches, only the hurt of the voice's disappearance, shattering my eardrums with silence.

I stopped at the clearing of trees, frantically searching for the owner of my alighted hope over the shore, but the beach and sand were void of life. Unwilling to accept inanity, my boots slid into the uneven sand, nearing the undulating waves as I prepared to call out.

"Hello?"

"Hello."

Then I saw her.

Standing waist-deep in the ocean, a dark-skinned, slender woman answered me, her voice sounding near despite the distance between us. Shells and pearls were entwined with her long, thick locks of hair, looking like the princess of the sea, and I was moving closer to her without my knowing. Her eyes were large and full of wonder; amethysts engraved into her entrancing gaze, her features like a melodic chord, sharp and beautiful, bringing harmony to the whole of her form. The ocean hid the lower part of her body, but the scales covering her abdomen clung to her perfect shape like a finely fit, sleeveless dress, colors of blue, green, and violet dancing over her middle and fading into ebony skin just beneath her collarbone. Each subtle movement she made was blinding with ocean hues, the sea reflecting her elegance through the waves that carried the woman's allure to the shore and threw it at my feet, casting the illusion that something so lovely was in my reach.

"You are..." I tried, but no words could encompass the sight that she was, and I was almost ashamed for looking upon her so freely, as though my eyes weren't meant to see this.

She smiled a youthful grin that was unbearable to look away from, causing her face to brighten in an unnaturally enticing glow.

"Thank you," she responded, as though she understood my feeble attempt at a compliment, her voice sounding like a caress to my ears, soothing my mind until there was nothing left but thoughts of her. "I heard you singing my song."

"It's yours?" I asked, guilt crawling up my throat, undeserving to utter anything created by her, but she didn't appear upset, rather curious.

"Yes, and it is rarely gifted outside of our kind. Tell me, who did you learn it from?"

"My father."

Her smile fell, and I had the sudden urge to apologize and claim to have heard it elsewhere, doubtful she would believe me, but longing for her smile to return. Her large, amethyst eyes searched my frame, sparkling as they moved, landing on my necklace.

"Come closer," she beckoned, and I was helpless to her call, the tide welcoming me in as it rushed at my feet, then knees, then thighs, then I was waist-deep in the ocean and finding the woman even more captivating up close. She circled me gracefully, examining me with more than her gaze, her hand sliding my hair over my shoulder and causing me to shiver unpleasantly as her cool fingers outlined the droplet on my neck, but I wasn't afraid. Rounding to my front, she cupped my face in her chilling palms with a look I'd always wished to see from Mother, pride in her eyes, adoration in her smile, and care in her face.

"You are finally here," she practically sang in relief, "After all of these years we have waited for you."

Pure joy bled from her expression, and I didn't know what to do with the emotions building in my chest, nor did I know how to release them, but they were crowding my lungs. My lips parted, preparing to speak, but the words didn't make it past my mouth, her glowing excitement leaving me speechless, but there was more she wanted from me.

"Will you give me your name?"

"ARI!" Kiernan cried, running to me from the edge of the forest, and whatever lulled state my mind had entered was broken at his shouts. His feet slipped over the sand, stumbling with every hurried step, his hands over his ears, and the panic in his eyes revealed the situation's severity. Startled, she didn't stop me, and I was free of the ocean's hold quicker than expected, Kiernan tucking me under his arm to block out other sound while he struggled to do the same for himself, hurrying us into the forest without a look back.

"Don't listen!" He insisted, huddling me closer to speak, but he hadn't cautioned me not to look. It saddened me not to see her in the waves as I glanced behind us, hoping to catch one more glimpse, feel the affection of her gaze. Kiernan didn't slow, hurrying us into the forest, only removing his hands from his ears after the tide's call could hardly be heard.

"Who was that?" I asked.

"A siren."

But that couldn't be true. She was beautiful, kindness illuminating her eyes, and I couldn't picture her as the evil Kiernan claimed.

"But that was Secret Beach. The sirens don't know those waters. Keagan told me so."

"She heard you singing. I don't know what I was thinking, letting you use your voice that close to the shore. My head is..." he shook it off, leaving the sentence unfinished and my worry to grow, his own fears audible as he stated, "They know you are here, Ari, and they will be coming for you."

The same chill I felt when she touched my marking ran down my spine, but again, I wasn't afraid, and I couldn't discern whether I was wrong for that.

"No beaches are safe anymore," he clarified, and I couldn't argue over his anxieties, not when he knew so much more than I did. "We must keep you away from them at all costs."

I didn't tell him the painful sting his words sent to my heart, the panicking need to breathe in the sea suddenly rising, and Kiernan was too exhausted to see how I paled.

Chapter Thirty-Nine

"Kiernan?"

He glanced up from his plate, and it was the first time he had looked at me in a while. We were both quiet since we returned to the cabin, thinking deeply on the siren in different ways, and though the tired lines under his eyes were gone, he still appeared exhausted.

"Is there something wrong with the food?" I asked as I eyed his untouched plate of raw salmon, while picking at my cooked version with a fork. I'd tried to do a little something with it: seasonings and lemon juice in hopes of making it more appetizing, because whether he thought I knew or not, he hadn't taken a slice of the bread we made together nor any other food in the three days since his brothers left.

"No. It looks delicious, Ari. I'm just not hungry at the moment."

"Okay," I put lightly, hiding the nervous lump in my throat while I gently moved my plate to the side.

"No, please eat," he urged, and he was such a hypocrite to sound worried about my eating habits when his were nonexistent. "I can finish mine later."

"So can I. I'm not hungry right now either."

I gave a kind smile, but he didn't return it, lowering his gaze with what looked like guilt, and I just needed him to smile. Removing the food from the table much too large for just the two of us, I grabbed the cards and took the seat across from him.

"How about a game?" I suggested, shuffling the deck, surveying how his expression emptied while watching the cards bend into place under my fingers, trying to get a read on something that there were no words for. I dealt us each three, considering my cards of a gold, a silver, and a fire, along with the possibilities I could create in a way that bent my argument to my advantage, distracted as Kiernan reached for the deck I'd set in the middle to draw two more.

"Five?" I questioned, and he assessed his new cards as he explained.

"It's different from playing in a group. You are allowed more cards, the topic changes each round, and since it's just you and me, it becomes more personal. You place down a card with a request or dare you'd like of me, and I can either counteract it or fold, then we move on to my turn, back and forth until we lose our cards."

I took two cards for myself, silently relived for the subtle rule change, now holding a diamond along with another silver and the ability to win any discussion, but I started lightheartedly.

"You can no longer toss me into trees," I exhibited, placing my gold to stand with my statement.

"I see how it is," he chuckled, but gave in too easily, setting a silver down, waiting for the use of the better cards I knew he had, hoping beyond measure one of them wasn't a diamond. He pulled out another silver then, refusing eye contact as he posed, "Sleep with the door open."

"I fold."

Kiernan's eyes shot to me, confusion lighting the greenery, and I was simply happy to be focused on with those jewels of sight.

"You don't want to know why first?"

"I'm curious, but I don't need to understand."

I trusted him with everything I was, and if there was anything I could do that would possibly alter this road he was going down, I would, without question, but Kiernan wasn't at ease with my blind willingness.

"Being closed off from you is... difficult right now, and the nights are getting longer. I won't pass the doorway, I promise, but if I could just see you every hour or so, it would help."

There were other things he wasn't saying, and that was the most concerning part, but we were lowing on cards, and I could ask my questions according to how the game ended.

"You sleep when I do," I posed, wishing I had a better opposition than a silver, and the fire Kiernan responded with burned straight through my request.

"You know that is impossible for me." I raised my eyebrows, and he didn't have to see my discriminating gaze to catch his mistake. "Sorry, I meant *improbable*. It's your turn."

I wanted to argue with him, to call a rematch and counteract him with a move he couldn't compete with, but I only had one shot, and I had to play it right.

"We refer to the stars as sun tears from now on."

Kiernan's eyes grew a little larger in surprise, his shoulders falling in a sheepish manner, and the fact that he didn't blush reminded me he hadn't permanently become human.

"You know about that?" he asked, sounding close to shy, no doubt thinking of the night he'd referred to me as that before I fell asleep, and I took pleasure in the emotions he showed.

"Keagan told me."

"The rat," Kiernan muttered to himself, and I laughed.

"I like that sound of it. Tears are a beautiful thing."

Kiernan's eyes skipped across my joy-crinkled face, staring at me with the same fascination he had months ago when he strived to understand who I was and how I worked.

"I fold," he spoke fondly, more affectionate than a yield should, his sight remaining on me as he placed a gold card, "Admit Sasquatch isn't real, and you went on that hunt with my brother to prove a point."

Talk of Keagan was making me miss him terribly; even if he was a ridiculous flirt, he was my best friend, and I strived to hide my sadness while adding a fire card to our growing pile of plays.

"I did it to get away from you and your tempting grin."

"This one?" He questioned, flashing a smirk that was unfair to use when he was across the table, out of reach, and unable to kiss. "One might call it mesmerizing."

I slammed a hand on the table in exasperation.

"Once! I said it once, and now you are fixated!"

"That's because I can't stop thinking about it," he admitted, still chuckling, "Someone as terribly breathtaking as you claiming *me* to be mesmerizing is nearly incomprehensible. I keep believing that I have finally experienced every emotion there is until you say or do something like that, and entirely new feelings awaken in me." It was the rawest amount of honesty I had gotten from him in days, and I didn't know how to respond. Kiernan started again before the silence became awkward. "I got sidetracked, sorry. State your provocation."

A nasty guilt coiled around my ribcage, knowing how I was about to ruin a precious moment I would cherish far into the future, yet that didn't stop me from flipping over my final card, resting the diamond on the wood, and uttering, "You go to Agrond."

Kiernan's face fell just as I had expected.

"Ari—"

"Flip your card over," I insisted, staring at his only available play.

"You can't—"

"Flip your card over, Kiernan."

"I fold."

"What?"

I was out of cards, and he placed his last, a silver, the weakest of them all, overpowering my play of nothing.

"You come with me. That is my final statement."

He'd yielded on the topic to win another one, a move I never anticipated and was unable to combat, leaving us both in a position of unpreparedness.

"There. It's either we go together or not at all," he affirmed, standing from the table and gathering the cards before I could spin something else on him in the form of a game.

"I'm not ready," I answered honestly, never considering a change to go when Killian was so adamantly against it, and Kiernan put his mask back on, closing me off from reading his feelings. That's how I knew I hurt him.

"Then we wait."

"You can't afford to wait," I shouted, getting to my feet to match his stance, ignoring how he towered over me, "Do you not think I've noticed? You are dying, Kiernan!"

He flinched, but it wasn't long enough to catch his emotions before he plastered on a cool indifference.

"I'm not dying. I just can't freely live."

"What do you mean?"

"There is a reason why banishment here is so fatal. Our essence is vital to our power, and in this world that is polluted with the suffocating air kelpies bring, it is weakening me to be alone without my brothers. I wasn't meant to live here. The horses were. The world favors nature, and anything outside the realm is harmed accordingly."

"So, you won't die?" I asked, but it wasn't quite relief in my tone, rather a pending fear I didn't know how to gauge.

"No. But I will forget what it's like to be a dragon," he answered evenly, more accepting of that fact than he should've been, rounding the table to close the open distance between us. "You, solely, are keeping me from losing myself because of your own essence. Sirens aren't like kelpies in that area. Dangerous as they are, their physical being does not harm us. I'd even dare to say it's more beneficial than other dragons, but I could just be biased."

It explained why he was always near me, why he wanted the door open when I slept, an easy access to my presence when he became too drained. It wasn't right that the one thing that kept him alive was the same reason he refused to thrive in a place that didn't rip his strength from him.

"As long as you are with me, I am fine," he assured, his hand lifting to brush my cheek, but the veins twisting unpleasantly in his arm gave me reason to back away.

"Prove it then. Shift. You haven't been in your real form for days."

"No. I'm not strong enough to change back and forth. I could get stuck."

"But this isn't who you are! You're trapping yourself in, and it's only making you weaker!"

A muscle ticked in his cheek unnaturally, proving my point as the skin he was hiding in became thinner and more see-through.

"I can't be who you need me to be in primary form. I can't talk to you. I'm unable to help you with everyday matters. I can barely even touch you. You are so easy to break, Ari. So easy and accidentally moving wrong could crush you against a wall."

"I don't care. Shift."

"No."

"Then I am leaving," I put defiantly, and I hated the torn anguish that came to his eyes.

"Don't do this," he pleaded, his unfeeling front crumbling, "Don't give me another ultimatum."

"I can't handle the thought of ruining two families. I messed up mine; now yours is broken, and even more than that, you are breaking. If you won't save yourself, then I will."

It was unfair of me to force him into a harsh decision when his family had just done the same; I knew that, but it was also unfair how fine he was with letting the most prominent part of him die away. He waited for me to change my mind, but I stood firm until he eventually gave in.

Transforming in the past has been no more difficult than breathing, but watching him struggle now, his arms shaking as they came away from his face, his scales taking time to form over skin and clothing, I felt personally responsible for his pain.

Kiernan stared down on me, his face all galaxy-dipped scales and misty forest eyes, and I relaxed myself right there, lying on my back, gazing in awe at the beast hovering over me, tracing the violet constellations of his scales with my eyes. He was right when he said we couldn't talk, but I'd learned to master communication without words in a house with a deaf parent, starting with the connection simple glances carried. Kiernan understood me almost instantly, lowering his head so I could run my fingers over the sensitive spot between his eyes, promising, "I'm okay. This is okay. I just need you to be the same."

He softly growled in response, and I interpreted exactly what he meant in the rumbling.

<h1 style="text-align:center">Chapter Forty</h1>

I didn't sleep that night, huddled close to Kiernan as though anything farther would revert him permanently, and in those long hours of silence, feeling every slow breath he took, heartbroken by the idea of separation, I decided I would go to Agrond. It wasn't a decision made from rash ideals, rather the understanding that Kiernan was my world, and this world, a place that didn't know how to make me feel warm, or wanted, or safe, had no more use for me.

For as much as he pushed me to leave with him, Kiernan hesitated when I agreed, staring at me with questioning eyes as though waiting for my mind to be changed, but it was already set. I withdrew from the cabin as it was, leaving every object and memory in its allotted place, not wanting to bring something along that could cause a sense of reminiscence over a life that didn't have the decency to do the same for me, and Kiernan seemed just as content to leave his home behind. He flew us to Secret Beach, stopping just near the shore, and though I knew I shouldn't have, I glanced at the water to see if the siren had come back. She hadn't, and Kiernan's focus was set on the horizon beyond the ocean. He stood behind me while I whispered my silent goodbyes to the sea, hoping it would have the mercy to release me from its call, and I hadn't known Kiernan shifted until he spoke.

"The caves," he began while pointing to the opening in the rock formation peeking out from the shifting waves, his voice shaking the ocean's mournful sounds from my ears, "They are portals between realms, only to be opened by that race."

"Then what are we doing on the beach?" I asked, stepping closer to him until we were nearly touching, but I still worried my nearness lacked the strength he needed to change back.

"I need to be sure this is what you want," he answered solemnly, lightly brushing his fingertips over the back of my hand, portraying his concern in an

339

action that gave me chills. "This isn't a small decision, and you shouldn't treat it like one. If we leave now, we won't be coming back."

"I know," I voiced softly, understanding his warning and the gravity that came with it.

"You don't seem ready for that fact."

It was my final opportunity to open up, to express my concerns and address their solutions before ending such a large part of my life, and it felt wrong to grieve something less than the loss of him.

"I'm truly never going to see them again," I responded in recognition, lowering my head, my limbs gaining the weight they attained when watching my family on Anders' birthday, now knowing that would be the final memory I had of them. "There still was a small, quiet, childishly hopeful part of me that wanted to believe they were still looking for me, that they cared enough not to give up. But this is for the best, I suppose. Everyone is happy in the end, right?" I wanted him to simply agree, to say there was no better outcome, but he was honest when I couldn't be.

"Are you happy?"

I couldn't remember the last time I'd been asked that. It's one of those sayings silently wondered but never voiced, something questioned in the back of the mind, and to hear the words aloud from Kiernan left me unable to fumble for any answer other than the truth.

"I will be. I'm with you. It's just..." I evened my breathing. "It's sad when you experience more comfort with your captors than your own family."

I felt him flinch.

"I wish it hadn't happened that way," he spoke in apology, soft and regretful, and I shook my head.

"I'm glad it did. You managed to make me feel safe despite being the reason I was in danger. You were so caring when I was resistant to nearly every help you offered."

"You were afraid. That is not something to shame yourself for."

"Yes, but I was also foolish. Even after trying to escape in the redwoods without proper clothing and an injured leg, I would've starved to death if you hadn't forced me to eat."

He chuckled, and while that alleviated some of my guilt, it started the embarrassed flush that crawled up my face.

"You still owe me an answer," he reminded teasingly, and I turned my confusion to him rather than the ground, blushing harder when he smiled at the color.

"What?"

"I finished the soup and left without finishing the exchange. According to our poorly formed rules, I still get one more answer from you."

It was possible he remembered every little insignificant moment we shared, every look, every touch, knowing exactly when to bring it back up to his advantage, and I wondered if he'd been waiting for something specific to ask or if he wanted to take my mind off of things.

"Do you have your question?"

His smile retreated as the intensity of his eyes scoured my face, his touch drawing from me to reach into his pocket, and the nervousness emitting from his strong build was palpable.

"I do."

He took one of my hands in his warm grasp, placing something small but solid in my hold, closing my fingers around the object until the sharp edges poked into my palm. I was curious to glimpse at the tiny gift, but his expression was altogether serious, hinting at worry, and I was too intently focused on what he had to say to let my eyes leave him.

"Ari, there is nothing I adore more in this world or any other, than you. I know you are uncertain about all of this, but I want to give you the assurance that everything will be okay. You have my love, my devotion, my *týpos*, and my heart, but if I gave all of who I am to you, each untamed side and every broken piece..." he paused to breathe just as I had, his mouth indicating a smile when the rest of his features appeared too anxious to match the joyous expression, and when his hand cupped my cheek, it was gently quivering. "*Agapité*, would you—"

Kiernan cut himself off immediately, eyes locking on movement behind me, his face contorting into something that sent a frightened shiver down my spine, and despite the fear fighting against my movements, I glanced over my shoulder.

A black horse too large to be normal stood at the end of the woods, and in the shadows cascaded by the trees, the figure morphed into something I knew, *someone* I knew, and the excited beating of my heart quickly changed to fear when his Scottish lilted voice yelled at me.

"ARI, GET AWA' FROM HIM!"

Then my arm was grasped, Kiernan yanking me behind him, the sheer and unconstrained strength of it throwing me to the sand, causing me to lose grip of the tiny object held in my hand. My head spun as I sat up, viewing Zadar return to his true form, galloping toward the dragon at unnatural speed, and Kiernan hunkered down, preparing for a fight I didn't want to witness.

"WAIT!" I cried, wobbly standing and rushing to get between the two mythical creatures just as Kiernan released the flames from his chest, aiming for the kelpie's face and hitting my left shoulder instead.

Suddenly, my skin was no more durable than thread, unraveling at the seam, breaking apart the line of my spine, searing the structured patterns of my left shoulder, and I screamed. The burning didn't cease even as I fell to the ground, writhing in the sand to put out the fire forcing its way into my nerves to singe them off one by one. The flames stretched into my blood, stealing my heartbeat until I felt the pulsations over half of my back, and nothing eased the ache. Through my anguish, I managed to end the massive fight before it could ensue, both Zadar and Kiernan losing focus of each other long enough to hurry to my aid, that was until Zadar got too close for Kiernan's liking. Darkness consumed me as the dragon's wings formed a dome around my being, the wind it caused blowing out the fire eating away at my body, but it failed to extinguish the pain, and his roar at Zadar masked my cries of agony.

"If ye dinnae let me near her *this instant*, she is goin' tae burn alive. Siren's skin is infectious tae fire, but ye ken that," Zadar sneered as though it'd been Kiernan's intention to harm me, and the way his wings curled protectively tighter around space, close off the proper flow of air, did not help counteract the assumptions. "*Let me near her.*" Zadar was typically skilled in blending in, but at that moment, he sounded far from human.

"Kiernan, *please*," I begged, using the last of my draining energy as the burning crawled up my neck and sweltered my throat, and as my pained noise broke off, I was blinded by the sudden light that came into view. My ears were ringing, but I could still hear the sand shifting as Zadar at last reached me.

"Een open, Ari," he directed, cradling my head as he resituated my body to lie on my stomach. I caught the briefest glimpse of Zadar slamming his bare fist against a large rock, the stone cracking after one hit and hollowing out the center to which he shoved into Kiernan's hold before instructing him, "Fill that wi' sea water and bring it back this minute."

Kiernan, in all his stubbornness, would've defied being ordered in any other situation, especially by a race combatant to his own, but after one look at the sweat dotting my weak form, he didn't hesitate in his run for the sea. Zadar wasted no time, either, ripping the already burned collar seam of Kiernan's shirt until it hung over my shoulder, exposing my scorched skin without fully removing the layer, and my body tensed as the wind scratched against the melted mess that was my back. Kiernan returned, stone carrying remnants of the sea set by Zadar's side near a sharp, broken stick I only then noticed before the dragon rounded to sit alongside me, his expression fearful and enveloped with guilt.

"I'm sorry," Zadar whispered before plunging the broken stick into my shoulder, ripping it down my back, and with energy I didn't know I still possessed, I shouted, grabbing hold of Kiernan's hand to squeeze. It was instinctual, I recognized, the way he braced to strike Zadar for intentionally hurting me, and if I didn't have such a tight grip on him, I feared he would've.

"What are you *doing*?" he practically growled, and Zadar answered evenly, as though Kiernan couldn't burn him down as well.

"Because o' ye, the fire's in her system noo, and if it's no washed from her blood it'll reach her heart and stop it beatin'."

Black, burnt blood dripped down my arms, outlining where I lay, and Zadar lifted the makeshift bowl to the open wound he created, pouring the contents graciously over my shoulder. The relief was instant, cool rushing in like the biting chill of the wind, and I had never appreciated the cold more. The world was regaining its colors around the edges, able to hear the continuous apologies Kiernan professed into my palm, and when I strained to touch his face, Zadar forcefully intervened with the demand for more water. Kiernan bristled more under the second command, but he complied nonetheless, my eyes following him to the shore.

"Right, Ari, I need ye tae breathe wi' me," Zadar insisted, turning my focus to him, "In through the nose for four seconds, hold for seven, oot through the mouth for eight. Can ye do that?"

I attempted to answer verbally, but my throat was too dry, making me swallow roughly as I nodded.

"Guid. In." He inhaled slowly, and I repeated, training my eyes on him even as Kiernan neared, handing the stone over and taking his place by me. "Hold." Zadar counted when my brain was too sluggish to put numbers in the right order, pouring more of the ocean's remnants over my cooling back, though the amount he used was significantly less than the first round. "Out." My whole body sighed with the exhale, releasing the tension from my muscles and the fading ache from my limbs, and Zadar tenderly brushed the damp hair from my face. "In." He removed his hand from my head, carefully eyeing the dragon who had his attentive sights set on nothing else but me. "Hold." Far too subtly, the stone bowl containing water was taken in his clutch. "Out." Without the slightest indication of warning, the rock was thrown at Kiernan's unsuspecting face, dousing his top half and trapping him in his weaker form, forcing him to use nothing more than human strength as Zadar swiftly made the first blow.

Despite his broad, strong build, Zadar's movements were nimble as he attacked, throwing Kiernan to the ground, striking with swiftness and precision. At first slow to understand what was happening, Kiernan acted just as quickly, dodging some of the impacts and grabbing the discarded stone and thrusting it into Zadar's temple, the hit strong enough to be lethal, but Zadar merely grunted and gripped his head, giving Kiernan a chance to kick the man off of him and get to his feet.

My sight was missing some color, my throat raw from screaming, my head throbbing as I sat up, but two people I loved were tearing each other apart, and I knew Kiernan was too fatigued to come out victorious.

"Zadar!" I called, tripping over my legs attempting to reach him, knowing if we simply talked, he'd understand Kiernan wasn't the danger he thought, but Zadar didn't appear in the mood for a conversation, fixing me with a sharp, illuminated stare that washed with a wave of peace.

I want to stay back. I want to keep low. I want to rest.

A nagging desire to lie back down and close my eyes, drift off to the contentment that suddenly flooded my body, but the thoughts were foreign to the voices I'd known, kinder and more gentle than the harsh accusations, and the comfort unnaturally easy to accept. The warped sense of safety wasn't difficult to combat, but the heaviness in my eyelids was different, determined to have its way through sleep, so I didn't have to watch my stepfather murder the boy I'd fallen in love with.

Against my best attempts, I must've fallen unconscious for just a moment because when I'd closed my eyes, Kiernan was holding his own, stone in hand, stance tall, ready for a fight, and when I opened them, Zadar had him pinned against a tree, throwing one punch after another to his gut, and not many could be blocked in their speed.

"Stop!" I demanded, trying to make it to my knees at the very least, but any thoughts of standing negated my heart, and there was not enough fight in me to struggle against Zadar and myself. He pretended not to hear me or acknowledge that he was beating someone to death, and I was more helpless than I'd been during the challenge between Kell and Kiernan. "You are going to kill him! Stop it!"

Kiernan slumped, too injured and overpowered to keep going, and Zadar picked up the stone, lifting his arm a final time to bash Kiernan's head in, ending his life right before my eyes.

"DAD, DON'T!"

Zadar halted, the name I hadn't called him since I lost my memories, giving him pause, and I choked on my sob, seeing Kiernan's blood all over my stepfather's hands. His hold on the defenseless dragon didn't wane, but his attention shifted to me, eyes wide and searching for answers.

"Ye remember?"

I nodded profusely, body trembling, desperate to keep his attention.

"Everything. I know who I am. I know who you were, and I can tell you whatever you want to know about where I've been and what's happened, but please don't kill him. I'm begging you."

Something shifted in his eyes, oceans illuminating like they did when he discovered Mother was pregnant with Anders, and whatever he saw in that moment was worrisome enough to calm his determination. Zadar shut his eyes and exhaled as though this truly hurt him to do.

"I'll no forgive masel if I kent he was oot free tae bring death as he pleases."

"He's leaving, Zadar!" I argued, preparing to offer up anything in exchange for his life. "He's going back to Agrond!"

"Is that true?" he demanded, turning back to the boy who could barely keep his head up.

"Yes."

I was sure my heart broke at the small rasp he gave, wanting to hold him and sing till he felt no more pain, but Zadar was still towering over him with the look of murder as justice in his eyes. His stare was cruel and unforgiving, searching Kiernan's bruised eyes for any signs of deception, and I was scared he had decided to kill him anyway when he released Kiernan's collar, observing as the boy crumpled to the ground. My heart leaped in painful hope, taking in every ragged breath and grunt of pain, but he wasn't pinned. My legs felt lighter, like I could run to him and place a comforting hand on his arm if I tried, but I was also highly aware that at any second, Zadar could change his mind and snap Kiernan's neck. I wasn't willing to take the risk.

Kiernan's hair still dripped, but it wouldn't be long until the dragon was dry, and fighting back wouldn't be a struggle. Zadar knew this, wasting no time as he leaned down and declared, "I'm only givin' ye one chance at life, and if ye e'er come back here, e'er even *think* o' harmin' her again, a stone'll be the least o' yer worries. That's my promise tae ye."

Of course, he had to look at me next, piercing me with those green eyes as that shattered my remaining composure, and I realized this was the only goodbye we were allowed.

"Go," I breathed, pleading with him in my eyes to take this chance I knew he wouldn't receive again, and Kiernan's gaze equally insistent, promising to come back for me.

Then he shifted, and I watched as the person I loved more than anything left this world and me with it.

Part 3

Patér was right to call this place paradise. The nights were longer, the sun's tears brighter, the air easier to breathe, and I would have thought living among my kind, in a world created for dragons to be free, would be much easier.

But all I could think of was Ari and how I left her.

Here, I didn't have to pretend. Every face I met was just as devoid of feeling as mine was before I met her, but now she was gone, and my emotions burned stronger, fighting the desire to keep her safe.

I didn't have to pretend, but I did, acting as though my worry wasn't growing by the second, that time could mock me across realms and keep me from her longer than was safe. She could die, and I had to pretend the thought didn't haunt me, as to fit in with society and not draw more attention from an already curious crowd.

But all I could think of was Ari and how her terrified, tear-filled eyes were the last thing I saw.

Basileús Draco was a very gracious ruler, allowing my family and me residency in his empire despite living our entire lives in the human realm. He personally greeted me as I arrived later than my brothers, offering a celebration in our honor, welcoming and accepting my family as though we weren't born from a disgrace of the law.

But all I could think of was Ari and how she was trapped with that conniving kelpie.

Killian used his free time to gain a deeper understanding of our native language as we were the only ones able to speak English apart from the *basileús*, while Keagan posed himself as the longing bachelor in search of a partner, and Kaid fought to prove his control in shifting forms to avoid being sent to the Children's Isle. Kell and I were sent to train with the rest of the embers, preparing for the inevitable war that would ensue when she was found. We were years behind in our combat skills, far from the warriors our age, and while Kell took it as a challenge, I was merely grateful to use fire in a manner that was controlled and without worry of drawing human suspicion.

But all I could think of was Ari and how I nearly killed her.

Evening meals were held in the royal dining hall with the *basileús* himself, feeding his curiosities of our lives foreign to the normalcy of Agrond while he fed our hunger and my brothers' desire for a new start. The conversations were as interesting as any emotion-deprived communication could be, Killian naturally doing most of the talking with our leader and only falling short when she was brought up. My shoulders stiffened when the title "your human pet" was used, giving away the severity of the feelings I attempted to hide as well as my extreme distain for the statement used, and seeing this, Keagan spoke up for me, deterring the conversation until the topic was far from the girl I fell in love with.

But all I could think of was Ari and how easily her innocent heart could be manipulated without my protection.

Even when I was alone, I could feel Killian's eyes on me, as if he could sense my anticipation to get back to her, and he portrayed his disapproval through silent action. This was the life he'd always wanted to give us, the same life our parents grew up in, and his fear of her coming and ruining our new beginning overruled my need for the girl I was tied to. She was never mentioned, even when it was only me and my family, and I hated how they acted as though she wasn't the very reason we learned how to properly smile and that she meant nothing until *Basileús* Draco's curiosity circled back to her. For as much as I respected the leader in his full pardon, I didn't like how he talked with Kell, in separate rooms or in distant hallways, sharing knowing glances over the most random topics, and I knew I wasn't the only one who picked up on it. Kaid was absorbed with the wonderment of this place, and Keagan, as always, was much too distracted by girls, but I saw the way Killian's eyes would fix on the ruler when he'd tap Kell on the shoulder and they'd step aside for a moment, and I was especially confused when Kell was announced as *diádokhos*, Agrond's second in command.

But all I could think of was Ari and how I would get back to her.

Chapter Forty-One

The sky was too vivid, too cheerful, bright with an electric blue as the black and violet faded away. He should've looked back and found me one last time with those unforgettable eyes, desperate to consume the few seconds we still had each other in our sights, or so my heart believed. I'd told him to leave, begged him to go, and now that he did, I realized the mistake it was. He was taking the best parts of me with him, my love, my hope, my *happiness*, leaving me the hollow, deprived girl I was before I knew him. Everything was deteriorating, crumbling into the ash from a burnt-out flame, and the only hands there to catch me were cold.

"Oh, Ari, whit have they done to ye?"

My eyes were torn from the sky vacant of the dragon who'd left the horizon far too open without his magnificent wings to overshadow the sun, and being turned to face the voice, I found Zadar crying. He was careful not to touch my injured shoulder when reaching for me, and while the pain dully throbbed over half of my back, I barely felt it, a numbing sensation spreading from my heart and through my bloodstream. The oceans in his eyes bled tears of relief mixed with sorrow as my view was impaired by the same waters of pain.

"I'm so sorry it took me this long to get to you. You are safe now. We are going to get you home."

The words never left his mouth, but the voice was his, speaking in my mind through the glistening stare, and I wondered how he knew the cabin's location. Too long, it took me to realize that he didn't, that the home he spoke of was in Crescent City, and that my real home didn't exist anymore.

Kiernan was gone.

Not coming back. Need him back. Need him. Need anything from him.

I suddenly tore from Zadar's touch, demeanor turning frantic as I search for the place I'd fallen. There was a gift from Kiernan I still had yet to see, and not having it felt like giving up on him, disregarding everything we fought for.

"Whit are ye doin'?" Zadar questioned gently, as though I was unstable, mentally distraught, able to snap at any moment, and I supposed he wasn't wrong. I should've been able to let him go, and the idea had seemed so feasible in my mind, but I didn't know how *terrified* of life I was without him. Zadar misread my searchings as frantic pacing, pitying me as I dropped to my knees, and I made sure my back was to him when lifting the object from the sand.

A scale.

Violet and onyx ombre in the shape of a triangle, one of the thousands of sun tears in his skin rested on my palm, sharp and beautiful and still here. He'd left me a piece of him, and my hand clutched it, holding tight to the sole remnant of his existence. With the smallest amount of peace it brought, I stood, facing the kelpie who analyzed my movements as though trying to read me, but even I was unable to identify my emotions apart from the growing numbness feeding away at my chest and fingertips.

"Would ye say somethin', please?" he requested, patient and concerned, sounding like the childhood still hazy in my memories, but it was a comfort, "What is going through your head?"

Subtly, I allowed my hand to slide into my pocket, releasing the scale into its hidden confinement without Zadar noticing, meeting his eyes once more as I answered truthfully.

"Home."

"You almost killed him," I said with an unexpected softness, and it felt strange to break such heavy silence after being consumed by hours of it. We'd walked seemingly endlessly, tracking our way on foot to the forest's edge where Zadar parked his car, and when night fell, still surrounded by the endless redwoods, we rested.

Zadar met my gaze over the fire he made, flames twisting in the oceans, and they turned hard like obsidian.

"I was doin' whit had tae be done."

I'd placed myself near the base of a tree that supported my back, observing his calm demeanor, much like translating a cryptic language, hoping to understand why he'd been so quiet during our walk and why I'd suddenly been afraid to be near him, but he'd been nothing but gentle.

"How can you say that?" I spoke as confusion and heartache pinched my features, "How can you justify cold-blooded murder? He'd done nothing wrong!"

Zadar dropped my gaze, poking at the fire until the flames sparked brighter, unintentionally making me flinch away, fearing it would latch onto my skin again, and we were far from the ocean.

"Dinnae fight me on things ye dinnae understand," he answered lowly, and a hot surge of anger rushed up my chest.

"And whose fault is that?"

I clicked my mouth shut, but that did nothing for the words already passed and the tone in which they accused, worrying how the kelpie who nearly committed a murder right before my eyes would take my resistance. Zadar met my stare again, his features firm but remorseful as he glanced me over, as though recalling something painful.

"Do ye really want tae ken?"

His tone was even more solemn than his expression, and it cooled my anger, taking in his words with a clearer mind.

"Yes."

"That lad was the one yer brother and I saw carryin' ye tae yer death," he answered, and I stopped breathing. His stare was too honest, too sincere, too haunted by the future, yet I couldn't believe. "I do not do things without reason."

"Kiernan wouldn't..." I was terrified to finish the sentence, the air tight around my throat and my mind shut down the idea. "You're wrong."

"I'm no," he argued with equal calm, and I stood as though it could give me leverage.

"You are *wrong*!" I shouted, desperate for him to agree with me, to prove his statements false so my heart could beat normally.

"I am no!" He bellowed, and the truth practically bled from his eyes. Still, I shook my head.

"You don't know Kiernan! He cares about me! He wouldn't—"

But I had begged him to, tried forcing him into a promise of ending me if I became all that they feared, and my argument died on my tongue.

"Ye trust far too easy, Ariella. Whit were ye thinkin' runnin' off into the woods wi' someone ye barely ken? A *lad* at that."

I tore my hands through my hair, pacing by the fire.

"It wasn't like that. He was gentle and kind, and if you weren't so busy trying to beat him to death, you would've seen that!"

"Dragons are deceitful creatures. That's why they're still alive today, and ye're lucky they played their tricks as long as they did."

I thought of Kell then, toying with my fear like it had been a game, an enjoyable play to gamble how long I lived, and just as quickly as he appeared, he was gone, replaced with Kaid and the confused knit to his brows as he wrote out the answers to his homework. Keagan would laugh at the ridiculously proportioned word problems, and Killian would lightly scold him, rarely harsh when it came to the people he loved most. When I thought of Kiernan, there was no one else, moments shared in private like they were a delicate secret, him softly kissing my neck or quietly confessing all he felt for me, him twirling me as we danced in the rain or counting the stars until we fell asleep. Just that morning he had given me a piece of himself, ensuring he'd always be there, that Agrond would be the relief we longed for, and I trusted that, because deep down, I hoped he'd come back for me.

"Ye really believed them," Zadar observed, and I'd forgotten he was there, lost in memories I held close to me as though they were meant to be stolen, "Ari, do ye understand who ye are—whit *they* are?"

"I know I am a part of a prophecy I want nothing to do with, and I know that because they told me. It would've been easier for them to keep me in the dark, yet they were honest with me anyway. I wasn't shut out, or forgotten, or left to compile this new terrifying information on my own, because that's not how family should treat—"

"Family?" Zadar interjected, his expression bordering a crinkling distaste along with cruel amusement, "Ye think they're yer family? A guid one that? They go on tae tear each other apart, and that so-called *perfect family* dies by the hands o' those who claimed tae protect them. Is that whit ye want tae be caught up in?"

My hands instinctively lifted as though to cover my ears, knowing this wasn't something I was meant to hear, terrified what my mind could do with the information.

"No, the future can be changed! It doesn't have to be that way! It *can't* be."

"Aye, the future can change, but there has tae be the will for it first."

"Then why didn't you kill him?" I finally snapped, breaking with a truth I was unready to handle, "If Kiernan is as terrible as you make him out to be, then why didn't you just end him when you had the chance?"

Zadar sighed, closing his eyes for a brief moment, and when he opened them again, a sadness swam in the blue.

"Because I looked at ye, and I saw my scared wee girl. It's been years since ye looked at me wi' any sign o' knowin' who I was, and I hated ye no rememberin' who I was. Then I saw myself goin' through wi' it, saving ye from that nightmare o' a fate, and I saw ye again, my scared wee girl, slittin' her wrists."

It was the one truth I didn't fight, the one that set well in my soul, and I could comprehend how dependent I had become on Kiernan.

"It wouldn't have mattered. If you murdered him, I would've died as well. I have his *týpos*."

Zadar was standing then, stalking past the fire to reach me, and the danger in his gaze had me stumbling back. He grabbed my arm, staring as though he had every intention to harm me, and I looked up at him with burning eyes. When he saw the green, he released me, the fire of anger in his expression remaining without the heat of it scorching me.

"That snake," Zadar spat, viewing as the emeralds in my stare dissipated, and the promised threat along with it, "So that's how they got ye tae bend tae their will. They infected ye wi' their claim, and noo the bond's could yer judgment."

"I am not *infected*! Kiernan did it to protect me. I would've died if he hadn't."

"Ye think that'll save ye later on? Yer tied tae him noo! Why would ye ever trust a dragon?"

"I love him, Zadar!"

I refused to break my stare, forcing him to see the honesty in my eyes, and sudden terror fell into his.

"Dinnae say that," he spoke as though I wounded him.

"Why shouldn't I?" I challenged, trying to fight back tears.

"Because yer mother and I already found someone for ye to love."

I immediately backed down, the shock of his admission hitting me like a pummel to the head, and the tears retreated when my outrage showed.

"You've arranged for me to give my life away to someone I don't know? Before I even knew who *I* was?" I shouted, grateful no one else was near to hear me, because I was yelling, and my anger was only growing.

"He'll make ye happy. I made sure o' it."

"No, you do not get to decide what makes me happy. This whole time, you've decided everything for my life! You chose to take my memories and let me believe I never had a parent who cared for me! You chose to leave me with an absent mother and raise Anders when I was only a child! You chose to keep the mythical world from me to figure out on my own! And now that I have decided who I am and what I want, you tell me who to marry?" My voice had cracked, shattering like my heart, and Zadar, too, appeared broken from the inside at my words.

"Those were never ma choices, Ari," he spoke in painful quiet, contrasting with my shouts and anger. "They were yer mother's."

"Mother's ideas? *My* mother? The one who couldn't look at me for eighteen years? The one who locked herself away to avoid communication with her only daughter?" The laugh that escaped my mouth was dark and bitter, aching with all the long years I shoved down the hurt. "My mother wants nothing to do with my life."

"That's a lie," he responded with well-practiced calm, unafraid to pin me with that sharp stare. "She cares too much. And she's scared, Ariella, *terrified* o' losin' ye efter losin' Avam. She acts this way because her mind's no sound, and it hasnae been since…" he held back his words, and it antagonized me to see him restrain the truth after all the painful claims he'd already made.

"Since when?" I demanded, readying to fight for answers I deserved, but his demeanor was calm again, unwilling to match my energy.

"Well, since she met yer father." He hesitated again. "He wasnae the best man. I ken ye looked up tae him , but ye were too young tae see how he hurt her and ye."

"He loved me. He cared for me. He taught me to sing. Lemon curd, I wouldn't even be here without him! You can say whatever you want about my death or how you've set up my marriage, but I will not hear you speak negatively of the only parent who wanted me."

"Yer mother wants ye. *I* want ye."

"No, you don't want me. You want the idea of me. You want the girl in that prophecy who is destined to create genocide for a kind you want gone. That's the real reason you came looking for me. Why else would you? I'm not your daughter."

Tears prickled at the back of my eyes once more, and the wounded look on Zadar's face is what caused them to fall. I didn't know it was possible for someone that intimating to appear that hurt, and I wished I could take the words back as he spoke evenly.

"Ye're my daughter, Ari, in aw the ways that matter."

I shook my head, not wanting to believe when that made it so much worse, thinking I could be truly loved in a home I didn't belong in.

"My father is dead, my mother can't even stand to *look* at me, and my brother is going to a place I can't follow! All of his life, I have tried to help him with things I didn't understand, but then you show up and teach him how to sleep through the night. You show up, and suddenly, Mother is alive again. Don't you see it? I'm the piece that doesn't fit! And I can't be upset with you for being happy with the family you created, but I can be upset with how you took the family *I* made."

"Ye werenae even gone a full month," he scoffed, and my heart constricted.

"And I was shown more acceptance and affection in that time than I have had in the last thirteen years!"

"Ye call bein' held hostage affection?"

"According to your wife, yes, it is. I was practically locked in that house my whole childhood."

He watched me for a moment, as though assessing what he could say that wasn't a lie.

"Yer mother's been through a lot."

"So have I! I almost died multiple times these last weeks, and I still came back for you guys—"

I closed my mouth, scrambling to gather up the mess that was my emotions, and Zadar latched on to the only claim I wished he missed.

"Ye escaped? When?"

"Anders' birthday. They let me go," I responded, wiping my eyes with the shirt that still smelled like Kiernan, "Not that it mattered. You three were perfectly content without me."

His brows lowered.

"We never gave up on ye. I ken ye were alive, just in danger, and we searched for ye every single day of ye were missin'. It got that bad Anders went two whole days wi'out sleeping, and when he finally did, it was only nightmares o' ye dyin'.

I made him forget. Just for the day. He's been miserable lookin' for ye, Ari, and he deserved a wee bit o' peace tae turn thirteen."

I lowered my gaze, guilt crawling up my spine because of course Zadar would do that, ease the heartache so Anders could breathe. It's what I would've wanted, and I hated myself for not thinking of that possibility and jumping to such conclusions.

"I didnae ken whit happened tae ye," Zadar continued, "but I ken whit ye went through wasnae easy. I want tae help. I could take awa' the pain o' this mess or even make ye forget it altogether."

"No. I don't want to forget," I answered, my heart fragile for the hollowed state Kiernan left it in, and with no anger to keep me upward, I plopped onto the ground, my gaze lifting to the sky. The stars were dimmer, but the moon made up for it, shining as though wanting to prove its presence, and though I wanted to smile, it didn't quite reach my lips as my fingers fidgeted with the scale in my pocket. If I'd been alone, I would've whispered to the moon or sung until the stars brightened, but I settled for the voice in my mind, hoping he could hear me.

Come back.

Chapter Forty-Two

The cold was a sensation I'd become accustomed to until I was introduced to the fire Kiernan brought to my heart, melting the icy claws of anxiety and heating my skin with flushing shades of acceptance. But he was gone, and the cold was so much worse, biting into my nerves as it fed into the fears that I'd feel this way for the rest of my life.

I wrapped my arms around myself, craving a warmth I could never produce, not with the chilling water covering my bare feet, ripples dancing around my ankles with each movement I made. Darkness stretched further than I could see; the air layered with hints of sweet muskiness; the scent of thistles dusted with the ocean salt. The thin surface of water at my feet was still, only making a sound when I pivoted to take in my surroundings, finding I wasn't alone.

Pale blonde ringlets crowned his head, falling into sea blue eyes, his light skin reflecting in the water he sat in cross-legged. His elbow was nestled over his knee, his hand propping a ruggedly handsome face with muscled features, peering at me with a delighted gleam as though he'd been waiting for me.

The boy from my vision—which could only mean I was experiencing another.

"Who are you?" I asked, surprised that my voice echoed back to me when there were no surrounding surfaces for the sound to bounce off.

He smiled, showing off two dimples as though aware of the perfect symmetry they added to his face.

"I've answered that already."

His accent was thick, possibly stronger than Zadar's, and while his words didn't echo, I could hear his serious response of "yer mate" repeat somewhere in the darkness behind me.

"What is your *name*?"

"I'm near affrontit ye didnae ken," he expressed, bringing a mocking hand to his heart and a disappointed shake of his head, "Efter aw Zadar made me pay."

It then clicked; the title he used for me, along with Zadar's intentions for my marriage, and an even harsher reality

"You *purchased* me?" I shouted, familiar sensations of anger bubbling in my chest, and he had the audacity to *laugh*.

"Paid as in sweat an' effort, Lassie," the handsome blonde explained, dropping a hand from his face to assume a straightened posture, "Zadar didnae make it easy tae win yer hand. The *Dákry's* man is nae simple title. Naw, I had tae *earn* ye. Prove masel' worthy, if ye prefer that idiom."

I attempted a scowl, but it felt wrong on my face, puckering my features into a pout.

"I'm sorry to disappoint, but I already found my person."

"Aye. An' whit did he dae tae win yer heart, then? Ca' ye bonnie an' bring ye flooers?"

The scowl came easily then.

"He has sacrificed himself for my well-being multiple times and protected me in every way imaginable," I defended, attempting to keep a polite tone, but I struggled when he scoffed, drawing lazy shapes in the thin layer of water surrounding his large legs. I noted how his pants remained dry where he lounged. My curiousity piqued as the freezing pools bit into my heels and left him untouched.

"Ye dinnae need protectin'," the man answered, "Mebbe a wee bit trainin', but ye're far frae helpless."

"I never said I was helpless."

"Mebbe no wi' words, but yer body's shoutin' it loud. Yer shooders are hunched, yer airms a' crossed roon yer middle, an' every muscle tight as a bowstring. Ye're makin' yersel' wee tae seem harmless, and though ye're bonnie beyond tellin', timidness disnae sit right on ye."

I was unsure whether his observation was intended to be a compliment or criticism, but I felt the need to huddle into myself further, attempting to explain my behavior with something that wasn't a lie.

"I'm cold."

"Ye're nervous," he corrected, his smile a bit too haughty, "An' I find that fair flatterin', though ithers'll see it as weakness."

Weak. Helpless. Insufferable. Nearly died to keep you alive. Won't come back. He'll find a girl of his kind. She won't be pathetic. He won't miss you. Only settled for you because he had no other option.

My fingers curled uncomfortably into my arms, wanting to disappear into darkness and cry, and if he were to judge me on my posture, I had no doubt he'd do the same for my feebly guarded emotions.

"Would you please leave?" I requested, but it came out in more of a plea, dropping my head to block his view of my growing tears, and I could practically hear the frown in his voice as he responded.

"Zadar never said ye were sae mannerly." I heard the shuffling of his clothing as he stood, stepping closer. "Or sae wee! Jings, ye're a bittie o' a thing."

When I faced him, it involved craning my head upward, tears slipping out through the corners of my eyes as I saw him towering over me, even taller than Kiernan had been. I was entirely average height, yet the way he acted as though I was abnormal in my stance reminded me too much of the boy I loved, like he was somehow being replaced. That thought repulsed me.

"Listen, I may not know who you are, but that doesn't mean you have the right to intrude into my dreams, claim to be my mate, mock the love of my life, and insult my height! I don't get what you plan to gain from being here, but if these are your tactics to 'win me over', you need some help. Either way, I'm not going to marry you. Whatever agreement you made with Zadar was out of my knowledge or control, but I have my own free will, and no *kelpie* will be taking that from me," I snipped, unpleasant and unforgiving, and his eyes sparkled with excitement.

"There noo. There's that fire," he marveled delightedly, and he seemed to be more pleased the angrier I became, "I kent ye'd it in ye. Ye're a redheid, efter aw."

"How dare you stereotype me!" I exclaimed, and his smile grew.

"Elle will hae a soft spot for ye, sure as sunrise."

He chuckled, taking a step closer, and out of habit, I almost backed away, but I wasn't about to let him overrun me so easily, instead meeting him head-on with a push to the chest, stumbling as my hand fell through his form as though he were nothing more than air.

"Ye might be sleepin', but I'm nae some dream ye conjured. Ye cannae shove me aside like a wisp o' yer imagination."

Which explained how he had stayed dry, and I hadn't, despite sitting in the pools; for him, all of this was conceptualized, and I wasn't fully convinced my mind hadn't created him in attempts to fill in the parts of stories Zadar had failed to finish in our heated discussion.

"Real people have names," I argued, beginning to recognize his enthusiasm stemming from the thrill of a challenge.

"Searlas, Ariella. Dae I feel mair real tae ye noo?"

"No."

He tilted his head, casting pale ringlets of hair directly above amused, blue eyes, and I hated how his grin made my heart work slightly faster, telling myself it was out of discomfort and aggravation but nothing else.

"D'ye ken hoo often ye lie? Or hae ye done it sae long ye believe the words yersel'?"

"Or maybe you are more confident in your abilities than you should be. You are lacking in tact—I wouldn't be surprised if that wasn't the only thing."

"Yet, I got ye tae stop cryin'," he pointed out, and the breath I'd built to argue with him fell loosely from my mouth, his smile altering into a self-satisfied smirk, "I'll be enjoyin' yer trainin' greatly once we get ye hame tae the Highlands."

A cold hand brushed over my arm, holding the same chill I would've expected from the touch of the one in front of me, but Searlas kept his hands by his sides. In glancing to find the source of the contact, he disappeared, and it wasn't the relief I thought it'd be. There was another soft touch and an echo of Zadar's voice in my mind, reaching through the dark abyss and rippling the still water.

"We're here."

I woke up.

My neck was sore from the awkward position in which I'd rested my head between the car door and seat, rubbing my eyes to better adjust me to the sunlight. I hadn't intended to fall asleep, but Zadar insisted on not lingering in one part of the forest too long, continuing our hike most of the night until we finally reached the road, and it had exhausted me.

I sat up with a groan, taking in my neighborhood, seeming more deja vu than reality, though that could've been blamed by my lack of total consciousness. As I exited the car, sea salt air filled my lungs, feeling like the first breath I'd taken in hours, and I wanted to close my eyes and blindly follow the tides call. Drowning didn't sound so bad right then.

"Ari," a gentle command followed by a sterner demand, "Inside."

His eyes fixated on something in the ocean I couldn't catch before being pulled to that bright orange door, making me think of Killian, and I feared if I found blueberries in the house, I would break.

"Dad!"

Anders' voice was enough to shake away any remnants of fatigue. It was the sound I thought of when I was most hopeless, when I needed a reminder of home, but it was deeper now than I'd been in my mind. His pounding footsteps from upstairs, however, were just the same as he trudged down at a quicker rate than when he'd hurry out right before the school bus. He never mastered the ability of walking lightly.

"Dad, you are going to be so proud of me! I know where we can find Ari! I had an even better vision of her this time that we can track— "

It stopped. The running, his shouts, the labor in his breathing the moment he saw me, freezing at the bottom of the staircase, fingers tightly clutching the handrail to keep him steady.

"That wonnae be necessary," Zadar answered, placing a hand on my shoulder to prove I wasn't a part of some dream, yet Anders stared like I was anything but real. I shouldn't have expected him to look like Kaid; I knew better than that, but he appeared the furthest thing from a child, his boyish features dissolving to a handsomely shaped face sharing a clear resemblance to his father's, but those wide, blue, innocent eyes were unmistakably Anders'.

"Hey, Buddy," I called, my vision blurring, and my voice posed as the cue he needed. Anders ran to me, wrapping me in an embrace that had me stumbling backward because he was much taller now. I didn't understand how a person could grow so much in a single month.

"I was so scared I'd never see you again," he cried, holding tightly to me, and I reciprocated the action, recognizing how needed the hug was for the both of us.

"I'm sorry, Anders," I whispered, trembling to suppress the sobs, "You didn't deserve that."

"I wasn't the one who got kidnapped," he lightly laughed, letting me fall from his embrace to get a clear view of me, "If there was someone who didn't deserve what happened, it's you." His hair, somehow curlier than before, was in desperate need of a trim, and he jerked away when I attempted to fix a few strands.

"You are a mess," I argued, reaching for his hair again while he shoved my arm, and I chose to blame Kiernan for my need to turn everything into a challenge.

"I don't like other people touching my hair. You know this," Anders complained, but that didn't stop him from smiling.

"So, are you going to fix it yourself?" I prompted, unsurprised when he didn't answer. He nervously giggled as his hands slowly neared my wrist, bracing for an attack, and he was right to do so. "That's what I thought."

I moved fast, but he was prepared, halting my reach with a grip around both my arms. Along with his looks and voice changing, he'd also gotten stronger, but that didn't stop me from fighting, randomly spinning to gain leverage. I pushed at him, and when he reciprocated, I almost fell, laughing as Anders did his best to keep me stable while containing my hands, laughing along with me. Zadar watched with proud amusement, but it was nothing compared to the shocked stare of Mother.

Anders and I noticed her at the same time, ending our playful fight abruptly, a serious air drafting in with her pale figure. She hadn't been there minutes ago when Zadar and I arrived, nowhere to be seen when Anders hugged me. In her hand was a container of paintbrushes in desperate need of cleaning, which I assumed she came to do. Mother had been noiseless coming down the hall that had those creaky floorboards, or it might've been that I'd been laughing too loudly with my brother to pick up the surrounding sounds.

"I'm going to go deconstruct the gadget I was building to help us find you," Anders said in way of goodbye, reading the room better than I was able to, and I tracked him as he took the path though the cold hall and up the dark staircase, the path I used to use at least five times a day.

I didn't love this house as I did before; it reminded me of the things I hadn't been allowed to know, and I was angry with myself for being content with a life disconnected from reality. Humans themselves were creatures I barely knew, living with two kelpies and a hollow mother, rarely did I share interaction with normal humans until I became a ranger, and that only happened to re-establish a relationship void of my understanding. My abduction was not much different than my childhood, kept to one place and forbidden to leave when everyone else could come and go as they pleased, apart from the fact that the Kallias' give me attention, positive and negative, at times entirely too much, but I was seen.

Mother was looking at me, but she wasn't seeing me, beautiful like glass, transparent and easy to shatter.

She crossed the room with a concerning calm, drawing me into a hug, and I stopped breathing. Mother hadn't touched me in years, and I was afraid to move, fearing to ruin a moment I dreamed of, but it wasn't all I wished it'd be. The way she held me was cold, distant, still managing to keep me at arm's length despite those arms being wrapped around me. I hoped the warmth would be in her eyes, that through a gentle look, I could find her care, but her stare was more lifeless than her touch as she pulled away, returning from where she came, rather paint than see her missing daughter.

"Bring her back, Zadar, please," I begged, watching as she left me once more, closing the door to her room, "I am eighteen now and no longer missing. She doesn't have a reason to be afraid anymore."

"It's no only ye," he answered sympathetically, taking hold of the paintbrushes Mother left on the counter, "She still feels the pain o' yer father. His voice has no left her mind. Much like a *týpos*, sirens can lay their claim on someone, keepin' them from leavin'. It's rarely used for love, but for prey tae trap their songs in the minds o' humans makin' them crave the source."

I turned from the hall, viewing Zadar start the kitchen faucet to clean the brushes. The water eagerly rushed over his dark skin, seeming to curl over his hand like it wanted to seep in as he softly smoothed the old paint out of the bristles.

"There has to be a way to make it stop," I urged, for once wanting there to be something I didn't know, a solution I'd not been presented.

"There is. She has tae hear him sing again."

"He's gone."

"But ye arenae," he answered, the red of the paint looking far too close to blood, and it didn't help that it was on Zadar's hands, flashing memories of the beach I strived to put out of my mind, "Ye've got yer father's gift, and in power, ye share his voice. If ye were tae sing her name, Evie would finally be free."

He spoke like he'd been longing for the day I could change everything for her, and that amount of hope was overbearing.

"But she's deaf."

"I ken. It's the reason I dulled her," Zadar explained, shutting off the faucet like he had her emotions, "Evie would've taken her own life years ago if I hadnae granted that wish."

"If you took away your dampening on her now, would she still be suicidal?"

"Naw," he responded, drying his hands and placing the brushes back into the jar, "But I'd never let that kind o' pain on her unless she asked for it."

I missed Kiernan and Keagan making fun of each other while Killian tried not to laugh. I missed them reminiscing over old stories and Kaid adding details as though he'd been old enough to witness any of them. I missed how threats were related to games, how arguments were settled with cards, and how fruits were fashioned into nicknames.

Thoughts of laughter and playful accusations somehow made the silence around the dinner table louder, the clicks and clanks of forks against plates deafening. It was my first dinner back, our first family meal with my memories intact. The chair I'd always seen empty in my past sat to my right, Zadar filling the space, now feeling too cramped. Anders' anticipation bounced through his leg, slightly shaking the table, dying to talk with me but unsure what to say.

"I dropped out of school," he announced abruptly, snagging my attention from the potato soup Zadar and Mother made together. His sign language had improved since I last saw him, using his words and his hands in conversation so Mother could understand.

"Why would you do that?" I questioned, concerned, matching his communications.

"You went missing," he answered as though it were obvious, "I wasn't about to go to class like your life wasn't in danger. We had to find you."

I lowered my gaze to the food, ashamed to have believed Anders would've given up on me when I knew he would've sacrificed everything to find me, and he did.

"Where did you go?" Anders questioned, and I couldn't help staring at the soup, willing it to change into the mushroom stew Killian had made as though to taste the warm memories it brought.

"A cabin in the redwoods near Brookings, Oregon."

"Who took you?"

"A family of five brothers."

"Five?" Zadar exhaled to himself, surprised and definitely alarmed, but I chose to focus on Anders' next question rather than Zadar's discovery.

"Did they... hurt you?"

The nerves in my shoulder tingled, pricking phantom flames in my skin, and I readjusted the side of Kiernan's shirt to stamp the memory away.

"That's enough for noo, Anders," Zadar intervened, understanding the meaning behind my uncomfortable movement, "This is still very new."

"Sorry," his son apologized, slouching into his seat from where he'd gradually leaned forward in conversation, "But now that she's back, we can finally go to Scotland! Right, Dad?"

"No," I interjected before Zadar could agree, not prepared for the stares my argument brought, shifting uncomfortably as I searched for an acceptable reason, "I need time to adjust."

"You are lying," Anders observed with a curious tilt of his head, reminding me of Searlas' accusations, and the warm soup began to burn me from the inside, layering my skin with heat. I stood from my seat and left without excusing myself, letting my skidding chair announce my departure as I made my way to the bathroom.

Locking myself inside, finally free from all prying eyes, I allowed myself to cry.

Kiernan was gone, and I hadn't had a moment to process it, even as I shook with silent sobs, I couldn't come to terms. Neglect had been my friend for far too long, whispering his hateful messages under the disguise of deserving it, and Kiernan had shown me what it was like to be whispered sweetly to.

"Come back," I whispered now to him, clutching my chest, stifling my agony enough to keep unheard. The object in my pocket poked my leg, gently requesting its freedom, and I pulled the scale from its confinement, wiping my eyes to study the subtle shimmer in the violet. I ran my thumb across the smooth surface, imagining running a comforting hand over his beast-like face, remembering how he pressed into my touch. "Come back."

It wasn't right to miss someone this much, nor to feel this strongly, yet logic chose to stay out of the equation, allowing my heart full control, and it *ached*. I held tightly to Kiernan's gift to me, wanting to embed part of him into my skin, permanently bonding us where even physical separation didn't have effects, but all the scale did was leave a mark in the center of my palm.

Curls fell onto my face, annoying at first, sparking an idea the next moment. One strand of hair burned the bright red of rebellion, untamable and shorter than the rest as it had been cut by Kell, and it only seemed fitting I braided the scale into that piece. I watched in the mirror while interweaving the small piece into my chin-length strand, strangely feeling closer to him with the purple peeking from the crimson of my hair, the violet bringing out my eyes that were far from human.

My reflection was someone I didn't recognize, those amethyst eyes nearly glowing and glittering with worry and hurt after the veil had been removed, my skin a sickly shade of pale, and yet he found me beautiful. I'd never felt pretty before him or that I was worth caring for, and I promised myself he wouldn't leave me forever. Every touch, every kiss, every word he dedicated to me was a promise, and Keagan was right. If there was something Kiernan believed, nothing was going to stop him from doing what was necessary, and the look he gave me before flying off was more than determined.

Kiernan would be back for me.

I left the bathroom after I'd composed myself, glancing in Mother's room while passing by, discovering what normally was a pristinely organized space was now a disaster. Barely started canvasses cluttered the floor while brushes and paint were scattered all over the place, as though distress had overcome the calm of painting.

Maybe Mother did care for me but didn't know how to express it.

The glint of a blade caught in the corner of my eye, and I found the knife with my lock of hair beside it on the nightstand on the opposite side of the bed she slept on. It was the knife I'd brought to the woods before I was taken, the memory of Kell's blood dripping from the edge, and before I could stop the thought, I pictured what it would look like with my blood on it.

I shook away the idea, reminding myself of all I had to lose, touching the scale tied into my hair.

He will be back.

Chapter Forty-Three

Blue.

I found it strange how much the color was in everything. It was in the sky and ocean, two things that were a large percentage of the world, yet the sky was primarily mentioned when the sun's rays changed it to orange and pink and the ocean when large waves washed white upon the shores. There seemed to be a hint of it everywhere, the cool undertone of azure in the air I breathed, layering the lungs with assumed life, tasting like salt and freedom just out of reach.

But what was most curious to me was the claim that blue related to sadness. I pictured gloom as a sort of grey, not bright enough to be white, and lacked the darkness of black, but despair had more vibrance than that. Things void of color were noticeable because why should there be concern around a person who is only blue?

And just as the color, the blue of emotion was rarely talked about. It was rather altered, adding yellow happiness to create a green life worth mentioning, a cover-up with a smile and a sunny day.

Which begged the question, was the universe depressed, and we'd been so use to seeing the signs that it went unnoticed?

I had a clear view of both the ocean and sky from my window, pondering how the clouds and sand shaped the sea and horizon, toying with the shell just beneath my collarbone. For wishing to be back in the forest, dancing with him, and playing games as a family, I truly missed Crescent City, the distant waves, the generous people, the friendly sunshine. It was home before I knew home was a feeling, a place that held all of my growing up, despite most of it being behind closed doors. Even at the age of eighteen, windows were some of my closest friends. I'd spent more time with them now than my actual family, concealing myself in a room that I couldn't quite call mine again.

I'd stared at the moon all night, wondering if Kiernan was looking at the stars and thinking of me as well. It was a struggle not to spiral without him around, overthinking everything I had said or done that'd give him reason not to return, and it made much more sense for him to stay in Agrond. Zadar had threatened to kill him if he came back, and I wasn't easy to love.

Yet, I still held out hope, unable to decide whether that made me naive or optimistic, brushing my fingers over the scale entangled in my hair when my doubts became too loud in the aching silence.

A knock at the door had me straightening, tucking the scale behind my ear, bracing for an interaction I doubted would end very well. I didn't like to think Zadar was a disappointment, but I'd hoped to see Anders' face rather than his father's, share a moment with someone who hadn't disguised who he was.

"I've a few errands I need tae run. Would ye like tae come wi' me?" my stepfather offered, keeping to the doorway, holding the handle.

"No, thank you," I politely declined, though I doubted Zadar came only to be turned down.

"Ari, please. Ye need tae get oot o' the hoose," he tried again, but I turned back to the view outside.

He didn't think that the last seventeen years of your life. Wanted to keep you in. Hide what you were. Prison with an orange door.

Zadar's sigh was deep enough to hush the voices, his tone less apologetic as he added, "I wasnae really askin'."

And I didn't have the energy to fight him.

Still, I kept my stare outside my window as we drove, searching for the life in blue, the call for help that'd been missed by so many.

"Whit keeps ye here still?" Zadar asked, prodding at conversations I avoided, and trapped in a car, I wasn't able to run away, "Your personal ties with this place have been cut. I saw it in your eyes the moment you stepped through the door."

"I can't go to Scotland," I answered, dragging my eyes over the quiet town, "That's a life change too large for me to handle, especially when nothing has stayed the same in months."

"But dinnae ye think it's better tae leave noo, rather than wait till ye get attached tae somethin' else?"

"I can't go."

Zadar took a deep breath in from his nose, his hands tightening over the steering wheel, and I braced for another accusation of lying as it seemed I'd been expressing more than the truth, unprepared for the doubts that were weighing in his mind.

"Are ye pregnant, Ari?"

I whirled on him, eyes wide with shock and brows lowered in offense.

"Excuse me?"

"It's a hard question, I'm sorry, but if there's even the slightest chance ye're carryin' a hybrid bairn, it changes everythin'."

"No, Zadar, I am not *pregnant*," I clipped, insisting he see my face to avoid any suspicion of such an absurd conclusion, "Kiernan wouldn't come into my room when I was resting, let alone use my bed—"

"I wasnae only talkin' aboot him. He's got brothers."

My offense altered to a sharp defense, angry that he could accuse them of such a thing.

"You would really think that lowly of people you never met?"

"I think that way *because* I never met them. Aw I ken is that ye were taken by *five* men, held captive in the woods alone wi' them for a month, and at least one o' them made ye believe he loved ye."

When he put it like that, the question wasn't unreasonable, but I didn't want to admit that, sticking to silence while returning my focus to the window. Not seeing him did nothing to stop the feeling of Zadar watching me once we pulled into the grocery parking lot, and I worried I hadn't hidden the braid behind my ear well enough when he affirmed, "Ye and that lad wouldnae have worked oot."

"How would you know?" I snapped, still dealing with the embarrassment of his last accusation.

"Ye're a siren. He's a dragon," Zadar affirmed, and I was tired of hearing *dragon* as though Kiernan wasn't a person, facing him again to argue.

"I'm a girl. He's a boy. It shouldn't matter past that."

"Dragons," he seemed to emphasize, and I bristled, "are possessive and lustful, and their loyalty drives them tae fix all o' that obsession on one soul. Others o' their kind are built tae wi'stand the intense nature, but a human would break under it in time."

"I'm not human."

"Part o' ye is, and sirens arenae much better. When it comes tae the body, they're nae stronger than humans."

Kiernan mentioned how breakable I was on multiple occasions, but I didn't think he could truly hurt me so easily. It made me wonder how often he held back with me in worry of causing harm, if he'd ever been able to relax when we touched, how long it would take him to find a girl he could be himself without fear.

"That's not true," I mumbled to myself, shutting the idea down before my mind could ground it, but Zadar couldn't read me as well as Kiernan could, assuming my words were intended in defiance to him.

"Have ye even met a siren before, aside from yer father?"

"Yes," I affirmed proudly, "She was strong and beautiful, and fully capable of loving whomever she wanted."

His brows lowered, his original thought process shifting directions behind his eyes.

"Whit did she look like?"

I tried to answer, but no words could fully encompass her beauty, sounding like a stuttering mess of an explanation that Zadar somehow understood.

"Tuuli," he said to no one but himself, a strange recognition overcoming his features as he instructed me, "Stay well awa' from her."

"Why?" I asked, but he was already out of the car, heading to the store and acting as though I never questioned him.

Inside, it was like no one had seen red hair before. There were double glances and unapologetic staring, gaping expressions and calculating eyes, all shocked, all curious, all on me. If Zadar hadn't been right by my side, tall and as intimidating as he was handsome, I worried some might try to approach me. To the citizens of this small town, I was no more than a deceased girl walking around the local grocery store, and though their questioning looks were entirely justified, I stepped closer to Zadar, wishing to hide away from the attention.

We reached the fresh produce aisle, and I kept my focus on the food rather than potentially making eye contact with someone who'd take it as an invitation for conversation, but when my sight caught on the basket of avocados, it did nothing to comfort me.

Zadar noticed my fixation on them, taking one in his fingers to give me.

"Would ye like one?" he offered kindly, but the sight of him holding an avocado left me unsettled, forcing memories of a rock in his bloodied hand, one strike away from murder, and I backed away from him on instinct, shaking my head while nearly tripping into the tomatoes behind me. I couldn't read Zadar's expression, just as I was sure he couldn't read my thought process, but he placed it down with a sigh. "Ari, I dinnae want it tae be like this between us. I've waited years for ye tae remember me. Why cannae we go back tae how things were?"

"I don't think I can," I answered honestly, sparing another glance at the avocados, "Too much has changed."

"Then we can start over. Put everythin' in the past. I dinnae like fightin' wi' ye, and it's no in yer nature either. Ye're goin' through hard things just noo, I ken that, but I'm here tae help. I'm no askin' ye tae forget, nor would I e'er expect that o' ye again, but I dinnae want the past tae spoil the good that's still tae come." He reached for the shelf over my head, bringing a carton of strawberries to my hands, smiling gently. "Peace accords?"

"Okay," I softly laughed in agreement, feeling the need to apologize for my opposition when a familiar voice interrupted.

"Oh. My. Gosh." Maddie was jumping down the aisle, her poofy hair bouncing with her, tugging me into an aggressive hug while practically shouting into my ear, "Jason was *so* right. You are alive!"

I went taut, pink bleeding into my cheeks from the memory of that night when Jason had seen Kiernan and me together. Apparently, he didn't believe me when I said I was safe or listen when I told him I wanted to stay dead to everyone else, and I shouldn't have been irritated when he seemed concerned. Or he was simply jealous; it was difficult to tell in the poorly lit room.

Unsurprisingly, Maddie didn't notice me stiffen under her touch, pulling away to look at me with eyes full of joy.

"Oh, Isabella, I've been so lonely—you have no idea! Everyone was leaving... or disappearing, and I'm so relieved to finally have a friend again. We need to catch up!"

"I think that's a grand idea. Ari needs a companion the noo," Zadar spoke up for me, and Maddie latched on to his approval rather than my discomfort, not even questioning how the man at my side related to me.

"There is a party Friday night—"

"No parties," I demanded sharply, not letting anyone overlook that insistence, and my boldness was the one thing that caught Maddie off guard.

"Okay, then," she laughed awkwardly, "How about shopping? I know the perfect mall we could go to."

I opened my mouth to decline politely, but Zadar answered first, placing a loving but firm hand on my shoulder.

"She'll be there."

"Great! I'll pick you up at eleven tomorrow," she cheered, somehow managing to have more pep in her step as she walked away, and I sidewardly glared at Zadar.

"For wanting to start over, you're not off to a great start," I stated, the bitterness in my tone unintentionally turning playful, and he chuckled.

"Ye'll forgive me."

"You really need to update your wardrobe," Maddie instructed, pulling out a bright turquoise shirt before eyeing my clothing as though picturing it on me, "Shirt dresses aren't really in style anymore." With a solemn shake of her head that I couldn't decipher was for me or the clothes she picked out, she hung the shirt back on the rack, muttering to herself through clamped teeth, "Nor were they ever."

I took a moment to survey her outfit, the stone-washed jeans and neon pink shirt tied together with a high-waisted belt, and I was grateful for the classic midnight blue shirt Kiernan left me with, oversized as it was. It was losing its marshmallow scent, but it was the closest I could get to him holding me.

Crinkling her nose in displeasure at an article of clothing I missed, Maddy decided it was time to move on, linking arms with me and leading us off to a new colorful store that caught her attention.

"Okay, so tell me about him!" she giggled, playfully tugging my arm, "Why did he let you go?"

I panicked over how she knew about Kiernan, still not ready to talk about him, choosing to play dumb with the question, "Who?"

Maddie moved even closer, glancing over her shoulder for no apparent reason, and her suspicious behavior gained more attention than when she was talking normally.

"The Silent Killer."

My muscles relaxed.

"Oh, I wasn't taken by the Silent Killer, Maddie."

"But that's what everyone said!"

"Most gossip isn't true," I informed, and her face scrunched into a pout.

"Then what happened to you?"

"I got lost on my way home from work."

"For almost a *month*?"

"The redwoods are big."

It was a pathetic lie, but Maddie had an extensive imagination, and I figured she could create the details on her own. We aimlessly walked while she thought, and I was curious as to how her mind worked, convinced that her brain was bedazzled with rhinestones just as her belt had been.

We were far enough away from town that I was able to get away with being any other person, avoiding the curious glances and unwanted attention, except for Maddie, of course.

"What a cute hair clip! Where did you get it? I need one."

My untaken arm lifted to touch Kiernan's scale, my heart beating a bit faster when thinking of him.

"It was a gift," I answered, and I should've done a better job at concealing my grin.

"From whom?" Maddie prodded, her tone turning mischievous, and when the truth hit me again, the smile was easy to drop.

"Someone who isn't here anymore."

"Ah, so that's why you have been so off," she concluded, guiding us out of the direct line of shopping traffic, allowing a slower pace, "You know, when I lost my cousin... Shelby? Shannon... Sheba—I don't really know. She was like three times removed or something—I never actually met her, but it was hard. Grief isn't a nice feeling, but that doesn't make it bad."

Was that what this was? Grief over Kiernan? I pondered how one could mourn another if they weren't dead, though I assumed I'd always have this hole in my chest whether he was gone permanently or not.

"What about Heather?"

Maddy stopped walking.

"Heather is okay," she assured, but it was the first time her smile ever looked forced, and I doubted it was me she truly tried to convince, "I mean, she's not like actually dead. For all we know, this 'Silent Killer' could be some teddy bear of a guy who takes hurting people into his magical home so they can be happy, right? You came back. Who says she won't?"

I studied her face, hoping to read her instead of asking questions that'd likely bring her pain, and I wondered if that was how Kiernan felt when he wanted to figure me out, prompting me to repeat the same inquiry he used on me just before he left.

"Are you happy, Maddie?"

She was surprised at first, quickly replacing the expression with something a bit too enthusiastic, lifting her shoulders in mock of a gleeful shrug.

"Who isn't?"

But her eyes looked bluer in the moment, deepening from the pale shade of clear waters to flowering forget-me-nots.

I didn't press her further, and it didn't seem like she wanted me to, moving into another store before the conversation could continue. We didn't shop much longer, grabbing ice cream on the way to the car and leaving the windows down as we drove. Maddie insisted on blaring the music, singing loudly and nagging me to join until I reluctantly gave in.

Using my voice made everything hurt a little less, and even if I really wanted to, I couldn't have forgotten all my heartache through song as Maddie had. Her eyes were back to the sparking blue of the little rippling rivers in the redwoods, laughing as she hurried to catch her breath between songs, and I giggled as well, exhilarated when the wind tried to force its way down my lungs. Maddie's excitement in everything was contagious, making me want to search for the all the color she saw in life rather than just the blue, and for as much as I wished to be upset with Zadar for making me leave my comfort zone, he was right. I needed a friend, and Maddie knew how to make life fun.

The sun was setting when she dropped me off, promising to do this again as she drove away, and I hoped she meant it.

If the lively night ended then, maybe I could've learned to heal, but someone was singing, and she was summoning me.

Ari...

Ari...

Ari...

It was hypnotic, the sound, the voice, the shape of my name. I thought only Kiernan could make it sound worth hearing, but this call held nearly as much yearning, and my heart constricted at the thought of ignoring such a plea. I surpassed the stairs leading down to the beach, needing to save time as I climbed down the rocky hill searching for the woman who put my name to song. I promised myself not to stay long, that just seeing her would fulfill my need to know her, but the closer I neared the ocean, the more personal the voice became, and I found myself not wanting the song to leave my ears.

The tide was angry, crashing against the rocks leading to the shore, but she remained in the middle of it all, undeterred by the motion of the waves that carried enough power to force her under. Her hair was tangled with shells, the necklace she wore casting the illusion of pearls floating around her collarbone, and the moonlight painted her scales from her chest and down the length of her slender body, hidden by the ocean's reflective blue, just as dazzling as her amethyst eyes when she smiled.

"Why do you call for me?" I asked, and her tone was clear over the roaring ocean, the waves submitting as though they knew whose sound held more power.

"Why does a dove cry for his deceased love unless he wishes to see her again?" she questioned in response, her voice like silk, soothing the ache in my mind that drew me to her.

"I don't understand," I pleaded, wishing to know everything told if only to hear her speak.

"Then you have not experienced grief, and for that, I envy you."

It felt wrong that someone as perfect as her could envy anyone like me, but that concept didn't hold my attention as it normally would. Something in her eyes shifted when she spoke those last few words, the night's restrictions playing tricks on my vision as I thought I witnessed her face transform more into something far from beautiful, terrifying in its monstrous appearance, but I blinked, and it was gone.

"I should go," I announced, but my attempts to leave were halfhearted, useless when the golden pieces interwoven in her hair glittered as she tilted her head.

"Is it Zadar who worries you?"

My brows lowered, and I blinked again as though it could change the words I heard rather than the things I saw.

"You know him?"

"Quite well."

"Are you friends?"

"I doubt he'd share the sentiment," she professed, and the strained bitterness of Zadar's earlier words paired with her voice.

"You are Tuuli."

"I am," she affirmed, her eyes sparkling pleasantly at the recognition, enticing her to ease closer to shore, "And from my understanding, you are Ari."

"Ariella is my real name," I explained, shame striking my heart when her lips dipped into a frown.

"You give it to me so freely?"

"Should I not?"

"Names hold power, and to pass that off without an exchange of equal value is a great loss on yourself. There is a cost to everything in life."

Zadar's warning chanted louder in my mind, contrasting with the excitement in my heart as she neared even closer, the waves reaching for my feet as though eager to introduce us, and I took a tentative step back.

"I don't think he'd want me talking to you," I answered in apology, and her smile returned.

"How interesting. I was just about to say the same thing to you about him."

"I trust Zadar," I informed defensively, glancing over my shoulder in fear she was right, that names truly did hold power, that speaking his would somehow summon his presence, and he'd see me with the woman he'd ordered I stay away from.

"Then why do you look as though you are hiding from him?"

I didn't respond, and she took my silence as a welcoming to advance, risking the shallow waters as her scaled stomach brushed against the sand, her arms propping her upper half above the sea while her shimmering tail peeked from behind, forming her in a graceful arch.

"Tell me, my sweet Ariella, what is your greatest desire?" Her fin flicked the surface, cascading ripples around the movement. "Wealth?" Every gentle breath she claimed shifted the iridescence of her form, changing from blue to violet under the light of the stars. "Fame?" There were no webs on her delicate fingers, no fins down her curved spine, or gills lining her neck as Kiernan had informed, just a beautiful girl with shimmering dark skin and large, innocent eyes. "To reunite with a soul that never returned?" I looked into those eyes then, a rapid heat rushing up my neck at her guess of something she shouldn't have known. "There it is," she affirmed, smiling in a way that made her face captivating, impossible to turn away from, "I could grant you that wish."

"How?" I asked before I could ponder the consequences, my desperation to see him again overbearing the memory of him tripping over the sand to save me from this siren.

"A deal."

She was too close, reaching distance away from grabbing the collar of my shirt and bringing me under, and it wasn't until that moment I realized I'd gradually been leaning in to speak with her, making myself stand up straight and step away to clear my head.

"No... I don't think I should. I'm sorry. I need to go. My family will be wondering where I—"

"Your father is alive."

"What?" I rasped, my knees feeling too weak to hold me as I listened to the words only uttered in my most fanciful daydreams, but Tuuli repeated herself, and it was real the way she spoke.

"Avam. He is alive."

"That can't be true. He died nearly twelve years ago. Zadar..." but I lost my words in the knowing gleam in her violet stare.

"I wouldn't put as much faith as you do in that kelpie, child."

"He wouldn't lie to me. He *can't* lie to me. None of the kelpies can."

"Is that what he told you?" she giggled melodiously, shaking her head in graceful movements that were close to hypnotic before mumbling to herself, "Very clever, Zadar."

"What are you saying?"

"Your mother loved your father dearly. I saw it myself. She is the only human to have known of us and lived. She was special, and Zadar knew that. He wanted her."

"But Mother was married. He wouldn't try to steal someone who was already taken," I countered, and the look she gave me was empathetic.

"Are you confident in the things you saw as a child, or were you too young to notice the signs?"

I had no response, for when it came to my childhood through the shifted memories and hidden appearances, there was very little I put my total belief in. Instead of leaving me to overthink her words, she reshaped the question.

"Who told you Avam died?"

"Zadar," I answered, honest as of my clear memory for that terrible day.

"Who was there when the grief became too much for your mother to handle?"

"Zadar," I answered with less assurance.

"Who was able to shape her emotions to his own pleasure?"

"Zadar," I answered hesitantly, a cold understanding stabbing at my heart.

"And yet... who became the hero that day?"

That time, I didn't answer, and it was the third time she left me speechless.

"You see, my dove, everything comes with a price, and trust is a cost that can make you a debtor if broken."

Zadar lied to me, used my naivety and the need for a parent to manipulate himself into my and my family's lives, and I had no proof against him. Mother didn't love him, but she believed she did, just like Anders believed his father could help him through his night terrors, and if I only found my father, it could prove his dishonesty.

"What is it you want from me in exchange for seeing my father?"

Another flick of her tail against the water.

"Your voice."

"You want to take my ability to speak?"

"No, no," she giggled, and I almost asked her to laugh again, my ears begging to listen to such a lovely sound, "I want to help you train your song. You are young, Ariella, and still have so much to learn as a siren. Let me teach you, and I will reunite you with your father."

My hand rested on my shell, so close to the heart pounding in anticipation, wanting to find him but fearing she was asking more than she let on.

"You are hesitant. I understand," Tuuli soothed, using her arms to push her back to deeper waters, "Life has given you reason to doubt. All I ask is that you would think on it and return to me when you have made your decision."

"How will I find you?"

"Sing, little songbird. I will hear you," she announced, and it reminded me of Kiernan, promising to come if I called. I had, and he was still gone.

Then she vanished into the ocean, remnants of her song announcing her departure.

Zadar and Mother were in the kitchen together when I returned, Anders already in bed upstairs.

"How'd it go?"

He was drying the dishes Mother washed, and I couldn't help overanalyzing every movement he made.

"Better than I thought," I responded, grateful he didn't see the way I nervously fidgeted with the hem of my shirt, facing Mother with an adoration in his expression I'd admired in the past. Now it was hard to breathe watching them so close, him lightly touching her back while she genuinely smiled, protectiveness taking over as I loudly announced, "In fact, would you be okay if I went again tomorrow?"

Zadar turned to me then, curious as to my blatant interruption while Mother, oblivious to the situation, went back to cleaning.

"Aye, sure," he answered, and nearly all of my energy was used to pretend I didn't want to hurt him for deceiving my family, that I was still that clueless, naive girl.

"Good. I want to see her again."

All I needed was for Zadar to see the truth in my eyes, not that we were talking about two very different people.

Chapter Forty-Four

*S*he's lovely. *She's beautiful. She's empathetic. Go back to her. Go back to her. Go back to her.*

I'd shifted my pillow under my head in every possible direction, searching for the only section that hadn't been warmed as I fought to fall asleep.

She knows everything. She brought you truth. She wants to help. Father is alive. Father is alive. Father is alive.

That last thought kept me awake more than the rest, pulsating in my mind until the anticipation matched the rush of my heart. All these years wishing to see him again, and now it was possible. It never stopped being possible, yet I couldn't fill in the holes of why he'd never attempted to find his wife and daughter again. I heavily believed the explanation included Zadar, as did the lie of Father's death, and it sickened me to know he was down the hall, sharing a bed with my mother, who was unaware of the danger beside her.

He'd done terrible things to make her his, breaking down and manipulating her thoughts to entrap her because no one with a sound mind would stay with a monster, pinning her reasoning for mental scars on her first husband. Zadar rarely used sign language to speak to her, staring into her eyes to pass the word into her conscience as he did once to me, and I didn't want to imagine all the twisted lies he caressed into her head. The signs were clear; even before my memories, something wasn't quite right about him, and I hated recalling how much I had sought his approval as a ranger.

Anders' mind, however, was a bit too clear, his dreams becoming a distinct reality, though that didn't make him immune to brainwashing, and I feared Zadar's influence on him the most. Unlike me, my brother was never forced to forget, and that only gave him time to grow the trust and love for his father, a longing to please and obey that Zadar could take full advantage of. I'd experienced that hope for approval in a woman who barely looked my way, and I couldn't imagine the false fulfillment Anders experienced with a parent's encouragement. Zadar had an ear trained on him that was unnatural, and I didn't even hear Anders wake up, only the footsteps too heavy to be Mother's passing my room to the young kelpie's.

I counted ten seconds before standing from my bed, careful with each step as I neared my door. I listened, and while it was obvious a conversation was being held, the voices were too muffled to detect even the tone surrounding the topic. Cautiously opening my door, I made my way across the hall, knowing exactly which floorboards creaked under pressure, and I didn't have to be right by his room to hear Anders' cries and Zadar's firm instructions.

"Shut yer een and set yer mind on it."

His voice was harsher now that I knew the truth, and I was unaware of how my hands balled into fists, ready to end anyone who dared harm my brother, and Anders' vulnerable exasperations only made it worse.

"I can't keep seeing it, Dad. It hurts too much. I can't get it out of my head."

"That's because ye're fightin' it. The visions'll keep hauntin' ye until ye learn tae accept them," Zadar insisted, and the only thing keeping me from barging into that room was the voice in my head echoing: *Father is alive. Father is alive. Father is alive.*

Breaking in now and declaring all I knew would do nothing more than present me as unstable, claiming observed accusations on someone who'd been without fault. I'd been endangered and could hardly speak of my abduction to Mother, hostage for a month, slowly going crazy from the helplessness in Anders' eyes, all while Zadar played the role of savior. That was his favorite act, I discovered, as he used it more than the rest, a hero of problems that didn't exist, just as Tuuli professed.

No, I had to wait until the hard evidence stood on my side, so I was forced to stay behind the closed door and listen as my little brother was manipulated.

"Whit is it ye see?" Zadar continued to press, and I wondered what Zadar intended to gain from this, whether it was control or a need to justify impregnating someone who wasn't his. Anders was the first thing he had that wasn't stolen, but that didn't mean his hold on his son was any tighter than my mother's.

"A dragon," he answered, and my heart spiked, "He steals her away again. In front of Mom this time. They are both screaming and... Dad, I can't do this anymore."

"Naw, focus. Dinnae let the image slip. Ye said they're screamin'. Can ye hear whit they're sayin'?"

Anders' breath was shaky.

"Ari. She has her arms pinned behind her, and she keeps yelling, 'I need my hands. She doesn't know. She doesn't know.' Mom won't stop crying. Ari is trying to comfort her, but they are taking her away."

"Who, Anders? Who is takin' her awa'?"

I could picture the furrow in his brow as he concentrated, but I'd tried to help him out of his dreams in the past when Zadar forced him to focus on them.

"There is more than one dragon," Anders answered after a time of silence.

"How mony?"

"Five."

Zadar paused to process that information, evidently thinking the same thing I was, that it wasn't only Kiernan coming back for me but also his family, though I couldn't understand why they'd be as forceful as Anders' presented.

"Is the one that kills her there?" Zadar clarified the thought, and hearing him address Kiernan as *the one that kills her* was even worse than *dragon*.

"No," Anders settled, and Zadar's tone held the same amount of confusion as my head.

"Then who is takin' her?"

"I don't know. I lost the vision. I'm sorry."

"Dinnae be sorry. Ye lasted longer this time. I'm prood o' ye."

And there it was, manipulation wrapped under the covering of approval, encouragement driven by control, and if I listened any longer, I knew I wouldn't be able to stop myself from causing a scene. Sneaking back to my room, I didn't sleep, driven by the need to free my family from a kelpie's lies.

Summer was approaching, and the waves greedily lapped up the sunshine reflecting into my eyes as I searched the seas for answers. I wanted to believe Tuuli, but I'd once believed Zadar, and I wasn't certain I could handle another betrayal. With Kiernan gone, my heart was more fragile than it had been before I knew him, and it was easier to hold everything at arm's length than to break again. So, when leaving the house under the lie of seeing Maddie, I sang for my father, the only person in this world who still held my whole trust.

"Wind on the ocean. Song on the Sea. Wished for the sky. Drowned in the—"

"Hello, my dove."

Her loveliness was startling, or maybe it was the cheerful demeanor she wore, contrasting with the solemn nature of the previous night, but never losing her elegance and serenity. She was bolder in her nearness, taking to the rock dangerously close to shore and perching herself there, head propped on her folded arms, which made her stature incredibly endearing.

"Have you given more thought to my proposal?" Tuuli questioned, and she was so exuberant I expected her tail to flick out of the water at the end of her sentence, but it only twitched as though it wanted to leave and was fastened to the sea.

"I have to see him," I confessed, watching as her eyes glittered brighter before she dove back in. When she emerged, her hand was around my wrist, cold and secure, bringing me into the water and closer to her reach. With her long fingers, she splayed my palm open, eagerly studying it until I was sure she was searching for the scar Kiernan healed when he kissed my palm to give me his *týpos*.

"And you will," she promised, swiping one thumb down the center of my hand.

Then she was cutting me.

I flinched as her sharp nails dug into my skin, carving a spiral into my palm that had me oozing black blood, dispersing when she lowered my arm into the water.

"What are you doing?" I asked, trying not to recoil as the water became like ice over the wound, biting at raw flesh as though a warning of how bitter the sea could become under broken promises.

"Marking our deal," she answered like all agreements held physical scars, yet when she let go of my hand, I saw no scars of her own.

"Where is your marking?"

"I have no need for one. The ocean already claims me."

Tuuli backed from the shallow then, staring at me expectantly, waiting for me to join, and I gripped my shell with my unmarked hand. The waves didn't look threatening today, but they hadn't the last time I was fully in the ocean either, the night I found out I was a siren and Kiernan nearly drowned. I could feel him now more than I had since he left, a lingering memory from behind, a touch at my back, a whisper in my ear, "Stay with me, *Agapití*."

"Ariella," Tuuli called sternly, and I was jarred by the sudden seriousness, the soothing, familiar warmth curving behind me shifting to a striking cold down my spine.

"I can't swim."

"That is the human in you speaking," she argued, glancing to where I stood, and the look on her face told me she was unsatisfied, jealous even, at my capability to walk, "You have the rare ability, Ariella, to be more than what you were born as. You've grown accustomed to your legs and lungs, ignorant of the sea in your veins. Can't you feel yourself thinning?"

I didn't answer, unsure what my response would lead to, and with my silence came more words spun beautifully that kept me in my speechlessness.

"Humans are like blood. We are like water. We run through them, nurture them, bring them to life with our song, yet they get the darker shade. They get the attention and association with life while we make up what they are." Tuuli lifted her eyes to me, and there was a type of ache buried too deep in the surface, but she allowed me one small glimpse into the pain she carried and the story that caused it as she stated, "Blood thins without water."

Unable to process the deeper message she meant to present, I studied her symmetrical face, and she smiled at the obvious uncertainty in my expression, her lips curving wickedly.

"Don't go fearing me now when we are becoming such good friends," she reprimanded playfully, her voice a blend of coax and taunt, her eyes glittering with mischief, and it was difficult to think ill of her when she looked so lovely, "Our exchange has already been made."

"What do you want with my voice?"

"You are too late to be asking those questions, my dove. Join me in the water."

"Give me a reason to trust you," I compelled, the tender warmth from behind returned as I spoke, the thought of Kiernan warning against this grounding more than anything else had.

Tuuli's smile grew, strangely pleased by my wariness, but she didn't advance.

"I have none apart from the fact that your father trusts me."

I wanted to argue and demand a better reason, but I didn't need one, and she knew it.

Cold shot down my spine as I entered the water.

Heart pounding, gathering one last breath, I was submerged by the chilling waves, shocking all the heat from my body. It was a jolt that terrified me, a rush of memories in these same seas where Kiernan and I struggled to stay afloat, to stay *alive*, but Kiernan wasn't here this time to save me.

Tuuli clasped my wrist when I realized what a mistake this was, holding me back from the shore and my craving for breath. I whipped my head around too quickly, my hair floating around my sight as I pinned her with a pleading stare, and the emotion swimming in her eyes was not one of empathy, but rather a possessive determination.

I needed her to let go. She had to know I would die if I didn't break the surface, but I couldn't afford to lose the small amount of oxygen I held on to.

"You are keeping to the human side, and to her, you are drowning," Tuuli instructed far too evenly, and I knew she could feel my pulse hammering in my wrist, but she was undeterred, "Release all the air from your lungs and give up everything that draws you to the land. Here, you are a siren. Here, you follow the sea."

My chest was straining to contain my last remnants of life, and when they slipped from me, it was an unexpected relief. Tuuli relinquished her hold when I emptied my lungs of all that was familiar to me, and I watched as the bubbles made their way to the surface, climbing to where they belonged. The desire to chase them and reclaim my right to land surfaced in my bones, but even that was shaken away with a violent chill overtaking my body.

Cold was painful when Kiernan was around because he offered the possibility of warmth when I never knew I desired it, but beneath the waves, he could not follow me, and I was surprised when it didn't scare me. My eyes slid shut as a sense of relief overcame me, not worrying over Kiernan, and I knew the longer I stayed, the easier it would be for me to let go of the paranoia.

Here, where my lungs didn't work, I could breathe.

Here, I was no more than a girl in search of her father.

Here, I was a siren, and I followed the sea.

I opened my eyes only to be met with endless blue and no siren in sight. It was too still, and the need for sound had me more uneasy than knowing I was suddenly alone in the ocean.

"Tuuli?"

A soothing hum answered in response, sounding near and out of reach all at once, and it wasn't until glancing down that I found its direction. I pictured myself still having legs and forcing them to work in unison, allowing more familiarity when I dove to the seabed, not sparing a glance to the sun begging me to return.

The humming grew louder the farther down I went, gradually losing light from the surface and fearing to lose her voice as well, but the sound was a coax to my heart, a reassurance that as long as I listened to her, everything would be alright.

Follow my song.

She hummed that verse of the lullaby over and over, warping through the ocean, filling me with the urgency to find her, and my willingness to comply with the voice halted at the mouth of a cave. The scarce light I still had was absent in the opening of stone, and I realized anything could be waiting for me in there. The voice reached for me through the abyss, and I reached back verbally, singing the rest of the chorus. I was startled when a line of light rolled through the cave, plants lining the edges of the stone tunnel illuminating where my song was carried, and when they lost their shine, I sang again. A trail of blues and greens sparkled across the darkness; their glow entrancing, and fascination enticing me to observe closer. Embedded in the walls and twined around the rocks, the roots were long, but it was the tips of the plants sprouting from every surface its stems touched that were the most enchanting. Little bulbs like antennae at the greenery's end quivered when sound was made, shuttering awake before swaying easily in the motion of water. They bloomed as flowers would, alighting the cavern to make it welcoming before beaming me with sharp vibrations and gleaming oceanic hues.

Though hesitant, I entered the cave, brushing my fingers along the inviting plants, a fuzzy yet stringy sensation against my hands, trailing the echo of her hum while singing in return. The cave had plenty of winding twists and tight spaces, enough that I struggled to remember where I had and hadn't been, suddenly afraid to be lost in this hopeless sea chamber where the moon could not shine. Suddenly, the tunnel ended, opening to a larger space still encased with stone, but Tuuli was there, mumbling to the radiating life, and somehow, in this lighting, she was even more radiant.

"There you are," she called, cheery in a way she hadn't been near land, "I was beginning to worry you wouldn't be able to find me."

"Why did you leave me?" I inquired, drawing to her side while trying not to stare at the illusion of sapphires embedded in her fin.

"To see how well you could follow. We can always locate each other if one is calling out. It's how I found you on that beach. Whether you knew it or not, you were calling for me."

Her fingers fiddled with the flowering buds, and they glowed brighter just for her, either in delight or reverence; I could not tell. The further we dove into the ocean, the more it seemed to exhibit its high regard for this siren adorned with the sea's mystery. Her smile shone luminously, as did the rest of her shimmering form while it quivered excitedly beneath her hand, and the entire space lit when she giggled.

"They thrive off of sound, and there is very little down here," she explained to me, but it felt as though she were speaking more for them, "Our voices were made to bring happiness and life, a joyful sense of pleasure for the hearts who did not know how to find it on their own. Plants are no exception to that."

Tuuli backed away, the lights dimming in sorrow, only to come to life once more as she hummed.

"Your turn, Ariella."

"For what?" I questioned, oddly nervous.

"Call out. Make the connection with one of us and follow their song."

Twiddling with my necklace, I sang as I always had, the melodies Anders fell asleep to, the sound Kiernan fell in love with, and while the flowers enjoyed it, I heard nothing in return.

"You are too gentle," Tuuli instructed, and the fear I was failing her tightened around my ribs, "The siren song is a powerful weapon, our greatest asset. You wouldn't use a sword as a butter knife, would you?"

"What are you saying?"

"I'm saying, Ariella, that your voice is unbelievably strong; you just don't know how to utilize it properly. I'm sure you have seen the effects on those around you when you sing."

"Father never wanted me to sing."

"But he did," she countered, "He was very excited for the day he was able to train your voice. You had a gift, and he wanted to watch it grow. Even so, we have to sing to others. It kills us not to. Sing with more than just your voice."

I thought of Father and the times I sang for him to return, releasing that aching longing in a melodic plea, and every plant visible shone sea green and sky blue. I inhaled the sea, unprepared for the intensity that escaped my throat, but it felt good to let go of.

A voice responded.

"Very well done, my dove," she encouraged, sounding genuinely pleased, "You may not need training after all."

I found the source we followed, but she led the way, and it took time for me to match her graceful pace.

"Does he ever mention me?" I asked as we approached another narrow tunnel, its tightness forcing her pace to slow, making conversation possible.

"He used to," she answered with a solemness in her tone, "You and Evelyn were all he ever talked about."

"You said he was alive," I accused, fearing the past tense of her words, heart preparing to break all over again.

"He is," Tuuli quickly prefaced, catching the panic in my voice, "There is a disease in the sea. It's killing us off one by one. Your father, along with the rest of the men, have been harmed the most. They've resorted to hiding themselves in the darker parts of the ocean so as not to infect the rest of us sooner, but we will inevitably fall under the same sickness in time. It's a part of our curse. You are the cure."

"I'm the cure?"

"Yes," she pressed, the severity of her words not going unmissed, "Avam is not dead, but he could be very soon. The ocean wants us out of her waters, and the longer we stay, the more she will punish us."

Yet deeper we merged through the underwater tunnels, and my discomfort grew by the second.

"Then why did he wait to train me?" I asked, if only to distract myself from the very tight space we were about to enter.

"You were too young to comprehend your power. Avam feared you'd mistakenly hurt someone on land where we were unable to aid."

"I could hurt someone with my voice?"

'You can hurt someone with anything so long as the desire is there, but I can see how pure your heart is. You remind me much of myself when I was young."

"Are you not young?" I questioned, allowing myself to look over the ethereal being she was, appearing not a day over twenty.

"Not unless you consider over four thousand years to be in my prime." She laughed softly at the shocked expression I gave her. "Time has been kind to me where the ocean has not."

Words built on my tongue, but organizing them into coherent questions proved difficult, especially when she began humming again, and voices echoed in response. Tuuli sensed my curiosity just as I was sure the whole ocean could, yet I was not prepared for her to explain.

"I had wings back then. Large, golden, *powerful* wings. They were what connected me to the sky, and there was nothing I loved more than the heavens. It was like they had a mind of their own most days. The feathers would catch a breeze, and I was forced to glide along the wind." Her eyes were dimming, and I almost began singing to return her glow. "It's difficult to feel the wind anymore. Does it still come in unexpected bursts that rush faster than your lungs can take in, and you are left unable to breathe, but exhilarated by its intensity?" She looked at me, but only for a second, and I couldn't decipher if she truly wanted an answer. She appeared so sad, and for some reason, my heart couldn't handle it. "Before the Storm. Before my wings were taken from me. Before pleading songs turned into screams of agony as the rain tore my feathers, I was just like you. I can still feel the pain as they were ripped from my back, the burning in my eyes as I sank deeper into the growing waters. It rained for days, and my wings were traded for a tail along with the entrapment to the sea. We will never fully return to what we were, the curse has made sure of that, but I miss the feel of the sun on my skin and breath in my lungs, and the freedom of running on dirt and sand. It's been so many years. I cannot remember the sensation of legs."

Something heavy built in my chest, a brick wall around my heart, ready to become whatever she needed to free them from this watery prison.

"Is there any way to break the curse?"

"There is, but it requires finding a certain dragon, and they are terrified of passing the sea." Her eyes fell on me then, hypnotic and contemplative, hopeful around the edges, "That boy on the beach when we first spoke. What was his name?"

"What are you willing to trade me for it?" I posed.

The pride was visible in her smile, which I was grateful had returned.

"No, it seems you won't be needing any training," she laughed softly, calling out another time as the responding voice quieted before continuing, "You give me the name of the one who holds your heart, and I'll give you the one who held mine."

"Kiernan," I answered, perhaps too quickly, perhaps missing the shape of his name on my lips, perhaps proving to myself I hadn't forgotten him, even down here.

This time, her hum was in acknowledgment and nothing more, a pause of silence that had the space darkening as though she was hoping to puzzle something out, but she didn't ask me anything else about him in that moment.

"His name was Rhodion," she instead began, very obviously watching me as she declared, "Firstborn from the line of Eryx, founder of Agrond, and the rightful heir."

I stopped swimming to look at her, process what I heard, and she stopped alongside me, expecting this type of reaction from the knowing expression she wore.

"You aren't the first siren to fall in love with a dragon," she said almost like a hum, and I was both shocked and relieved at her words. Tuuli wouldn't show judgment or tell me the impossibility of its nature because she had experienced it herself.

"His father wanted me as his family's personal songbird. I sang for them in the mornings, and I used to hide away to see him any other time. Eryx was not pleased that his heir was spending so much time with a siren. In the king's eyes, I was meant to sing and remain quiet if not. Our voices healed the dragons, and the dragons protected us. That's how it was always supposed to be."

"What happened?" I pressed, and she didn't look at me as she answered.

"He died."

She began swimming again, her movements limp compared to the grace she carried before, and I guess the subject was too difficult for her to talk about. Quietly falling beside her, she glanced at me, and immediately, her demeanor shifted, pausing her swim again.

"He gave you his scale?" Her eyes glittered, amethysts sparkling in intrigue. My back went straight, realizing I'd forgotten to tuck the strand of hair behind my ear during her story. "How long have you known him?"

"Five months."

"Someone is forward," she giggled, reaching for my braid to lightly touch the only part of Kiernan I had left, "*Obsessed*, I would even dare to say."

"It's just a gift," I contended, hoping to downplay her fixation.

"Did he not explain when he offered you a piece of himself?" That was a strange way to put it, sounding more consequential than something to remember him by, and I wondered if there was some joke I was missing.

"There was something he wanted to say, but we were... interrupted."

She giggled again, lively and excited, dropping her hand from my hair to focus on me with enough enthusiasm to make me rethink everything Kiernan said on Secret Beach.

"Ariella, a dragon bestowing a scale is the equivalent to a human offering a ring."

"Are you saying Kiernan was proposing?"

She nodded.

"And by the looks of it, you accepted," she offered, gesturing to the scale tied in my hair.

I didn't know why this revelation scared me, especially when I'd known for some time that he was the one I wanted to spend the rest of my life with, but it felt more like a fantasy than reality, a dream I'd always awake from eventually, but this was real, and it was jarring. Despite my uncertainty about the situation, I took comfort in one understanding, and it made everything easier to take in. Kiernan would be back; I could no longer deny it.

In his mind, we were engaged.

"Your song—it's in Greek," I observed as we neared the voices we'd been following, now close enough to depict words.

"It is," Tuuli affirmed at the same time I heard the word calling to me.

"*Dákry?*"

"Teardrop," she explained, "You are our teardrop of hope."

I thought of the deeper meaning through it all, how Father was trying to warn me from the beginning. This song had been a call for help, and I'd sung it as a lullaby most of my life.

At last, the end of the tunnel was in sight, the voices close enough to nearly touch, and I didn't know how to process the wave of excitement. I reached the mouth of the cave before Tuuli did, but it was her that exited first, undeterred by the magnificence before us, feeling worthy to enter when I didn't.

A ravine glittering with illuminated flowers and vines rested in front of me, caves dotting the walls, containing piles of gold remnants, shells, and pearls that glittered amongst the turquoise lights. Chandeliers of pure gold were strung everywhere, adding extra light as the stems coiled around the arms of the lavish lamps, the blue buds in place of white fire, and song ignited it all. Harmonies such as I never heard passed through my ears, touching my soul, reshaping the song I knew by heart into something magical.

"This is Esrin," Tuuli encouraged as though this place frightened me, and maybe I feared how attached I'd already become to a crack in the earth.

"You live here?" I whispered, astonished and afraid to ruin the melodies that echoed in each chamber of this place, coming together to blend in the open center.

"As could you, with the rest of your kind, if you so choose."

Being offered a chance to stay here, in a place full of mystic enchantment, was an undeserved gift, yet Tuuli spoke as though she truly wished me to permanently reside here. She led me by the arm when I hadn't moved for some time, and the gravity of the ravine overcame me once more with its intricacy. Spirals like the one now on my palm were etched on every surface smooth enough to mark, adding a shading that appeared symbolic.

Now that we were out in the open, I could see the sources of such hypnotic sounds at the same time they saw me. Sirens with various features and activities all paused the moment I came into view, all female, none of them my father. He was sick, Tuuli told me so, but that hadn't stopped me from searching for him in the crowd of violet eyes. The fear that I may not recognize him after all these years surfaced in the back of my mind.

With the siren's hesitance came silence, and with silence came darkness, leaden and thick, and suffocating.

"Do not be afraid, Sisters. I have found us our *Dákry*," Tuuli called, the plants acting as a spotlight for her, disappearing after her words ended.

"Did she call?" a siren questioned, the section where she resided brightened at her words, revealing dark hair and light skin, before returning to shadow.

"She did," Tuuli affirmed, and a girl from the opposite side of the room was the one to speak next.

"We hadn't recognized her voice."

"What is your name?" a yellow-haired girl followed up, speaking directly to me.

"What is yours?" I countered, neither of us getting our answer before another question was brought to light.

"How old are you?"

"Eighteen."

Whispers from all directions teased the light, but I could barely make anything out in front of me.

"Where have you been?" asked a siren in an unsure voice, her hair also uncertain it wanted to be red or brown.

"Near Pebble Beach. My mother is human."

"You've seen land?" someone shouted from behind me, and I was too slow to catch her appearance, answering to the darkness.

"Yes. I lived there my whole life."

More whispers followed by quiet gasps, and I was hyper paranoid over what they were saying. I turned to Tuuli, forming whispers of my own.

"I thought you said you lived on land years ago."

"There are only three of us still living who'd seen that time," she answered equally quiet, "All of these girls have known nothing more than the ocean, and most haven't had the courage to reach the shore."

"Are you here to free us?" another interrupted, and I opened my mouth to speak at the same time Tuuli placed a hand on my shoulder and answered for me.

"Ariella has come to give us our right to land. She will be treated as nothing less than one of our own."

Her words were firm, a command not to question me any longer, but I doubted they caught that detail over the sudden cheer filling the dark place, song rupturing from their mouths. Their voices were soft, their words curious, their tone gentle, and while their beauty was immeasurable, it was the innocence in their gaze that was impossible to look away from. They swam around me, giggling and kicking their fins with an elegance I doubted I'd ever have, and with their bubbling excitement, Esrin was alive.

Tuuli had yet to leave my side, and her loosened posture at her sisters' joy didn't go unnoticed. She'd been different from the beginning, less willing to trust, and more distant, and I realized it was for the rest of them.

This was a race that needed protection, and with the protectors abandoning them, Tuuli took on that role, a leader they'd willingly follow to the death. She was hardened so the rest of them could be soft, and the reverence they looked to her with showed their undying loyalty. It seemed dragons and sirens had that similarity.

"Tuuli!" A siren shouted, emerging from one of the caves, and all attention was drawn to her. She was beautiful in the way fresh snow was, her hair sparkling white while her skin neared pink, moving in a blur as she rushed to Tuuli. "She has gotten worse!"

"Show me, Brisa."

She led Tuuli, and I followed, feeling more secure when I was around her. We came to another cave opening, but this one was veiled with kelp that was pushed aside to enter. Inside, a siren lay on a bed of torn sea grass and kelp, and she was unlike anything I'd seen. From viewing the others, all sirens shared the same kind of tail, the small scales and large fins with iridescent hues of blue, green, and purple, but there was nothing entrancing about this siren. Her skin was the same texture and color as her tail, a swampy blue-green that was a shade lighter than her stringy hair. Sharp fins jutted from her spine, webbing between her fingers, and though her eyes were closed, I somehow knew they were soulless. She was the sea monster the Kallías' feared.

"What happened to her?" I breathed in horror, and Tuuli swiftly brushed past me to reach the terrifying creature.

"The curse," Tuuli quickly answered, taking the girl's head in her hands to press their foreheads together, softly singing, "Heed my voice, Melten. *ákouson tes phonés mou.*"

A soft noise in the back of her throat proved she was alive, yet she did not possess the strength to open her eyes, and Tuuli pulled away to look at her with a fear that was uncharacteristic of the confident siren I had made a deal with earlier in the day.

"She needs to sing," Tuuli directed, and the pale enchantress she'd called Brisa responded.

"She won't be able to present on her own."

"Which is why we will go with her."

"But it has been days since we have had someone to sing to," Brisa reasoned, staring at the weak siren with an anxious worry in her amethyst eyes, "The humans who have come to the ocean weren't looking for help."

"Then I'd call it rather fortunate we have someone who knows land." Tuuli faced me, leading the others to follow her action, and I had to remind myself not to shrink away. I'd promised to help. "Do you know a human who is in need of relief, Ariella?"

Taking in the hopeful stares and the dying girl, I nodded, thinking only of wild curls and unsuppressed laughter that'd grown colder in recent days.

"I do."

Chapter Forty-Five

"And you are close with this Maddie?" Tuuli asked unsurely, as though she had wanted me to say someone else.

"Enough to know she could use help," I answered, trying not to stare at the horrifying creature resting by us, reminding myself it was not her fault she looked that way. The curse was killing her, and I was going to be her cure.

Brisa had left to gather a group willing to join us venturing to the shore, leaving Tuuli and me alone with the barely conscious Melten.

"What pain has she suffered?" Tuuli questioned, and it took me a moment to realize she was referencing my friend's situation.

"She lost someone close to her several months ago, and I don't think she knows how to let her go. Maddie would rather hope miracles happen than grieve."

"What is the name of the one she lost?"

"Heather."

Something passed over Tuuli's face, there and gone, and subtle as though to be hidden, but Brisa returned before I could question it.

"Ianira and Nereyda agreed to come with us."

"Good. You three guide Melten while Ariella and I lead. We must leave as soon as they are ready."

"Agreed."

Brisa exited the cave and called for the girls while Tuuli brought me to the less inhabited part of the ravine, and I hadn't been able to notice the gaping cavern below us that the plants didn't reach.

"What is down there?" I asked, peering at the sheer darkness.

"Those who cannot afford to be up here."

I lifted my head to meet her eyes, unable to control the anticipation in my voice.

"Father?"

The look she gave me was strange and seemingly unlike her.

"He is unwell, Ariella. You cannot see him now."

"But is he down there?"

"Yes."

I turned my attention back to the darkness, diving into the abyss with my heart beating wildly.

"Avam!" I shouted, cut off by the much faster Tuuli placing herself in front of me, her hands grasping my shoulders.

"Do not *disturb* the resting," she hushed, and her voice was concerningly serious, making me whisper in response.

"But he must know I'm here. He must know I've been looking for him."

He has to know I miss him, I love him, I'm afraid of life without him. I have to know he is okay.

"If you go down there, all you will find is death." I thought I saw a flash of something over her face, dark eyes and green skin, but it was gone in an instant, replaced by the beautiful, dark face before me, and I took it as my eyes playing tricks on me from the lack of light. "Be patient, Ariella. The ocean is not forgiving to those who demand."

"Is it true the sun scorches you if you are in its presence?" Nereyda asked, making it her fifth question about the surface.

"And that it will blind you if you dare look on it?" Ianira added, eyes wide with fear and wonder, and I smiled at their curiosity.

"You'll have to find that out for yourself," I teased, and they nearly lost their careful hold on Melten in their disappointment. Brisa was there to support, and I was grateful she swam in front of the three, blocking my view from Melten. I didn't know why, but my soul seemed to ache if I stared at her too long.

"Another time," Tuuli interfered, leading us through the winding maze of a cave, "It is night now."

"Already?" I questioned, because it'd only felt like a couple of hours passed since I was last on shore. Tuuli didn't respond.

"So, it's the moon that could hurt us?" Ianira piped up, her voice like a pleasant little bell.

"The moon is benevolent. He would never cause hurt unless to protect those he cared for," I clipped, pursed my lips, calmed my defensive heart, and followed with, "Have you never been to shore?"

Ianira blinked at me, startled, innocent eyes brimming with apologies for causing an offense, and guilt prodded at my abdomen. She wasn't Zadar, I reminded myself, and her words were not an attack.

"Only when we need to sing," Nereyda answered when her sister stayed silent, "and we can do that without reaching the surface. Tuuli, Brisa, and Melten are the only ones comfortable enough to be near the land because they used to live there."

"And you will too, Ianira and Nereyda, when our *Dákry* breaks the curse."

The guilt remained, joined by a heavy weight constricting my chest and hanging over my shoulders because I was their hope, the light they'd been waiting for, and I barely knew how to swim.

When we reached the shore of Pebble Beach, I was disappointed to find the moon wasn't there to greet us, clouds hoarding the sky's midnight jewels while we emerged into darkness. The younger sirens were hesitant to break the surface, but after my encouragement, they did. The breeze was warm, welcoming me back after my longest time away from air, smelling of salt and my youth. Nereyda remarked how the world felt lighter up here, while Ianira complained about her golden-brown hair sticking to her neck, but my focus was set on the house just above the hill, the orange door hardly visible in the blackness.

"Call to her," Tuuli commanded, startling me with her sudden closeness, and I spun to face her, catching her sight on the same house, dropping to me next.

"Maddie? Now?" I asked, and she responded with her eyes, flickering like violet flames, "She could be anywhere."

It would be very Maddie-like to be out partying at this hour, and the possibility of her being in an entirely different town was feasible. There was a long pause before Tuuli answered, staring at me as though there was something obvious I wasn't acknowledging, and once she did speak, her attention was turned back to my old home.

"You know her name. Tell the wind, and it will carry it to her."

As if agreeing, the breeze picked up, tussling Nereyda's raven locks into her face, causing Ianina to giggle at someone else's hair struggles. Brisa held Melten upright on her own since we reached the air, and I allowed myself one glance over her harsh, sunken features before calling out.

"Maddie," I sang in a whisper, worried I'd wake someone, terrified Zadar would find me here. I didn't want to imagine he'd hurt my family as a punishment for disobeying his direct orders of avoiding Tuuli, but I'd never thought him one to brainwash the people he claimed to love, either. I couldn't trust him, and I wouldn't risk Mother or Anders.

I called again, and those who were able joined, blending into a harmony that had me wanting to relax into the sea and drift away. I thought of life like this, living among my kind, never discouraged for who I was, never thinking I was a monster. So many years I debated life with Father, opposed to with Mother, and this would've been it.

"A human!" Ianira squealed, grabbing hold of Nereyda's pale hands in her tan ones, and I followed their gaze to the frazzled Maddie struggling to reach us in her light pink floral nightgown.

"She moves so strangely," Nereyda observed, "Do all awake humans act that way?"

My brows furrowed, wondering how she knew what sleeping humans looked like when they'd never left the water, but Melten was appearing weaker by the second, and now was not the time to question.

"She's running. It's the faster way of walking," Brisa explained, but Nereyda's nose still crinkled in confusion.

"It's not a very graceful form of movement."

"It is, just not for Maddie," I chuckled, watching her stumble her way through the sand, though I really had no right to laugh. Brisa rested Melten on the shallow end of the beach while Ianira and Nereyda stayed back, not quite comfortable being near the ocean's end. I swam to meet Maddie halfway, remaining in the ocean with my top half exposed, appearing human to the half-asleep girl in front of me.

"Isabella?" she questioned, genuinely concerned and extremely out of breath, "What are you doing in the ocean? It's the middle of the night!"

"Maddie! I'm going to help you!" I shouted over the waves, grabbing her hands and smiling encouragingly, "Come into the water! Quickly!"

If she'd been looking where her feet were going, she would've seen my tail shimmering turquoise and blue, but she was fixated on the others with the same fins, her grip tightening.

"It's okay. They are my friends," I eased, but she didn't glance at me as she was dragged from shore, nightdress wetting up to her thighs.

"You are friends with mermaids?" she gasped, and I couldn't tell if it was from awe or fear.

"Ah, mermaids," Ianira giggled, gaining the courage to near land, and the others followed.

"Humans struggle with the difference," Brisa offered, graciously smiling, and she was just as entrancing as Tuuli when entertained.

"They are pretty things, but have terrible voices," Nereyda informed, studying Maddie with a wild intensity, as though this was her one opportunity to gaze at a human. Typically, Maddie loved attention, but she was more focused on giving it this time, staring openly at each siren with amazement, and I was waiting for her to spew her fascination.

"Dearest Maddie, what is your greatest desire?"

I watched the way her tense posture relaxed the moment Tuuli spoke, putting her at an ease I didn't think was possible for Maddie. She opened her mouth, closed it, opened it again, only for nothing to come out, and Tuuli smiled.

"Heather," she spoke gently, taking Maddie's hand, brushing a thumb down the back of it, her eyes claiming the section of skin, "You want to be with her once more."

I never thought I'd see Maddie cry again, not when she fought to always be smiling, but hearing Heather's name spoken so sweetly shattered her feigned happiness.

"I lost her," she choked out, this vulnerability nothing like the Maddie I knew, and it was eating me alive, "I lost all of my friends, and I'm afraid of being alone."

"You have nothing to fear any longer. Help my friend, and I can ensure you never feel alone again," Tuuli promised, creating a deal when Maddie just needed a hug, but she'd always been too quick with her decisions, too rash.

"I will do whatever you want."

Those six words marked her before Tuuli did, carving a spiral onto the back of her hand and forcing her to touch the sand beneath the waves, causing the water to reach her elbow. The blood, black with oaths, dispersed in the sea, and Melten stirred at its touch, underwater and out of sight from the human.

"Ariella, would you like to begin?" Tuuli asked, letting go of Maddie to face me, her expression making me wonder how much choice I truly had.

"I thought Melten was the one who needed to sing."

"She will, but I want to see your capability first," she answered with a strange excitement in her tone, "Sing and take her sorrow."

I glanced at the sirens, and they all watched me, waiting for my next move, but Maddie's attention was on the newly made scar over her skin. She traced the spiral with her finger, her face pained before she was cut, and mine on my palm tingled in response. I'd seen the look on those I was closest to, an ache that was deeper than the surface, darker, like the seabed of the ocean, and I'd only found one way to lighten such hopelessness.

So, I sang.

Gently, quietly, I began the lullaby, and Maddie's face snapped to me. Her eyes were glistening with tears, the icy blues of her vision matching the waves at her waist, but she said nothing. I missed the Maddie who hadn't understood how to stop talking, who didn't know my actual name in her insistence to start a new conversation. The Maddie who was eager to squeal, and laugh, and invade personal space, and be unapologetically loud.

This Maddie was silent, and it scared me.

"More," Tuuli softly pressed, her voice behind me, her leverage in the back of my mind. My song kept its quiet nature while attempting to lose its gentleness, but Tuuli was over my shoulder, observing Maddie as I did.

"More," she insisted, something akin to greed lilting her tone, but I obeyed, seeing the relief it brought. Maddie tipped her head back with a sigh, her eyes falling closed, and it was like she had no control over her body as she swayed in time with the waves.

"More."

But it felt like I was taking so much more than her pain.

"This isn't right. I think I am doing something wrong," I answered, turning to Tuuli, and her eyes were sparkling with excitement.

"No, Ariella, you are beyond perfect. You have her enthralled." She didn't contain her delight, and I almost wished she had because she was overjoyed by something that felt so very *wrong*.

"Melten should—"

"We will find someone else for Melten. Maddie is yours."

I blinked at her shortness, catching Brisa's sharp, questioning look toward Tuuli in my peripheral vision, but Maddie was sniffling, and my heart was cracking.

"Oh, please don't stop," she cried, drawing my attention back to her anguished face, "Just let me listen a little longer. Isabella, I'm begging you."

"Your hesitation is hurting her," Tuuli warned, but it felt like a threat. My muscles were locking up, bracing to run, but the ocean kept my legs together, my hands shaking.

"*Please*," Maddie whined, falling to her knees, so willing to give herself to the sea.

"What have you made me do to her?" I spoke, watching as Maddie clutched her chest. A cold hand rested over my shoulder, and its softness was lost in the moment, calloused, rough, and *webbed*.

"A trade of her essence for your song," Tuuli soothed, coaxing me as my back went rigid, and the power she held through simply speaking terrified me.

"You were planning for me to enchant her," I breathed, cold, brutal understanding settling into my chest, forming icicles around my heart.

"To make her happy," she corrected as though it justified everything, leaning in to softly profess, "She wants to be reunited with her friends. Carry her to the place I took Heather."

I broke from her touch, her calming whispers in my ear, shutting out any unnatural longing to please her in one abrupt movement, and it was then I saw her.

Green, scaly skin covered every inch of her, bones nearly protruding out of her body, while sharp figurations managed to stretch from her spine. I was trembling at the memory of how those decaying nails slit my skin, those deformed hands touching me, and during it all, I thought there was nothing more beautiful than her. In the moonless night, her eyes posed the most terrifying part, black and soulless where white once was, a ring of violet iris was the sole color left in her stare, a stare I felt trying to steal my own soul.

"What *are* you?" I voiced in horror, and her features twisted into something even more sinister, sending painful chills through my entire body.

"Someone who has been contained for far too long," she answered plainly, because I was no longer under her enchantment, and she could sense her sway slipping, "Do not make the mistake of forgetting your actions, Dove. I *own* your voice, and you will use it as I command."

The spiral on my palm began biting into my skin, an aching reminder of what I'd done, and what it might lead me to do. I wasn't aware I'd stopped breathing, just that when I tried to respond, my body couldn't decide if it needed water or air. Maddie was whimpering, and it was enough to snap me into focus, my lungs claiming air while blinking the ocean out of my eyes.

"You want to leave, but you can't," she demanded, reinstating her control as my focus remained on Maddie trembling in the water, "I have promised to make you great. Don't let your human heart be so willing to give that up."

"And you are so willing to let another die for it?"

Her sharp disapproval sent fear shooting down my spine.

"Feigning innocence is a hindrance. I understand your fears because they were once mine. I was afraid of hurting those I cared for, but that's not *this*. She wants this. She wants to let go and feel peace. The only way to bring eternal happiness is to rid them of this cruel world. How could you keep that from her, and believe you were doing right?"

My mouth had gone dry, but my eyes were wetting, wanting to bleed tears and erase everything I was seeing.

"You are our sister, Ariella. You've had your time with the humans. We want to know you as well," Ianira joined, sounding sad and perplexed that I'd possibly not choose to stay, undeterred by Maddie's mental torment.

"Free her and come back with us. Esrin will adore you," Nereyda agreed, and the thought of being adored by my own kind felt good, right, natural, and it scared me more. They didn't know any different, and like a mirage, their beauty remained, revealing I was still under their enchantment and needed to break free. Brisa was silent, her sight set on Tuuli with an emotion I couldn't read, but Tuuli's fixation was on me, covetous and controlling.

"We had a deal. If you leave now, you will be indebted to me," Tuuli stated sternly, and I hadn't realized I'd been gradually shifting toward Maddie until I felt a warm, human hand reach for my arm, a touch as desperate as her tone.

"Isabella."

It was her last cry for help, and I took it, grabbing hold of her hand as I forced us to shore, bracing for the unsteady sensation of legs. I hadn't looked back when we first moved, but I did when my feet were firmly planted on the sand, unsettled by Tuuli's indifference to her one hope fleeing, Ianira and Nereyda disappointed, and Brisa still tending to Melten.

"Blood thins without water, and you are nothing without me," Tuuli said like a promise, those blackened eyes trained on me, waiting for my next move. I bettered my grip on Maddie's arm, and she swayed, drawing my attention to her glass eyes and snapping me back into focus. This time, I didn't glance back, running for the orange door, for someone who would know what to do, and Maddie stumbled behind me. They began to sing, an overwhelming, compelling melody with perfect harmony to persuade us back, but we were already out of the ocean, and I'd shut away the part of me compelled to the sea.

"Run!" I shouted over their voices, pulling Maddie in front of me and pushing her forward, "Don't listen to them! Keep going!"

My throat ached to join in on the song I knew by heart, but I didn't have time to think about myself when Maddie kept glancing back, her face not hiding her longing to be back in the water. I gave her another push, another command, if only to satisfy the need to scream, and it was with pounding hearts and heavy breathing we made it to my house.

There was no hesitation in entering, no pause as the door was unlocked, no breath before I was dragging Maddie to my room, telling myself my harsh clutch on her was from adrenaline and not the desire to hurt her. She protested with each step down the hall, but I couldn't hear her over the remnants of Tuuli's voice swirling in my mind like a raging hurricane.

Blood thins without water, and you are nothing without me.

I blinked the ocean out of my eyes to see Maddie pleading with me, her beautiful features pinkened in distress as the sea tumbled down her cheeks.

She was still enchanted, and I still wanted to sing.

I backed away, closing the door between us, locking her into separation from me. Maddie banged on the exit, and I stumbled backward, catching myself just before falling down the staircase.

"Isabella! Let me out, Isabella! It hurts!" she shouted until she screamed, and I trembled thinking how beautiful the sound was, all the ways I could harmonize with it.

I'd never been more grateful Mother was deaf.

"Ari, what is going on?" Anders exclaimed, rushing down the hall to me, and it was the first time his presence brought me dread.

"Where is Zadar?" I demanded, knowing he would've woken the moment the door was thrown open.

"He went looking for you. You've been gone for hours. We thought you were taken again. Where did you go?" he pressed, advancing to a dangerous distance from me, and I matched his strides, attempting to keep space, unintentionally backing myself into his room.

"She tricked me," was all I could manage, my back meeting the wall, and I slid down it, pulling my knees to my chest.

"I'm going to go try to find Dad."

"No!" I shouted, my arm extending to him before I pulled it back, "Anders, I need you. Don't let me leave this room. Please. I still want to…"

Kill her.

I swallowed the words.

Anders took his time observing me, possibly witnessing a vision through my crumpled form.

"Okay," he agreed softly, closing the door behind him and sitting on the floor across from me, "I won't go anywhere."

My shoulders loosened, and my head dropped into my knees, allowing myself to take control of my mind now that Anders was here. I'd sung to him nearly every night the very song I tried to escape now; if there was anyone who could survive my voice, it was my brother.

The sea in my veins had yet to give up on me, freezing the mark on the palm that I secured around my leg, beckoning me to fulfill my promises.

Free her. Free her. She wants to die. She wants to hear you sing. Beautiful voice to bring her peace.

"Stop!" I cried because now the voices were singing, echoing in my mind louder until they sounded right next to me, and my hands moved from my legs, gripping the back of my neck while my wrists covered my ears, "*Please.*"

Blood thinning. Blood thinning. Nothing without her. Need to go back. Back to her. Back to her. She is patient. She is relief. She is death.

My shell weighed heavily on my neck as though wrapping around my throat, a present from a father I hadn't reunited with.

Father who told you not to sing. Father who is still missing from your life. Father who you will never see again.

"Do you want a hug?" Anders consoled, his voice elevating among the screams he couldn't hear.

Yes.

"No," I forced out, unable to glance up, knowing I would break if I saw his sweet face, "I don't want you near me right now."

"You are scaring me, Ari."

My breath shuddered, my fingers trembling because only in my darkest fears did he say that. I was a monster even the sun was frightened by.

"I'm sorry. I'm so sorry, Anders. I'm sorry. I'm sorry. I'm sorry."

And those were the words I continued to say until my eyelids grew heavy and the burning in my throat ceased.

When I woke, Anders was gone, and the small clock he owned told me I hadn't been asleep for more than forty minutes, yet the sun was full and shining through the window. My head was foggy, my limbs unbalanced as I tried to stand, falling twice while trying to remember how to separate my legs. My voice was raw from screaming, and I hoped it would only get worse. I hoped I'd lose my ability to speak entirely. Chills racked my body, a cold sense of dread at the memory of Tuuli's words.

I'd broken the deal I'd foolishly agreed to, and I didn't want to know what being indebted to a siren entailed.

The house was quiet, but that didn't come as a surprise to me; rather, the volume of the silence was harsh and buzzing. I turned on the radio to fill the void where cries had been less than an hour ago, and taking a leveling breath, I moved to my room.

"Maddie?" I called gently, throat aching, knocking once.

Silence.

She must've still been mad at me for locking her up, which I couldn't blame her for. I doubted we'd be friends after this, and that was for the best.

"Maddie, I am going to take you home."

This time, the silence came with a painful twist in my heart, a chilling awareness that something was wrong, and I didn't ask permission as I opened the door. I feared to see her on the floor, pools of blood around her ears with pencils in her hands, an attempt to deafen herself just as Mother had, but it was so much worse than that.

The room was empty.

And the window open.

My heart stopped at the sight. It was the same window I'd used to escape to the redwoods the night I was abducted, when I'd been warned of the mythical existence and still decided to discover it myself.

"Maddie!" I shouted while frantically scouring the house for anything to disprove my fears, that she hadn't left while I attempted to calm myself, that she hadn't returned to them while I cried. A voice responded in the kitchen, but it wasn't from Maddie or any of my family.

"Nineteen-year-old Maddie Schiever was announced missing as of last night. Her parents reported last seeing her going to bed at 10 P.M.—"

The radio continued, but I heard nothing more than static.

Maddie was missing.

Maddie was dead.

Maddie was dragged beneath the waves, where no one could find her, just as the others that were never found.

My blood was thinning.

My eyes were bleeding.

My lungs were shredding.

My knees were buckling.

My throat was closing because screaming could never take back what I'd done.

I was the Silent Killer.

<h1 style="text-align:center">Chapter Forty-Six</h1>

Blue was the color of sorrow because it was the color of the sea. And the ocean mixed with the scarlet drops of blood created violet, the color of vengeance and my father's eyes.

The two hues spotted my vision despite my eyes being closed, head pressed to the floor, and arms clutching my chest. I wailed to release the need to sing, sobbed to cope with the understanding of what I'd done.

I killed Maddie.

The girl who found joy in every situation, who befriended me when no one else had, was dead because of me. She never knew my real name. I didn't have the heart to tell her, and now it felt as though I was entirely heartless.

There wasn't blood when Maddie died.

There could be. Bleed for her. She deserves it. Red covered in blue. Your eyes for hers that cried. Your hands for hers that were marked. Your life for hers that was taken.

Mother was deaf, yet I still kept quiet entering her room, cautious when rounding the bed she slept in to approach Zadar's nightstand. The large kitchen knife rested in the same place it had the day of my return, unmoved as though afraid to touch the memories behind the blade, yet I wasn't scared to take the weapon into my possession. With Mother asleep and Zadar and Anders gone, I assumed I would get by unnoticed, but the framed pair of eyes proved me wrong. Father's brush stroked gaze followed me from the darkened corner of Mother's art room, and I drew near to the amethysts I'd been unable to find, failing to be the daughter he hoped for.

"I should've listened," I confessed, studying the painting in hopes of reverting the damage violet had done to my mind, "You told me to keep my voice a secret, and I shared it with too many." I wished he'd come through the painting and scold me, if only to hear his voice one more time, but he didn't, and I lowered my head in submission. "Please don't be too disappointed with me, Father. The world will never hear me sing again. I'm going to make sure of it."

I felt his eyes on me as I left, closing the door to Mother's room to escape them, heading for the bathroom, the only room in the house with an inside lock. Anders would come back eventually just as Mother would awaken, and I didn't want them to have easy access to the scene.

For a moment, I debated filling the tub and dying in pools of blood and water, giving up my legs and heartbeat all at once, but I ultimately decided against it.

I never wanted to become that monster again.

Adrenaline rushed in my ears as I stared at my reflection in the blade, green eyes replacing violet, Kiernan's protection from anyone who intended to hurt me, including myself. I could see him in my eyes, the pleading for me to stop as a stroke of heat brushed my shoulder. A phantom in its warmth, as was the distant whisper in my mind.

'Stay with me. Ari. Ari—'

"Ari!"

The bathroom door was forced open, tearing my attention away and losing the illusion of Kiernan. Zadar's hand was on mine, ripping the knife away from me at the same time Anders' arms were around me, embrace firm to detain my need for harm, but I responded to neither motion, staring blankly at the tile floor.

"Where's Maddie?" Zadar demanded, looking distressed, watching the knife as though it was still meant to end me despite being out of my reach. He'd seen my death by that same blade, and he'd broken down the door to prevent it. Anders must've gone looking for him the moment I fell unconscious.

"Dead," I uttered shakily, yet I hadn't meant to speak, my voice betraying me once more. Anders hugged me tighter, and I foolishly held my breath, hoping one of them would say it wasn't true, that she was okay and simply got lost on her way home.

"How'd it happen?" Zadar pressed, and my eyes filled with tears, because he didn't deny it, and I had no hope left.

"Window," I choked out, Anders releasing me to face his father, understanding in his eyes that the elder lacked. He began rambling to Zadar about the previous night, a hurried explanation that I intended to retain, but his words were too rushed for me to process.

"If only I'd been able tae speak tae you, Maddie would still be alive," Zadar sighed, keeping the weapon a maddening distance from me, "Aw ye needed tae do was sing tae her, and she'd have been freed from Tuuli's enchantment."

Zadar told me I was cold, but I didn't feel it. He said my body was confused, that siren was still in my blood as I stood human, but he didn't know it was thinning.

He'd sat me on the couch, wrapped a blanket over my shoulders, but I hadn't registered the actions. The ocean was in the window, and it was waving to me.

"She's calling," I mumbled, observing the sea, the color, its movements, how many corpses it held, "She keeps calling to me. Her voice is in my head constantly." I looked at Zadar. "Can sirens enchant other sirens?"

"Naw," he answered, "but ye cannae forget there's human in ye, and human minds are the easiest tae control."

I faced the ocean again.

"If I shut the human out, I won't hear her."

It was silent for a moment, I used the time to count the waves, the number of times they crashed against shore, how the heavy currents enjoyed dragging others down.

"Ye're thinkin' o' goin' back."

It wasn't a question, and I wondered if Tuuli had been honest when stating Zadar could lie.

"Father will die if I don't," I answered, and he looked genuinely confused.

"Whit're ye talkin' aboot?"

"The sickness in the sea. The disease will kill my father if I don't free them."

Zadar shook his head, confusion replaced by realization, and then indignation.

"There's nae *disease*. Only a curse keeps them from leavin' the ocean. Tuuli wanted ye tae use Maddie's essence tae extend yer youth. It's the only reason she and her enchantresses arenae extinct since the males were wiped oot annihilated in the last battle here."

"But," I struggled, my voice cracking as I felt my heart crumbling once more, "But he is sick. She told me Father was alive but needed help. She said—"

"She lies, Ari. She tricks and ensnares ye wi' deals that bind ye tae her will." Zadar's arm lifted, and I waited for him to bring it down, striking me in the reprimand I deserved, but his fingers slid through his hair instead, uncovering the hidden spiral carved on his temple.

"You made a deal with her, too?" I asked, though I knew the answer. I could almost feel the amount of pressure she used to give him that marking.

"It was years ago. I was in pain, learnin' tae live wi' grief and guilt aw at once, and she appeared when I was at ma weakest, offerin' tae grant ma heart's desire. It was the first time the dragons tried tae wipe oot Nessie, the first battle I e'er fought in. I was young, and cocky, and a right fool. They didnae finish their mission, but they didnae leave empty-handed either. Ma recklessness got Isleen, ma partner, taken from me by those foul beasts. Aw I wanted was tae get her back. Tuuli knet that, and she preyed on it."

"I didn't know you had a love before Mother."

"It's no like that. Kelpies dinnae love the way ye do. We're paired at creation nae one's left alone, and that soul becomes yer life-long companion. Isleen wasnae ma wife; she was ma sister."

"But you love Mother, don't you?"

"More than onythin', but it didnae start that way. I've kent Evie since she was a wee lass. Her father owned one o' the last survivin' fishin' businesses left in Scotland, and I captained his ship. She'd fight tae come along every time our crew sailed oot. Her love o' the sea was too fierce. The older she got, the bolder she became, but her heart grew wi' it. If Evie wasnae singin' wi' the crew or sketchin' aw she saw in that clever heid o' hers, she was chatterin' tae whoever would listen. Hawf the men on the ship were smitten wi' her, but she didnae notice.

"I kent the day Evie was enchanted. Her een werenae as bright. She lied when I asked whit happened, but I'd fallen for siren trickery afore so I kent the signs. I never saw Avam at first, but I felt his presence in her. Bit by bit, Evie stopped talkin' and singin', and the wee glimpses I caught o' her art were dark and monstrous. She'd nae answer ma questions, and she wouldnae leave the sea though I begged her tae. Then she was gone."

"Gone?" I asked, brows lowering, "Where did she go?"

"I wasnae sure, and that scared me most. He could've taken her anywhere and done onythin' in the middle o' the ocean. Efter losin' Isleen, I'd shut masel' aff ma vision, hopin' tae escape the kelpie blood I felt unworthy o', but I brought them back tae find her. I couldnae lose yer mother too. It took me months tae track her doon, and I was too late tae protect her. Avam had her mind bound. Yer father twisted yer mother's till she believed she loved him, and there was near nothin' left o' her will he didnae own."

"Tell me you are able to lie," I begged, clutching my shell as though holding on to hope, "This can't be true."

"I wish I could say it wasnae," he answered solemnly, continuing as though this revelation wasn't tearing me apart, "When I finally found Evie again, ma visions came crashin' back tae me, and everyone one o' them circled roon ye. Evie was carryin' the *Dákry*, and that was something I should never have kent."

"Why not?"

"Because that's whit Tuuli wanted. In our bargain, I swore tae find the *Dákry* and bring them tae her. Noo I kent where ye were but nae whit she'd do tae Evie if I obeyed. Sirens survive through the corruption o' humans."

I'd seen that for myself, yet I struggled to imagine the father I longed for doing so to my mother.

"I didnae tell Tuuli aboot Evie," Zadar continued, "And she cursed me for it. She'd seen yer mother afore, how close we were on the sea, and she made me fall in love wi' her."

"How would falling in love be a curse?"

"Evie was already in love then, but I dinnae think that was Tuuli's reason. She's cleverer than that. There's somethin' in our agreement I've yet tae un-earth."

I folded my limbs around myself to keep from falling apart, swallowing down the cries as I said, "She said she'd fallen in love with a dragon once, and asked me about Kiernan."

"Did ye tell her?"'

My heart stilled as I met his startled eyes.

"Was that a mistake?"

"She is seeken' tae end the line o' Rhodion," Zadar answered evenly, but the straightness in his tone was unnatural, "He's the reason the sirens are trapped, and wi' the death o' his blood, the sirens'll roam land once again."

"But that was hundreds of years ago," I argued, hoping for a solution to at least one of my faults, "His line could be all of Agrond."

"There was... one indicator that reveals the stained nature o' that line. His family was obsessed wi' the sirens in a hunger far beyond their usual hoardin', and that has been passed doon. The one obsessed wi' the *Dákry* is the one whose blood holds the key tae their freedom."

"Kiernan," I breathed, tears pricking my eyes as chills ran through my body.

Tuuli was after Kiernan next.

I slept in the living room that night, though resting proved difficult. She was still in my head, soft and gentle, where the other voices had been harsh. I supposed that was how she effortlessly deceived her victims, posing as a source of relief when things of land became a burden, attacking vulnerability under the cover of care. Evil prefers the weak.

I was that weakness Tuuli sought after.

If I were strong, I wouldn't have stepped outside knowing the danger that swam not far from my home. If I were strong, I wouldn't have cried to the moon, desperate for him to hear me.

"Don't come back," I whispered, trembling because my limbs were too weak to carry me.

She was there. I could feel her watching me with those soulless eyes, and if I were strong, I wouldn't have made the mistake of glancing at the beach. Seeing Tuuli made my muscles loosen, the voices silence, becoming the relief she promised to be. The temptation to follow her beckoning down the hill, and dive into the waters had a firm hold on my heart, desiring to drown myself as Maddie was forced to. But I knew Tuuli wouldn't let me die while I was still of use to her, so I fisted my hand and showed her the back of it instead, and she smiled, knowing its meaning—a symbol of disrespect in dragon culture. Tuuli didn't sing for me as we stared at each other, and I didn't give her the satisfaction of letting her see me cry, though my resilience would only last for so long.

If I were strong, I wouldn't have hesitated to slit my throat when I had the chance.

Chapter Forty-Seven

She was crying. I was screaming. She died. I lived.

It was the same every night.

I was the one with the nightmares now, and no amount of comfort Zadar or Anders attempted to provide could change that. Each close of my eyelids was stained with visions of her death I hadn't fully witnessed, and my brain went through drastic, tormented fantasies to fill in the unknown.

Tonight, Maddie was out of the water, lying painfully still on the shore with her back to me, and running felt slower than ever before. I collapsed on my knees when I reached her, rolling her body over with the intention to rest her head in my lap, but the blood on my hand halted me. Through her nightgown, plunged into her chest, was a hole, red, gaping, and missing her heart.

They ripped out her heart.

"It hurts, Isabella. It hurts," she said weakly, but my head echoed the screams, the last words I heard her say.

"Help!" I cried, "She needs help! Somebody! Please!"

But with each shriek and plea, the ocean roared louder, drowning out my noise. Maddie stared blankly at me, hazy, but alive enough to project her innocence, deepening my heartache when she didn't even have a heart of her own. She said nothing, tearing my soul apart with her glassy eyes, until the waves neared, washing over both of us, and she was gone.

"Maddie!" I panicked, scouring the endless, thin layer of water I now kneeled in, terrified I lost her when she was so close to living this time. It didn't matter that a vital organ was missing, or that she didn't take a single breath as I held her, because she had spoken to me, and her eyes were awake, "Come back, Maddie! Where did you go?"

"I reckon ye ken that answer already," a familiar, heavy-accented voice answered from behind, humor hinting in his tone, "Ye really should stop askin' such obvious questions."

My head turned to see Searlas and the dark abyss that was this dream-like connection, water lining the flood that he, once again, sat cross-legged in.

"What are you doing here?" I demanded, but he gave no distress to my bite.

"Answerin' a call, that's aw."

"Go away," I choked, hating that I had no control over my tears, "I don't want to see you."

"Did ye ever stop tae think that ye were the one that reached oot tae me?" He posed, letting me ponder a minute, "That mebbe, just possibly, ye want me here?" I held my tongue, and he tilted his head to present himself as more endearing. "Ye've tae admit I'm better than the nightmares."

"That's debatable."

"Then aye, go back tae yer ghastly visions if ye must. I'll be here when ye cry oot for help again as ye will." I turned my head back to my empty hands, picturing the blood staining them, and I could feel Searlas staring at me as he softly added, "They didnae torture her, by the by. Yer friend walked intae those waters o' her ain will, an' she passed in under five minutes. I saw it."

The relief his closure brought was insignificant compared to the guilt.

"Why would you tell me that?"

"Because I dinnae want it tae haunt ye."

His answer was honest, and I wondered if one day I would be able to move on from her death, or if that blue stare would forever torment me. He held my stare and its intensity had me wishing to avert my gaze, abashed for looking that deeply into eyes that weren't green.

"Do you visit everyone's dreams?" I voiced, hoping to shift whatever unspoken message had flowed between us.

"No everyone. Yer different—special," he answered in almost a mock, grinning when I couldn't manage to.

"Can all kelpies do this?" I pressed, and he turned more serious.

"Naw. It takes a kind o' devotion most o' us dinnae hae tae bridge wi' another species. Aw our power comes frae Nessie, so we're born connected, an' for ony ither it takes patience. Ye've tae ken the soul deep enough tae step intae their head."

"You've never even met me."

"But I ken ye. I ken ye cannae sleep through the night 'cause ye're that used tae soothin' Anders. I ken ye stumble on yer feet 'cause ye were never meant tae hae legs." He paused, debating whether to voice his following statement, his tone quieting as he decided to continue, "I ken yer greatest fear is that ye'll never be enough for the folk that need ye most." I swallowed, because he was right, and I never understood it until then. All those years I fought for Mother's approval were simply a need to be enough for her, and I never was. I failed her, just as I had Zadar, and Anders, and Kiernan, and Keagan, and Kaid, and— "An' I ken the guilt ye carry ower Maddie is deeper than ony wound."

I sat up straighter to mask the nerve he'd struck, but it only drew more attention to me, voicing the darkest longing my heart had yet to utter.

"Dinnar let Tuuli win, Ari. She's taken enough from ye. She cannae hae yer will tae live as well."

"How do I stop it?" The voice in my mind. The song in my ears. The guilt in my chest. The ache in my soul.

"Train wi' me." I met his eyes again, and there was no sympathy in them, but a song promised for change. "Nae soul should hae power ower yer but yersel'. Ye're the *Dákry*."

I bristled, the tears turning angry.

"If someone tells me that one more time, I swear..."

"Whit?" he prodded, an enthusiasm coming to his tone, "Whit'll ye dae?" I kept quiet, but it didn't discourage him in the slightest. "This is whit I'm seekin', that fierce light burnin' inside ye. Ye've still tae learn whit ye're capable o'. In time, ye could drown the world, Ariella."

"Don't tell me that. I don't want to know," I begged, thinking only of Maddie. In the distance, echoing from an unforeseen wall, a beeping sounded.

"Then ye'll never be enough for those still drawin' breath, Little Thistle."

Nausea had me waking rather than the alarm going off, sickened by the idea he presented, the *truth* he stated. I was nothing if not a monster, and it was time to visit Maddie's vigil.

It was cruel, the understanding that the Silent Killer murdered through sound, yet the most depraved concept was how I could join the vigil on the same beach she was murdered, without consequence, grieving right alongside people who prayed for her return.

It should've been a funeral, but why mourn someone who still may be alive?

A candle was in my hand while dozens of little flames surrounded Maddie's portrait, a beacon for her to find a way back home, and I was the only one who knew her own light had gone out. So many gathered in support, many more people than I'd ever been acquainted with. I placed myself in their shoes, picturing the agony of the unknown, the desire for closure they would never receive, forever hoping the following day would be the one in which she returned. Out of respect, I lingered behind the group of heartened visitors, their prayers and wishes a waste of breath, and I bit my tongue till it bled when they broke into uplifting song.

Tuuli was not by the shore, I knew, because her voice wasn't in my head, yet I glanced at the ocean time after time, fearing her thirst for blood would reach her last victim's relatives. Or maybe I was a coward. Maybe I was afraid to see her photo propped in the sand, knowing those lively eyes were dead, that her body lay next to my father's, and no matter how much I begged, I couldn't be forgiven by a person who lost their voice as water filled their lungs.

Zadar walked with me to the beach under the claim he couldn't trust me alone for the foreseeable future, but he didn't have to stand by me when the preacher began speaking, or place a soft, reminding hand on my shoulder when I forgot to breathe for an extended time. I couldn't understand why he still attempted to comfort me when I'd so easily believed the worst of him from Tuuli's lies, but I was grateful for it, even as he remained by my side when everyone else left.

I was the last one to leave, long after the vigil had commenced, yet I couldn't bring myself to be near her smiling photograph. I lost time watching the flames flicker in the ocean breeze as the sun fell, frozen in pain and regret, wondering what apology could measure to the torment I inflicted.

"Would ye like me tae do it?" Zadar questioned gently by my side, and I was unresponsive, fixated on the light surrounding her wild hair like a halo around her head, yet I didn't fight him as he gently lifted the candle from my hands, setting it beside the others.

The candles were all the same shade of off white, and I found it to be a disgrace. Maddie would've wanted them in different colors and shapes, some even sparkly, and scented, at the very least. I thought of how important colors were to her, how vividly she saw every shade of the world, wanting to know my favorite hues before even knowing my name. I pictured her scolding me for wearing something as drab as the color black, or that my hair needed to come down from the bun I had it pinned in. Normally, I left it down to hide my unremovable symbol, but I wore a scarf around my neck as my hair was pulled from my face, wanting to clearly see the pain of her loved ones, to always remember this moment. Maddie was nothing but a happy human who spread her joy everywhere she went, and I was the evil who stomped out her light. It wasn't fair that I got to live while she didn't.

"I can take this pain awa'," Zadar reminded, watching me too long like he knew the thoughts that circled my mind, and blue didn't look cursed when it was in his eyes.

"Things can't heal unless they have first hurt, right?" I spoke through a forced smile, though tears paved their way down my face, "I did this to her. Forgetting would be a disrespect to her life."

Zadar didn't push it further, going silent while his presence assured I wasn't alone, and I swallowed, gaining the courage to voice the decision I'd set on.

"I want to go to Scotland."

Even as I said it, my voice cracked from the shattering of my heart. I kept my head turned away from him, refusing to let him see the lie in my eyes, and there was a long silence before he responded.

"If it's the sirens ye're tryin' tae get awa' from, Ariella, Tuuli will follow ye wherever ye go."

I loosened a breath, forcing my feeble legs into submission as I moved toward home, leaving the candles and ocean behind me.

"I'm counting on it," I mumbled quietly enough to only reach my own ears, thinking of the blood she was now after.

Chapter Forty-Eight

Zadar left the following morning, preparing for us to leave as he had the last time we planned to move, and I spent my day packing. Anders kept me company as I gathered my things, and it was harder to be sad when he was around. Darkness was repelled by sunshine.

"What even is this outfit?" Anders exclaimed, pulling a dress from my closet I hadn't seen in years, triangles and circles patterning it with bold colors of orange, blue, yellow, and purple, "It looks like something you'd see on a humannequin in one of those big stores."

It looked like something Maddie would've worn.

"They are called mannequins, Anders," I corrected, focusing on the conversation at hand rather than the sudden overwhelming need to spiral.

"Then why are they shaped like humans, Ari?" he combated, tossing me the dress so I could fold it with the growing pile of my packed clothing.

"Lemon curd," I exhaled, rolling my eyes, knowing just how long this argument could go on if pressed forward.

Once we had finished boxing and cleaning out everything in my closet, Anders and I moved to my dresser, and I quickly snatched the small piece of paper I'd been writing on earlier that day before he noticed. My fingers fiddled with the message behind my back, folding it multiple times as I realized I couldn't put this off any longer, even as my heart dreaded going through with it.

"I have something I need to do," I explained to Anders briefly, exiting my room and heading to the front door.

"Okay. Where are we going?" he prompted, bouncing on his feet as he followed me downstairs.

"We?" I chuckled, but Anders wasn't smiling when I looked at him.

"Dad told me to stay with you anywhere you went until he gets back."

His stare was as apologetic as it was determined, and I bit the inside of my cheek, struggling to answer in a way that he'd agree to, knowing he could see when I was lying.

"His worries are justified," Anders added after a beat of silence, "I think you can agree with that."

I sighed.

"Go get in the car."

The drive was silent, and I preferred it that way. It gave me time to think about what I was doing, why it needed to be done, and how to keep my hands from shaking. My brother wasn't the least bit surprised when I parked at the entrance of one of the redwood trails, opening his door before I had a chance to unlock my own.

"Anders, please. I want to do this alone," I pleaded, and while he paused, he didn't fall back into the car, "I am not here to run away."

"You weren't the first time," he reminded, and I wetted my lips, bothered by how easily he'd been able to corner me.

"I will be right back," I promised, relieved when he saw the honesty in my eyes, sighing as he took his seat. His sight tracked me as I headed toward the trail until the trees hindered his view, engulfing me in the beauty of nature, and it felt like a hug from the forest. It was alive as always, bustling with excitement at my reappearance, and I was helpless to the way my mind fell into memories of him in this beautiful place. I walked along the path we raced each other on, stopping to run my fingers through the brook we drenched ourselves in, sitting in the place we rested as he confessed his happiness our time together brought.

'Only with you.'

Kiernan told me he loved me many times before the words left his mouth, whether it was saving me from a bear or securing a blanket over my shoulders, that care had always been there, yet I had missed it. The night he kissed me under our tree for all the stars to watch, I'd been truly bewildered, not that a beast like him could love so gently, but that he would choose to devote all he was to a monster like me. I wondered if our tree of secret meetings and tender moments held a more mystic nature than the rest of the redwoods as

I circled back to it, for it seemed each instance spent here was heightened with a magical intensity, prompting behavior that didn't sync with my lack of confidence. Or perhaps it had nothing to do with the tree and was all about the boy who brought me here. Kiernan made me feel safe enough to be bold, and I worried I would never gain that strength again.

Unclasping my necklace and pulling the note from my pocket, I stared at both, feeling such weight in objects that barely fit my palm. The shell was all I had left of my father, a liar, manipulator, murderer, and the person I looked up to most in my life. I lost count of the times I read the tiny piece of paper, thinking of every possible scenario the message would bring, but I couldn't leave him with nothing. *Don't come looking for me* it read, and I could only hope he would respect my wishes, believing this was what I wanted, though it was far from the truth. The only thing I wanted more than Kiernan, was him alive.

Folding the note tightly, I slid it into the opening of my shell before weaving the silver chain into the branches, the pendant dangling like the tree bore fruit. He would come for me, and when I wouldn't be found at either of our old homes, he'd come to our tree, our hideaway from the rest of the world, the secret place only we knew, where he would find the only piece of me left in Crescent City.

"Tell him goodbye for me," I gently requested to the forest, my friend, hand resting over the moss-covered bark on our tree, and a tall, dark figure moving in the corner of my vision had my heart spiking. Foolishly, I thought it was him, nearly calling his name like I had when he'd playfully hide out of sight, but the shadow was gone as I rounded the tree that I caught it peeking behind. The only proof I wasn't slowly going insane, catching glimpses of things not there, was a mark in the mud, a print of a big foot, and a smile pulled at my lips despite the lump clogging my throat.

I would never get to tell Keagan.

Mother was in the living room when Anders and I came home, and the sight was alarming, like a sundew plant in a bed of flowers. A cup was in her hands, and she'd occasionally sip from it, though her attention was fixed on the sunset reflecting orange and yellow hues off the ocean. I halted, unused to seeing her, especially as resigned as she was, and I hated how desperate I was to have her simply look at me.

'Does she know?' Kiernan had asked me the night before he confessed his feelings, back when he was here, pressing the ache away with the most tender touches, *'Does she know how she hurt you?'*

And I now realized she didn't, consumed by the belief that if I were just more respectful, more thoughtful, more understanding, then surely, she'd love me. Surely, she couldn't hate me if I were perfect in everything I did.

But I wasn't perfect. I was a fool.

"Why don't you go upstairs and start packing your things, Anders? I'll join you in a minute," I offered, but my eyes never left Mother.

He hesitated at first, as though expecting me to run away the moment he turned around, and it saddened me to realize that's why he'd been with me all day. Not because he wanted to, but to ensure I didn't disappear a third time.

Shouldn't be surprised. Better off alone. Better off gone. Death to a murderer. No one wants you.

"But he did," I whispered to myself, tucking his scale behind my ear because that didn't matter anymore. I was never going to see him again.

Too consumed by my thoughts, I hadn't noticed Anders leave, only that Mother was out of her room, and I was dangerously close to her. The couch dipped as I sat next to her, moving slowly as not to upset her, and another sip of her drink was all the acknowledgment I attained.

"Killian spoke of you," I started, surprised by the light that briefly came to her eyes as I spelled his name, hopeful she'd open up, "He said you were like an aunt to him. Is that true? Did you care... about them?"

I wondered if she knew Kiernan when he was younger, knew I'd fallen in love with a dragon. Mother averted her gaze, and I lightly placed my hand on her knee, readying to draw back the moment she flinched, but she stiffened instead, directing her focus to my mouth as I pleaded.

"Talk to me. Why do you close me off? Why am I never enough for you?"

"That was a long time ago," she mouthed, standing to gain distance, to flee from my touch, and the years of her rejection were something I never figured out how to handle, but it hurt, and I snapped.

"I lost my memories *for you*! Zadar said you were sick, and I chose to let him take my childhood from me because I love you!" I shouted, matching my signs with my volume, standing because I was tired of her looking down on me, "Why is it Killian gets to know what it's like being loved by you while I can hardly remember? I'm your daughter! I was kidnapped for a month, and you didn't care. I nearly died, did you know that? More than once. But it doesn't matter. You would've gone to my funeral with the same face you gave me the day I got back."

We stared at each other, and I searched for any glimpse of remorse or care in her chocolate eyes, broken when it remained the same empty gaze I had seen for years, and she had the audacity to take another sip of her drink in dismissal.

"You chose this!" I broke, my voice, my composure, my mockery of strength, "You chose to forget the pain and fear of losing Father, while I could barely remember who he was! You hide away like I don't exist instead of facing emotions like an actual human, a *real mother*. You'd rather live numb than feel anything for me, but did you ever stop to think how it could hurt *me*? I needed you, Mother! I *need* you." Tears welled in my eyes, and my arms fell to my sides, hands balling into fists as my entire body tensed to speak, "You are a coward."

She didn't cry. She didn't nod. She didn't blink.

She was nothing who felt nothing, and I was the girl who felt too much.

In time, I believed I would regret my words, but in that moment, I gained the leverage she held over me, and I never felt so free. I left her there, hoping she would listen to me only once, though I knew better. Mother was deaf, after all.

I took a moment to breathe before entering Anders' room and opening his door to the sight of him standing tall and unashamed in the center of the place where he cried nightly from visions of the future he couldn't control. He was so young, yet held more strength than I could possibly imagine.

"What is it?" he questioned when noticing my stare, lightly chuckling at whatever expression had formed on my face.

"You've grown up so much."

Never needed you. Haven't helped him. Only been a burden. He would be better off without you.

"I didn't unpack much since boxing everything a month ago," he explained for his nearly spotless room, picking up the Rubik's Cube off his nightstand to mindlessly play with, and the question was tumbling out before I could stop it.

"Are you happy, Anders?"

His head lifted, then tilted, looking at me curiously, but I couldn't spot the scrutiny in his gaze.

"I am," he answered easily, smiling warmer than the sun ever could, while fiddling with the Rubik's Cube, "I think we all will be in time. Continuing down this path is the most promising our lives can be, and—"

The toy slipped from his hands, hitting the ground hard, shattering the cube into pieces.

"Somebody's clumsy," I teased, moving to pick up the shards, but Anders didn't laugh, staring blankly with wide eyes bluer than usual, and my smile was quickly wiped away. "What do you see?"

He shook his head, tears beginning to pool, but he didn't blink. I reached for his hand, confused when he pulled away as though I had shocked him. The electric blue of his eyes dimmed, and I knew he was seeing me and my concerned expression, yet he still wasn't telling me, which worried me the most.

"I... I can't—"

"Anders, what is it?" I demanded, and my brother sealed his lips shut, determined to keep his truths in while his eyes gave it all away, glancing to the window behind me before finding their way back to my face.

"Ari, no!" he yelled, but I beat him to the window, throwing the curtain to the side, only for my heart to still.

Kiernan was on the beach, and he was staring at the ocean.

Chapter Forty-Nine

"**A**nders, under *no* circumstances do you leave this house!" I shouted, rushing down the stairs, not processing that Mother had left the living room or how closely my brother trailed behind me.

"Don't go out there, *please*!" he begged, panic edging his tone because he knew something I didn't, he saw something he wanted hidden from me, and it terrified me.

"I have to!" I insisted, grasping the door handle, and Anders stopped several feet from the exit.

"No, you don't! You can choose us!"

His voice was earnest enough to give me pause, glancing at him over my shoulder. Anders' eyes were oceans bleeding, waters doing everything they could to wash away the fire in my heart, but it wasn't enough to make me stay, so he added, "He will kill you."

My knuckles whitened around the handle, my knees trembling, needing to run, but fearing the future he saw. My sunshine was breaking, but on the beach, my moonlight would soon be drowned, and a storm was growing inside me, needing to decide between the brightest lights of my life. But my mind had been set the second I saw him out the window, a life cut short better than a long existence without him, and taking a deep breath, pain encompassed the words I spoke over my shoulder.

"Then take care of Mother for me."

"Ari—"

I closed the door, taking off to the beach, and there was no thought, no plan on what to do, just rapid urgency pulsing through my limbs as I raced to him. He stared at the water, hopeless about the idea that I was with them, that he was too late to save me from myself.

I'm here! I wanted to shout. *You didn't lose me. I'm here!* But the ocean's roars kept me from it, however, afraid to scream and draw the very attention I wanted to keep him from. He seemed unaware of his surroundings, staring unmoving at the water reaching for his boots, the sea drowning out his senses, but I would've assumed he sensed me from the fear tightening every one of my muscles.

"Kiernan!" I cried when I was near enough, hoping he could hear the warning in his name, but when he saw me, he appeared too relieved to understand anything but the familiarity of my voice.

"My angel!"

He was so happy, and I couldn't wait to feel that rush of excitement once I knew he was away from the danger to his life. Reaching the shore, I hurriedly surveyed the ocean, Tuuli not in sight, but that did little to calm my racing heart. She would be here any second, and she would force me to watch him drown as punishment for dishonoring our agreement.

I wrapped my arms around him, practically jumping into his embrace, needing him in my hold before anything else could claim him first, and the impact had him stumbling backwards, feet falling several paces into the sea.

"You are okay. You are okay," I reassured myself, holding tighter to him. My mind was racing with questions, but as water soaked into the legs of my pants, one thought rang louder than the others.

"Get out of the ocean," I tried to say while separating our embrace, but his lips were on mine the second I spoke, pressing his mouth to mine over and over, kissing me into silence, and the water splashed against my shins. He pulled me closer, and the heat of him distracted me from the initial cold of the water, lulling me into a false sense of security. I lost myself in that moment, looping my arms around his neck to press further into his warmth, my dire need for safety he brought overriding my retreating instincts. This kiss was different than the others, hurried and urgent, when I knew Kiernan to savor each tender moment with me, but I was just as desperate to have him, unaware of the sea waiting to take my legs.

One of Kiernan's hands held to my waist while his other dipped into the water, dripping the waves over my skin as he danced his fingers across my collarbone, smoothing a soaked palm down my arm. He took another step backward, tide eager to welcome us, but Kiernan's mouth dipped, trailing kisses along my jaw before I could voice anything. He subtly lowered himself to cup a handful of water, never faltering as he kissed the places along my neck that left me unable to think straight while lifting his hand to my head, petting the sea into my hair, threatening the ocean's claim on me as his lips trailed my throat, and I could feel my legs weakening, losing my stance about to shift—

"Kiernan!" I insisted, pushing him enough to look at him, but I couldn't read him. He was touching my arms, and my hands were on his chest, but I couldn't *feel* him. His heart was gently beating under my palm, nothing like the erratic thrum he experienced when he kissed me, his breath far from matching the wild exhalations heaving my chest. The green was dulled in his eyes, emeralds there, but not sparkling, and the ocean was reaching my waist. "Kiernan?"

"It's okay, Ariella. You trust me."

He never used my real name.

An eerie discomfort ran down my spine like a chill, complementing the ocean's biting cold, and taking a step away from him proved to be the wrong decision.

Kiernan's grip turned forceful, and I nearly collapsed into the sea trying to escape from his clutching hands, confused and scared, backing to the shore just as she emerged from hiding. Bits of gold and pearls glittered and gleamed from her stringy, sea-green hair as she lifted herself onto a rock, her scaled stomach stretched over the stone while her tail remained in the water, the curse holding tight to her.

"You've been ignoring me, my dove," she coaxed as though we were old friends, and her blackened eyes contrasted with her gentle smile. My hand reached for the shell no longer around my neck, grasping for the phantom comfort to ease my mind, but I had given it away. My eyes flicked to Kiernan, begging him to run with nothing but a glance, but his sight was obediently set on Tuuli, watching like he was waiting for another order, and my heart fell from my chest.

I was too late; Kiernan was enchanted.

"It saddens me I have to use him to bring you back when your heart so clearly yearns to be home," she spoke, and the marking against my palm began to throb, "I know you are aching to join us."

Two others made their appearance then, Melten immediately recognizable as her horrifying physique never changed, but she was alive now, and I hated to think Maddie was sacrificed for her. It took me longer to identify Brisa, her mannerisms and sidelong glances at Tuuli giving her away when her pale hair and light skin couldn't. Tuuli's voice was sweeter than my mind remembered, though her monstrous appearance stayed, and the relief that she could no longer enchant me was insignificant compared to the dread of her control on Kiernan.

I had known his emotionless mask, having spent months with him where the only smiles he knew were fake, but this despair covering his features wasn't the same. Kiernan's eyes were cast to the waves, viewing his impending doom with no hope of salvation, and the oppression weighed heavily on his shoulders.

"Let him go, Tuuli, please. I can't live without him," I begged, and she didn't understand the honesty of my statement, how I was forever tied to him in life or death, nor would I tell her. If her cruelty destroyed him, then she couldn't have the satisfaction of keeping me.

"Your spirit is broken," Tuuli eased, speaking as though she cared for me, and in her corrupted mind, I believed she truly thought she did, "Heartache continues when you feed hope to that which is hopeless. It is you who must let him go." A pointed glance was given toward Brisa, and she nodded, swimming to the defenseless Kiernan, grabbing his arm to pull him under—

"I will do anything you want!" I shouted, rushing into the ocean without a second thought, and my actions gave them enough pause to listen, "I will become your *Dákry*. I will give you my voice. Just free him." Every part of my heart was breaking, snapping, crumbling apart, and Kiernan reacted to it. It was barely anything, but his eyes lifted to mine, sensing the antagonizing terror that bristled under my every nerve.

"There is nothing you can give me that I do not own," Tuuli snapped, suddenly harsh as she came down from the rock, and I feared she noticed the subtle movement as well, "You signed your life away to me the moment you pathetically chose your heroism. What did it get you, little siren?"

"No," I pleaded, shaking my head as tears gathered in my eyelashes, hands trembling as they once more reached for a necklace that wasn't there, but it didn't stop Tuuli.

"Maddie came back to us, begging for relief from the agony you put her in. Was that your idea of salvation?"

"Stop," I choked, clutching my neck as the memory of needing to sing burned in my throat, "It-it was an accident! I didn't... mean to—I shouldn't have..."

"We want to help you, Ariella," Brisa joined, letting go of Kiernan to focus on me, her soulless eyes doing all they could to appear sympathetic.

"Let us help you," Melten echoed, swimming closer to reach for me, but I moved back before her cold, scaly hand could touch my skin, and she frowned.

"Why do you reject your kin?" Tuuli questioned, her head high as if to look down on me while she spoke, "To humans, you are a killer. To dragons, you are their downfall. To kelpies, you are a mistake. Who else do you intend on turning to?"

My eyes fell on Kiernan without my permission, seeing him fixated on me, the tiniest twitch in his brow proved his strain to break free, even as the sea gradually lulled him forward, preparing to lay him down to rest in his watery grave for eternity.

"You think he could be anything for you?" Tuuli prodded, following my line of vision, "He's a dragon; a foe."

"You were in love once!" I fought back, "Rhodion, you told me. He was dragon, and you loved him. Was it all a lie?"

"No," she answered cooly, and the worried stares Brisa and Melten gave their sister didn't go unnoticed, "But I didn't tell you why we were trapped in this world while they were saved from the Storm. I didn't tell you that I cried for Rhodion's help, and he held my gaze as he closed my only chance of escape. He took my heart and crushed it in his palm. He took my freedom and threw me to the sea. *He took my wings!* He took everything from me!" Her voice broke off, pain straining her most powerful weapon, and the ocean reflecting in her eyes cast the illusion of glistening tears. She neared Kiernan, causing my breathing to still. "This boy will be no different, no matter how much he claims to love you. The dragons have damned us, Ariella! Do not give them your loyalty."

"You expect to have it then?"

"You gave me your loyalty the day your skin was marked. I own you, *Dákry*, and already you have done my will. Kiernan was the final piece I needed to free us, and you brought him right to me. I'm proud of you, Ariella. You may not appreciate my words now, but you will one day."

I was disgusted with how eager the human part of me relished in her approval, gaining the acceptance I never had from Mother. I focused on the songs in my head and the sea in my veins instead, fighting the instincts to dive beneath the waves. Tuuli circled Kiernan as I struggled, studying him for an uncomfortably long time, and I imagined her searching for similarities between him and Rhodion.

"My song has a verse your father never gave you. Would you like to hear it? Or would you prefer I whisper it to him?" she asked with a cruel smile.

"I won't let you take him from me," I expressed, despite not having a plan, and the excited glow that came to her eyes was unnatural. Whether Tuuli would admit to it or not, she wanted to witness what her long-awaited *Dákry* was capable of, and that was the only reason Kiernan was still breathing.

"If you are so confident he will hear you, then show me your power," she prompted just as I knew she would, "Use your voice, and I will use mine. When he gives in to me, he will succumb to the sea, and you will come home with us."

"And what will happen when he listens to me?"

"Sweet, naive girl. Your loss is apparent, for he is already gone," she explained, indicating his hollowed face, but his eyes were on me, and that was all I needed.

"I don't believe that."

"Then go on, Dove, cry for your deceased love as I did for mine. He will not see you again."

I steadied myself in the waters that did their best to move me forward, bracing my lungs that craved the sea for air, and when I looked to Kiernan, searching for the boy who sat outside my door while I slept and asked permission before kissing me, Tuuli was already in his ear, singing her liquid poison into his mind.

"Long I have waited for your return."

Her hands lightly trailed over his arm, and I knew it was to distract me, yet I couldn't help the unease and anger that raced through my blood. I hated how someone so vile could sound so lovely, and it took all my strength to block her out, only having eyes and ears for one person, my voice for him and him alone.

"Follow my song, rest for long."

So began the brawl between sirens, and warfare had never sounded so beautiful.

Lovely disguised.
I offer all that you need.
Now I discern.
Heed my voice.
Amber honey.
Take my choice.

Shattered by green.
Let your heart lead you to me.

I finished, begging those last words, tears slipping down my cheeks, yet he only stared.

"You took my wings..." Tuuli projected unending, her fingers forcing their way through his shoulders until I could see the blood her nails drew from the grey-blue shirt he wore, "Now your scales will bleed."

He gave no reaction to the pain on his body or in his heart, and all too quickly, I realized I failed him. He'd let his own brother rip him to shreds to keep me safe, and I wasn't even strong enough to sing where he could hear.

"Kiernan," I cried one final time, wanting my last word to be his name in song, and that's when he snapped. He blinked first, recognition coming to his eyes, heavy breath to his lungs, and he was so magnificent awake. Tuuli may have lied and deceived with most things she spoke of, but she'd been honest when saying names held power. I felt that electric surge of power as Kiernan used all of his chest to speak, his drawn back emotions releasing as he voiced one word.

"Ari!"

Then he was shoved under the water.

Chapter Fifty

I wasn't sure if I screamed or lost my breath as I jumped, but my lungs ached when I submerged myself beneath the ocean.

The sea pulsated through my blood, the sensation equally numbing and throbbing under my skin, and everything seemed to slow.

As though gravity didn't exist, the only heaviness I felt was in my chest, a force I couldn't use to thrust myself downward. The ocean was its own universe, its own space where cosmic dust was sand and ravines were broken asteroids, but there were no stars to light this blackened galaxy, and the moon-light was rapidly diminishing.

Brisa and Melten were dragging Kiernan into the darkness, each one grasping an arm, carrying him to lie with their many other victims. I outstretched my hand to him, and Kiernan reached for me with his eyes when his arms couldn't: Eyes that had stared at me with adoration, that saw something in me that I had yet to find myself. My marked palm pulsated, straining for him, the spiral shooting aches through my body, slowing my already faltering swimming. He kicked and pulled, but this wasn't air, his body unfamiliar with the motion of waves. How horrible it would be to die embraced in the matter that kept you weak, forever to remain powerless.

No. He won't die. Can't let him. Can't lose him.

With all my waning strength, I fought to save the memories we never had the chance to make, and moments I wished to relive, muscles groaning in protest, but I couldn't hear their complaints over the water rushing in my ears.

Tuuli didn't chase after me, nor did she aid her sisters, observing from above with hopeful intrigue. Still, she believed I was the miracle she'd waited thousands of years for, more than a broken girl terrified of losing everything, and I was seconds away from that fear becoming a reality.

Even in ending life, the sirens were graceful, gliding beneath the tides with no urgency, unbothered by attempts to save the captured because they were faster, and I was not a threat. Blue, teal, and violet flickered in my vision, threatening to blind me with the shine of their tails, but I focused on the green, the color of land and life, breaking the illusion the sea hoped to lull me in. I felt the need to rest, to sleep and never wake up again, exhausted and without air. The water was too heavy, fighting against my foreign limbs, and the pain rushing through my body began to dull along with the rest of my senses. My eyes were open, yet I struggled to see, my limbs losing weight as all feeling was taken from me.

Thinning. Thinning. Thinning.

My heart faltered, my body giving out, and my head lowered, catching a glimpse of legs beneath me.

Human legs.

I never shifted, forcing my way through the currents in a form unable to combat the sea, and I hadn't breathed in what felt like years. Someone shouted my name, but I didn't hear them, nor did I notice Tuuli diving to me, reaching the understanding at the same time I did.

I was going to die, and for me, the realization was a comfort. I was exhausted, and the shore was a distant memory, land, the redwoods, and our little orange door. Silently, I said goodbye to it all. If hunger was what the sea needed to quell, I was content to take his place.

Take me. Let him live.

And with no breath left to give, I parted my lips, inhaling the ocean, drinking in my end.

For a moment, there was nothing. No color, no voices, no heartache, no relief.

Then there was everything.

A new life erupted in my being, filling my blood and burrowing in my bones, and the contentment that encased my soul broke away. My heart was sputtering sudden symphonies, the ocean's call melodic as she woke me, and a song was in my ears. Seconds went by before I recognized the voice as Tuuli's, that I was being drawn upward rather than down, trying to bring me to land, singing to occupy my mind as she did so. Her song ceased when I resisted her hold, startling me with the anxiety lining her monstrous face when she looked at me.

"You... weren't submitting," she stated, and it was the first time her voice wasn't soothing in my mind, sounding jittery as though the sight of my lifeless state had petrified her, "I was waiting for you to give in to the sea, but you stayed human, and I... I didn't think you would—"

Her soulless eyes were frantically examining my face, staring at me as I imagined a frightened mother would look at her endangered child. She kept her grip tight over my wrist, gripping me in the way death had clutched me moments before.

"Let me go, Tuuli," I said softly, "I'm not who you want me to be."

Slowly, her grasp loosened, but as soon as I moved, her fingers clamped back down on my arm.

"You cannot save him, Ariella. Again, I will tell you, he is already gone."

"You are wrong. If he were gone, I wouldn't have woken up," I answered clearly, unafraid to keep her hardened gaze.

She released me then, abruptly and without an indication as to why, and I didn't trust her graciousness to remain. Not wasting a second, I dove to save my dragon, and she didn't follow.

Forsaking my human mind and body, I sang out to the depths, tracking the voices responding, and the water moved in time with my swim. Darkness engulfed me, yet I didn't slow my pace, forcing me to raise my voice and light the shivering blue and green plants. The cave felt smaller entering a second time, tunnels more narrow as my body twisted through several openings, closing around my form as though to suffocate me, but I'd already given up on air. Each rock and opening I hurried by looked the same as the last in the dimming shades of turquoise and sea green, confusing my direction. There was a ticking in my heart, a clock counting the beats that I still hadn't found him, and there was only so much time a person could fight for life. My cry for him was strangled, a call I could hardly distinguish between the songs of those in the cave and the others responding in the echo of the ravine. I began to panic, spinning to view the multiple entries the sounds echoed from, readying to pick a random tunnel in my haste when the sea hummed in my mind, whispering me to follow. Her current rushed comfortingly along my scaled skin, beckoning me with warmth, calming the shuddering vines until their light fell away, and sudden pressure on my chest told me to stay silent. Alone, in the watery black, I closed my eyes to focus on the feel of the ocean, the currents in my veins, guiding me blindly deeper into the stone passage, and with my sight rejected, my ears enhanced in direction, capturing that the sirens I searched for were near.

Not wide enough for the three of them, Melten dragged an unconscious Kiernan through the tunnels while Brisa led, lighting the way with her voice so that darkness trailed behind them, and me along with it. I was silent when stealing their captive, swift when pulling him down a side chamber that concealed us both in the absence of light, even as Melten's sudden shriek brought all surrounding plants to life.

Kiernan was cold against my touch, the fire in his skin washed away, and the foreign sensation filled my body with dread. I looped my arms beneath Kiernan's shoulders, holding his back to my chest to fit through the tight spaces, and he was unresponsive to each movement.

Voices of dismay sounded from behind us, looping around the caves and reaching the ravine, prompting more songs to question such noise, and I knew it wouldn't be long until all Esrin was after us. The weight of his limp figure slowed my swim significantly, but the sea brought us out of the caves, the moonlight reaching our skin, shining over Kiernan's emotionless face, eyes shut, and brows smoothed.

Not enough. Not enough for him. Didn't get him out. Failed him.

My thoughts shifted to panicked words, pleading for him to stay with me, singing his name over and over.

Get his head above the water. Can't breathe. Head above the water! Can't let him die!

I hadn't known the strength in a siren's tail till that moment, and I ignored the pain in my body because it was nothing compared to the shattering of my heart.

Can't lose him. Didn't get to say goodbye. Need him to stay.

I fixed my sight on the moon, fighting to reach it, to feel the breeze against my skin, but even after breaking the surface, the water held to my form, straining on my back rather than my forming human legs. I shouted into the open air, the stars blinking at me in question, noticing the sea's bond to me before I did.

Kiernan's head was above the water, along with the rest of his body, hovering just above the ocean in air too thin to climb, and I nearly lost my hold on him in my shock. My teeth gritted, re-adjusting my hold, eyes reaching for a solution, and the opening of a large rock formation posed as the safe haven I needed.

Singing rang in my ears once more, and I spotted Tuuli on a rock, the look of mercy gone, calling back what she had let go moments before. My mind struggled to combat her when all my strength fought to keep Kiernan in my hold. My muscles were tearing, my thoughts begging to listen to the alluring voice behind me, and I released a yell of agony, pushing to the cave with a resilience deeper than my being could offer. I didn't look back, not even when Tuuli abruptly ended her callings, feeling myself breaking down, unable to combat a single thing more.

And in the chaos of it all, I failed to notice Anders standing in the doorway of our home, watching everything from a distance, unlike the siren whose attention diverted to the young kelpie with a curious glint in her violet eyes.

My body collapsed at the mouth of the cave, Kiernan falling beside me, unawakened by his head hitting stone. Every part of me ached, trembled, dwindled, my chest sore from trying to keep up with my heart, but Kiernan was on his side, facing me, and his body was doing nothing to keep him alive. My nerves were stretched thin as my arm reached to touch him, weakly tracing the cold features of his profile while he blurred in my sight, my tears falling unapologetically.

"Don't leave me," I cried, out of breath and longing for him to be the same, "Open your eyes. Please, Kiernan, *breathe.*"

My hand barely made contact with his chest when the water rushed out of his lungs, escaping from his mouth in deep coughs, and his heart sputtered to life under my palm. His spirit awakening gave me hope strong enough to sit up, brushing hair from his closed eyes, holding his face while his breathing shuddered, and I quietly pleaded, "Hear my voice. Hear my voice. Hear my voice."

I was too late to save Maddie from enchantment, but I wouldn't make the same mistake for him, pressing the song into his ear until Kiernan gently took one of my wrists, moving my hand from his cheek.

"I hear you," he answered, blinking his eyes open, their magnificence striking me as though I were looking at him for the first time, "I see you," he assured, those emeralds trailing each line of my face as though to make sure I appeared the same as he'd memorized, brushing a tear from my check to promise, "I love you."

I couldn't hold back then, wrapping my arms around him and burying my face in his neck, wishing to hide away from the heartache and guilt, to melt into his embrace and think of nothing but him. Kiernan was just as eager to have me, revealing how needed my touch was through the fingers splayed over my back, securing my safety as his hand cupped the back of my head. Not even the sea could wash the smoky, sweet smell of him, the scent of warm memories and home.

"You came back," I whispered over his skin, relieved that it was regaining warmth. Despite having a place to comfortably live, despite Zadar's threats, despite everything, he came back to me.

"I never wanted to leave you in the first place."

"I missed you so much."

"*mou éleipes, Agapité*," he breathed, bringing his hands to my upper back, his fingers tracing the divots of my shoulder blades while uttering, "Ari... how long have you had wings?"

"What?" I questioned, following where his mesmerized stare was captured behind me, losing my breath when turning my head.

The sea waved hello in the shape of two wings, humming power at my back, and the currents pushed through my bloodstream. My eyes widened as I examined the puddles, disregarding gravity altogether as they straightened in the air, droplets twisting inside to form intricate designs that adjusted as I moved. Touching the back of my neck, I felt a line of water traveling from the droplet on my nape, down my spine, and outstretched across the middle of my back. The ocean now was embedded into my skin, woven into my blood, and it hadn't been until Kiernan's life was on the line that I'd willingly sacrificed my human side.

"They make you glow," he whispered, suddenly close, brushing a hand down my arm, now bright with a radiance I didn't know how to control. The light reflected off my wings, casting glimmering rays of luminescence across the darkened area, making the cave glitter from inside. "Such a beautiful sun tear." He kissed my mouth once, twice along my jaw until his lips were at my ear, "My sun tear."

"Kiernan," I tried to say evenly, failing because he was being so gentle to a murderer, and it hurt too much to feel cared for when Maddie would never again, "I've done something terrible."

"Oh, Ari," he softly spoke, examining the spiral on my palm I opened for him to see, unveiling the center of my regret.

"It was a mistake."

"I'm not going to let her take you."

"I need you to take me first."

"What do you mean?" he asked, his tone edging suspicion, and I was unable to maintain eye contact while confessing.

"I killed her." My emotions broke free, a dam collapsing as water demanded out, and I attempted to suppress it all through a quivering inhale to continue, "Maddie is dead, and it's all my fault." His eyes were full of pity, concerned as I showed him my shattered pieces, but he was supposed to be angry with me. "You were next, Kiernan. Tuuli thinks you are a part of the curse. She was going to kill you tonight, and I'd given her your name. I never wanted to hurt you. I never wanted to hurt anyone. I'm sorry. I'm sorry."

I was being lowered then, tucked under his chin, but this wasn't right. He was supposed to hit me rather than gift me with gentle touches, show his disgust for the creature I was, rather than deep affection.

"Cry. I have you," he soothed when screaming accusations were meant to come from his mouth, and it only made the guilt worse.

"Kill me. I need to die."

Kiernan's body went tense, physically affected by my request, releasing me to look me in the eyes.

"You are thinking irrationally again," he stated sternly, and it bothered me how truly he believed it.

"I know you will. Zadar and Anders have both seen it. Please, she is going to use me again. I can't—I can't watch anyone else die. It *hurts*." I guided his hands to my neck, bracing my fingers over his wrist as his brushed the droplet on my nape. "I want you to do it. It won't take much. I know you struggle not to fracture me every time we touch. It's in your nature to want me dead, but I want it too. And you said yourself you were the only one who could hurt me. You can still live the life you wanted—"

"*Stop*," he groaned, using his grip to bring me back to him, resting our foreheads together, "Stop, *Agapití*. I'd rather harm the entire world than touch you in any way that isn't to prove my love. Bringing you harm is something I will never be incautious enough to do again. I made a promise to protect you."

"Don't," I begged, gently shaking my head, "I deserve your cruelty. I murdered a girl I called my friend. I'm forever indebted to the woman who would do anything to have you killed. You shouldn't want me anymore. I'm ready to go."

"Then let me take you home," he posed, taking my hands, smiling when my brain wanted him to scowl, "Come back with me. Agrond is everything I could not give you here. We can start a life there—a real life, where you don't need to be afraid. Tuuli can't reach you there. You can leave all this weight on your heart behind. We can start over. Be free with me."

I stared into those eyes that held so much promise. Though I may have deserved death, he deserved happiness more, something he experienced *only with me.* And until I helped him find an equal source of joy, I would stay with him, just as I promised the night I gave him my heart.

"Take me with you."

Dear Reader,

This is separate from my story, but I am writing it specifically to you, because I care for you, and would be so grateful if you read it all the way through.

I have a question, one that I am sure you have either thought of or heard before.

Where do you think you will go when you die?

Something happened when you read that sentence, didn't it? You felt a stirring inside of you, and that, my friend, is the Lord.

There are only two possible answers to that question. Heaven or Hell. No reincarnation. No simply ceasing to exist.

You will end up in one of those two places, and it will be for eternity.

Let that sink in. Eternity.

The Bible says in Romans 6:23 "For the wages of sin is death, but the gift of God is eternal life with Jesus Christ our Lord." All of us are sinners; it doesn't matter how good a person you are. Have you lied? Stolen? Cheated? Coveted? Dishonored your parents? Those are all a part of the Ten Commandments, and none of us are guiltless. There was only one sinless person, and I'm certain you know His name. You may have spoken it flippantly without understanding that one name is powerful enough to rebuke demons. Jesus, the name above all names.

God cannot accept sin, but He wants you. He wants you enough that He sent His one and only Son to take on our sins and die in our place as sacrifice, so that you could have the choice to be with Him. John 3:16 "For God so loved the world that He gave His only begotten Son, that whosoever believes in Him should not perish but have everlasting life." God is just, but He does not force us into things. It is up to you to believe in Him to forgive you of your sins and become your Savior. Romans 10:9-10 "that if you confess with your mouth the Lord Jesus and believe in your heart that God has raised Him from the dead, you will be saved. For with the heart one believes unto righteousness, and with the mouth confession is made unto salvation." I implore you not to take this lightly.

I don't know who you are, or what you believe, but please consider this one thing. Say you are right: that there is no God, or your only way to Him is through works, or you just aren't certain of anything. What do you have to lose? Nothing, right? But say I am right: that the words God has given us through His word are true. What do you have to lose by not accepting Him? Everything. Your life, your soul, your peace, your eternity will be placed in a torturous, very real place called Hell with permanent separation from your Creator. My friend, I do not want that for you. Please think over these words and the weight they carry. The Lord is coming back, and I want to be with you in Heaven.

Cry out to God. Admit you are a sinner. Repent and turn away from your sins. Ask Him to forgive you. Believe that Christ died for you and rose again. Trust that He will save you.

It's truly that simple, but the outcome is grave.

The Lord is waiting for you.

With love,
Bree Ireland

Acknowledgments

Oh my lemon curd, we finally made it! This book has put me through every emotion possible, and if you've come this far, I am incredibly grateful! It means the world to me that you set aside the time to invest in my story!

Before we get to all the people who deserve so much appreciation, I want to thank the One who even gave me the desire to write. I give God all the glory that comes with completing this book and the many books to come. He is my Savior, my Heavenly Father, and my friend, and if not for Him, I would be alone, without ambition, depressed, hopeless, and on my way to Hell. There are a billion things I could thank Him for, but this book alone has been an incredible blessing to me and my life, so thank you, God, for being with me through this incredible journey and using it to help me grow closer to You!

All right, starting with my song, I have Caleb, Ana, and Nae to thank for that. I worked for months on this piece, messing around on the piano to best find out what didn't kill the eardrums, but their help is what really made it possible. Hours they individually took out of their schedule to work with me, and their talents are immeasurable, especially the lovely Miss Ana and her ability to portray emotion on the violin. All three of you are amazing!

I have a lot of people to thank for aiding or inspiring this book, but I truly don't know how I would go about my day-to-day life without my dad, my mom, and my Aunt Chelle. Mom introduced me to my love of romance, Dad helped deepen characters and plot twists, and Aunt Chelle encouraged worldbuilding and the magic of storytelling. (Not to mention the MONTHS she spent editing it all. She's stared at this book nearly as much as I have, and I couldn't ask for a better editor because no one understands my writing like she does. Aunt Chelle and Nae both worked so hard to make my very messy manuscript as perfect as possible.) I look up to them more than anyone else in this world, and the fact that they have supported me through this very long and challenging process is the only reason this book is in your hands now.

Thank you to all of my beta readers, Dad, Mom, Loch, Aunt Chelle, Aunt Kaitlin, Aunt Jeanna, Grandma, Nae Nae, Lys, Adri, and Emi for all of your feedback and encouragement! When writing was difficult, I thought of you all, and how kind you were with every chapter, and it kept me going. Through the typos, undeveloped ideas, and extended periods of time waiting for me to write, you guys stuck it out for me. I love you all so much! And a special thanks to Adri and Emi, who would spam text me as they read, freak out over plot twists, and laugh with me over characters I created. Loch as well, my wonderful sunshine, for becoming just as obsessed with my story as myself. You have no idea how encouraging it was!

But to Kaylee and Lexi, I want to express my gratitude for beginning my love for writing all the way back when we were kids. If you hadn't suggested we write Love for the Wicked or GPS, I would've never even thought of creating Eroded Ember.

And to all of my lovely readers, I am grateful for every single one of you. I hope you know you are wonderfully and beautifully made. Please never feel ashamed for being soft in a world that is so hard. I see you. I understand. But don't give up! There is so much waiting for you.

Eroded Ember Lullaby

for Piano & Violin

Bree DePoppe

Bree DePoppe
Arranged by [Bree DePoppe]

Copyright © 2024 by Bree DePoppe

2
17
(8)
23
(8)
28

About the Author

Bree Ireland loves anything involving books. She started writing at the age of eleven, and by thirteen, she knew story telling was her passion. She wrote books, short stories, and scripts all while finishing book reports and research papers. After graduating high school, she began her work on Eroded Ember, and cannot wait for the rest of the series.

If you have an obsession with reading, love stories, or prefer fictional over reality, you can follow her Instagram @booksbybree where she shares all of that and more.

www.ingramcontent.com/pod-product-compliance
Lightning Source LLC
Chambersburg PA
CBHW051254130726
47987CB00004B/1521